THE HIDDEN KING BOX SET

JEN L. GREY

Created with Vellum

DRAGON MATE

THE HIDDEN KING TRILOGY

CHAPTER ONE

My phone buzzed beside me on my end table. I hadn't slept all night, nervous about this moment. Clutching my phone, I turned the alarm off and waited for any noise to indicate that someone else was up.

It was four in the morning and a safe time for Mom and Aunt Sarah to be asleep. But so much terror coursed through me that I was afraid to even breathe as I listened for anything out of the ordinary.

Pure silence greeted me.

I threw my black sheets off and stood, glancing around my dingy bedroom. The walls were off-white, and the room was only large enough for a metal, full-sized bed and an end table. The closet, positioned right across from the bed, was four feet wide at most. But it didn't matter. It wasn't like I had much stuff anyway.

My aunt had ensured I had the bare minimum, and my codependent mom never noticed. This was a four-bedroom house, and the third bedroom was twice the size of mine.

I squatted and reached under the bed. I pulled out my small duffle bag, which I'd packed last night. It sucked, but this was all I was taking to college with me. I'd buy more clothes and school supplies once I got to Kortright University, but it wasn't like I'd have more to carry if I weren't sneaking out.

After all, I couldn't stand living with my aunt for one more day. The constant insults she threw around and the way she'd smack me or worse when Mom wasn't looking had gotten out of hand. The older I got, the worse her abuse became.

I shouldered the strap of my bag as dread pooled in my stomach. What if Aunt Sarah caught me? She would do whatever was required to make me stay. She enjoyed having a punching bag.

The house remained quiet, so I headed to the door, but then I realized I'd forgotten my cell phone. I snatched it from the table and went into my settings to disable the GPS tracker.

My heart raced as I reached for the doorknob. The door tended to squeak when I opened it, so I prayed the WD-40 worked; I had put some on last night before bed. My aunt's bedroom was right beside mine so she could keep tabs on me. Mom stayed in the master bedroom downstairs, so she wouldn't hear Sarah's and my violent fights.

As I slowly opened the door, my body sagged with relief, until the door groaned right at the end. Dammit, I'd almost opened it the entire way.

Something bumped in Sarah's room. "Jadie?"

I hated that nickname, and she knew it. That was why she insisted on calling me that. Hell, I wasn't really a fan of Jade, either. My eyes and hair were dark, and my skin tone was olive. Why had my parents named me that?

My head grew dizzy from me holding my breath. It wasn't like she could hear me breathe, but I didn't want to chance it. Maybe she'd go back to sleep.

Of course, that was when something hit the ground. It had to be her feet.

"Damn, girl," she muttered as her footsteps headed to the door. "If you're trying to sneak out after all I've done for you, I'll beat you to a bloody pulp," she said loudly.

There was no getting out of this gracefully. I inhaled sharply and took off down the hall. I needed to get to the stairs before she beat me there and woke up Mom to play the role of needy mother. I always caved.

I reached the stairs right as her door opened.

"Get your ass back here!" she yelled, stepping into the hallway. Her long caramel hair was disheveled, and her cold, ice-blue eyes stared at me with disgust. "Where do you think you're going?"

She expected me to obey, but not today. I had to take this chance ... for me. I barreled down the stairs and heard her running after me. When I hit the bottom of the staircase, Sarah rounded the corner and bounded down behind me.

Dammit. She was in almost as good of shape as I was, but I had youth on my side. By the time I unlocked the front door, Sarah was halfway down the stairs. I yanked the door open and raced out to the front yard.

The middle-income neighborhood was quiet and dark, without a light on in any house. Everyone was still sleeping like Sarah should have been.

I ran left, hoping my crappy, old Toyota Corolla was still parked in the dead end. I'd bought the car only ten hours ago for this escape. It was the only thing I could afford without blowing all of my savings.

Sarah slammed the front door shut as she ran out into the yard. "Stop running this instant."

No, that was definitely not happening.

I ignored the command and channeled all of my energy into getting away. Adrenaline pumped through me, but I could hear her gaining on me. The duffle bag was making it so damn hard to run.

Right as I reached the edge of our half-acre front yard, Sarah slammed into my back. I fell to my knees hard, and she kicked me in the side.

"Do you know what happens to people who disobey me?" Sarah hissed and kicked me again.

Pain throbbed deep in my side, but I refused to let her know how much it hurt. I understood physical pain and welcomed it on occasion, just not when I had so much at stake.

She pulled her leg back to kick me again, and my instincts took over. I caught her foot and lifted, throwing her off balance. She landed on her back.

The one good thing Mom had done for me since Dad had died was put me in martial arts and self-defense classes to make sure I could protect myself in ways she never could. It was part of the reason she was so broken now; she felt responsible for Dad's death.

"How dare you!" Sarah groaned and rolled onto her side.

A dog barked in the distance, and a light turned on in the neighbor's house directly across from us.

We were going to wake up the whole neighborhood, which was partly her goal. If she could make the neighbors come out, she could manipulate them into getting me back inside. She'd lied about things I'd done before.

I climbed to my feet and adjusted the shoulder strap as I prepared to take off again toward the car. I had to lose her before she could see my car and get my license plate number. She'd have the police searching for me within minutes. I had to figure something out. Each passing moment jeopardized my escape.

My aunt grabbed my foot, and I again found myself falling forward onto the grass. Then it hit me.

I had no choice.

I had to fight her.

She crawled over to me and punched me in the ear. A loud ringing pierced my brain.

Tossing the bag a few feet away, I ignored the sound and turned toward her. I punched her in the nose.

The bones crunched, and blood ran from both nostrils.

I grimaced internally, knowing Mom would be mortified and ashamed when she heard about this. But I needed to do this even if it was selfish.

"You." Her eyes narrowed into slits, and she spat on the ground. "That won't slow me."

I was sure it wouldn't. Crazy held no limits.

Getting into a fighter stance, I made it clear I wouldn't back down. "Good. This is long overdue." I was bluffing. I didn't want to hurt her even though she took every opportunity to cut me down. I needed to knock her out or force her to retreat into the house. The latter wasn't an option for her, though.

"Yes, it is." She used the back of her pajama shirt to wipe the blood from her mouth. "I've always held back, but not now."

That was a lie. One day, she'd punched me so hard she'd broken her hand. But I'd try the bare minimum to convince her to back off.

"I'm giving you one last chance." Sarah breathed raggedly. "Get back in the house now, or I will make your face unrecognizable."

"No," I said slowly and with force. That wouldn't happen.

She tried to knee me between the legs, but I'd anticipated the cheap shot. I took a few steps back and kicked her in the stomach. She flew back a few feet and landed on her ass.

Not giving her a chance to stand, I rushed behind her and wrapped my arm around her neck. I tightened my arm around her, cutting off her oxygen.

As I waited for her to pass out, I kept my eyes on the neighbor's front door. She hadn't come out yet. Granted, she could be watching from the window. I had to get out of here.

Sarah dug her nails into my arm. Blood pooled under her fingertips as she desperately tried to get me off her, but I pushed through the pain.

Just as the pain became unbearable, her hold on my arm slackened. The lack of air was finally making a difference. Within the next few seconds, she'd be out cold.

The front door of the house across the street opened, and the older woman peeked out. When her eyes landed on us, her mouth dropped. She gasped, "Oh, dear God," and shut the door.

She'd be calling the cops.

Sarah's head rolled to the side, and I released my hold, gently putting her on the ground. If the neighbor hadn't seen us, I would've put her inside the house, but I had to cut my losses.

I ran over, grabbed my bag, and ran for my life.

My hands shook as I drove toward Kortright University. An hour ago, Mom called over and over to the point where I turned my cell phone off and chucked it before Sarah had the cell phone company track me. I managed to grab a prepay one at Wal-Mart a few miles back and was finally able to use the GPS to find the University without worrying about being located.

It was ridiculous. I kept glancing in my cracked rearview mirror, expecting to find a cop car chasing me. No one knew this was my car, and I'd parked far enough away that the neighbors hadn't seen me drive away. For all they knew, I was on foot, which would bode well for me.

The phone rang, startling me. How the hell had Mom gotten this number? That should have been impossible.

I glanced at the caller ID, and my shoulders sagged. It was a number I'd never seen before, proving I was way too anxious. I had to calm down before I did something stupid like wreck my car. The vehicle couldn't survive a hard bump, let alone a fender bender.

Kortright University's all-brick sign became visible, and butterflies took flight in my stomach.

It was real. I had made it to Hidden Ridge, Tennessee. For a second back there, all had seemed lost, but here I was, further validating that this was destiny.

As I turned onto the street that led to the school, I suddenly felt self-conscious. I passed by brand-new Hondas, SUVs, and a few BMWs.

I stuck out like a sore thumb, which was never a good thing. Blending in had always been my motto.

None of that mattered. It was only a stupid car I would rarely drive. I drove past the large-ass stadium as football players ran around its perimeter, wearing gold shirts and black shorts—the university's signature colors.

This school had been around for over a hundred years and had quite the reputation—another reason I'd been surprised to get a full ride mid-school year.

I found myself in a large parking lot close to two huge buildings. From all the pictures I'd seen, those were the dorms.

My car squealed as I pulled into the closest parking spot. A couple of guys a few cars down chuckled at me.

Whatever. I wasn't trying to impress them.

With as much dignity as I could muster, I shouldered my strap and climbed out of the car. I tried not to visibly cringe as the door groaned shut.

The guys hollered, but I held my head high and walked past them, pretending they didn't exist. I didn't need anyone anyway. Getting close to people only got you hurt or in trouble.

I marched to the sidewalk, on a mission to find my room and settle in. I needed time to decompress after the hellacious start to my day.

But when I turned the corner to walk past the boys' dorm, I stopped in my tracks, unable to process what I saw as drool pooled at the corner of my mouth.

CHAPTER TWO

I blinked. I had to be imagining this. The sexiest guy I'd ever seen was walking towards the front door of the boys' dorm.

He was easily seven feet tall, a good thirteen inches taller than me, and built like a freaking Ford truck. He wore a simple, loose, royal blue t-shirt, but it molded to his muscular chest and arms. His blue jeans also hugged his body in all of the ways they should on a man, but he might as well have been wearing sweatpants because his manhood was outlined. His longish blond hair was styled upward with matching scruff on his chin.

I'd never felt drawn to any guy before, so it caught me by complete surprise.

My gawking must have caught his attention because his golden eyes turned to me, and his pupils turned to slits.

Slits. That was freaking impossible.

I tore my gaze from him, freaked out by the experience. I was both turned on and petrified.

Forcing my feet to move, I pretended that nothing had happened. I kept my eyes forward and focused on putting one foot in front of the other.

Something inside me knew he was watching me. Without permission, my head turned back toward him, and I almost cried in relief when his pupils were normal. Sleep deprivation had hit me hard, causing me to imagine things.

He stepped toward me, and everything inside yelled at me to flee. I jerked my head forward and picked up my pace. Part of me wanted to go to him, which made the rest of me more desperate to get away. A guy could destroy you. That was what had happened to Mom. I never wanted to end up like her.

"Hey, wait up," the guy called out. His accent was strange and alluring. I'd never heard one like it before.

Without acknowledging him, I continued on like I either hadn't heard him or thought he was talking to someone else. In all fairness, he could have been. There was nothing special about me.

I forced him out of my mind and focused on the weather. Knoxville was a good twenty degrees warmer than Indianapolis. Of course, my rushing around probably kept me warm too. My blood was definitely flowing.

I entered the dorm and stopped at the front desk. A girl with light brown hair pulled into a ponytail looked up from her cell phone. Her chestnut brown eyes locked on me, and she arched an eyebrow. "How can I help you?"

"Oh, um." I pointed at my duffle bag like that should make it obvious. "I'm new here. I need to find which dorm room I'm assigned to."

"Yeah, okay." She tapped a clipboard a few times. "Are you Jade Storm?"

"That's me." I tried to make my voice sound light, but it fell flat ... and sarcastic. This was why I avoided people.

"Alrighty then." Huffing, she reached into the drawer and pulled out an envelope with 501 written on it. "Here you go."

"Thanks." In an attempt to avoid making the encounter even more awkward, I turned and scanned the lobby.

For an older school, this surprised me. Single light bulbs hung from the ceiling every few feet, and the walls were a medium gray. A group of couches created a huge square in the center of the wide open space, each one a different primary color that offset the walls.

Straight back sat a large elevator with a door on each far side of the wall that had to be the stairwells. I already felt underdressed in my holey jeans, which hadn't been designed that way, and the thin sweater hanging off my frame. The few girls I'd passed were dressed in trendy outfits such as skinny jeans, boots, and cute fitted sweaters.

I rushed past the couches, ignoring the strange looks thrown my way. I hit the button on the elevator and prayed the double doors would open and swallow me whole. I needed time alone, which was crazy, seeing as I'd driven for over five hours in the car by myself.

Whispers filled the air, choking me. As the weird loner, no one wanted to associate with, I'd been made fun of throughout high school. Sure, guys would hit on me, but they always only wanted one thing. It was like a challenge to them since I never paid any of them any attention.

The doors slid open to reveal four of the most beautiful girls I'd ever seen. The most striking one was in the center. Her shoulder-length, rose-gold hair and piercing blue eyes would have stopped any guy in his tracks. She was a tad shorter than the striking redhead, who had her head thrown back in laughter, but not by much.

"Oh my God, Roxy." The brown-haired girl at the end cringed, narrowing her light brown eyes, which had an auburn tint to them. "We don't want to hear about your sexcapades with Axel."

"Speak for yourself." The girl with black hair and even darker eyes laughed. Her eyes had a red hue that made them unique and gorgeous. She wore a long-sleeved, flowy black shirt with dark jeans. "I'm not getting any, so I have to live vicariously through someone. Sadie doesn't kiss and tell."

"I don't want you thinking of Donovan that way." Her blue eyes glowed faintly. "He's all mine."

The air around them was comforting, unlike most girl cliques I'd seen. They didn't have jealousy or animosity floating off them. For the first time ever, I was jealous.

"Hey," the girl I assumed was Sadie said gently as her eyes locked on mine, "are you okay?"

What? Reality swooped back in on me when I realized I was blocking them from exiting the elevator. Once again, I was gawking. "Yeah, sorry." I moved aside and waved them on, waiting for their laughter.

But none of them laughed.

Instead, the girl with the lighter brown hair smiled. "It's no problem."

The four of them walked by me more gracefully than I'd ever seen anyone move. I'd have bet they had their pick of any guy they set their sights on.

I jumped into the elevator as the girls on the couches snickered again. Now *they* were cold-hearted bitches who were only out for themselves.

On the fifth floor, the number of girls chattering in the hallways almost overwhelmed me. After scanning the area, I turned right and headed to the very end of the hall. My room was the last one on the right.

The fact that I wouldn't have to deal with neighbors on both sides excited me way too much. I unlocked the door and walked in.

The room was four times the size of my bedroom at my aunt's. Twin beds sat across from each other against the light gray walls. A small window in front of the unclaimed bed overlooked the boys' dorm. A desk occupied the space at the foot of the bed, no wider than the bed itself, leaving enough space for me to walk around it to look out the window. The half of the dorm room that would be considered mine gave me more than enough space to feel comfortable.

I'd learned how to live minimally at Sarah's. When Mom and I had moved in after Dad died, Aunt Sarah had sworn up and down that she needed the third bedroom that had been twice the size of the room I wound up occupying for storage. The kicker was that the room wasn't close to a quarter full. I'd been eight years old and had just lost my father, but it had rubbed me wrong even then. Yet, this had been just a tiny taste of what the next ten years had been like for me. Still, at least it prepared me for dorm living.

Brushing off the memory, I entered the room, and a short, thin girl who wore glasses with thick, dark plastic frames faced me. Her stringy caramel hair hung down her face and across her sable eyes. She wore a white Star Wars shirt and plaid pants.

Her outfit was interesting, which was saying a lot coming from me.

When my eyes met hers, she jerked forward and stiffened. She was breathing so hard I could hear her from five feet away.

"Uh ... hi." I wasn't sure what to do, but if we were going to be roommates, I couldn't be a complete ass, could I?

"H-hi," she stuttered and moved her focus back onto a textbook on her desk. "I was hoping I'd have the room to myself again, especially since it's halfway through the school year."

At least, she was as socially awkward as I was. That would either work out well for both of us or be a complete disaster. Only time would tell. "My name is Jade."

She tugged at her ear and kept her eyes cast downward. "I'm Vera."

I glanced at her side of the room and winced internally at the Star Wars sheets on her bed and the poster against her wall. Our room had a sort of style.

The fact that she'd picked the side of the room that butted up against our dorm neighbor surprised me. I'd gotten the side that I preferred. "What's wrong with the bed?" That was the only explanation why she'd choose the lesser side.

"Nothing." She cleared her throat and bent over, hiding her face from me. "It's just ..."

"What?" Before settling in, I wanted to know what I was up against. Bed bugs? Lumpy mattress?

She cringed. "I'm a—afraid of heights."

I hadn't expected that. The window was three feet above the bed and small. It would take a lot of effort to fall through it. It would have to be purposeful, not an accident. "Okay." I nodded, trying to keep my expression indifferent.

"Please don't make fun of me." Her bottom lip quivered. "I know girls like you don't understand what having irrational fears must be like."

"Girls like me?" Just when I'd thought she was timid.

"Beautiful and confident." She waved at me. "I won't bother you, I promise."

I'd never been described like that before. "Thank you, but I'm neither one of those things, and there is no reason I'd make fun of you." I understood what it was like to be cut down each and every day.

She licked her lips. "Okay."

Silence descended between us as I unpacked my bag and made my bed with the light sheets I'd brought. I hung up my clothes in the closet right behind my desk.

It was kind of sad. Within five minutes, I'd unpacked everything I'd brought. "Is the bookstore open?"

"Yes, for another hour or two." She peeked up, looking at my chin, avoiding my eyes. "If you need books, now's the time to get them."

"No shit," was on the tip of my tongue, but I bit it back. That'd been the whole reason I'd asked. "Got it." I grabbed the cash from my duffle bag and walked out of the room. I wouldn't find peace until I felt somewhat prepared for tomorrow.

I took the stairs to the first floor. That way, I wouldn't have to pass the fakers.

At the bottom, I took the side door instead of going through the lobby. A chilly breeze hit me as I stepped outside.

I'd have to buy a jacket soon. In my haste to leave Sarah's, I hadn't thought to grab one.

I wrapped my arms around myself and hurried to the building right across from the girls' dorm. According to the map, it had to be the Student Center where the bookstore and cafeteria were. My stomach grumbled at the thought of food, but I wanted to get my books first.

I hurried along the white concrete sidewalk between the two buildings. Several groups hung out at the benches, and three huge oak trees shaded the entire area. Even with the cool breeze, people were unaffected here.

The back entrance to the Student Center appeared, and I rushed over, wanting to get out of the cold. A strong gust of wind slammed the door shut behind me.

I practically jumped out of my skin.

Dammit, I was way too on edge.

To my right was the university bookstore. I glanced inside and realized that most of the books had been picked through. I'd been banking on purchasing used books. This meant I needed to find a job as soon as possible.

A few students were doing last-minute shopping like me, including—no. Tall, blond, and sexy was across the room, scanning the science section.

That was fine. I'd get that book last. I figured he should be out of here by then. I rushed to the English section on the opposite side of the store. I found the book and moved on to find the other two.

Now, I only needed my science book. I glanced over at that section and found him still standing there. What the hell? Were all of his classes science?

I considered checking out and coming back later. Then it occurred to me that I was letting a man affect my decision, breaking my most important rule: I would never give anyone that much power over me.

I straightened my shoulders and marched over to the science

section. I was making way too much over this. It wasn't like the guy would notice me. He screamed "important," and he'd need someone wearing Versace or whatever the hell those designer clothes were called on the girl standing beside him.

Steadying myself, I walked down the aisle, looking for the Chemistry 101 book. Of course, as I walked past the Biology and Physics sections, I noticed the book I was looking for was at the end, right next to him. *So, he must be taking that class too.*

My heart pounded, and I was so damn glad that no one but I could hear it. How did simply looking at someone make me turn into this pathetic girl I refused to be? Even if my nerves were raw, I'd be damned if he ever knew it.

He stood directly in front of the stack of books I needed, but I could do this. I had to prove it to myself. I cleared my throat, but he kept scanning the books. The only hint that he might have heard me was the corner of his mouth tipping upward.

"Excuse me." I cleared my throat even louder, glaring at him. My annoyance made me feel better. Maybe I was overreacting. "I need to get that book."

"Sure," he said, his faint accent catching me off guard. "I'm sorry." He stepped out of the way, but his huge body was still partially in front of it.

Fine. It was fine. I reached past him, making sure not to touch him, and snatched the book as fast as possible. I turned and rushed away, taking the long way out so I wouldn't have to walk past him. I'd been close enough only moments ago.

No one was in line at the cash register, so I rushed to the front and threw all of my books down on the counter.

The guy behind the counter raised an eyebrow and shrugged, ringing up each book and notepad. When he read off the total, my stomach churned. I didn't have enough on me. "Oh, can I leave these here and run back to get more money?" I hadn't imagined school books would cost this much. The day had progressively gotten worse.

My throat dried as tears burned my eyes. I'd have to look for a job tomorrow if not tonight.

When a huge presence appeared beside me, I wished to become invisible.

CHAPTER THREE

I didn't have to look to know it was him. His presence towered over me. What I didn't understand was why he was here.

"Is there a problem?" Dead Sexy asked, and my stomach tightened.

His voice added to his allure. Maybe I needed to invest in earplugs for when he was around. Wait ... no. That wasn't the solution. The real answer was keeping my distance.

The cashier nodded. "Yeah—"

"No," I cut him off. I refused to be humiliated more than I already was. "There's no problem. I just need to run back to the dorm and get more cash." Not eating a large dinner would teach me self-discipline, which I was obviously lacking, thanks to Golden Eyes.

Ugh, I wasn't sure which nickname was worse: Golden Eyes or Dead Sexy. Both made my heart flip-flop. Stupid, traitorous heart.

Golden Eyes placed his books down beside mine. "Here, ring mine up too." He pulled out a credit card and set it on the counter. "I'll get both of ours."

"What?" Did he think I needed a handout? "Thanks, but no. I have enough back at the dorm."

"It's cold, and you don't have a jacket." He frowned as he glanced at my clothes. "This will keep you from getting sick."

"What are you, my mother?" I cringed; I was being rude. I didn't mean to be, but for him to buy my schoolbooks put red flags up everywhere. No one did anything nice unless they expected something in return. I blurted, "I won't sleep with you."

The cashier snorted and covered it up with a cough.

"Damn, Egan," a guy said, not three feet from us.

I snapped my head in the newcomer's direction and wished I could turn back time. I wouldn't have gotten the damn chemistry book.

The guy who'd spoken had buzzed dark hair and was only a few inches taller than me. His dark eyes filled with mirth. "You just got burned."

"Axel." The third guy, who was taller and even more handsome, chuckled beside him. He was larger than his friend but only half the size of Golden Eyes—Egan. He had longish black hair and piercing blue eyes. A tribal tattoo peeked past his short-sleeved shirt on his right arm.

Who wore short sleeves in winter? And here Egan was, concerned about my lack of a jacket. He needed to worry about his friends.

Egan ignored them and handed the cashier the credit card. "No sex is expected."

"Or blow jobs. Anything sexual is off the table." Why couldn't I shut up? It was like all logic had left me.

His friends tried not to laugh, but smirks were sliding right across their faces.

"Nothing is asked of you." Egan's face turned red as he pushed the card toward the stunned cashier. "It's really not a big deal."

Those books cost more than I earned in a week back at the Italian restaurant I had worked at. The tips hadn't been great but steady. So this was a huge deal. However, I'd already been rude enough, and honestly, I could use the help.

Taking the card, the cashier swiped it, obviously uncomfortable and wanting me to go away. I couldn't blame him. Awkward silence grew thick around Egan, his friends, the cashier, and me.

"We're heading to the cafeteria," the taller friend said. "Want us to save you a seat?"

"You know he does." Axel snorted. "The guy will probably eat most of the food anyway."

"Maybe you and Roxy aren't such a good thing," the other guy replied. "You've gotten more of a mouth on you since you two became ma—a couple."

Mae? I had no clue what he'd been about to say, but he'd obviously changed the wording because of me, piquing my curiosity.

No, Jade. Interest in people was not allowed. I had enough on my plate, without adding more complications, because that was what any relationship created.

Egan took the card back from the cashier and signed the receipt. "I'll be right there."

The two guys waved and headed off.

The cashier divided up Egan's and my books and handed us each a bag. At least, he was smart. I grabbed my bag and stayed put. After him buying my books for me, it wasn't like I could run away. So far, he'd only been nice. It wasn't his fault I found his damn sexy ass attractive.

After putting his wallet in his back pocket, he took his bag and held his right hand out to me.

That was a new one, but okay. I quickly and limply shook his hand. The less touching we did, the better. My fingers buzzed when I touched him, telling me way too much. This was the type of stuff I'd overheard girls describe right before their hearts got destroyed beyond recognition. Yet another reminder of why I needed to gain distance.

He chuckled and shook his head. "No, I was going to carry your bag for you. All those books are heavy."

"You don't think I can handle it?" This wasn't anything. I lifted weights six times as heavy every day.

"What? No." He lifted his hand. "That's not what I meant. It's just, you're a lady—"

"So I need a strong, burly man like you to help me?" He considered me helpless, and it infuriated me.

He blew out a breath. "This is all coming out wrong." He dropped his hand in defeat. "I was trying to be a gentleman."

Maybe that was the truth, but it didn't improve the situation. I tried to swallow my anger, except the best I could do was turn it into annoyance. "I can pay you back." I held out the money I had in my back pocket. "I'm only short a hundred. If you let me run back to the dorm—"

"That was the whole point." He waved the money away. "And it's fine. I don't mind doing that for you."

"Look, at least, take this." He was making me feel pathetic even if he didn't mean to. It was important that I stand on my own two feet. He was a strong man, so he wouldn't understand. "It'll make me feel better."

"It would make you feel better?" His brows furrowed. "Really?"

If I hadn't been so upset, the confusion on his face would have been comical. I wondered how many girls he'd done this for. Obviously, none of the others had complained. "Yes, that's a lot of money, and I just need to do this."

"But it's no big deal." His shoulders sagged in disappointment.

"It is to me." He looked like he was crumbling, so I applied more pressure. "I really do appreciate it." And I did. By him covering what I didn't have, I'd have enough money to eat for a few days if I budgeted. I'd have to go find a job and run to the grocery store. I'd be eating a lot of PB&Js. I held out the money, needing him to take it.

He pursed his lips and scratched the back of his neck. "Okay."

Once he'd taken the money, I turned, ready to get the hell out of there. Since he was meeting his friends at the cafeteria, I'd skip lunch and come back later to grab dinner. In the meantime, I'd raid the vending machine downstairs in the dorm. Besides, I didn't have any cash on me to get food even if I wanted to.

"Hey," he called right as I entered the hallway.

I wished he'd leave me alone. The more time I spent around him, the harder it would be to keep my distance. I wasn't sure how I knew that, but I felt it in my bones. On their own accord, my feet stopped and turned me around. "Yeah?"

"My friends and I are grabbing lunch." He placed a hand in his jeans pocket. "Why don't you join us?"

This guy couldn't be real. He actually seemed decent, which scared me. Assholes I could handle, but sincere people petrified me. "Remember, I don't have any more cash." I forced a grin. "But thanks." I couldn't remember the last time someone had invited me to hang out with them.

He took a few eager steps toward me. "I can buy your lunch."

"You just covered a hundred bucks on my books." My head screamed at me to run. "Thanks, but no. Have fun with your friends." I took off again, back to my dorm, needing to clear my head.

My alarm blared, barely waking me from a deep sleep. After the traumatic start to my day, I'd passed out hard last night, but I didn't feel any better. I'd dreamt about Mom and Dad and the day before he died. It was strange. We'd gone to the beach as a family and had the best day. I'd even made a friend, whom I'd felt like I'd known all my life even though we'd just met. At first, my parents had hung out with his parents, and they'd all gotten along until something had freaked out Mom.

I hadn't dreamed or thought of that day in so long. It hurt too much. It was the last time everything had felt perfect in my life.

Vera grumbled, "Are you going to turn that thing off?" She put her pillow over her head.

Good to know she had the dramatic air of a normal teenage girl.

I'd started to think she was abnormal, which wouldn't have been a bad thing. After I'd gotten back from the bookstore, we'd kept to ourselves. Being roommates might work out for both of us.

"Yeah, sorry." I snagged the phone off the ground and stopped the alarm. All I wanted to do was go back to sleep, but then I'd be late for my class.

I had to take this seriously since I ran away for this opportunity when fall semester hadn't panned out at the local community college. Mom and I agreed that I'd attend there for the fall semester. We'd compromised since Mom didn't want me to leave. I'd at least get an education. But when Aunt Sarah had found out about our little plan, she'd informed Mom that if I went to college instead of getting a job to help cover our expenses, we'd have to move out. Mom had broken down, and I'd done the only thing I could: I'd let the opportunity go—or I'd planned to.

But when I'd stumbled upon an online ad for Kortright University. Something had pulled at me stronger than ever before. This was the place for me, so I did what I had to do. I'd paid for a post office box and applied. I hadn't expected it to amount to much since it was a private college, but then they'd offered to cover my tuition, including room and board, and only books and other expenses were my responsibility. I'd have to work, but the brunt of the financial burden had been eliminated. I'd considered it destiny.

With every ounce of strength I had, I put my feet on the shaggy brown carpet and stood. I hadn't showered after my rumble with Sarah, so that was a necessity. I grabbed the one towel I'd brought and a change of clothes and forced myself to enter the realm of an all-girl bathroom.

It was worse than I'd expected for nine in the morning, but luckily, I got the last shower stall and was in and out within minutes.

Back in the safety of my room, I sighed with relief as I finished toweling off my hair, slipping on a pair of ripped jeans and a long-sleeved shirt. As usual, I didn't put on makeup. I had no one to impress anyway.

I grabbed the textbooks I needed for my first day, a folder, and some cash for breakfast. Since I didn't have a bag to carry my items in yet, it was a little awkward, but I'd make it work.

I'd wound up hiding out for the remainder of the night in my dorm, eating Doritos and Funyuns instead of going back to the Student Center. I hated to admit it, but I'd been too nervous that I might run into him yet again, so I'd stayed put. Those two run-ins with him had been more than enough.

The buzz of conversations hit me when I entered the Student Center. I scanned the wide-open area of booths and tables, and most of them were full. It felt like high school all over again. Everyone had their clique, and I was the outsider.

I made a beeline toward the food counter on my left. There were ten different service stations, and each one was pretty full. It surprised me that there were so many options. The pictures on the internet hadn't done them any justice.

Saliva pooled in my mouth as I considered the different options. When I spotted the fresh cinnamon rolls one of the workers put out, I practically ran right to them.

I snagged two and a cup of coffee and headed straight to the cash register. On my way, my eyes found him—Golden Eyes. Wow, when his friends had said he ate almost all of the food, they hadn't been lying.

Egan had two trays, and each one was full of every type of breakfast. It had to cost at least fifty dollars, all in one sitting. Who could afford to eat like that?

Didn't matter. It wasn't any of my business. I forced my focus back in front of me and quickly checked out before I had yet another run-in with him.

The safest spot for me was outside, despite the chill. After class today, I'd go find a job and pick up a jacket. I marched right outside and sat at a bench in the sunshine. It wasn't quite as bad there.

Taking a bite, I enjoyed the cinnamon and vanilla frosting that hit my tongue. I hadn't had a cinnamon roll in years. Well, about ten years. That was what Dad would make me every morning on my birthday. It had been my favorite growing up. The fact I was now eating one wasn't lost on me. Maybe I could finally put a little bit of the pain behind me.

The pink-haired girl from the other day walked out of the Student Center and frowned when she saw me. "Hey, are you okay?"

I looked around, expecting to see one of her friends, but then I realized she was talking to me. "Uh ... yeah. Why?"

"You look sad." She made her way over, watching me with a tilt of her head. "And you're sitting out here alone while it's chilly by Tennessee standards. Did something happen?"

Maybe I wasn't leaving any of my pain behind after all. "Yeah, I'm fine. Just a little overwhelmed." I wanted to slap my hands over my mouth. Why had I said that to her?

"You're new here." She nodded. "Are you lost or something?"

Her question hit me hard. "Yeah, I am." But I didn't mean it in the way she thought. I meant lost in life. It was probably the most honest moment I'd had in a long time.

"Then where are you heading?" The girl smiled, somehow becoming even more breathtaking.

"American History." At least I knew that off the top of my head.

"I am too." Her sky-blue eyes lit up with enthusiasm. "Come with me." She gestured for me to follow her.

Eh ... I could eat the other cinnamon roll in class. I stood, gathered my things, and walked beside her, feeling awkward. I wasn't used to talking to people my own age.

As we strolled past a Student Center window, the back of my neck tingled, alerting me that someone was watching me. My heart raced, and the urge to flee overwhelmed me.

CHAPTER FOUR

The chill sank deep into my bones. It felt like the times Sarah would be watching me through the window, thinking I hadn't noticed her.

It was creepy, unsettling, and straight-up disturbing.

The rose-gold-haired girl stopped and turned to me. "Is something wrong?"

"Nope," I said way too quickly. Great, let's add paranoid to my list of winning personality traits. I picked up my pace and glanced over my shoulder. Something flashed behind a tree by the side of the building as if they were hiding from me.

It was probably a cat, rabbit, squirrel, or some other animal that hung around during the colder months. It wasn't like it was a person. But I couldn't shake that feeling. No wonder talking to people gave me such anxiety.

"So, I'm Sadie." She gestured to herself.

The name suited her. "A unique name for a unique girl."

Her eyebrow lifted, and a corner of her mouth turned upright. "Um ... thanks?"

"Unique as in different." Oh, God. I'd just insulted her when all she'd done was be nice to me. "I mean, you're pretty."

She chuckled. "Are you going to share your name with me?"

"Jade." I tried pointing at myself but wound up shoving the plastic food container into my chest, nearly popping it open, and coffee sloshed out and trickled down my hand.

"Do you need help?" She held out her hand to take the container. "You need to get a backpack or a bag or something."

Yeah, I did. But I'd have to wait until I found a job. Right when I was about to tell her no, that I had it, she took the container out of my hand.

"Let me get the coffee too." She snatched the coffee and picked up the pace, leaving me behind.

Adjusting the books, I hurried to catch up. "Thanks." I jostled the books to one side and wiped my hand against my jeans to remove the coffee.

"No problem," she said, eyeing me like she expected me to snatch the food and drink back.

Part of me wanted to, but I ignored the urge. Yes, I'd mainly come to college to get away from my aunt and make something of my life, but maybe I could be a little more open with people. Like, not go crazy by dating or anything but, at least, have an acquaintance I could copy notes from if I missed a class.

Even thinking about dating had my heart beating erratically, but I couldn't become a weird, reclusive cat lady, could I?

The thought wasn't all that unappealing, proving how bad I'd gotten.

Instead of continuing down my train wreck line of thoughts, I focused on our surroundings. We headed right, passing the sidewalk that led to Kortright Stadium, and stayed on the path of the large circle, passing Wilson Hall. American History was held in Grey Hall, which sat across the grassy area from the Student Center with Webster Hall to the left and Wilson Hall directly opposite.

As we approached the standard two-story brick building, I

observed the students buzzing by. Our class was on the top floor. If memory served me right, there wasn't an elevator in this building. The entryway was flat, and I held the large single door open for Sadie. It only seemed right since she was carrying my food and drink. It also helped that she knew where she was going. I followed her as she turned right to the single stairway that headed upstairs before entering the large hallway of the main floor.

People squeezed past us as we walked up the narrow stairway barely wide enough for two people to pass by comfortably.

I should've taken my stuff back from Sadie. If her clothes got ruined, I couldn't afford to buy her any new ones.

But I soon learned I didn't need to worry. Even as people shoved past her, she had the most grace I'd ever seen before. It was like she anticipated the movements before they jarred her and shifted to prevent anything from spilling on her.

I was extremely envious. Even with all the martial arts, I still tripped over my own feet.

On the top floor, Sadie entered the first classroom on the right, and I dutifully followed. There were four rows with eight seats each. The classroom was half full, and most of the front seats were already taken.

Odd.

Didn't everyone get to class early to sit at the back? That was always my motivation.

Sadie walked past the first two rows toward the back. She glanced over her shoulder. "Mind if we sit back there?"

"Nope." That was exactly what I preferred. Maybe we were meant to be friends.

Two guys in the middle almost broke their necks to watch Sadie walk by. Girls like her commanded attention even though it wasn't on purpose, unlike the popular kids back in high school, who would flip their hair and wear revealing clothing to capture guys' attention. Sadie wore jeans that weren't skin tight and a thick, black sweater that was stylish yet simple. Her hair was short compared to most girls our age, and her face was gorgeous despite wearing very little makeup.

As I walked past another row over, no one turned my way, which was fine. I didn't want the attention anyway. I plopped into the desk next to Sadie and dropped my Spanish book on the ground.

"Here you go." Sadie held out my food and coffee.

"Thanks for the help." Those were words I wasn't used to saying.

"No problem," she said as she set her purple backpack on the ground and pulled out her own items. She got situated as I finished my food.

A petite girl entered the room. Her teal eyes, which matched the shade of her hair, locked on Sadie, and a smile spread across her face, emphasizing the golden-pink hue of her skin. What was it with the girls here? This girl was gorgeous too.

"Sadie," she said, and her voice sounded like a bell. She rushed toward the back and took the other seat beside her.

"Naida." Sadie sounded thrilled to see her. "How are you? It's been a few weeks."

"Yes, I'm sorry." Naida's voice held a slight accent similar to Golden Eyes. "Just everything is crazy in Fae—"

"The family." Sadie laughed loudly then cringed. "Those damn family members."

"Right," Naida agreed, and her eyes brushed over me. "They are something."

It was obvious they didn't want me to know what they were talking about. Maybe I'd misjudged them. I kept my eyes forward, not bothering to glance at them. I recognized when people were excluding me.

Class ended, and I grabbed my books and stood, eager to get the hell out. I tried to be patient with all of the people in front of me, but I didn't want Sadie to feel obligated to talk to me. As long as I looked busy, she'd be off the hook. It helped that Naida had leaned over and begun whispering right when class was dismissed.

Every seat had been taken since this was a fundamental class at a coveted university. I'd bet all my classes would be packed.

Luckily, my next class was in the same building, only on the first floor. People finally moved out of my way, and when I stepped into the hallway, I breathed a little easier. I bounded down the stairs and entered the wide main hallway. I found my classroom, which was the last room on the left.

As I entered the empty classroom, my shoulders sagged. Maybe I'd actually get a few seconds to myself. Back home, I was always in my room and only came out when absolutely necessary. I'd only been here one day, and the constant swarm of people was getting to me. I'd figured coming here would be an adjustment, and that was just part of it.

I tossed my trash in the garbage can and headed to the back where I liked to be. This classroom was set up the same way as the one upstairs, so I took a seat and leaned my head against the dark gray wall behind me.

A few people trickled in but didn't sit near me. I'd never understood why, but most people kept a decent amount of distance between themselves and me as though they sensed something weird inside me, or maybe I had a resting bitch face. That seemed plausible too.

Even before my dad's death, I hadn't felt like I fit in with anyone until that day on the beach when I'd met the boy. For the first time in my life, something had clicked. Between losing that connection and my dad within a day, I couldn't breathe when I thought back on it. I had no clue why all of this was bubbling to the surface. Maybe it was because I'd gotten away from Mom and Sarah.

Something inside me shifted as heavy footsteps entered the room. My eyes opened, and there stood Golden Eyes. His attention was locked on me as he made his way toward me.

Every time I'd read a book where a character caught their breath,

I'd laughed. Like, how did one actually do that? Did they stop mid-breath or maybe look constipated? But now I understood it. Every part of my body was focused on him and couldn't expend any extra energy beyond that.

"Hey," he rasped as he somehow fit into the desk beside me.

Any other guy would have looked ridiculous squeezing into something that small for them, but he looked damn sexy. The worst part was that I was noticing and couldn't stop.

"Hi," I said, forcing the word out.

He scanned my books on the floor and frowned. "Where's your backpack?"

"Oh." That snapped me out of my stupor. "It broke this morning," I said, lying through my teeth.

Egan's face wrinkled like he smelled something bad.

Dear God, please tell me I didn't fart. I'd have noticed if I had, right? I was tempted to sniff the air to see if I could figure it out, but I had already embarrassed myself enough.

"Well, why don't we go to the Student Center and buy you a backpack after class?" He smiled like it was the best idea he'd ever had.

What was it with him and wanting to buy me things? That wasn't normal, was it? "No, I'm good. I can probably fix it. No need to waste anything that can be fixed." That would be another item to pick up while I was out.

He pinched the bridge of his nose as it wrinkled.

Okay, I had to know. "Do I smell bad or something?"

A girl sitting at the front of the class looked back at me. Her low-cut red top left little to the imagination, and I probably would've been able to see her vagina in that super-short skirt if she hadn't been wearing tights due to winter. Her cinnamon-colored hair fell across her shoulders as her ebony eyes landed on me. "If you have to ask, it probably means yes." She patted the seat next to her and did a duck face while looking at Egan. "You can come sit next to me. I promise I don't smell."

"I'm pretty sure skanky stinks too." It was one thing when people talked shit about me behind my back, but when they were blatant enough to do it to my face, I had to put an end to it. Otherwise, I'd be bullied my entire existence. "And I'm sure if anyone gets within a foot of you, they risk getting an STD."

Egan's eyes widened, and his lips mashed together, but he couldn't hide the shaking of his shoulders.

"You bitch." The girl jumped to her feet like she thought she could do something about it. Her platform shoes had heels that were over six inches tall.

All I needed to do was break a kneecap, and she wouldn't be able to stand on the other foot or crawl back to her dorm. "Maybe." It was true, and even though everything inside me told me to put the girl in her place, I already made a big enough scene. I was tired of people shitting on me. Still, I didn't want to become like Sarah.

"Listen here." She stomped her foot like it didn't make her look like a toddler throwing a tantrum. "You're the one who said it. I just agreed and gave him another option."

Egan shifted in his seat, and I turned toward him, not able to hide my surprise. Was he really going to go sit next to her after offering to buy all of these things for me? Maybe he was looking for a lay.

Leaning over the desk, he arched an eyebrow and looked me directly in the eye as he responded to the girl, "There is no other place I want to sit than back here. I want to make that perfectly clear."

My blood pumped, and my body warmed. What the hell was wrong with me? I had to be falling sick or something.

I didn't know how to respond, and for a second, it felt like he and I were the only two people in the room. None of this made sense. He seemed familiar, but I'd remember someone like him. He'd be impossible to forget.

The professor entered the room and cleared her throat, forcing me to come back down to reality. While I'd been distracted by this guy, the classroom had completely filled, and she began class.

The entire time in class, I tried to keep my eyes forward and on the whiteboard, but I couldn't repeat a damn word that the professor said. I kept wanting to look in Egan's direction. At one point, I stole a glance, which was a huge mistake. He was staring at me, and I wasn't sure if I should be thrilled that he was struggling too or scared that he'd caught me.

After class, I'd be going off-campus. I needed to run errands, but it was so much more than that. I had to reflect on what was going on with me. It was unnerving.

Class ended, and I stood, wondering if the girl would try to start shit with me again. Luckily, she darted out, eager to leave. At least, that problem was solved.

I heard Egan climb from the desk beside me. I'd taken a step toward the door when his sexy voice called out, "Hey."

The smart thing would have been to pretend I hadn't heard him, but my feet stopped.

CHAPTER FIVE

I hated the hold Egan had over me. Whenever he spoke, it affected me in forbidden ways, especially since I'd only met him yesterday. It warned of an unhealthy dose of attraction. I waited for him to finish whatever he wanted to say.

He moved closer to me and ran a hand through his hair. "Maybe after my next class, we could grab lunch together?"

"I don't date." I cringed at how he might take that. "Or sleep around."

Oh, crap. What if he hadn't meant as a date but as friends? No one like him would actually want to date me. He looked like all the statues of gods that littered textbooks—chiseled abs visible through his shirt and bulging everywhere else ... and I meant *everywhere* else. My eyes almost flicked to his crotch. I lost all sense around him.

"Okay, good to know." He chuckled, but the smile didn't reach his eyes. "And that's too bad about the dating thing."

My heart picked up its pace. It had to stop doing that. "Really? You want to date me?"

His smile turned into a sexy smirk. "Why wouldn't I? You're beautiful, strong, and stand your ground."

I almost corrected him. I wasn't strong; I was scared. There was a huge difference, but for him to call me beautiful had caught me off guard enough that I was speechless. I welcomed it for a minute because, at least, I wouldn't babble something else embarrassing. "No, you're beautiful." Scratch that. There it was.

"I'm beautiful?" His eyebrows shot up as his forehead creased with confusion or surprise.

Right now, there was a fifty/fifty shot it could be either emotion. "God, no."

Startled, he tilted his head. "No?"

"I mean ... you're sexy." I needed to shut up, pronto. "Dead sexy." My mouth wouldn't quit, meaning there was only one thing left to do. I turned and ran out the door.

Dropping Spanish, or never leaving my dorm room again, wouldn't be a big deal. Both were viable options.

In the hallway, a large, warm hand gently grabbed my arm and turned me around. Tingles ignited from where his skin touched mine. He was so tall I had to lean my head all the way back to look into his eyes; otherwise, I'd be staring at his nipples. I bet guys didn't like that any more than girls did. Granted, his chest was pure muscle and no fat. I was tempted to reach out and touch it to confirm it'd be hard against my fingertips.

His eyes glowed. "You finding me dead sexy is a good thing."

The fact that I wasn't more freaked out by his glowing eyes and that I actually found him hotter petrified me. Something was broken in my brain, and I had to get my hormones under control. "I've got to go." The longer I stayed, the worse it would be. It took every ounce of willpower I had, but I pulled from his grasp and rushed back down the hallway. I needed fresh air.

Right before I turned to head out of the building, I glanced over my shoulder, worried and excited at the possibility of him chasing me. However, he stood right outside the classroom, watching me go. A frown marred his gorgeous face, and it bothered me that I'd put it there. I wanted to go back and make it right.

Instead, my survival instincts kicked in, reducing the urge, and I headed outside. I'd planned on going back to my room and changing to look for a job, but I needed a second to collect myself. The woods called to me. Maybe nature would help settle me.

No one watched as I broke through the tree line. At first, the trees were spread apart, but the deeper I walked, the more clustered they became. Growing up, I'd hang out in the neighborhood woods every Saturday morning when Sarah would leave to run errands or meet up with someone. It was the only thing that had kept me sane.

Hiking had quickly become my favorite pastime, and as I walked deeper into the woods, the burn in my legs brought relief. My arms grew heavy from the books I carried, so I found a bush to stash them in. A thirty-minute hike should snap me back to myself.

Sunlight trickled through the trees, casting long shadows in certain areas. Moments like these brought me peace. I never challenged why. Maybe it connected me to my father because we used to go on short hikes together.

With each step, my body warmed until I no longer felt cold. A slight breeze picked up, blowing my hair out of my face. The ground became an incline, forcing my calves to work even harder.

Even though the trees were bare, birds and squirrels scurried from branch to branch. The chirping and rustling were like music to my ears, which most girls found strange.

As a kid, I'd believed I was connected to nature. I'd declared to Dad that I could shift into an animal if I wanted to. He'd laughed and asked me which one. I remembered pointing to myself and sticking my chest out proudly, saying, "A unicorn." His response had been perfect, especially for a little girl.

He'd replied, "If anyone could ever be a strong, powerful unicorn, it's you." Those words had made me so happy.

Of course, I wasn't a strong, powerful unicorn, and boy, had Sarah enjoyed teaching me that hard lesson. At first, I couldn't defend myself, but after years of martial arts training, I'd gained the skill and confidence to stand up for myself. And I'd defended myself one time. Sarah had cried out, alerting Mom. Mom had come upstairs, and my aunt had pointed out how I'd hurt her. Seeing my mom's disappointment had devastated me. I never defended myself again until yesterday.

A branch snapped a few yards away from me, and I stopped, scanning the area for anything out of place, but nothing stuck out, except for the silence.

All of the happy animal noises were gone, which meant a predator was out. I hadn't even considered a wolf would be out here, but I should have. The hundred and fifty acres of woods that surrounded the college had drawn me here. With that much land, large predators were a given.

My breathing quickened, and I turned around in place. I tried moving slowly and silently even if it was futile. Wolves had excellent hearing, but I hoped it was a different hunter that didn't have such enhanced hearing and sight. Moving slowly was my best option.

I put one foot in front of the other. Luckily, the way back was downhill, which would help me move a bit faster.

With each step, I prayed I put more distance between me and whatever was back there. The back of my neck tingled again just like this morning. It was probably my paranoia and nothing more, but if something was chasing me, it could be gaining ground, and I wouldn't know.

God, I'd been stupid to come out here alone. I should've known better since I didn't know this area. The real kicker was the fact I could be out here dead for days before someone even missed me. Maybe a professor would follow up with the business office to see why I'd missed class, or parts of my body would show up on campus from whatever animal had killed me. It really proved how alone I was in this world, and for the first time, I regretted it, which was strange. Normally, I didn't care, but now, it made me sad.

Another branch snapped behind me, closer than before.

No. Something was hunting me. There was no question now.

I took off running, acting like the prey it wanted, but dammit, I didn't care. Maybe its instincts to hunt and kill would drive it crazy and I could outthink it. Hunting was ingrained in whatever was chasing me.

In other words, I was dead.

Every rational thought left me, and I ran harder than I ever had in my entire life. The leaves crunched underfoot, telling the animal where I was going.

But I couldn't stop.

Something made a noise behind me, but I couldn't make out what it was, and I refused to turn around. It would only slow me down, and I was hell-bent on getting back to campus—hopefully in one piece.

My feet slipped on the leaves, and I slid a few inches before landing hard on my knees.

More noises came from behind me, and I couldn't help but turn around. Pure terror coursed through my body, and when I didn't see anything behind me, my fear went into overdrive.

Whatever was chasing me didn't want to be seen until it was ready. It would be less terrifying if I knew what I was up against, not that it would make a bit of difference.

I jumped back to my feet and took off again, running a tad slower. If I kept falling, it would take me longer to get back. Every few feet, I heard another noise. The predator was having fun and closing in.

The realization that I wouldn't make it back to campus slammed into me.

No, I couldn't give up. I'd risked it all to get away. I couldn't let it end just when I'd gained my freedom. Renewed energy invigorated me, and I kept steadily on my feet.

A low chuckle filled the air.

A fucking chuckle.

I didn't know of one damn animal that could laugh. A person couldn't be hunting me, right?

If so, they were a sick psycho. Now I couldn't force myself to look ahead. I needed to know what was behind me. I ran haphazardly forward as I looked back, and I slammed into something hard. As I bounced off, strong, solid arms wrapped around my waist, and I screamed louder than I had in my entire life.

My knee instinctively slammed upward, and a loud groan vibrated from his chest. This guy was huge.

As he crumpled to the ground, one hand released me to cup his balls. Using that in my favor, I punched him in the face. Something popped, and pain coursed down my arm.

Of course, it would be some douchebag guy, but how the hell had he circled in front of me?

"Stop, please." The too familiar, sexy-accented voice groaned. "I didn't mean to scare you."

"Egan?" Wait ... there was no way it could be him. I'd left him behind at the school. What was he doing out here? I stepped back so I could see him.

His face was red and scrunched in pain. "Yeah."

"We've got to go." He didn't need to be here. Now we'd both get eaten alive.

"What's wrong?" He straightened and looked behind me. "Did something happen?"

"Something is chasing me." My voice shook with fear, but I didn't care. "We need to go. We both could be in danger now."

"No, it's fine," he said as he placed his hands on my shoulders. "You're safe."

What was crazy was that I actually felt that way, but I didn't want to analyze those feelings, not after what I'd just gone through. "How do you know?"

"I just know." He sighed. "Stay right here and let me go take a look. I'll be right back." He stepped in the direction I'd been running from, and I grabbed his hand.

"Don't." I didn't want him to get hurt. "Let's get back to campus."

He shook his head, ready to argue, but I didn't want him to leave my side.

I pressed, "Please."

Something softened in his eyes. "Okay," he said gently. "I won't leave you."

I exhaled a breath I hadn't realized I'd been holding. "Thank you."

"Of course." He looked deeper into the woods one last time before turning and standing close to me. "Why don't we head back to campus and get you settled?"

"I'm all for that." Words had never sounded sweeter.

We trekked back toward the university in silence. A few minutes in, Egan looked at me and asked, "Why did you come out here all alone?"

"Wait ..." That reminded me... "I thought you had a class right now." He'd asked me to go to lunch in an hour.

He chewed on his bottom lip. "I saw you head out here, and I came looking for you."

Wow. He really was a nice guy. For some reason, that made this all worse. "You missed your class because of me?"

"It was just the first class to calculus." He waved his hand dismissively. "I took it last semester for a few weeks, so I already know the material."

"Oh." I guessed that made sense. "Did you drop it?"

"Yeah, something came up, and I had to leave." He shrugged as he looked at me again. "So I'm back and retaking the same classes."

He obviously didn't want to tell me more, and I wasn't one to push. God knew I had my own secrets. "Well, I hope everything is okay now."

"It is." He grinned. "What about you?"

We were getting closer to campus, and the bush where I'd put my books came into view. "Oh, this is my first semester at college." I didn't have too much to share.

At the bush, I stopped and grabbed my books.

He held his arms out. "Here, I can take them."

I almost handed them to him before I stopped myself. "No, I'm good. Thanks, though." He'd saved my life. Every time I was around him, he took care of me in some way.

Something fell behind us, and I spun around. At least, we were close to campus. "We better go. That's what was going on earlier."

"Head back." His shoulders stiffened, and he grew rigid. "I'll be right behind you."

"I'm not going without you." Was he crazy? I couldn't leave him alone out here.

"Fine." He waved me on.

I took off running back to campus. After I'd run about a hundred yards, I realized I didn't hear Egan behind me. I stopped when more noises sounded several feet to my right. There was more than one predator. We were so screwed.

CHAPTER SIX

I wanted to yell for Egan, but that would only put us both in more danger. Maybe he'd heard the person and was hiding. I wouldn't blame him. After all, people only looked out for themselves. Since I was already at risk, it was my turn to protect him. "Who's there?" I dropped my books and spread my feet shoulder-width apart, crouching into a fighter's stance. Whatever it was could likely kick my ass, but I wasn't going down without a fight.

Footsteps approached me from behind a tree. I sprang into action and reached for whatever it was. My hand touched smooth skin, freaking me out, and I jerked the person toward me, prepared to knee them in the face. A flash of rose-gold hair flashed.

Sadie yanked her arm from mine and dodged my knee. It should have been impossible, but she moved fast.

"Jade." She stood and lifted her hands. "I'm not here to attack you."

"Then what are you doing out here?" None of this made sense. First Egan and now her. "I could've hurt you."

"I heard a noise and thought someone might be in trouble." Sadie gestured to the tree line several feet away. "But apparently, all I did was scare you."

"You shouldn't be out here." I snatched my books from the ground and glanced over my shoulder again. Egan was still missing. "But thanks for checking on me." I turned to go back deeper into the woods when Sadie grabbed my arm.

"I shouldn't be out here, but you're about to run back in there?" She shook her head and tugged me to the tree line. "Nope, that's not how this goes. You're coming with me."

"But ..." I tried to pull out of her grasp, but she held on firmly. I really wasn't getting out of this situation without causing a big scene. I didn't have much of an option, and after what I'd seen of her, I had a feeling she could kick my ass. "Okay." I sighed. "I'm coming."

"Good. You can join me and the girls for lunch." She continued to tug me toward the buildings. "I'm supposed to meet with them now."

"Uh ... I've got errands to run." Being around them didn't sit well with me. I didn't feel comfortable around others.

"Come on." Sadie stopped and turned to me. "You almost messed up my face. The least you can do is eat lunch with me." She pouted.

"You're manipulating me." For some reason, I didn't mind.

She pointed at herself and winked. "I'm not even going to deny it."

If I told her no again, she wouldn't push it, but after what I'd experienced in the woods, maybe it wouldn't be so horrible to make friends. I didn't have to get close to them or anything. "Fine."

Her mouth dropped. "Really? I figured you'd say no again."

"Oh." She hadn't expected me to say yes. "I totally don't have to. I really do have errands to run."

"Nope." She smiled, and it even reached her eyes. "You already said okay."

"Technically, I said fine begrudgingly," I teased, which surprised me.

"It's a form of yes." She looped her arm through mine and tugged me toward the Student Center. "And there are officially no take-backs."

Being around her felt easy when she wasn't having elusive conversations with other people. I wasn't sure how she would be around the other girls. "I can't stay for long."

"Middle ground." She nodded. "I can handle that."

We walked toward the Student Center in amicable silence. My thoughts kept going back to Egan, but I had the odd feeling he was all right. *How the hell could I know that?*

We walked into the building, and Sadie zeroed in on her friends all the way in the back corner of the overcrowded place. I could barely make out Roxy, but it was like Sadie knew where her friends were. It was strange, unless those were their normal seats.

She dragged me with her, and we squeezed by various tables to get to the booth. The two darker-haired girls sat together while the vibrant redhead had a vacant seat next to her.

The two girls sitting across from Roxy each had a travel cup and no food, while Roxy held two plates that each contained a double cheeseburger and fries. Roxy put one plate down in front of the open seat beside her.

All three girls glanced at me periodically, making me feel extremely paranoid.

"Thanks," Sadie said as she snatched a chair from a vacant table and put it at the end. "There, you can sit here, Jade."

At least I wouldn't have to stand here awkwardly, pondering my next moves. "I'm going to grab a bite."

"Okay, we'll be here." Sadie smiled and bit into her burger.

I placed my books on the table and hurried away. When I stepped into the cafeteria, my heart calmed. I hadn't noticed, but adrenaline still pumped through my body from whatever had gone down in the woods. At times, it had sounded like an animal, but at other times, it had sounded like a person. It couldn't be both, so what the hell was it?

Scanning the food stations, I made my way over to the cheap

chicken nuggets and fries baking under a hot lamp. They looked like they'd been out there a while. The chicken looked shriveled, but it was the cheapest food they had here. After packing a container and picking up a bottle of Coke, I quickly checked out at the register and headed back over to the four girls. They stopped talking as I approached, making me feel uncomfortable.

I quickly sat down and shoved a nugget into my mouth.

The girl with brown hair smiled. "Hi, I'm Katherine. I don't think we've met yet."

"No," I said around a mouthful of food. "We haven't. I'm Jade."

"I don't think any of you have met her," Sadie jumped in. "That's Lillith," she said, pointing to the darkest-haired girl. "And that's Roxy."

"Nice to meet you." I pretended not to know any of their names.

"Sadie was telling us she found you in the woods." Roxy took a sip of her water. "What were you doing out there?"

That was kind of odd and random. "Just needed to get away, so I went for a hike."

"Those woods aren't the best to go in alone." Lillith lifted her drink. "Last semester, a few people went missing in there."

After what I'd experienced today, I wasn't surprised. "Yeah, there was something out there. I have no clue what, though."

"You heard something?" Sadie frowned. "No wonder you were about to break my face." She chuckled.

"Yeah, it sounded like something was chasing me." And here I'd thought I was paranoid. There was no telling what had happened there. "A friend found me but didn't follow me out."

"That had to be scary. Where did your friend go?" Katherine asked with concern.

"I don't know. Egan told me to head back to campus, but when I looked back, he was gone." Talking about it had made me lose my appetite. Maybe I shouldn't have left him.

"If I know Egan, there's nothing to worry about." Sadie patted my arm reassuringly. "He has an uncanny way of always coming out on top."

Of course, they'd know him. "You know him too?" I shoved a fry into my mouth, trying not to let my insecurities bubble to the surface. When I imagined the type of girl meant for Egan, Sadie popped into my mind.

"Yeah." She smiled. "We all started here last semester together. He was in a class of mine."

I wondered if they'd ever dated and tried pushing it from my mind. It didn't matter.

"So, where are you from?" Roxy asked as grease dribbled down her chin.

"Ew." Lillith grabbed a napkin from the holder and threw it at her. "Leave greasing up for the bedroom and just verbal details for me. I don't need a visual."

Oh my God. They were going to talk about sex with me here. Hell, I didn't even know how to do that. I'd never even kissed a guy. Okay, that was a lie. I'd kissed a guy when I was thirteen, but there'd been so much slobber involved that I did my best to forget it.

"Most of the time, my mouth isn't involved unless he's been extra good." Roxy wiped her face with an exaggerated motion. "And that doesn't need greasing up." She wiggled her eyebrows.

I choked on my food.

"Aw, you're embarrassing her." Lillith tsked. "You should really learn when to keep your mouth shut."

"Oh, bite me, va—" Roxy's eyes widened, and she stuttered. "You meanie."

Katherine glared at Lillith. "You started it."

"Whose side are you on?" Lillith stuck her tongue out at her friend.

"The right side." Roxy motioned to herself. "Which is also known as Roxy's side."

"Just ignore them." Sadie turned toward me and rolled her eyes.

"Those two like to give each other a hard time. It's the foundation of their friendship."

That was clear and amusing to listen to. I'd bet those two never let things get boring.

"Hey." Roxy wrinkled her nose. "Don't tell our secrets."

Lillith snorted. "I agree. I don't like being called out."

Katherine lifted her cup. "Yet you two are the first to call anyone out."

Roxy's forehead lined. "What's going on here?"

"I don't know." Lillith pouted. "But I'm thinking we need to do something."

"Please don't." Sadie shook, feigning horror. "We don't want to scare Jade off after just a few minutes."

"Fine." Roxy flipped her hair over her shoulder and smiled at me. "Only because she seems cool."

Now *that* made me feel awkward, so of course, that meant my mouth opened. "So what, are you two on a diet or something?" I glanced at Lillith and Katherine, who only had drinks.

"Oh ..." Katherine grimaced.

"No, we aren't," Lillith interjected and ran her finger along the top edge of her lid. "We just enjoy drinks with lots of protein."

I hadn't heard of that, but to each their own. I finished the rest of my food and glanced around. The place had become even more packed. "Well, thanks for letting me join you all, but I'm going to get going." I needed to find a job. The food here was more expensive than I'd realized.

"No more going into the woods alone, okay?" Sadie narrowed her eyes at me, driving home her point.

"Don't worry, that won't happen again."

"What's your number?" Roxy asked as she pulled her phone from her pocket. "We can bug you later about dinner."

They actually wanted to be my friends. I rattled off my number and waved, turning to the door.

Outside, a cool breeze lifted my hair, and my eyes instinctively went to the woods. Egan stepped out of the tree line. He wasn't injured. The only thing different was that his perfectly styled hair was messy, adding to his allure.

His attention remained firmly locked on the woods, and the other two guys from the bookstore the other day stepped out and talked to him.

At least, he wasn't alone.

My body wanted to go to him, but I'd been around him enough for one day. I forced myself to turn toward the dorms and took off without looking back. It was probably one of the hardest things I'd ever done.

In my dorm room, I breathed a sigh of relief. Vera wasn't there, so I'd actually have a moment alone. Setting the books on my desk, I flopped onto the bed and removed my cell phone from my pocket. I unlocked it and searched for places that looked promising to work.

The best establishments were upper scale, but not too uppity that only the rich could afford. It still shocked me that the rich were usually the worst tippers. They'd order multiple bottles of hundred-dollar wine but leave a ten percent tip.

One place caught my eye—Haynes Steakhouse. The restaurant was located only ten minutes from here, making it an even better option if they were hiring. I hoped they didn't ask for references, but I'd figure that out later.

I stood, grabbed my black slacks and white button-down shirt from the closet, and quickly changed. I put on some mascara and nude lipstick to look a little more professional. Now it was time to go since the restaurant was open for lunch.

I PULLED into the parking lot of the older building with new charcoal-blue siding. There were two dark, cherry wood doors right in front with a bronze sign displaying "Haynes Steakhouse." Mercedes-Benzes, BMWs, Lexus, and other high-end cars were in the parking lot, and my crappy car definitely looked out of place. I parked in the parking lot farthest from the door, underneath a tree, praying to God that the people inside wouldn't notice my car.

Grabbing my wallet, keys, and phone, I climbed out of the car and slammed the door. As I approached the entrance, a worker opened it, allowing me inside. A grin filled his face. "Welcome to Haynes Steakhouse."

"Thanks." I entered the building and walked up to the large cherry wood hostess desk.

"How many will there be?" a girl my age asked and picked up a few menus. Her amber eyes stayed locked on me as she turned toward the seats. Her white shirt and black slacks fit her like a glove, and her long, light auburn hair, pulled into a French twist, completed the look flawlessly.

"Actually, I'm hoping you all are hiring." At least, they didn't think I looked too underdressed to eat here. "I'm hoping to apply for a server job."

"Sure." She smiled and lifted a finger. "Give me one second, and I'll get the manager. He just got here. I'll be right back." The girl walked away, leaving me alone.

The restaurant had booths along the walls and several tables scattered throughout. The place was packed, but the seats were spaced out enough that it wasn't overwhelming. The tables and chairs were made of dark maple and covered in thick white tablecloths.

This place wasn't as nice as the one I'd worked at back home, so hopefully, the tips would be better.

The hostess reappeared with a man only a couple of years older than me. When his eyes landed on mine, warning and dread filled me. A smirk lifted his lips, and everything inside me told me to leave.

CHAPTER SEVEN

"Here she is, Ollie." The hostess waved at me. "She wants to apply for a server role. I wasn't sure if we're hiring."

"We just had an opening come up," he replied, and a chill ran through me. With each step, his golden-brown hair bounced, and his cognac eyes scanned me. He was taller than me by a couple of inches, making him around six feet tall.

"Who quit?" she asked and placed a hand on her hip.

"Daryl," he answered distractedly, his focus locked on me. "He turned in his notice last night."

This line of work had a high turnover rate. That was one reason I wasn't too worried about finding a job.

"And," he said, snapping his fingers, "I happen to have time for an interview."

"Really?" Her brows furrowed, and she glanced back toward the kitchen. "I thought there was an issue going on."

"It's fine." Ollie gestured for me to follow him. "I can make time for this."

Maybe this had been a mistake, but I couldn't turn down an interview. Perhaps the guy was awkward like me, and that was what was putting me on edge. I needed the money, so I obliged and followed him to the very back of the restaurant where no one sat.

"It's after the lunch rush, so we can have some privacy back here." He walked to the booth along the back corner wall and pointed for me to sit across from him.

Pushing away any doubt, I followed his instructions and sat at the table. The only thing that prevented me from standing and running out the door was that I could hear people walking by. This section was close to the kitchen, so if I needed to scream, someone would hear me.

He held out his hand over the table toward me. "I'm Ollie. And you are?"

"Jade," I said breathlessly but loud enough for him to hear. I had to become more confident or I wouldn't get this job. "I'm Jade," I said louder. When I touched his hand, it was cold and clammy, and it took everything in me not to jerk my hand back.

"Nice to meet you, Jade." He leaned back in his seat, the corners of his mouth tipping upward like there was a hidden joke I wasn't privy to. "Are you looking for a full-time position?"

"No." I hadn't even considered they'd want someone full-time. "I'm looking for a part-time job. I'm a student at Kortright University and need to work evenings or weekends."

"Good." He placed a hand on the table. "We are looking for a part-timer to work during the dinner rush, so that's perfect. Friday evenings and the weekends are the busiest hours."

"That would be great." I wasn't sure if I should be excited. This whole situation seemed peculiar. "I served at an upscale Italian restaurant back home, so I do have experience

"Then you're hired." He lifted both hands and chuckled. "You sound like the perfect fit."

"Wait ..." I didn't want to discourage him, but he'd only asked me two questions. "Don't I need to interview with the other shift manager and fill out an application?" *Please don't ask for references,* I chanted internally. If Sarah went by my old workplace and Ollie called, she could find out where I was.

"I'm the manager over the weekend evening shift, so you only need to meet with me." He sounded so proud of himself. "And yes, I'll need you to complete an application, but it's just a formality for your paycheck. I'm assuming you can start Friday."

Thinking about my entire situation, I couldn't turn this down even if I'd wanted to. Any other place would have called my old job. "Sure. I can. Thank you."

"Of course." Darkness rolled into his eyes. "I need to help out a fellow classmate anyway."

That caught me off guard. "You go to Kortright?"

"Sure do." He tapped his fingers on the table. "I think I might have seen you on campus."

"Maybe." I didn't remember seeing him, but hell, I couldn't point out most of the students I'd seen today.

"Oh, I most certainly did." He leaned over the table. "I could never forget a face like yours."

I wasn't sure if he was being nice or hitting on me. Surely, with him being my boss, he was trying to be nice. "Is it your first year?" Changing the topic was my best bet.

"Yes, but I'm a junior." He leaned back and crossed his arms. "I transferred this semester since an interesting opportunity popped up."

"Well, a manager and a student." I had to admit, I was slightly impressed. "I bet that's hard to juggle."

"Nah." He shook his head. "I work the weekends and a few evening shifts during the week. It's not too bad, but I've always been ambitious."

"Good for you." I had no clue what to say. "Thank you for giving me this job. It looks like what I'm wearing is the standard uniform."

"Yes, another sign it was meant to be." He stood and pulled at his own white button-down shirt. "I need to get back. Tell Betty to give you the application on the way out, and just have it completed when you return on Friday. Be here at five sharp."

"Betty?" He'd have to give me a little more information than that.

"The hostess." He frowned. "Sorry I can't walk you out, but I need to return to the kitchen to ensure the problem was resolved."

"No worries," I said too eagerly. I just didn't feel comfortable around the guy. "Thanks again."

"Sure. I'll see you around." He chuckled as he stayed firmly in place.

I stood and forced a smile in return. "I'm sure you will." I stepped away slowly, ensuring that I didn't run to the door.

As I turned the corner to the hallway, I looked back at where we'd been sitting, and he was standing there, watching me walk away. It unnerved me.

My pace quickened, and by the time I reached the hostess desk, I was faintly out of breath.

The girl smirked. "Are you okay?"

"Yeah." I sucked in a breath and got my act together. "Ollie told me to get an application from you."

"Really?" She shrugged and pulled a drawer open. She snatched a paper and handed it to me. "There you go."

"Thanks," I said and headed for the door.

Outside, a tingling feeling ran down my spine. It was similar to what I'd felt in the woods earlier today. I tried to brush it off as I rushed to my car, but the feeling only intensified. I glanced over my shoulder at the restaurant, but there was no one but the doorman near a window, and his attention was firmly on his phone.

I wondered if my imagination had gotten carried away earlier today in the woods. There was zero reason for me to be feeling this way. I was in a small, bustling, picturesque town. It wasn't like something could get me.

I tried to appear calm, cool, and collected as I walked to my car. If any regular customers or coworkers saw me acting strange, it would make my first few days of work that much harder. I didn't need to be labeled a complete outcast. At work, I needed to be friendly so people would cover for me if I needed to run to the bathroom.

My hands shook as I pulled the keys from my back pocket and went to insert them into the lock. Having a nicer car with keyless entry would really come in handy right about now. My hands jerked, making the key scratch the handle, and some of the paint flecked away.

Dammit, something had to give.

Something hit the ground right behind me, and I jerked in that direction. My heart hammered as I saw a twig not even a few inches from me. I glanced up at the tree I was standing under. Dear God, a twig had scared me.

I'd never been like this until yesterday. It had to be stress or my mind playing tricks on me. I hadn't run away to lose my mind. I had this.

Turning back to my car, I held my hand steady and unlocked the door. Mind over matter. That could be my new motto until whatever this was settled down.

My urge to jump into the car and get the hell out of here surged, but I'd expected it. I climbed into my car and shut the door, proud of myself for not slamming it. I started the car and pulled out like a normal human being, but when I pulled onto the road, I stomped on the gas pedal, my instinct taking over.

I ARRIVED BACK at school close to five. I'd stopped at Walmart to pick up a few things, only to realize I couldn't afford more school supplies and a backpack until after my first night of tips. I'd settled on picking up a jacket, some granola bars, peanut butter, and bread to get myself through the rest of the week. Those weren't my favorite things to eat but having money for gas was more important.

I found Vera sitting at her desk as usual. She chewed feverishly on her lip as she read.

When I shut the door behind me, she jerked her head up and slammed the book.

"Sorry." I hadn't been silent when I'd entered. "I didn't mean to startle you."

"No, it's fine." She waved it off like it was no big deal. "I was just caught up in the book."

The book she'd been reading was bound in leather. "Wow, that looks like an old book."

"It is." She opened the desk drawer and placed the book inside. "It's my grandmother's journal. She left it to me."

That sounded strange, but who was I to judge? "That's nice."

I placed my bags on the desk, and she wrinkled her nose.

She stood and glared at the bags. "Please tell me you aren't planning on eating in here."

"No?" I hoped this was a trick question and she was messing with me. Otherwise, I'd be taking my peanut butter and bread down to the lobby to eat. I wasn't sure if that option or the Student Center was worse.

"Thank God." She sighed, clearly relieved. "I was worried for a second."

Wow. I hadn't pegged her to be worried about eating in our room. "Nope, no problem here." But I was willing to do whatever was necessary for us to get along. My stomach rumbled, which was perfect timing. I didn't want to be up here much longer anyway.

"On that note, I'm going to go eat." I pulled out a plate from the small package of paper plates, the jar of peanut butter, a couple of slices of bread, and a plastic knife. "I'll be back shortly."

"Take your time." She sat back at her desk and pulled out a textbook. "I'm going to get on my homework."

She had homework already on her first day of a new semester. Neither of my classes did. Maybe she was taking harder courses. I walked out of the room and took a deep breath. The lobby had been pretty empty, so now would be the best time to eat before it got busy.

The hallway was deserted, so I made my way to the elevator and pressed the button. Within seconds, the door opened, revealing Sadie, Roxy, Lillith, Katherine, and the teal-haired girl from class earlier.

Roxy's eyes zeroed in on my bread and peanut butter, and her mouth dropped open in horror. She breathed, "For the love of God, tell me that isn't your dinner."

I stood there and blinked in response. Her reaction baffled me.

"Oh, stop." Katherine rolled her eyes as she lifted the hand holding her coffee cup. "Peanut butter is a staple in the American diet."

"Everyone needs meat." Roxy grabbed my arm and pulled me inside the elevator. "Please tell me that's just a snack."

"No?" That was the second time in less than five minutes that I'd answered in the form of a question. "It's my main and only course."

"I don't eat meat," the teal-haired girl responded. "Not everyone does."

"That's because you are ..." Roxy paused like she was searching for the right word.

"Unique," Sadie blurted, clearly uncomfortable.

Her awkwardness made me laugh. "Didn't I call you that earlier?"

"Yes, you did." Sadie laughed, returning to her usual demeanor. "I guess I can't give you hell about that any longer."

I turned my attention to the drinks the two dark-headed girls carried. "You're drinking coffee or protein again?"

"Protein." Lillith lifted the cup to her lips and took a large gulp. "It never gets old."

The elevator opened again, and I stepped off first, heading to one of the vacant couches.

"Where do you think you're going?" Sadie asked as she caught up to me.

"My roommate doesn't want me eating in the room, so I'm stuck down here." I raised the food. "This is where I'll be eating my dinner."

"Nope." Sadie shook her head. "No one is meant to eat alone. Join us."

"Nah." I was tempted to go, but it was better that I hang out with them in moderation. Besides, they were only asking because they'd seen me. "You all go and have fun. I don't want to impose."

"How are you imposing?" Roxy's forehead lined with confusion. "If anything, we should be hurt."

"What?" Her words made no sense. "Did I do something?"

"Yeah, you ignored my texts." Roxy tapped her foot. "For a peanut butter sandwich."

She'd texted me? I set the plate on the couch and pulled out my phone. Sure enough, I had a text asking if I wanted to join them for dinner.

"Now you have no excuse." Lillith snatched the plate and headed to the door. "You're stuck with us."

They were putting so much effort into inviting me that I couldn't say no. "Fine, but only because you're all so desperate for me to join." I grimaced, realizing what I'd said.

Roxy burst out laughing and wrapped an arm around my waist. "You'll fit in just fine."

We walked into the Student Center, and my eyes darted to Egan and his two friends sitting in the middle of the seating area with several tables pulled together.

"And there is my sexy man," Roxy said to me and pointed right at the buzzed-haired friend.

Holy shit. They really were friends with Egan. I had to get away.

CHAPTER EIGHT

When the girls told me they knew Egan, I hadn't expected this. But as I pieced together their comments, it made complete sense. Of course, this would be their group of friends. The guys looked strong, sexy as hell, and commanding. They'd want girls like them beside them. I wondered which one was dating Egan. My gut said Sadie. "Oh, I didn't know you were meeting up with more people." I couldn't watch him fawn over someone. It would bother me. "I'll just head back to the dorm."

"Nope." Roxy tightened her arm around me. "You, dear girl, are stuck with us."

As she dragged me over to the table, Egan walked over to Sadie. The buzzed-haired guy raised an eyebrow but didn't say anything.

"Here, let me help," Egan said as he took my plate from her hands and headed back to the same side of the table but two spots down from the guy with the tribal tattoo at the end. He placed the plate in front of the chair right next to himself.

Strange, I thought Lillith had been carrying it. I guess that just proves my focus was off, again. Ugh.

The tribal tattoo guy chuckled. "You think that bread will fill you up?"

"Stop." Lillith pursed her lips. "He's always been a gentleman. Don't give him hell because you two act more like apes."

"Oh, please." The buzzed-haired guy motioned to the chair next to him and pointed at Roxy. "Just taking care of my girl."

Roxy bounced over and kissed his lips before sitting down. "Now, go get me food. I'm hungry."

"Come on." Sadie tugged my arm and sat next to the guy with the tattoo, leaving me to sit between her and Egan. I wanted to remain standing, but that would make this worse. There had to be a way out of here.

The other chairs filled in with Lillith and Katherine sitting in front of Egan and me and Roxy across from Sadie. The teal-haired girl sat at the end between the two guys.

"This is Jade," Sadie introduced me to the two guys. "This is my boyfriend, Donovan." She faced him with an adoring smile. "And that is Axel."

"So the girl who burned Egan officially has a name." Axel placed an arm around Roxy's shoulders. "I'm hoping to see more instances like that occur."

"Burned Egan?" Roxy arched an eyebrow. "What haven't you told us?"

I wanted to die. Coming here had been a huge mistake. "It was nothing." I placed the jar of peanut butter and the knife on the table.

"Doesn't sound like nothing." Lillith leaned across the table. "Spill."

"She's obviously uncomfortable," Egan said with annoyance. "Why don't you cut her some slack?"

The table went quiet as everyone's attention landed squarely on Egan.

At least, it wasn't on me. I opened the jar and spread some peanut butter on the bread, wishing to hurry and eat.

"And you said he was a gentleman," Sadie joked, eliminating the awkwardness from the table.

"I'm going to go grab something to eat." Egan turned to me. "Do you want anything?"

"Nope." A bottled water would've been good, but he'd already done enough for me. I could choke down the bread. "Thanks."

"Okay," he replied and walked toward the cafeteria, leaving me behind with everyone pretending they weren't staring at me.

Sadie turned to Donovan and smiled sweetly. "Mind getting me a Philly steak? That way I can stay here with Jade and protect her from these vultures." She waved her hand from Lillith to Katherine to Roxy.

"I may be many things, but I'm no damn bird." Roxy harrumphed and crossed her legs. "I'm almost offended by that."

"You'd have excellent vision." Katherine sipped her drink. "So, it wouldn't be horrible."

"My vision is amazing enough already." Roxy stuck her tongue out at her. "And I'm thinking red wouldn't be a good color for feathers."

Lillith bobbed her head. "Red's not a good color for anyone."

"I think her hair is pretty," the teal-haired girl interjected. "There are many people back home that would kill for hair like that."

"See?" Roxy smirked. "Naida knows how it is."

How the girl had referred to her home made me curious. "Where are you from?"

"F—" She began.

"Finland," Roxy interrupted. "She's from Finland."

"Really?" She had an accent, but not one I'd expect from there. "That's neat. I've never been anywhere but the southeast." One day, I hoped that would all change.

"While you ladies gab, we'll go get some food." Donovan kissed Sadie and looked at her adoringly. "One steak sandwich coming up." He turned to Naida. "Your usual?"

"Yes, please." She smiled genuinely. "Thank you."

The two guys walked off, and Roxy's focus landed on me. "What's the story with you and Egan?"

I should've known she'd be like a dog with a bone. "It wasn't a big deal." It really was a big deal to me, but if they knew that, then they really wouldn't drop it. The five girls' faces wrinkled like they smelled something disgusting. I sniffed, trying to figure out what the hell it was, but I didn't smell a damn thing. "What's wrong?"

"Nope." Roxy pointed at me. "Not happening. Don't change the subject."

"I was short on cash while buying my books, and he happened to overhear and helped me out." I left out the part where he'd been perfectly fine getting all of my books. What kind of guy did that?

"Whoever winds up with him will be one lucky lady." Lillith almost purred. "Sexy, kind, and an overall good guy."

I wanted to slap her hard. The overwhelming urge caught me off guard. I had to stay away from him.

"Hey." Katherine's brow furrowed. "We aren't trying to upset you."

"Oh, I know." I was acting irrationally. So what if Lillith wanted him? If they were single and wanted to ... I couldn't even get myself to say the word internally. But I couldn't have him. "I'm not upset."

Sadie covered her nose with her hand and winced. "Stop pestering her."

"What did you do?" Egan asked, sliding into the seat next to me. "I thought I told you to leave her alone." Protectiveness laced each word.

However, I couldn't focus on that. Egan had brought back two trays overflowing with food. He had a little bit of everything—pizza, hamburgers, pasta, a few desserts, and two drinks. I moved my plate toward Sadie to give him more room.

He picked up one of the cups and a wrapped burger and handed them to me. "I hope you like Dr. Pepper and hamburgers."

My stomach rumbled even though I'd eaten a peanut butter sandwich. It smelled good, but I needed to save my money.

"Wait." Roxy narrowed her eyes as they flicked from Egan to me. "You're sharing your food?" She stood and reached over to grab a fry.

Right before her hand got near one, he smacked her hand away. "I'm sharing it with her, not you."

"I'm fine." If I got too hungry, I'd go out in the hallway and eat a granola bar. "I don't need your food." He must have thought I was a charity case. That had to be it.

"Nope, I got too much." He winked and nodded to the burger. "We don't want it to go to waste."

I should've argued more, but it smelled way too good. "Thank you." I wouldn't even pretend I'd pay him back. I barely had enough for gas before Friday.

A huge smile spread across his face. "You're welcome."

Avoiding everyone's gazes, I kept my eyes on my burger and took a bite. Blissfully, the other two guys came back.

I remained quiet for the rest of the time, trying to process why I felt so drawn to the sexy man beside me.

By the time I finished the hamburger, Egan had put a piece of apple pie in front of me. For the first time in a while, I was stuffed. The others were chatting and having a good time, and I enjoyed listening to the back-and-forth banter. Every few minutes, one of them would glance in Egan's and my direction like they were trying to figure out something. I wanted to tell them, "So am I," but that would have made this situation more uncomfortable.

I crumpled up my wrapper and stood. Now was the perfect time to run away. "Well, thanks for letting me join you all tonight, but I'm going to head back to the dorm and call it a night."

Egan stood and picked up both trays. "I'll walk you back."

His attentiveness stunned me. Sure, he'd asked me out earlier, but when I'd turned him down, I'd figured that would stop his attempts. "It's fine. Stay here with your friends."

"Not after what happened in the woods," he rasped and stepped toward me. His citrus scent filled my nose, causing my brain to short-circuit. I nodded before I even realized what I'd done.

"Good." He took my wrapper from me and threw away the trash on the tray.

Concern flashed across Katherine's face before she smiled. "We'll see you later."

"Yup." I needed to get away from all of the awkwardness. "See ya." I rushed to the front of the Student Center without waiting for Egan. The more I was around him, the more I lost my head. I pushed the door open and stepped outside.

Even though the group had been nothing but nice to me, I'd felt every one of their glances. Egan's attention had them focusing on me even more.

The door swung open, and a sexy, deep voice called out, "Hey, wait up."

"Look." I had to end this now. I kept my back to him, not wanting to see his reaction. If he looked relieved, it could really hurt me. "I don't need your pity."

"Is that what you think this is?" He gently grasped my arm and spun me around. His head jerked back like he'd been slapped. "That's not it at all."

"You paid for my books and now my dinner." I sucked in a breath, forcing myself to loosen the grip I held on my pride. "I really do appreciate it, but I'll be fine. I don't want you to feel obligated. I can take care of myself."

"Of course you can, and there is absolutely no reason to pity you." His eyes locked on mine. "I know it sounds crazy, but all I want to do is take care of you."

"Why?" I asked before I could take it back. My body was on alert, desperate to hear his reasoning.

"There's something about you." He cupped my cheek and looked deeply into my eyes. "Something I can't and don't want to shake."

The gold in his eyes lightened, and the stubble on his chin

reflected the moonlight. He licked his lips, and I wondered what they tasted like.

Everything inside me wanted to kiss him. I stood on my tiptoes as his head lowered, feeling our connection too. My heart pounded in my ears, and my stomach roiled with anticipation. Right when his sexy, full lips were inches from mine, my brain screamed.

I was here to get an education and make something out of my life. Not piss it away on a guy. I shoved him away, pushing him off balance. He hadn't expected that.

"No, I can't do this. I'm sorry. Please don't follow me." I turned and ran toward the dorm, hoping he'd respect my wishes. When I didn't hear his footsteps, I breathed a sigh of relief and glanced over my shoulder to find him watching me. A frown marred his face, and so much hurt wafted off him that I could even feel it. I hated that I'd done it, but I couldn't turn out like my mother—barely surviving.

As I opened the door, he turned to go back inside the Student Center and rejoin his friends. I watched him disappear inside, tempted to rush back to him, but I wouldn't do that. I couldn't afford to be stupid and become more broken than I already was.

A cry for help pierced the air, coming from near the library. After another moment, a girl screamed again, "Please don't!"

I took off running in that direction. I couldn't let someone get hurt when I could hear them. No one else was outside or within hearing distance.

I ran as fast as possible and stopped by the library building. I had no clue where the scream had come from beyond there. I stood still, trying to pick up cries, heavy breathing, anything.

But I heard nothing. "Hello?"

A bird took off from the woods, flying high into the sky. Something dripped from its beak and left a trail behind.

I rushed over to the liquid, pulled out my phone, and turned on the flashlight. I stuck my finger in the warm liquid and placed it under the light. My heart sank, and I gagged.

It was blood.

A whole lot of blood.

Enough for a thick trail to be left behind.

What the hell kind of bird was that? "Is someone here?" An eerie feeling overcame me as I slowly followed the trail of blood. Surely, a bird hadn't caused the girl to cry out.

I wiped my finger on the grass, desperate to get the blood off me. It could have come from anything. Even after the blood was gone, I could still feel it. I needed to wash my hands, but first, I had to make sure someone didn't need help.

Following my gut, I pulled myself together and proceeded toward the tree line. When I reached the first line of trees, I stopped. I wouldn't be making the same mistake in complete darkness.

Hands shaking, I used my phone to cast a light on the ground. A cold breeze picked up, chilling me to the bone and making the situation even scarier. I took several steps, scanning the area for something out of place, but nothing showed.

Maybe someone was playing a joke, or the scream hadn't come from this direction. Standing out here in the cold wasn't smart. I had to get back inside. But when I took a step back toward the dorm, the blood trail popped back into my mind.

I'd missed something.

When I spun back around and lifted my phone, my light shined a little farther back, and my blood turned to ice.

CHAPTER NINE

No. There was no way this was happening. I screamed, unable to process what the hell I was seeing.

A girl I'd never seen before lay on the ground, dead. But that wasn't the worst part. Something had pecked out her eyes and not delicately. They'd gone deep, and blood still trickled from the wound.

Throwing caution to the wind, I moved to go inside the woods, but strong arms that were already way too familiar wrapped around my body and turned me around, burying me into a hard chest. I hadn't realized I was crying until his hands were rubbing my back as I sobbed.

"Hey, it's okay," Egan said comfortingly. "It's going to be okay."

"No, it's not." Even though I no longer faced her, the image had been burned into my brain. "I think she's dead. We need to check."

Footsteps rushed over to us, and Donovan said, "Why don't you take her away from here? Axel and I can handle this."

"Handle this?" I pulled away from Egan's arms and glared at him. "You mean call the cops, right?" Hysteria bubbled through me. "She is a person."

"Yes, we're going to call the police." Donovan lifted a hand. "I just meant you can go back to the dorm."

"But I found her." The police would want to question me. "I can't leave."

Axel ran toward the girl and stopped short of her. He faced us. "She's dead."

"How the hell do you know?" I marched over to the girl, pushing by Axel, and dropped to my knees. "You have to check for a pulse." I placed my fingers on her neck. There was nothing, but her skin was still warm to the touch.

If I'd only gotten here a few minutes earlier ... I wrapped my arms around myself, and tears fell to the ground.

"Guys," Donovan groaned. "Get her out of here."

Hands scooped me off the ground and cradled me against a warm chest. I almost fought against him until the citrus smell slammed into my nose.

It was Egan, not Axel, but I hadn't heard him walk over, and he must have moved super-fast. I glanced into warm, golden eyes. I was losing it. "I need to stay."

"They'll tell the police where to find us," Egan reassured me as he walked out of the woods toward the library. "We'll just sit at a bench outside of the Student Center."

He really wasn't giving me much of a choice, and I was too tired to try to get out of his arms. My emotions rolled inside me like tumbleweeds in the desert.

"Let me know if you need anything," Egan murmured.

I closed my eyes and cuddled against his chest. My brain yelled at me to stand on my own feet, but I pushed the voice away. There was no other place I'd rather be.

His heart beat steadily, calming mine inside me. I'd never felt so safe in my entire life, and for once, I allowed myself to feel it. I couldn't be strong on my own right now.

"Is she okay?" Sadie's concerned voice startled me.

Again, I hadn't heard anyone approach. I lifted my head to find Sadie and the other four girls standing next to us.

"She's " Egan started.

"I'll be fine," I cut in. I wouldn't allow them to treat me like I wasn't there. I might not want to stand on my own two feet, but I wouldn't be ignored.

"Says the girl being held," Roxy snorted.

"Well, if you'd just stumbled upon a girl with her eyes pecked out, I bet you would be a little unstable too," I snapped back, ready to defend myself.

"What?" Katherine's mouth dropped open, but her reaction fell short. "You saw what?"

"People don't just stumble upon death like that." Naida pursed her lips. "It's not something they're used to."

See, she got it. "Thank you. Each one of you would be struggling too if you were in my position." I smacked Egan gently on the chest and pointed to the ground. It felt imperative that I stood. "The death is a lot easier to process when you're not the one who saw all the blood."

"You're right." Sadie glared at her friend and gave me a friendly smile. "I'm sorry you saw that. Is there anything we can do?"

"No." Egan shook his head. "Donovan and Axel are handling it while Jade and I hang out here to wait for the police."

"Okay." She glanced at her friends and sighed. "You have our number if you need anything. We'll head back to the dorms."

"I'll keep this," Katherine said, lifting my jar of peanut butter, "with us for the night."

Oh, damn. I'd forgotten it when I'd been desperate to leave Egan behind. I kept being an ass to him, but here he was, treating me great. I wasn't sure what to make of it. "Thank you. Just make sure you don't get tempted to eat it due to your all-liquid diet."

Lillith laughed hard. "We will try our best, but no promises."

The girls headed back toward the dorm.

Now that we were alone, I felt awkward. He'd seen me have a

complete meltdown. He must have been ready to get the hell away from a train wreck like me. "Look, I'm sorry."

"For what?" He took my hand and tugged me over to the bench. We were the only two out here, most likely due to the chill in the air. I hadn't been able to get a jacket before the girls had pulled me from the lobby, so my teeth rattled together.

"It's cold out here." He scooted closer and wrapped an arm around my shoulders, pulling me into his side.

The warmth coming off him comforted me. "How are you so warm in just a dress shirt?" I'd bet my skin was cool to the touch.

"It's all the fat." He glanced down at his stomach. "It keeps me insulated."

"There is not any fat on your body." The memory of him carrying the box sprung to mind. I'd seen the outlines of everything he had to offer. "So that can't be it."

"You've looked?" A smile tugged at the corner of his mouth as his eyes ran over me.

This would have been the perfect opportunity for me to stay silent. "It's hard not to." My breath caught on the last word. He was damn sexy, and he had to know it.

Now, I wanted to die. My cheeks had caught on fire.

He brushed a fingertip across my cheek. "I'm glad because you're extremely beautiful and sexy."

Sexy.

No one had ever called me that before. Sure, a few guys had called me pretty in passing, but that was it. Sexy was a whole different caliber than I was. "Thanks." I bit my bottom lip and stared at the ground.

This was wrong. A girl was dead, and here I was, getting all swept up in a golden-eyed god.

He must have realized where my thoughts had gone because he pulled me even closer against his chest. "I'm sorry about tonight."

"Me too." The image reappeared in my mind. "I still can't get over it." I probably wouldn't get any sleep tonight. "I heard a cry for help, but I didn't get there in time." That made me wonder. "How did you find me?"

"I heard the scream too." He sighed and ran a hand through his hair. "I wish I could've gotten there first. It would've been nice for me to find her and not you."

"Nice?" That sounded like the wrong word to use.

"Okay, maybe not nice." He blew out a breath and lowered his forehead against mine. "But I would've preferred it. You should've never seen that."

"And you shouldn't have either." Being with him felt so natural. We'd only met yesterday, and not under the best circumstances, but I felt like I'd known him my whole life. "Unfortunately, we both saw it."

"I hate to ask." He cupped my face. "But did you see anything?"

"You wouldn't believe me." I still had a hard time processing it.

"Try me."

"Okay." I pulled back to gauge his reaction. "When I got to the woods, a bird flew out with blood dripping from its beak." My gaze went straight to the finger that had touched the blood.

He remained stoic. "Any clue what kind of bird?"

"I'm pretty sure it was a falcon." I tried to recall the bird. I'd been locked on the liquid since I hadn't expected it. "It had all white feathers underneath because the light from my flashlight app reflected off it clearly, and dark gray on top. Part of it blended in with the darkness."

"Well, it's not here now." He looked skyward, searching for the threat. "And you're safe."

He actually believed me. "I've never heard of a common bird doing something like that."

"Me neither." He frowned like he knew something that I didn't before he sighed. "Maybe it had rabies."

"Really?" That was a stretch, but I didn't have any better ideas. "Do you think the cops will think I did it?"

"No." He shook his head. "You had only left moments before from a crowded Student Center. You'll be fine."

I hadn't thought of that. It was a damn good thing I'd gone with them. Imagine if I'd stumbled upon her and no one had seen me.

I laid my head on his shoulder, enjoying his closeness. The silence descended between us, and fatigue hit me hard. The horror I'd witnessed had taken a lot out of me. I breathed in his unique scent.

His cell phone dinged, startling me.

He huffed, "I'm sorry." He pulled the phone from his pocket and glanced at the text. "The police want to talk to you."

"Okay." I was ready to get it over with.

My alarm blared, waking me. I blinked, trying to figure out where the hell I was. Last night was a huge blur, and I'd dreamed about it all night.

I sat up, and the familiar bed and sleeping roommate made things click. I was back in my dorm room.

Now that my brain was working, I remembered Egan walking me to my room after the police had dismissed me as being traumatized. They didn't believe the bird story and told me the coroner would figure out a more plausible explanation. Egan had stood protectively over me and shut the police down when they'd become condescending. For the first time ever, I'd let someone take care of me. When he'd walked me to my room, he'd reassured me and kissed my forehead. I never would've believed a man like him could exist.

Vera rolled over and glared. "Turn that blasted thing off."

"On it." I sat up, grabbed my phone, and turned it off.

"Why are you taking such early classes." Vera propped herself on her hand. "Who was the guy last night, by the way?"

"Oh, his name is Egan." I couldn't believe I'd managed to sleep, but his presence made me feel calm. I'd been so tired I hadn't changed out of my clothes. "Sorry about passing out on you last night."

"You were out." She snorted, which oddly fit her. "I don't think I could've woken you if I'd banged on drums."

"I'm sorry about that." I'd barely been able to talk when the exhaustion had hit. I'd wanted to sleep and not think about the bird and the girl anymore. "I saw something that took a lot out of me."

"Oh, what?" She sat up in bed, her attention fully on me. "Did something happen?"

She hadn't said more than a handful of words to me, and now she was acting like we were best friends. She had watched me last night, but I hadn't cared. Ever since coming here, I'd felt like I'd entered a whole different dimension. "I found a girl dead in the woods. Her eyes were gone."

"Yikes! The university sent a letter out about it last night." Vera shivered. "I didn't realize you were part of the group it referenced."

I didn't have much to say in response, so I grabbed my towel and headed to the door. Her morbid curiosity had gotten to me.

After getting ready, I left the dorm, munching on a granola bar. I'd been stupid and actually put makeup on in case I ran into Egan. At this rate, there was no stopping me. The one thing I hadn't been able to buy and bring to the dorm was a coffee pot, so I rushed into the Student Center to get a cup. The place was packed with everyone whispering about the dead girl. Despite them whispering, they might as well have been screaming in my ear.

I felt the need to get away as the images of last night flashed inside my head. I hurried to the cashier, threw five dollars down, and didn't wait for the change. I couldn't afford it, but I didn't care.

Outside, I inhaled and slowed my pace. I didn't want people to think I was stranger than they already believed. I headed toward Grey Hall and stayed on the sidewalk, passing the woods. Part of me wanted to go inside to see if I could figure out what was out there hunting, but a larger part of me was in survivor mode. I didn't need any more trouble than I'd already found.

But the *kak, kak, kak* of a falcon call caught my attention. I turned my head, and a bird flew out from the trees. Then it stopped and hovered in the sky. Its round eyes locked on me, and I stopped in my tracks.

My body froze when I noticed the crimson dot on the pure white feathers under its beak.

The bird and I stared at each other for God knew how long until it swooped down, heading directly at me.

CHAPTER TEN

I stood frozen in disbelief. The entire world had gone insane. A fucking bird was attacking me. It was close enough that I could hear its feathers against the wind. I needed to duck, but I was entranced. All I could do was stare at the blood spot. It had to be the same bird from last night.

"Jade!" Egan called out, and I heard footsteps pounding in my direction.

He wouldn't be able to reach me in time, but his words snapped me out of my mental fog.

The falcon was only two feet away when I tossed my coffee and books at it and hit the ground. The bird dodged everything, buying me time to crouch.

A large body shielded me, easily covering all of me, and I knew exactly who it was. But how had Egan reached me in time? He had sounded several yards away.

Another round of *kaks* came from the bird, close at first, then sounding farther and farther away. There was definitely something wrong with that damn bird.

"Are you okay?" Egan slowly moved off me and sat on the sidewalk in front of me. "Did he get you?"

"He?" Out of everything that had happened, only I would focus on his mention of the bird's gender. "How do you know it's a he?"

"Intuition." He surveyed my body for any injuries. "Are you hurt?"

"If my pride counts, then yes." A stupid bird had taken me down. "What the hell is wrong with that thing? Someone needs to shoot it." I didn't usually advocate for killing, but that bird was an exception.

"Don't worry." Egan stood and held his hand out to me. "I plan on handling it."

"You're good with guns, eh?" There probably wasn't much he wasn't good at. Of course, that put my mind right in the gutter. "Are you okay?"

"Not so much guns, but I can fend for myself." He kept his hand extended, waiting for me to take it. "And yes, I'm just glad I got to you in time."

Not wanting to be a jerk, I grabbed his hand, and something shocked between us where our skin touched. The jolt was strong but not unpleasant. Once I got to my feet, I pulled my hand away and wiped it on my jeans. "Thanks." It still tingled from where we'd touched. It had to be static electricity. That was the only thing that made sense.

He bent down and scooped up my books, frowning at my coffee cup; the lid had popped off, its contents staining the white sidewalk. He sighed. "It looks like we need to go get you another coffee."

The thought of going with him was alluring, but I had a class to get to. "Thanks, but I'll be late." I stepped closer to him without meaning to. His body drew me in, and the overwhelming urge to touch him rocked through me.

"Then let me walk you to class." He turned toward Grey Hall. "I can carry these for you."

"Okay." The words were so soft he might not have heard them, but his responding smile told me otherwise.

We walked toward the building in amicable silence. Just being beside him brought me peace, which bothered me again. Last night had been a moment of weakness, and look at what happened after I let my guard down a little—I desperately wanted to be beside him. He was consuming way too many of my thoughts.

He held the door open for me, and I slipped inside, heading through the main corridor to the hallway. My class was on the first floor and midway down. I stopped and held my hands out, ready to take my books from him. "Thank you."

"Anytime." His eyes landed on my lips.

My brain screamed at me to go into the room, but my body refused to budge. "Thank you for that out there." He'd protected me once again.

"You don't need to thank me." He pushed a piece of my hair behind my ear, and a jolt warmed my body. "I'll always protect you." His words were a promise, and I liked them way too much.

He didn't remove his hand, and it felt like we were the only two people in the world. His touch felt good, and I found myself stepping into him. Damn traitorous feet. My eyes flicked to his lips, and I licked mine, wondering what he tasted like.

"You can't always protect me." I laid a hand on his chest, feeling his hard muscles. It felt like a spell overcame me as the jolt connected us, making me crave him even more. "You can't be around all the time."

His lips were only a few inches away. "I can try." His breath hit my lips, and I closed my eyes as I rose onto my tiptoes.

His lips touched mine gently, and a shock like I'd felt between our hands hit me hard between our lips. It hurt but in a pleasant way, and I almost moaned. He tasted of vanilla, which caught me by surprise, and I never wanted to taste anything else ever again. The thought startled me out of the moment.

No, I couldn't get attached to a man. Not like this. In just two days, I'd felt things for him that should've been impossible. If something happened to him, it could break me like my mother had broken when Dad had died.

Some say she'd survived my father, but not in a healthy way. Sarah had sucked her into their unhealthy, codependent relationship, and Mom had never been the same. I didn't want to become like that.

I jerked away and shook my head. "I'm sorry." I spun and entered the room, leaving him behind.

THE ENTIRE TIME in both classes, my mind kept replaying our kiss. I couldn't pay attention to either teacher. The connection between us was indescribable, which meant we couldn't do this any longer. Our relationship would only end with one or both of us getting hurt.

I walked out of my chemistry class and outside Webster Hall. The all-brick building was my favorite. Though similar to the others, it was a little larger because of the science labs. This building had four stories and a slanted roof. From the school's website, I'd read that it had been built between the times of Wilson Hall and Grey Hall.

No stairs led up to the double wooden doors, and more people were heading into this building than the others. People's bags bumped into me as I hurried to the courtyard outside the Student Center. It wasn't quite as packed here since there was still a chill in the air.

Desperate to get back to my dorm, I picked up my pace, ready to lose myself in a good book or show.

As I passed by the Student Center, I noticed Egan's large frame standing in front of the girls' dorm. He stood there like he was waiting on someone. I both hoped and dreaded that it was me. And that was the crux of my problem.

Dang it, I didn't need to run into him. I had to avoid him. His presence made me do stupid stuff.

I kept my gaze down, but I felt the moment his eyes landed on me, almost like they were part of me, and it petrified me. At the split in the sidewalk, I cut toward the library about ten feet from him and walked faster.

"Jade!" he called out, fracturing a piece of my heart.

This was not normal. Getting this emotionally involved with someone in such a short amount of time wasn't rational. If this wasn't the first sign of a very unhealthy relationship, I didn't know what else was. It already felt like the only way to find peace was to be near him.

No, I couldn't do this. His footsteps pounded on the pavement, catching up to me. He grabbed my arm, gently turning me around. Eyes locked on me, he asked, "What's wrong?"

"I ..." I'd never had to say such hard words before. "I need space."

He blew out a breath as he flinched. "What? Why?"

"It doesn't matter." I decided to escape before I caved. I had to protect myself. "Please, give me space." I jerked my arm out of his hold and ran, refusing to look back. My heart and body screamed, but I ignored them, pushing through. In time, the pain would ebb. It had to.

THE NEXT TWO weeks flew by in a blur. I worked the busiest shifts at Haynes Steakhouse and made pretty decent money. Ollie was as strange as they came, but he mostly left me alone. I got there when it was busy and left around midnight, completely exhausted after cleaning up.

A few more deaths had happened on campus, but luckily, I hadn't stumbled upon any of the bodies. Everyone was on edge because some of the victims had had their throats cut. I'd thought this place was supposed to be a safe haven, but apparently, something similar had happened last semester. People had gone missing and were never found. This time, dead people were being found all over the place.

When I wasn't working or in class, I hid in my room like a coward. I even tried hiding from Sadie and the other girls. They were a little more persistent. One night, they'd forced me to hang out in one of their rooms, promising that Egan wouldn't show up. The first time Roxy had brought him up, I'd gotten up and left. I knew where their loyalties lay, and they weren't with me.

For once, Vera sat up instead of bitching about my alarm. That was unusual.

"You okay?" I asked.

"Oh, yeah." She yawned and closed her eyes. "Just going to the library this morning for a paper due in Composition II."

"Considering how much you read and work, I'd think it'd already be done." Every time I walked in, she was usually reading her grandmother's journal or a textbook of some sort. "I don't know how you can fit so much in and still have more to do."

"There's a lot more to studying than just the basics." She flipped her long hair over her shoulder and stretched. "Besides, it's not just school work I want to focus on. There's a lot about me you know nothing about."

That was fair. "Got it. Well, I'm going to go get ready for classes." This conversation was already awkward, so I wanted to escape quickly.

"Whatever happened to that guy?" she asked as I gathered my things.

She must have meant Egan. "Nothing. We just haven't been hanging out." Each day, staying away from him got harder instead of easier. It was ridiculous and didn't help that he sat beside me in Spanish class. I'd see him watching me out of the corner of my eye, and it would thrill me. He looked as miserable as I felt.

"He seemed into you." She pulled the covers off her legs and placed her feet on the ground. "And he's hot. I was hoping you'd be dating and he might have a brother."

Okay, that shocked me. We barely talked, and now she wanted to double-date with me? "Uh ... no clue if he has a brother." There were so many things I didn't know about him, and her question added to my curiosity. Damn her.

"You're really going to let a guy like that pass you by?" She reached for her thick glasses on the nightstand and placed them on her nose. "I get we aren't friends, but you're my roommate. I want the best for you."

"Thanks." I grabbed the rest of my clothes and opened the door. "I really appreciate the concern, but I'm good."

I stepped into the hallway, and right before I shut the door, Vera yelled, "Someone else will get his attention if you keep acting like that."

The door closed behind me, but I couldn't move. It was like I couldn't even fucking breathe. The thought of him with someone else hurt. How had I let this happen?

It didn't matter. I repeated the phrase several times, but my heart screamed in protest. It did matter, and I wasn't sure what to do.

Needing to get outside and clear my head, I quickly showered and got dressed. I foolishly put mascara and lip gloss on because it was Friday and I'd see him. I'd been doing so well until Vera had put those insane thoughts in my head.

I rushed back into the dorm room and grabbed the new black backpack I'd bought after my first weekend working. It'd been a godsend, not having to carry all my books around while people gave me strange looks. Vera had left, so I didn't have to deal with any additional awkward conversations.

Throwing my bag over my shoulder, I strolled over to the Student Center, grabbed my standard cup of coffee, and put in the cream and sugar. Something tickled at the base of my neck. Almost every day, it felt like someone was watching me, but I'd never felt it in here. I turned around, but like every other time, nothing was there.

At first, I'd assumed it was my aunt, but now I needed to admit I was paranoid. I wondered if anything had actually chased me in the woods that day. Brushing it off, I rushed to class, eager for the weekend.

I WALKED INTO SPANISH 101, and Egan was already there. I hated when he got there first because he'd watch me the entire way to my seat. At least, when I beat him, I could have my book pulled out, pretending to read.

As I settled into my seat, his attention stayed locked on me. He always made me feel like I was the only person in the room ... like I was special.

While I leaned over to pull my book from my backpack, he leaned toward me. The edge of his shoulder touched the front of mine. The jolt sparked between us even through our clothing. I couldn't be the only one feeling this ... could I?

Trying to pretend I hadn't noticed anything, I sat up and opened my binder. I took out my pen and tapped the paper over and over again. Nervous energy ran rampant in my body.

He scratched the back of his neck and cleared his throat like he was about to say something.

No, he couldn't talk to me now. I still wasn't strong enough. I needed fate to intervene and help me stay strong.

The professor entered the classroom, saving me from talking to Egan, and I exhaled loudly.

She clapped her hands several times and smiled at us. "As you know, your first test is coming up next week, and one section will be on pronunciation. The best way to do well in this section is to practice speaking. I will pair you up with a partner to practice for the first twenty minutes."

Good, that meant I could turn my desk away from Egan. That would help some. At least, he wouldn't be tempted to talk to me.

As she paired off students and got closer to me, it became crystal clear that fate had a dark sense of humor.

"And you two," she said, pointing to Egan and me, "are a pair."

There was no getting around this. I would have to talk to him. I just hoped I could stand my ground.

CHAPTER ELEVEN

"All right." The professor twirled her finger around. "Get to work with your partner. Use the vocabulary words we've learned in the first five chapters."

I didn't move my desk; I was hoping this was all a bad dream. I'd been keeping him at a distance, and boom—just like that, it was over. Him sitting next to me had been bad enough, and now I had to talk to him. The more I saw him, the harder this all was.

The corners of Egan's mouth tipped upward, infuriating me. He scooted to the side and pushed his desk right next to mine so that his leg brushed against mine. The jolt between us was stronger than I remembered, stealing my breath.

Dammit, all of those feelings crashed into me, more powerfully than before, and my hand itched to touch him. The memory of how it had felt to have his hard chest pressed against mine and strong arms wrapped around me almost undid me.

How the hell was it possible? I'd kept my distance to prevent this exact thing from occurring. But the connection between us had strengthened, and I was at a loss as to why or how. Even the vanilla taste of his mouth flitted into my mind as his citrus scent surrounded me. My body buzzed with the need to feel more of him.

Him being so damn attractive made it harder to think straight. How could I be thinking about all the things I wanted to do with him right here in the middle of the classroom? It was so inappropriate, but I didn't care. I wanted to cave, but I couldn't.

"Hola," he rasped, adding to his damn sexy allure. "How have you been?"

"That wasn't Spanish," I bit, coming off like a bitch. Ugh, I didn't want to be like that, but my survival instincts had kicked in. "Muy bien, gracias."

"Look, I know we need to study, but can we talk for a second?" Egan leaned over his desk to catch my gaze. "I've been trying to respect your wish of needing space, but I don't understand what happened between us."

Me neither, and that was the entire problem. "We can't do this right now. We're supposed to be studying." If I let my grades slip, I would lose my scholarship, which was unacceptable.

"How about after class, then?" He rubbed a hand down his face and sighed. "At least, give me that. I want to make things right."

"Yes" almost formed on my lips, but I squashed it down. If I let him talk, I wouldn't be able to stay strong. "I'm really sorry, but there isn't much to say." I bit my lip, wishing he would drop it, but I was thrilled he hadn't. These conflicting emotions were wearing me out. "And right now, I really need to study. Please?"

He huffed, clearly disappointed, but nodded. "Okay." The hurt in his eyes bothered me more than I'd like to admit. But I focused on the task. It was the only way I'd come out of this unscathed.

I RAN out of Spanish class so fast it wasn't even funny. I didn't even pack my books. I grabbed my stuff and got the hell out before Egan could process what I'd done.

After dropping my books off in the dorm, I stayed in the room to get myself together, enjoying this rare moment alone. Since I took earlier classes, this was my little reprieve from Vera.

Once I got situated, I opened the window, allowing a cool breeze in the stuffy room, and took my phone from my pocket. I lay on my bed and logged into my Facebook Messenger account. That was the social media platform Mom used, and there were more messages from her. She begged to know where I was and to please come home. I'd broken down a few days after getting here and responded, needing her to know I wasn't dead.

I might have run away, but I still loved Mom.

We talked a little back and forth, but I limited my responses. I didn't need to accidentally drop a hint of where I was.

I made sure to never post anything and turned off the locator. I needed to remain hidden, but Mom had made it clear that Sarah was pissed and doing everything in her power to find me. The police refused to look for me since I was of age and was in contact with Mom. I wasn't a missing person, after all. So, that had been a relief.

When my stomach rumbled, I forced myself to my feet. I headed down to the Student Center to grab something to eat before Egan and his friends got there. The one time I'd gone through the line, Sadie had chased me out, trying to get me to eat with them. She'd frowned the entire time I'd turned her down. I needed to stay away from them since they were close with Egan. So, once again, I was utterly and completely alone. But it was for the best.

From outside my window, a familiar voice caught my attention. "What the hell do I do?" It sounded like Egan.

I peeked out the window and saw Egan sitting next to Sadie on a bench outside the guys' dorm. His hair was messy, revealing he'd run his fingers through it.

"I couldn't even go to my next class, Sadie." He lifted his head skyward. "She won't talk to me."

"She needs time," Sadie reassured him and patted his arm.

"Remember how Donovan acted at first. Strong feelings like that are overwhelming."

Ugh, the fact she could tell how attracted I was to him further embarrassed me. I had to be drooling or foaming at the mouth whenever he was near.

"What if she doesn't feel it, though?" Egan's shoulders sagged. "Maybe my intensity is scaring her."

"You're being insecure. The way she looks at you proves she does." She dropped her hands into her lap. "And maybe you're being too nice."

Yup, there was my proof. She could clearly see my attraction to him, but who wouldn't find him sexy? He deserved someone not broken. The thought of him with someone else didn't sit well with me, though. Something inside demanded for that girl to be me.

"But she asked for space," he growled and glanced around to make sure no one could overhear them. "What kind of mate would I be if I didn't give her that?"

Mate? My heart dropped. That was either an odd way of saying "dating interest," or he viewed me as a friend. But if we were friends, would he be that upset about me not talking to him? I had to stop being stupid. I was the one who'd pushed him away, not the other way around.

I shut the window harder than I should have, but I was that damn desperate to not hear anymore. Everything inside me wanted to run down there and ease his pain. Stupid, sexy man with his god-like biceps and ample lips that I wanted to devour and ... Oh, dear God, I had to quit. If I kept going, I'd run down there and lick him like a lollipop.

Snatching a notebook off the floor, I used it to cool my ass down. I needed a cold shower before heading to work. I glanced at the clock and realized it was noon. At least, my homework would distract me now so I wouldn't have to do it later, and I'd eat another peanut butter sandwich since Egan was hanging out outside. It was time to get my act together and not obsess over the conversation I'd overheard.

I FINISHED PUTTING lip stain on my lips and took a step back. I'd been wearing more makeup to work, hoping it would increase my tips. I didn't know if it worked, but I earned more than some of the other servers.

The clock read three-thirty. I had only thirty minutes to get to Haynes. Given how reliable my car had been lately, I might need every second.

Outside, dread pooled in my stomach. My eyes darted to where Egan and Sadie had sat a few hours before as if I still expected them to be there. Each day, my paranoia increased, and I had no clue why.

The weird feeling tickled down my spine. I spun around and found nothing out of the ordinary. A *kak* sounded nearby, indicating a falcon was near. I swore that sound followed me wherever I went. Even at Haynes, that damn bird followed me, but there was more than one falcon in the area, so I was just being hyper-sensitive to them since that night. A shudder rocked through me every time I remembered.

I ran to my car, unlocked it, jumped in, and peeled out of the parking lot. My poor car sounded like it was dying, but I didn't let up. I would outdrive that bird.

I got to Haynes several minutes early, which was what I liked. I hated arriving right on the minute. If you pushed being right on time and something went wrong, you could easily be late. I entered the bustling restaurant. The older crowd always came in first, followed by the younger customers.

I passed by Betty and waved as I rushed to the back to get my apron and notepad. A few servers stood in the back, talking as one shift changed to the other. The room was smaller, so I squeezed between a few people and grabbed the black apron.

"Hey, Jade," Michael called as he walked up to me. "You're taking over my section." His shaggy charcoal hair hung in his eyes, emphasizing his ice-blue irises. He was a couple of years older than me and always nice.

"Got it," I said and held my hand out.

He handed over the paper with his open orders and smiled. "There's a party tonight if you wanna meet up after your shift."

This was the second time he'd asked me out, and I didn't know why, but it rubbed me the wrong way. "Sorry, not interested. We've been through this." If I were going to date anyone, the guy I'd choose was back at Kortright.

"Fine." He shrugged. "You can't blame me for trying."

"Yeah, I can," I said teasingly but didn't really care if it came off that way. He knew I was serious. "All right, let me get to work." I squeezed past everyone and turned toward the back section of the restaurant. I actually preferred it to the other sections. At the front of the building, near the hostess stand, it got a little chaotic once the waiting room got overcrowded. You'd have tables complaining about people hovering over them or their food and whatever else they could come up with.

As I stepped back into the hallway, that eerie feeling washed over me. I was getting so sick and tired of it. I turned around, expecting not to see anything, but I squealed when a thin frame hovered close by.

Instinct took over, and I grabbed the person's arm and punched him in the face. The guy's head flew back and hit the wall so hard it left a hole in the sheetrock. I turned to throw him over my shoulder and onto his back when the guy groaned, "God, Jade. Stop."

I paused and looked the guy in the face. It was Ollie. I dropped his hand and stepped back, asking, "What the hell are you doing standing in a dark corner like that?"

"I just got here and was looking to see who was on time." He stepped toward me, getting a little too close for comfort, and rubbed his jaw. There was a large red mark where my fist had connected with his face. Despite the pain, his eyes glinted darkly as he chuckled. "Why are you so jumpy?"

The asshole enjoyed scaring the shit out of me. He really was off his rocker. "Sorry for punching you." I'd needed to say it so I wouldn't lose my job. "But you caught me off guard."

"You've got strong instincts." He grinned, revealing yellow teeth. "That's good. It'll come in handy."

"Look, am I in trouble?" I gestured to the hole. "I can pay to fix that if it's any consolation."

"No, I'll handle it. After all, I scared you." He cleared his throat and smiled. "The way you rush around, I should've realized you'd startle easily. It doesn't help that so many girls are showing up dead on campus."

He always gave me the creeps. A rational person wouldn't stand there, smiling about dead girls. Each time I saw him, the worse the creepy feeling got. He didn't affect anyone else the same way, but I sensed a darkness around him I couldn't explain. He reminded me of my aunt when she was out in the real world. Somewhere deep inside, he was unhinged. "I don't rush."

"Sure." He lifted a brow and winked. "We can go with that."

Yeah ... creepier by the minute. "Okay, then. Sorry again." I took a few steps back, ready to get away. "I need to check on my table. See ya around."

"Be careful, Jade."

The words sounded like a threat, but I chose to ignore them. I had customers to wait on, and I didn't need extra drama in my life. Maybe next week, I'd look for another job after school. Getting away from him was becoming more and more of a priority. At least, my attack against him might make him think twice about stalking me.

I walked to the table, checked on their order, and got straight to work. Losing myself in orders brought me some comfort. Those types of conversations were easy. The customer would tell me what they wanted and what was wrong. There was no guesswork. As long as I did my job effectively and with a smile, I got paid and moved on to another set of customers. It was mind-numbing and busy.

Out of the corner of my eye, I saw Betty seat three people in a middle booth. I dropped off the drinks at one of my tables and headed over to the new customers. When I approached the table, I almost stopped in my tracks. Sadie and Donovan were on one side, their eyes locked on the table, with Egan on the other side, smiling worriedly.

Of course, they'd be seated at my table, and I couldn't run away without causing a scene. Egan might just get his way and force me to talk to him.

CHAPTER TWELVE

"Hi, I'm Jade." I cringed internally, but I would be professional and play my role. "I'll be your server tonight."

"You work here." Egan sighed and closed his eyes. "Of all the places."

His reaction felt like a slap. He was usually so eager to talk to me, but it was clear he was less than thrilled to see me. "Not sure what that means, but okay." I tried to keep the hurt out of my voice. "So, what would you like to drink?" The quicker I could get their orders, the faster I could get away. I hadn't been prepared to see him.

"Egan?" Amber squealed from behind me. "Is that you?"

She was my least favorite coworker here. She wore over-the-top makeup, unbuttoned her shirt to give customers a peek of her cleavage, and flipped her hair so much I swore it had to be a compulsion. However, she was the only server who earned more tips than me.

Pushing past me, she slid into the seat right next to him, and irrational anger overwhelmed me. That stupid bitch knew him. My heart sank. "You know each other?"

Egan winced, and his eyes locked on me. "I used to work here."

"And he disappeared right before we got to know each other."

She turned to me, forming her dark red lips into a pout. Her moss eyes glowed with power like she knew this affected me. She flirted with everyone and competed with me for the most tips, but this was something more. She wanted to make it clear that Egan was hers.

"That's a bit of a stretch." Egan tried scooting away from her, but he was so large, and she'd basically sat right on top of him, so he didn't have much room. "We never even talked outside of work." His cheeks turned pink, and I wanted to snatch her by the hair and yank her away from him.

"Oh, stop." She ran a hand down his chest and purred, "You know we have unfinished business."

Sadie glanced at me with pure pity. "I'd love a glass of water."

"Same." Donovan tugged at the collar of his polo shirt. "If you don't mind."

"Got it." I kept my attention on them, refusing to look at Egan. If her hand was somewhere near his southern region, I'd come unglued, and that wouldn't be good for anyone.

"Why don't you get me and Egan here a few shots of whiskey?" She placed a hand possessively on his arm. "We can start the night early."

"I am actually here with my friends," Egan said.

"Don't worry." She giggled. "I don't mind." She turned her body into him. "I'll need to get to know them eventually."

Wow, this girl was more brazen than I'd thought. But Egan wasn't trying too hard to tell her to fuck off. "If you want whiskey, you'll have to get it yourself." At least, she'd have to gain distance from him. "You may be off duty, but you're not twenty-one." I glared at her. "And I refuse to serve anyone underage." I spun on my heel and marched off to the kitchen, needing to catch my breath. I hadn't even asked if Egan wanted anything else to drink. For all I cared, he could drink his spit.

In the kitchen, I leaned against the wall and closed my eyes. I'd never felt this angry and out of control in my entire life. I didn't have a right to feel this way. I'd pushed him away, but it didn't matter.

Seeing him with someone else highlighted the mistake I'd made. He couldn't be interested in her, but the words tasted bad in my own mind. Why wouldn't he be? She was gorgeous and into him.

I had to get out of there. I couldn't watch him show interest in someone else. I had enough money saved from the past few weekends to leave early tonight.

With a renewed goal, I went searching for Ollie. It was like the prick had disappeared.

A thin sweat broke out against my skin at the realization that I might not be able to leave and I'd have to watch Amber with him all damn night.

"Hey, are you okay?" Jerry, the assistant manager, stepped from the back of the kitchen, his brows furrowed. "You don't look so hot."

I didn't have to lie. My stomach was upset over it all. "I'm not feeling great, and I can't find Ollie anywhere."

"Yeah, I was looking for him too." He shook his head, causing the lights to reflect off his balding spot. "One minute, he was talking to me about the schedule tonight, and the next, he was gone. I'll split up your tables. Go home and get some rest."

"Are you sure?" It was a godsend that I'd run into him instead of Ollie. I had a feeling the actual manager wouldn't have been so nice. "I can try—" I prayed this didn't shoot me in the foot, but I had to pretend I hated to go.

"No, it's fine." His eyes warmed, reminding me painfully of my dad. I tried staying clear of him because of that. "Go on. You don't need to be serving food if you aren't feeling right. Let me know if you need anything."

"Thanks." I removed the apron and placed it on the hook. I drew the keys from my pocket and headed to the back door. I refused to give Amber the satisfaction of seeing me leave.

Outside, the tingling feeling hit me again. What the hell was going on with that? It didn't even register until I heard a noise behind the dumpster a few feet away. The disgusting smell of rotting food hit me, and I almost lost my lunch.

I had no interest in finding out what was making that noise, so I turned and ran out of the dark alley and toward a street light.

More sweat coated my body as I rushed around the side of the building and onto the grass that led to the parking lot. Right in front of the entrance, several large groups of people were waiting for a table, so I slowed down to appear more casual.

My head inadvertently turned toward the restaurant, and I searched for Egan. Obviously, I was a glutton for punishment, but it wasn't like I could see them. They were at the back of the building.

I wasn't sure which one was worse—seeing Amber draping herself over him or imagining what they were doing together right at this moment. I forced myself to focus on my car and tried to push him from my mind.

But I couldn't do it.

The way she'd run her hands all over him kept replaying in my mind. What kind of hussy did that? The kind that wasn't afraid to go after what they wanted. Someone completely opposite of me.

Maybe I was more like my mom than I liked to think. I was so worried about getting hurt that I was letting things fall through the cracks. But as long as he was happy, I figured I would survive.

I sobbed the entire way back to the dorm. Once I got into that room, Vera would probably pepper me with questions about him, and I'd have to hold myself together. I refused to appear weak in front of anyone. Showing weakness made you vulnerable, and when you were vulnerable, people took advantage of you. Case and point —Sarah.

My tires squealed as I pulled into my normal spot as far away from the buildings as possible. The car didn't necessarily embarrass me, but it stuck out like a sore thumb. I turned off the engine, unbuckled, and sat there for a moment. I wiped the tears from my cheeks and took deep, calming breaths.

They didn't work.

In fact, I only cried harder. The void deep within me got bigger. A piece inside me had always seemed cold. I could touch it, but it wouldn't warm no matter what. It'd been there for as long as I could remember, and years had passed since I'd thought about it.

No matter what, I would survive this. I refused to give in.

Minutes ran together as I allowed myself to break down for the first time in ten years. The last time I'd cried like this was on the day of my father's funeral. Little had I known that day would be the last one of my childhood. My life had changed the moment we'd gotten into Sarah's car to head back to live with her.

My body shook with emotions as I mourned the loss of not only my dad but my mother too. And of the sexy stranger I'd only known for a handful of weeks.

Someone pounded on my window, startling me. My head jerked left, and I found Egan staring right at me. His body sagged as he took in my state.

Embarrassed, I used the sleeve of my white shirt to wipe away the tears again. When I pulled it back, black mascara streaked it.

My eyes flicked to the rearview mirror, and I wanted to die. My worst fear had been confirmed. My eyes were red, and the mascara was smeared under my eyes. I looked like a damn raccoon.

"Jade," he said deeply. "Please unlock the door."

The way my name rolled off his tongue made my heart flip-flop in my chest. "I ..."

"Please," he said again. "We need to talk."

He was right, and I was being ridiculous. My refusal to get out of the car wouldn't prevent him from telling me he was dating someone else. And here I'd thought he'd been trying to talk me into seeing him while it had probably been about Amber the entire time. Gathering all of the strength I had, I unlocked the door.

"Thank you." He opened it and held it for me. "Are you okay?" He straightened, focusing on me.

"No." I didn't have the energy to lie. There was no point. I had to be honest. We deserved that. "I hope I didn't ruin your night with Amber." I wanted to spit her name, but I managed to only grunt it. The fact that I was being irrational pissed me off.

"That's what I thought this was about." He touched my face, and our strange connection buzzed between us as tenderness reflected in his eyes. "You heard her. She hadn't seen me since last semester when I disappeared. She means nothing to me. I didn't go there to see her."

"Right, but you didn't seem upset with her lying all over you." Oh God, I had to stop. I sounded so pathetic.

"Jade—"

"No, it's fine." I pushed him away. It was time to remember this was for the best. "It makes sense that you'd be interested in someone else. Hell, we've only kissed once." Tears burned my eyes again. How the hell was there any liquid left in my body?

"Stop." He gently grasped my arm and pulled me out of the car and against his chest. "I will never move on from you."

"What?" I sounded stuffy, and I pulled back to look up at his face. "But you let her—"

"I shouldn't have." His forehead lined as he cupped my face. The jolt flowed between us. "She surprised me, and I didn't want to be rude. But I hurt you, and I wish I could undo that."

I nearly denied that he had, but that wouldn't accomplish anything. "How is this possible? I feel such a strong connection to you after only a matter of days." If he was on the fence about me, that would make him run miles away. I braced for his rejection.

"Thank God." He lowered his forehead to mine. "When you stopped talking to me, I was afraid my feelings were completely one-sided."

"You're relieved?" Most guys our age didn't want to hear girls talk about strong feelings. They wanted to be single and to mingle. "You aren't freaked out?"

"I was until you said that. The past two weeks have been pure hell." He pulled back, and a huge smile spread across his face. "I feel the same thing, if not more, for you, and I understand that the intensity can be scary."

"Can be?" I still didn't understand how he wasn't freaking out.

"That's why I stopped talking to you." Now that I'd started telling the truth, it was like my mouth had diarrhea. "This scares me. I didn't want to give you the opportunity to hurt me, and we can see how well that panned out. Even with distance my feelings for you grew, which makes no sense. Seeing you tonight, thinking you'd moved on ..." I couldn't finish that sentence.

"I'm so sorry." His head hung to the side. "I never meant to make you feel that way. It's the last thing I ever wanted to happen. You're the most important person in my life, and there is no one else who could ever capture my attention."

I believed him. I felt the exact same way. "But that's not normal to feel so strongly after such a short amount of time."

"In my family, it is." With his free hand, he curled his fingers into my hair. "When we find our person, we're all in."

"And that person is me?" The fact that his family commonly found someone they had these crazy feelings for was unbelievable.

"Yes." He stepped closer, his scent overloading my senses. "No one holds a candle to you."

Those words warmed the void inside me, and for the first time, my head didn't yell at me to stop. It had taken tonight for me to realize I needed him. I stood on my tiptoes and pressed my lips to his, wanting him to know I was done fighting. The jolt bolted between us, and my tongue licked across his mouth. Everything around us disappeared, and my focus was entirely on him.

A low growl emanated from his chest, throwing my hormones into overdrive. He opened his mouth, and his tongue swept into mine. The vanilla taste was better than I remembered, and my head grew dizzy.

I slipped my hands under his thin sweater, enjoying the feel and warmth of his skin on mine. I'd never been so brazen before, but he was driving me mad.

His hands dropped to my waist and pulled me against him.

Then someone cleared her throat, tugging me back to the world around us.

CHAPTER THIRTEEN

I wanted to bury my face into Egan's massive chest and hide. I had an inkling it was Sadie who had caught us in our passionate embrace. I licked my lips, enjoying his lingering taste.

But I wouldn't cower, not this time. I pulled away slightly, but Egan's arm wrapped around my waist, anchoring me to him. He wanted me to stay close, and it thrilled me more than I'd ever admit.

"Is ... uh ..." Sadie grinned. "Is everything all right?"

"Really, babe?" Donovan chuckled and took her hand. "I'm thinking they're more than okay."

My face was on fire, so I changed the subject. "I'm sorry about earlier and the past few weeks. I've been rude to all of you, and it was uncalled for. I just got ..." I paused, searching for the best word.

"Overwhelmed?" Donovan threw out. "Unsteady? Scared?"

That brought my struggle to light. It hadn't been one thing but all three. "How did you know?"

He turned his focus on Sadie and took her hand. "Let's just say you aren't the only one who's experienced something like this. It's a lot at first."

"You have a connection like this too?" I'd only read about stuff like this in books, and now I'd learned that another couple had this.

"Yes, we do." Sadie nodded. "It was a similar situation to you and Egan; I knew there was a chance to have a connection this strong with someone, and Donovan had no clue. We fought the connection at first too."

"She's right." Donovan scrunched his face. "I was a complete asshole."

"I wasn't much better." Sadie kissed his cheek. "But we've made it, and that's all that matters."

I completely understood that sentiment.

"Roxy and the others told us to meet them at the Student Center." Sadie lifted an eyebrow. "Do you two want to join us?"

"It's up to Jade," Egan said, his focus only on me.

My heart screamed no, but I'd been an ass to all of them. "Do you mind?"

"If that's what you want, then of course I don't." He pressed his lips to mine. "Whatever I can do to make you happy."

Okay, maybe I'd made the wrong call. We could be doing more of this instead, and honestly, I'd kind of prefer it.

Donovan laughed. "You better snatch her before she changes her mind."

"Leave them alone," Sadie chastised. "I'm thrilled for them."

There was no way I could've fought this any longer. Each day had chipped my will away. Even if I hadn't seen Amber all over him, I would've said screw it, just not nearly as fast. In a way, I was thankful she'd made me wake up sooner and put myself out of this misery.

"I need to do something about my raccoon eyes first." I gestured to the pronounced bags under my eyes.

"Oh, I can help with that." Sadie opened her purse and pulled out a makeup remover tissue. "Roxy makes me carry these around in case my makeup messes up. It does come in handy at times, but I'll never admit it."

Yeah, telling Roxy she was right would make her gloat for days. She and Lillith were forces to be reckoned with.

I pulled away from Egan, grabbed the cloth, and wiped under my eyes until no black rubbed off any longer. "Thanks."

Egan ran a finger along my chin. "Let's go. I'm starving."

"Didn't you eat already?" I had no clue how long I'd been in my car, but I figured it had been long enough for them to have eaten and come back to me wallowing in self-pity.

"Of course not." He moved so only one arm remained wrapped around me as he faced the Student Center. "When we realized you'd left, we were out of there in minutes."

That meant so damn much to me. "I hate that I ruined your night out."

"We didn't really want to eat there anyway." Donovan shivered. "Egan and I used to work there, and they weren't too happy about how we left, so we welcomed the excuse to get out of there."

"Then why go there in the first place?" That sounded like they'd been asking for punishment.

"We were looking for someone." Sadie tugged Donovan's hand and strolled toward the building, turning her back to us. "But they weren't there."

I quickly locked my car. Then Egan and I followed behind them. I asked, "Who was it?"

"I'm not sure of his name." Sadie glanced over her shoulder at me. "But we would know if we saw him."

That was vague and ominous, but I didn't want to push. They were already being super nice about me blowing them off for the past two weeks.

I was relieved that the Student Center wasn't super packed. Most people were hanging out off-campus and partying, being college students and all. That wasn't how I rolled. I liked being firmly in control, which was the opposite of what happened when alcohol was involved.

My eyes located their crew at the back of the room. Naida was the only one missing. Two tables were pushed together, making room for eight. Lillith and Katherine sat across from each other at the end. Axel and Roxy had their backs to us.

"Holy shit." Lillith rubbed her eyes and smirked. "Are my eyes playing tricks on me?" She looked at Roxy, who sat right across from her, and pointed at me.

I wasn't sure if I'd rather they give me a hard time or ignore me out of anger. I hated being the center of attention.

Roxy faced us and waggled her eyebrows. "I don't believe they are, and a certain huge guy has an arm wrapped protectively around her, so I'm thinking he finally locked her down."

"You two, stop." Katherine smacked Lillith on the arm. "Don't embarrass the poor girl."

"You're right." Lillith pouted. "She might disappear and hide for another couple of weeks."

I stood on my tiptoes and whispered in Egan's ear, "I'm never going to live this down, am I?"

"No." Axel rubbed Roxy's shoulder. "You aren't. Roxy is as loyal as they come, but she'll throw out every wrong thing you've done to her any chance given."

How the hell had he heard me? I'd been quiet. "Do you have supersonic hearing?"

Egan tensed beside me.

"Phew. Please." Roxy rolled her eyes. "You aren't nearly as quiet as you think."

Apparently not. I squared my shoulders, needing to own up to how I'd treated everyone. "I just wanted to say I'm sorry about everything." I'd keep it vague since I had a feeling Roxy would drag it out as much as humanly possible.

Roxy tapped her finger on her lip as she pulled at the gold dress that hugged her body and complemented her complexion. "For what, exactly?"

"Roxy," Egan warned. "She's had a hard enough time. You should understand that."

"Fine." She placed her hand on the table and pursed her lips. "Take all my fun away."

"She should understand?" My attention went straight to Egan. "What do you mean?"

"They have a connection like ours." Egan's hand swallowed mine whole. He was huge, warm, and the kindest person I'd ever met. "They struggled at first too."

"Are you all family?" He'd said that his family knew connections like this existed. I hadn't considered that a group as close as them could be blood.

"I sure hope not." Roxy snorted. "Otherwise, we've been doing some pretty illegal stuff every night."

"Seriously?" Lillith groaned. "You guys were making sexual innuendos less than two minutes ago. I was hoping for a longer break."

"Stop the hate." Roxy pulled out the chair beside her and patted it. "Come sit with me, Jade. We have plenty to catch up on."

"Do I have to?" I glanced at Sadie for help. "She's going to make me uncomfortable."

"It builds character." Roxy pointed at the seat. "Now get your ass over here so we can chat."

Sadie shrugged. "Sorry, but you'll have to fend for yourself on this one."

I deserved that. I walked over and plopped onto the seat next to her. My body tensed until Egan sat next to me and took my hand in his. Just his touch calmed me. I'd experienced the same thing the night I'd stumbled upon that dead girl.

"What's up?" I asked just as I inhaled the delicious scent of her hamburger. My stomach rumbled, and I realized how famished I was. I'd skipped dinner because I usually snacked throughout my shift, but now that I'd calmed down, I was starving.

Egan released my hand and stood. "Hey, I'll be right back." He kissed my cheek and headed toward the cafeteria.

"I'll join you." Donovan jumped to his feet and brushed his fingers on Sadie's arm. "I'll grab us something and be right back."

"Don't be long." Sadie blew him a kiss.

"Maybe I should go join them." Axel shook his head as he scanned the table full of women. "It was bad enough when it was three against one, but now we're talking about five."

"Oh, grow a pair," Roxy teased as she pushed his arm.

"No, but seriously." Lillith leaned over the table, her eyes more maroon than normal. "What's it like to kiss him?"

"What?" I knew women kissed and told, but I hadn't expected to be asked so blatantly. "Egan?"

"Have you been kissing someone else?" Roxy's eyes grew so wide they looked like they might pop out. "Who?"

"No one." This was bad. I didn't want Egan thinking I'd touched anyone else. I would never want to. "I'm just surprised you asked me that here."

"That either means it was remarkable or god-awful." Lillith leaned back in her seat and crossed her arms, causing her black long-sleeved shirt to wrinkle. "I'm hoping, for Egan's sake, that it's the remarkable one."

"Guys ..." Sadie giggled despite trying to maintain a solemn face. "Leave her alone."

Katherine leaned forward to see her around Lillith and said, "That isn't very convincing."

My mouth started running like every time I felt uncomfortable. "His lips are amazing. He tastes like the best part of a cinnamon roll—the vanilla frosting—and his tongue feels like velvet. When he touches me, it's like the world rights itself and I've finally found something I've desperately been missing without realizing."

"Velvet, eh?" Roxy chewed on her thumb. "I could see that."

"Really?" Axel's mouth dropped, and he stared at his girlfriend in disbelief. "I'm right here."

"You know you're it for me." She gestured to her neck. "There's no getting out of it, but Egan has always been a mystery and somewhat removed. To see the girl who turned him into a blubbering idiot and hear about that side of him has us all intrigued." She kissed Axel. "You have nothing to worry about."

"Damn straight, I don't," Axel growled and pulled her harder against his lips. "But you keep at it, and I'll have to kill him to make sure."

"Just kill her." I swore she and Lillith tried to embarrass us every chance they got. It was like they liked the shock factor and fed off each other. "Problem solved for all parties."

"Hey." She jerked in my direction. "What the hell kind of traitor are you?" She smiled, clearly happy I was dishing it back.

Egan appeared, somehow balancing three trays. "Don't talk to her that way. I'd hate to have to drop all this food to come to her rescue."

"Don't worry. You wouldn't have to." I crossed my arms. "I can handle her on my own."

"And if you need help"—Lillith hit her chest and pointed at me —"I've got you."

"Man," Axel said, eyeing the three trays Egan placed on the table. "And here I thought you couldn't eat any more."

"Oh, stop." Egan put a tray in front of me that held chicken pasta, a cinnamon roll, and a Coke. "This one's for her."

I hadn't expected him to get me anything, but I couldn't say I was surprised. I'd planned on eating a peanut butter sandwich after getting settled, but this looked and smelled so much better. "Thank you, but you didn't have to."

"I know." He winked. "I wanted to."

For once, I believed him. He'd been trying to take care of me since the moment I'd seen him. Sadie and Donovan joined us, and we enjoyed our meal.

EGAN and I left the others and slowly headed back to the dorms. The entire evening had been fun, and I let myself relax and enjoy the company. We approached the girls' dorm, and I walked over to the brick wall, leaning against it. A group of girls was hanging out in the lobby, and the last thing I wanted was for Egan to walk me upstairs and Vera to ask more questions. She was nice enough, but I wasn't ready for an interrogation.

He placed an arm on each side of me, trapping me.

If anyone else had done it, I would've freaked out, feeling claustrophobic, but not with him. It made me feel safe, and my body warmed at his close proximity.

"I had fun tonight." He looked deep into my eyes and sighed. "Having you there like that felt right."

"I know what you mean." I propped my head against the brick so I could see his handsome face. "Granted, it'd be nice if you and I could hang out alone sometime."

A large smile spread across his face, and his eyes appeared to glow faintly. "I am all for that, but I don't want to rush or pressure you."

"You're not." And that was one reason I trusted him completely. He knew what I needed. I placed my hands on his chest, enjoying the feel of his muscles. "And I'm all in."

"You have no idea how glad I am to hear you say that." He lowered his lips to mine but stopped a breath away. "I really would love to kiss you again."

"Then why wait?" I closed the distance between us, needing to reassure him. I was done letting fear rule me.

I focused on his lips and taste. Even after eating, he still tasted like warm vanilla. I moaned before I could stop myself. I'd normally be embarrassed, but I didn't give a damn. I didn't want to stop.

His arm slid down my body and wrapped around me, pulling me flush against him. The feel of his front pressed against mine made my body turn hot. I'd never felt this way before, and I realized why people did stupid things in the heat of a moment. My mind was foggy, and I wanted more.

When I licked his lips, he opened his mouth, allowing me in. He matched me stroke for stroke, and a low groan came from the back of his throat. My hands snaked up into his hair, and my mind focused on everywhere that he touched.

"Egan," Donovan said right next to us. "I hate to interrupt, but we need your help." His tone held an edge. Something was definitely wrong.

CHAPTER FOURTEEN

Egan pulled back from me slightly and looked at Donovan. His voice was low, raspy—sexy. "This can't wait?"

"No, man. Sorry." Donovan's gaze darted to me and back to Egan. "It's something we need help with now."

"Is everything okay?" Not too long ago, we'd all been hanging out and having fun. Their demeanor had completely changed. "Is there something I can do?"

Axel lifted a brow at Egan.

"Nah, you go in and get some rest." Egan kissed my forehead and smiled. "You've had a long night, and I'm hoping we can hang out tomorrow." Fear filled his eyes.

Him worrying that I might say no gutted me. I'd really done a number on him and wished I could take it all back. "Of course, but I don't mind helping."

"I know." He leaned down and kissed me once more. "But I'm sure it's nothing. I'll come by in the morning, and we can have breakfast together.

"Sounds perfect." I wanted to insist on going, but exhaustion overtook me. The night had been an emotional rollercoaster, and the bed called my name. I pulled my phone out of my pocket and unlocked it. "What's your number? I'll text you so you can let me know when you're heading my way."

He cupped my face and rattled it off. He then kissed my forehead, walked over to the door, and opened it for me. "I'll see you soon."

Donovan and Axel fidgeted, ready to get him and go. I was holding up whatever they needed to do.

I almost pushed, wanting to join them, but Egan had made it clear that he didn't want me involved. I guessed it was something guy-related.

"Be careful." I brushed my fingers along his chest as I walked by and entered the building.

He shut the door and stayed in place, watching me the entire way to the elevator. The guys talked to him as I stepped into the elevator. As the doors shut, Egan turned, and the group hurried off, but the doors slid shut before I could figure out which direction they'd rushed off in.

I regretted not forcing myself on them or following them to see what they were up to, but the elevator was already moving, and I doubted I could find them.

Oh well. It was probably for the best. I fired off a quick text, of **It's me**, so he'd have my number.

When I reached my floor, I walked slowly down the hall. It wasn't bubbling with people like usual. Most of the rooms were silent, indicating people were still out partying; the few people who'd stayed in had their televisions on loud.

I opened the door to my dorm room and was surprised to find that Vera wasn't inside. She always was at this time. Her normally tidy side of the room had an open bag on her bed with clothes thrown everywhere.

She must have been in a hurry. Strange. But I wouldn't worry about it; I was going to enjoy the alone time I'd found. She almost always sat at her desk, pouring over books all the damn time. I didn't get it.

After putting on pajamas, I climbed into the bed, facing the door. Right as my eyes began to close, my phone vibrated on my desk. I picked it up to find a text message from Egan.

Good night. I can't wait to see you tomorrow. Be there to get you at 9.

The amount of happiness I felt from a stupid text was insane, but I was giddy as fuck over the fact he'd made it a point to tell me good night. I typed out my response: **Good night. I can't wait either. I'll be ready.**

I placed the phone back on the desk and fell asleep with a grin.

Red and blue lights flickered against the gray walls, waking me. I sat up and looked out my window, which overlooked the boys' dorm and the parking lot. Four police cars and an ambulance were pulled right up to the curb, all with their lights flashing.

Something bad had happened. Could it be another dead body? That surely couldn't be why Egan and his friends had run off. They wouldn't get involved with something like that on purpose ... would they?

The doubt alone made me stand and glance at Vera's bed. It was after one in the morning, and she was still gone. What if she'd gotten hurt? Maybe I should've gone looking for her instead of going to bed.

Not bothering to put on blue jeans, I stayed in my long flannel pants and long-sleeved shirt. I grabbed my jacket and slipped my tennis shoes on, rushing to get down there. If I'd gone to sleep while my roommate was being tortured or worse, I might not ever get over that.

Racing out the door, I opted for the stairs. I flew down them, each step faster than the last. I reached the bottom of the stairs in half the time it normally took me. File that under "weird" and something to address at a later date.

Outside, two paramedics pushed a stretcher out from the walkway between Webster Hall and the library. A breeze blew the sheet off the person's face, and my eyes landed on familiar dark hair, a white button-down shirt, and black slacks. My stomach roiled.

Amber.

But, why? She didn't go to this school. She went to the local community college.

Egan and their entire group of friends stepped out from between the two buildings behind the paramedics.

Somehow, they'd known about this girl. And of course, the girls had been included, but not me.

"Jade," Egan called out. His eyes had taken on a glow. "Go back inside."

Really? He thought he could tell me what to do? That was not how this worked, and he'd be finding that out right now. I marched a few steps toward them, but Amber's neck caught my attention, stopping me in my tracks.

Her throat had been gouged over and over like something had repeatedly stabbed it or pecked at it. Blood congealed around the wound, but her eyes were frozen open, now a dark green color instead of the sparkling green I was used to seeing. Unable to look into them any longer, I focused back on her neck. The markings reminded me of the girl I'd found with her eyes gone. My stomach roiled again. How did this keep happening?

As the paramedics pushed her past me, I couldn't look away. Deep frowns marred the two men's faces, and their shoulders drooped. There was no helping her. Someone would have to call her parents and inform them that their child was dead.

Egan reached me and pulled me into his arms. "Jade."

"You knew." I pushed back from him and glared. My hands shook with anger. "That's why you ran off earlier."

"Look, I need you to go back inside." He opened the door and waved me in. "It's not safe out here."

He wasn't listening to me. He was too hell-bent on forcing me away. "But it isn't too dangerous for them?" I pointed at Sadie and the other girls. Even Naida was here. It burned. I'd let my guard down and thought I might actually be part of their group, but clearly, I wasn't. "Just not me. Why? I'm not part of your clique?" Something white-hot coursed through my body, burning me. Oddly, it didn't hurt. Rather, it was invigorating.

"No, that's not it." Egan lifted a hand. "We didn't ... Just, please, go back inside."

"Egan," Sadie warned. "We need to go somewhere else."

"Like hell! You're not leaving me behind." They had to know more. Something deep in my gut told me that. "I want to know everything. What aren't you telling me?" They wouldn't push me away like a nobody any longer. If I let them discard me, they'd continue to do it.

"Honey—" Egan pleaded.

"She's either in or out," Naida said. "I told each of you that getting her involved was a mistake, but none of you listened. It's time to decide. Pick a side."

"Look at you," Roxy snickered. "Learning some slang. It's about damn time."

Ignoring Roxy, I asked Egan. "What is she talking about?" Out of all of them, I was surprised Naida wanted them to tell me everything, but he would be the one to tell me. If he believed in our connection, it was time for him to prove it.

"They're coming," Donovan whispered. "We need to at least pretend we aren't fighting."

I scanned, seeing no one, unsure what he meant until four police officers marched from the woods, coming into view. "How did you know that?" There was no way he could've known unless they weren't entirely human. But that was impossible. Those types of creatures didn't exist outside of stories.

"Please, stay calm," Katherine said with concern. "Naida's right, and if he won't tell you what's going on, I will."

That was enough for me.

The officers approached and stopped a few feet away.

The oldest one nodded, and the lines of his face deepened. "That's it for tonight. Give us a call if you remember anything else." He handed Egan a card. "And all of you need to go inside."

"Yes, sir," Egan replied. "Let us know if we can help out with anything too."

"You guys finding her was enough." The older officer hung his head. "I only wish we could've saved her."

"Us too," Sadie said with remorse.

The youngest officer grimaced. "With that kind of wound, it wouldn't have mattered."

"That's enough for tonight." The older one motioned to his men. "Let's get moving."

Donovan nodded. "We will do just that."

The officers headed to their patrol cars as we stood there, watching them go. There was no way in hell I would even pretend to go inside. If Egan had his way, he'd run off to keep me out of the loop. I stayed firmly in place and turned my full attention on him. "Spill."

"Not here." Egan scanned the area like he thought someone might overhear us. "We can talk tomorrow."

"No." I stood tall and lifted my chin. "I let my guard down with you. With all of you." I looked at each one of them, except Naida. "And I regret it."

"Don't say that." Egan grimaced and reached for my hand. "We're only trying to protect you."

I dodged him and clenched my teeth. "I am more than capable of protecting myself."

"You are *mine* to protect," Egan growled. His eyes glowed, and his pupils turned into slits. "There is nothing more important to me."

The first day here, I'd thought I'd imagined his pupils doing that.

Fear rocked through me, and I blinked, thinking my mind was seeing things. But they stayed the same.

"Egan, you need to calm down." Sadie grabbed my arm and pulled me toward her. "You're getting too wound up."

"Do not touch her!" he roared and pushed Sadie off me. "No one but I can."

"Hey now." Donovan sprang into action and shoved Egan hard. "Calm down."

I stood there in shock at what he'd done. He'd always been caring and sweet, but he'd just pushed his best friend.

Sadie didn't seem angry, though. She placed a hand on Donovan, and as soon as she touched him, he calmed down. I'd never seen anything like it before.

Egan took a few menacing steps toward Donovan, ready to fight. He fisted his hands, prepared to punch him.

"You need to make him focus on you," Roxy said, pointing at Egan. "Or they're going to fight, and it'll cause a huge problem."

A little more direction would've been nice, but instinct took over. I stepped between Donovan and Egan, effectively shutting Egan down.

I clutched both of his fists. "Calm down. They aren't doing anything. You're acting irrationally."

"You do realize telling an irrational person that they're being irrational isn't the smartest move," Lillith scoffed. "I know it pisses me off more."

"That's because you're female," Axel retorted.

"Oh, hell no," Roxy gasped and smacked him on the back of the head. "That's not cool."

None of them were normal. I hadn't noticed how much until this moment. Who cracked jokes when two friends were about to beat each other down?

Egan's breathing calmed, but his pupils remained slitted.

Even though part of me was freaked out, an equally large part wasn't fazed by his odd-shaped eyes. "Please, tell me everything," I said, soft and non-threatening.

"Okay." He sighed and glanced around the group. "But not here. It's late, and we all need to get our rest."

"If this is your way of getting out of it—"

"It's not." He ran a hand through his hair. "I promise. But we just found Amber dead, and you're in your pajamas."

When he laid it out like that, I couldn't argue. Damn him and his logic. "Then, first thing in the morning." I wouldn't let him get out of it completely. They were holding back something huge, and not knowing was driving me insane.

His face fell. "But I kind of wanted to enjoy some time with you."

"No, you obviously have secrets." I gestured to the library and to Naida. Not to mention his eyes doing freaky shit. "I'm not going anywhere with you until I know what you're hiding. I opened up to you, and you're refusing to do the same?"

"It's just—"

"Let me make it clear." I placed my hands on my hips. "Don't bother coming tomorrow if you aren't going to tell me everything." His hesitation about telling me what it was threw up giant red flags. I'd let my guard down too soon, but I wouldn't be treated like I wasn't an equal. I'd rather be alone.

I turned on my heel and walked into the dorm, letting the door slam shut behind me. I left a part of my heart behind, but I forced my feet forward.

The door opened behind me, and he called out, "Wait."

CHAPTER FIFTEEN

Everything inside me demanded I stop, but he was playing a game I didn't like. Somehow, I continued my march to the elevator. If I caved, it would set a precedent I wasn't okay with.

"Wait." Egan's footsteps grew closer as he rushed to catch up. "I'll tell you." His voice sounded broken.

I stopped and turned, facing the empty lobby. "When?" I was tired of bending to the will of everyone around me—my mom, Sarah, and now Egan. Committing to a time would push this along.

Childhood memories flashed in my mind. The times Sarah would punch me for being five minutes late from school. When Mom would purposely turn a blind eye to the abuse. The near-constant insults about being worthless and an annoyance. Telling me daily since I was eight that I would never amount to anything and I was lucky to have a bed because I didn't even deserve that.

I was done being the victim and letting others make the rules. That had been the point of running away to Kortright. Not being with him would hurt like hell, but it would be worse to lose myself.

"It's late." He scratched the back of his neck. "And you really need your rest, so you should sleep in tomorrow. We can put off our morning like initially planned."

He offered to tell me everything, and then in the next breath, he tried to push off the conversation. "Whatever." I shouldn't have been surprised. I gestured to his friends, watching outside the door. "Go back to them. There's nothing left to say. You know how to get a hold of me when you're ready."

It hurt so damn much that he was keeping things from me, but I couldn't change that. I inhaled sharply like the air around me could strengthen my resolve, pivoted toward the elevator, and pushed the up button.

He exhaled loudly. "Okay, let's talk now. You're right. You have a right to know." He sounded gutted. "But we need to go somewhere private to talk."

His words validated my fear. It had to be bad. "My roommate isn't here." Under normal circumstances, being alone in a room with him would be a bad idea, but that wasn't a problem tonight. He couldn't distract me from what I wanted to know, and if things went south, I was surrounded by girls who'd hear my screams.

"Of course she's not." He laughed without humor. "Well, okay then."

My nerves frayed even more. There was no reason I should be feeling trepidation. The elevator doors slid open, and Egan waved to his friends before getting in.

I had to keep reminding myself they were his friends. They were almost a family, one I wasn't part of even if I felt like I had a connection with them.

Time crawled the entire way to the room. Now that I knew answers were imminent, I was equally thrilled and terrified. I might finally understand the connection between us.

I steadied my hands, opened the door to my room, and waved him inside. "Come on in."

He hesitated then sighed and entered the room. "Do you know

when she's coming back?" His focus settled on the Star Wars poster on her side of the room.

"No, but I don't think it'll be tonight." We really didn't keep each other abreast of our schedules. I only let her know when I worked so she wouldn't be scared when I got in late. "She's never been gone like this, so she probably went back home. She's not a social butterfly."

A frown marred his face as I sat on my bed.

I placed my hands in my lap and arched an eyebrow. "So get on with it."

"Once you learn everything, there is no going back," he said ominously.

"I don't care," I said, my voice cracking. Surely, this didn't have anything to do with the girls' deaths. I'd found the first girl, and they hadn't been anywhere around. I'd left them in the Student Center. "I want to know, or you need to go."

"All right." He ran his hands through his hair, mussing it up. "This will sound crazy, but I need you to keep an open mind."

"That's not surprising." There was something different about their group. I'd felt it on day one, but the more time I spent around them, the more things I noticed. "What are you, spies?"

He barked out a laugh, but his eyes were devoid of humor, making me even more uncomfortable.

"I wish that was it." He paced between the beds. "My friends and I are different."

"Tell me something I don't know," I snapped, my patience wearing thin. "But how are you different?"

"You really are like Sadie." He rubbed his temples. "You just cut through all the bullshit. That's one of the things I like about you."

The comparison to Sadie rubbed me the wrong way. "Are you saying you're into Sadie too?"

"What?" His mouth dropped open, and he blinked. "No. Not at all. You're it for me. It's just a similar trait that I find endearing."

I wanted to push it, but I had to keep my jealousy at bay. There were more important factors at hand. "Can we stop talking about *her* and get to the point?"

"Jade." He stared deep into my eyes. "There is absolutely nothing to worry about. Sadie and I are just friends. Nothing more. We were never anything more. You don't need to feel threatened. I was stupid to compliment you like that, and I'm sorry. I keep messing up."

"Why shouldn't I feel threatened?" Sadie was like the perfect person. "She's gorgeous, kind, and there's something about her that puts me at ease."

"But she's not my mate." He sucked in a breath. "You are."

"Of course I'm not all those things." Tears stung my eyes. "So that's what we are? Friends?"

"Dammit." He dropped my hand and pulled at his hair. "I'm doing this all wrong. You're more than that. You're sexy, infuriating, and so damn strong. When you smile, it's like everything in the world gets righted. You're becoming the oxygen I need to breathe." He cupped his hands around mine.

"But you just said we're mates." I didn't think he'd be so cruel to mess with me like this. He'd say we were friends in one breath; then in the next, he'd give my heart hope. All of these confusing emotions were driving me insane.

"Mates as in fated mates. Some call them soulmates," he said as he angled his body toward me. "That's what I'm trying to say. We are two halves of one soul, and we found each other."

"Fated mates?" I tried to scoot farther back, but my traitorous body wouldn't do it. I needed to be near him. "Those aren't real." Those were my favorite type of romance stories to read, but that's what they were. Stories.

"They are in my world." He winced. "In *our* world."

"What the hell does that mean?" My voice rose in anger and frustration. "Just tell me." My mind was racing at all the possibilities, but each one was impossible ... wasn't real.

"My group of friends and I aren't human." He rubbed his hands together. "We're supernaturals."

"Egan, stop fucking with me." He had to be messing with me, but the explanation made sense. How Egan had heard the scream that night when he'd been back in the Student Center. How his eyes turned to slits. And how they could hear me when I whispered. But that was insane.

"I'm not." He rubbed his finger along the top of my hand gently. "I know it sounds crazy, but that's why you feel the connection between us the way you do."

"So what are you?" My mind was running so fast I couldn't even process my thoughts. "Vampires?" Of course, *Twilight* was the only thing I landed on.

"Katherine and Lillith are."

Their all-liquid diet made all kinds of sense now. "Are you serious?" I touched my neck as a chill ran down my spine.

"Yes, but they don't drink straight from humans, and they don't kill." He tightened his hold on my hand. "You are completely safe. If they were a threat, I wouldn't let them near you."

"So what is everyone else, then?" I was struggling to remain calm. I pulled my hands from his.

"Donovan, Axel, and Roxy are wolf shifters." He watched my reaction and flinched. "Naida is a fae. Sadie is a hybrid of fae and wolf shifter. And I'm ..." He trailed off.

For him to act like that made me even more nervous. "You're what?"

He stared at me looking for something. "A dragon shifter."

"A dragon?" His eyes turning to slits made sense now, but they were huge and scary. "You've got to be kidding me." I had to be dreaming. I was sure this was just a nightmare. I chuckled, and he frowned.

Hurt turned his eyes almost black. "Look, I know it's a lot to take in." He raised his hands and dropped them into his lap. "But if you think about it—"

"I don't want to think about it." This was all too damn much. A bird or some other animal had killed Amber tonight, and I'd just learned that supernaturals were real. "This is insane. You're telling me that everything I've read or watched on television is real?"

"Most parts are." He rubbed a hand down his chin. "Usually, stories are based on real things. It's just that supernaturals don't want humans to know about our existence. It would cause mass hysteria."

"Then why are you telling me this?" I stood and backed against the wall, needing distance from him. If he was a dragon, he could hurt me without trying. "That defeats the purpose of keeping it a secret."

"Because you're my mate, Jade. Those rules don't apply to you." He took a step toward me. "You're different. You and I are meant to be together, meaning you're now part of this world."

His fingertips brushed my cheek again, and I felt so safe despite everything I'd learned. I inadvertently stepped into him, drawn to him, proving our bond was extraordinary.

"Please don't." I pushed his hand down, not wanting him close. Every time he touched me, my mind turned fuzzy, and I needed a clear head. "What you're telling me is crazy." Hurting him was the last thing I wanted to do, but this was too much.

He flinched and dropped his hand to his side. "I can only imagine." Concern etched into his forehead. "I don't want to throw you into a world you want no part of."

"Yet you did." He'd taken care of me because he felt like he had to, and he'd kissed me while knowing about our connection. His actions felt like a betrayal. "You should have told me straight away." By not doing so, he'd allowed our connection to grow. Unshed tears burned my eyes. I'd trusted him completely. "Instead of manipulating me."

"I didn't manipulate you." His shoulders sagged, and he closed his eyes. "I was scared to tell you. You're too important to me, and the thought of losing you petrified me."

"You're right. Manipulation isn't the right word, but you lied to me." Hurt coursed through me, and the cold spot inside my chest felt like a weight, adding to my pain. Not only had he not told me, but none of the others had either, cutting me deeper. "I thought I was going crazy. I didn't understand what was going on, and you let me struggle. I'm human, and I've never felt even half of what I feel for you for someone else before. The connection is so strong it takes my breath away at times."

He hung his head and brushed a tear off my cheek. The jolt between us came to life. Our bond had already gotten stronger tonight.

"You're right. I did." He closed his eyes and shook his head. "I'm so sorry. I never meant to do that to you, but the urge to be close to you was overwhelming. I needed to be near you. When we're apart, it's like a piece of me is gone."

"Maybe you didn't mean to hurt me, but you did. I should've known before we kissed tonight. You should've told me everything." I shuddered and rubbed my hands along my arms as cold settled in my bones, adding regret to my emotions. I needed to sort through everything. If he stayed, I'd say things I would regret. "I'm sorry, but you need to go." Saying the words physically hurt me. I didn't want him to leave, but him staying would only result in us hurting each other.

"What?" His head snapped up, and his eyes darkened to a rustic gold. "No."

"Yes, you do." Something brushed against my skin, urging me to hold him, but I pushed it away. I didn't need to make any decisions right now. "I need time alone to process."

"Can I come back in the morning?" He sounded like a little boy.

"I'm not sure." I picked up my phone. "I'll text you when I'm ready."

"Jade." He reached for me.

"Stop." If he touched me, I'd crumble into mush. "Please, just go."

His eyes glistened as he ran his hands through his hair. Somehow, he looked only about half of his normal height. He rasped, pain clear in his tone, "We always come back to here." He stepped toward the door. "At first, you asked me to 'Please give you space.' Now it's, 'Please just go.' You're always pushing me away."

"That's the thing." I glared at him. I wasn't sure if he was trying to make me feel guilty. "It's not about pushing you away. It's about processing everything in my own time."

"Okay." He opened the door and paused. He turned toward me. "This time, I'll give you all the space you need." His breath caught as he glanced at me, looking so broken. Then he walked out the door, and when the door shut behind him, I crumpled to the floor.

I WOKE up with a pounding headache. This had to be what a hangover felt like. In all fairness, I had one—an emotional hangover. I'd stayed up till four, crying like a newborn baby. If I'd thought the episode in my car was bad, I'd been wrong—so damn wrong.

My eyes were tender, so I grabbed my phone and turned on the camera immediately regretting it. My reflection staring back at me was one of horror. My hair had knots in it, and my eyes were almost swollen shut. The slits I could see were dark red. I looked like I'd been ridden hard or gotten the flu.

There was no way I could make it into work today. I snatched the phone off the desk and felt a little disappointed when I didn't have a message from Egan. But I had to remember, I'd asked for this.

Quickly texting Ollie to inform him I felt worse than yesterday, I tossed the phone on the bed and flopped back onto my pillow. I had no energy to get out of bed.

The shock of Egan's revelations last night still hadn't fully processed. That his friends were various kinds of supernaturals was insane. The fact I believed him made me certifiable.

Each one of them was so genuine and embraced who they were, unlike anyone else I'd ever met before. Maybe that was the missing piece that made it all click together. They were confident in themselves in a way no human could ever be.

Growing up, I'd been petrified of the dark, so to have my childhood terrors come to life and be real unsettled me. Had I somehow known as a child that the supernatural stories were real since I was a dragon's destined mate? It sounded crazy, but right then, that was my norm.

Egan's handsome face appeared in my mind, and just seeing it brought a sense of calm over me. Surely, if he were a real threat, I'd be naturally inclined to fear him, not tugged toward him. But could I knowingly enter into a life that was so hard to accept?

I didn't understand what being part of that life meant. I had a feeling it was completely different from what I'd ever known.

At the same time, the thought of not being with Egan was too painful to consider. But what would I have to give up to be with him?

Whichever decision I made would require a sacrifice.

On Monday morning, I stepped out of the dorm room. The entire weekend, I hadn't left except to run to the bathroom. Vera had never returned from wherever the hell she'd gone, so I was able to eat and drink in the room.

Egan had left me alone as he'd promised. I'd expected a few calls or texts, but it was radio silence.

That worked, though, since I'd been in hiding. I'd finally come to a decision, one I wasn't sure about. But when had anything ever truly gone my way?

It was early as hell, but I couldn't sleep and needed to do this. With shaky hands, I pulled up Egan's name and sent him a message. **Hey, can you come outside so we can talk?**

My heart pounded against my ribcage. That was how nervous I was. Then my phone buzzed. **On my way.**

CHAPTER SIXTEEN

Waiting for him outside the dorm was probably the hardest thing I'd ever done. I didn't know what to expect, and the fact that I would be solidifying my decision churned my stomach. He must have been going through the same thing this past month while being around me.

The sky was still pitch dark, and the cold was penetrating without the sun to warm the air. I tapped my fingers on my jeans. I wore a thicker black sweater and jacket since it was below freezing. Every breath puffed out in a cloud.

The campus was still asleep, and no one was around since it was before six in the morning.

Footsteps came from behind, startling me. I spun around, ready to defend myself, and found Egan walking toward me.

"Couldn't sleep?" I'd been worried about waking him up, but obviously, I shouldn't have been.

"No." Dark circles lined his eyes, and his hair was in complete disarray. He wore his usual jeans and a thin sweater, but they were wrinkled. I was pretty sure it was the exact outfit he'd worn the last time I saw him.

"Are you out here alone?" I hated the thought of something happening to him.

He stopped several feet away like he didn't want to come closer. "Yeah, keeping an eye out for anything strange."

It burned. Maybe he'd decided he didn't want me. Like he'd said, I'd been difficult this entire time. Maybe my last breakdown had been his tipping point. I kept pushing him away. "With all these deaths, you shouldn't risk it."

"Would you care if something did happen?" His expression was unreadable as he watched for my reaction.

His question stung, but I deserved it. "Of course I would." I couldn't survive him not being alive. "That's why I need you to stay safe."

"You have a funny way of showing it." He crossed his arms, unapproachability radiating off him.

"If you aren't up for talking, we can meet up later." I cleared my throat. "Or not at all." With the vibe rolling off him, he might not be interested in talking to me ever again.

He lifted an eyebrow, and his nose wrinkled. "Is that your way of telling me your decision?"

That was when it hit me—he expected me to end things with him. "No, it's not, but you look like you can barely stand. Have you slept?"

"It's hard to sleep when the one person who holds my heart wants nothing to do with me." He lifted his hands in front of him. "Please, just tell me what you want instead of dragging this out."

"First, I have a few questions." I didn't know how any of this worked.

"You'll be safe." His eyes glowed. "I'll make sure of it. You can pretend that the supernatural world doesn't exist. You can pretend I don't exist."

He looked like a heartbroken man. He only needed me to confirm what he expected. "That's going to be hard to do."

"I can leave if you want me to." He put his hands into his pockets. "I can be gone in a few hours if that's what you need."

"But I don't want you to leave," I whispered, knowing he could hear the words.

He stilled, and he blinked. "What are you saying?"

The cold spot in my chest warmed as I watched his face change from broken to hopeful. The warmth had to be linked to him. That would've sounded insane two days ago, but not anymore. I had so much to learn.

My heart raced as I moved closer to him, but I stopped a few inches away, not confident enough to bridge the entire distance. "I'm sorry about everything, but you've got to understand that my life hasn't been the easiest. I ran away to come here."

"What do you mean you 'ran away'?"

"My dad died when I was younger, and Mom almost didn't survive it." I'd never talked about this with anyone. It hurt too much. "She couldn't hold a job because she could barely function. So we went to live with her sister." That was when my bad dream had turned into a nightmare. "My aunt hates me, and she's made my life a living hell. I was supposed to go to a local college fall semester, and she threw a fit, so when I got accepted here, I ran. Neither one of them knows where I am."

"I'm so sorry." He scratched at his longer-than-usual stubble. "I had no clue."

"No, don't." I hated when people apologized for things they had no control over. "But you need to understand that I came here to figure out who I am and what I want to become. I swore I'd never allow a man to have that much control over my happiness like Dad had over Mom."

He frowned and nodded. "I understand that. So meeting me has been very problematic and horrible timing."

"The worst timing." I touched his arm, and the jolt crashed into me. "But I wouldn't change it for anything."

He sucked in a breath, and his eyes flicked to mine. “What do you mean?”

“Thank you for not giving up on me.” I licked my lips, still unsure. “I’m all in if you still want me.”

His strong arms wrapped around me, pulling me tight against his chest. “I’ll always want you. Even if you decide you don’t want to be with me, I’ll never get over you.”

“I couldn’t get over you either.” I pulled back and stared at him. “And I don’t want to try.” Our connection came to light, and I stood on my tiptoes as his mouth pressed against mine.

I had so many questions, but we deserved to have this moment. I opened my mouth, inviting his tongue inside. His sweet vanilla taste overwhelmed me in the best way possible. A shiver coursed through my body as his scent and taste surrounded me.

He leaned back, his eyes light gold. “Let’s get you inside. It’s freezing out here.”

“My roommate is still gone,” I offered. “Why don’t we go up there?”

“Okay.” He nodded and took my hand, and we headed inside.

In my dorm room, I stood between the beds and faced him, feeling awkward. I was very inexperienced when it came to guys.

“You don’t need to be nervous.” He took my hand and pulled me onto the bed beside him. “There are some things we still need to talk about, and I would never want to do anything that made you feel uncomfortable.”

“There’s more to tell?” The last bit of news had been a doozy, so I hadn’t expected there to be any more.

“Yeah, you freaked out and didn’t give me a chance to tell you everything.” He played with my fingers. “But before you get in too deep, I need to tell you all of it.”

“Shoot.” I scooted closer to him. I was pretty sure nothing could scare me off. “What else is there?”

He swallowed, his doubt resurfacing. “The more we connect, and especially when we complete the bond, our souls will connect.”

That didn't sound as bad as he was making it. "I think I'm still missing something."

"Essentially, you'll slowly change into a dragon shifter like myself." He patted his chest. "You'll become a supernatural."

All right, I'd spoke too soon. "How is that possible?"

"The connection causes us to become one, in a way." He avoided my gaze completely. "And since I'm already part shifter and human, I won't change. But since you are fully human, you'll be impacted the most."

"Can I control it?" I knew so little. "Will it hurt?"

"Wait ..." A huge smile crossed his face. "You don't need to think about this again?"

"No." Being with him felt right, and even considering the alternative ripped my heart wide open. "This past weekend put things into perspective. I was afraid our connection would make me weak, but being without you felt like I wasn't whole. Why would I put us through that when we could be so much happier together?"

"You have no clue how scared I was." He rested his forehead against mine and ran his fingers through my hair. "Thinking of a life without you in it ..."

"Hey, it's okay." I kissed him gently. "I'm not going anywhere. But will it hurt?"

"Mom said it didn't." He shook his head. "It's strange, but it didn't hurt her."

"Wait, your mom was human too?" I hadn't expected that.

He booped me on the nose. "A little secret that only dragon shifters know. All mates are human in the beginning."

"Others have gone through the same thing?" That was strangely comforting. At least, I wasn't odd or going against the grain. Maybe his people would be more accepting of me that way.

"Yes, granted I'm the first dragon who's found their mate in decades."

"Why is that?" This whole new world fascinated me.

"Because we were hunted." He paused. "We had to hide, but

then we couldn't reproduce, so our kind started dying off. We can only reproduce with our fated mates. We had to do something, so that's one reason I'm here."

"To find mates?" Now he was telling me he was a matchmaker.

He laughed hard. The sound was breathtaking. I'd never heard him so happy before.

"No, that would be a disaster." He cupped my cheek. "But learning how to coexist with other supernaturals and humans again. That way, I can help the others adapt better and more strategically so they'll have a better chance at finding their mates."

"What if they can't find their mates?"

"Why did you come here?" He ran his fingertips down my arm. "Why Kortright?"

"I don't know." The day I stumbled upon the ad flitted through my mind. "I saw the campus and knew I needed to be here."

"The bond pulled you here just like it drew me here too. That's how dragons find their mates."

That sounded beautiful. "We were destined to find each other?"

"Yes, but boy, did I think we wouldn't get here," he said and kissed me.

My brain short-circuited at the feel of his lips and the pleasant jolt running through my body. I wanted to lose myself in all things Egan.

I pushed my hands into his hair and pulled him closer to me. I craved his touch. He eagerly returned each kiss and stroke of my tongue. A hand slipped under his sweater and my fingers traced his six-pack.

He groaned, "You'll be the death of me."

His words empowered me. I placed a hand on the back of his neck and slowly lay back on my bed. He crawled over me and placed his arms on either side. Feeling trapped had never excited me before.

Both hands slipped under his sweater and I tugged the hem toward his head.

He paused and pulled away. "We don't have to rush things."

"We've waited long enough." My body burned for him, literally. "Unless you don't want to." Doubt crept in.

"You have no idea how bad I want to." His pupils turned to slits. "But I don't want to scare you away again. This will really kick in the bond. Having sex pretty much completes it, except for the formal mating ritual done in front of our thunder."

"Thunder?" The way he looked at me nearly had me purring.

"That's what a group of dragons is called," he breathed.

My hands trembled as I unbuttoned his jeans. "You won't scare me. I need you."

"But you're shaking." His breath hit my face. "I don't want to pressure you."

"It's just that I'm a virgin." I closed my eyes, completely embarrassed. "I'm nervous, but there is no doubt in my mind."

"Hey." He pulled his sweater off and discarded it. "I am too. There is no reason to be nervous or embarrassed." He kissed my cheek and peppered kisses down my neck.

"Really?" I'd figured he'd been with a ton of women. He was sexy as hell. I noticed how many girls watched him. "You're a virgin too?"

"Yes. I never wanted anyone until you." He straightened to look into my eyes. "I figured there was no reason to have sex until I'd found my mate."

I'd been such an idiot for pushing him away. He was an old soul and a genuinely good person. His actions and thoughts proved just how rare of a treasure he was. I raised my lips to his. "Make love to me." I pulled my sweater off and tossed it on the ground.

A low growl emanated from him as he lowered himself on top of me. His hand snaked around my back to unfasten my bra. In seconds, I felt it unlatch, and he helped remove it from my arms.

"You're so beautiful." He captured my nipple in his mouth and sucked then nipped. A hand grazed down my stomach toward my pants.

New emotions flowed through me. His tongue flicked, and my

entire body warmed even more. A deep ache inside caught me off guard.

His mouth worked magic on me as he unfastened my jeans. Words left me as I lifted my butt. He pushed down my jeans and panties, kissing down my stomach. My skin tingled where his mouth devoured me.

He stood and discarded the rest of his clothes then grabbed my pants and underwear, discarding them as well.

My eyes devoured every inch of him. His sun-kissed body deserved to be licked, and that day I'd seen the outline of him had grossly downplayed what he had to offer.

His eyes glowed as he dropped to his knees, placing his fingers on my core, and devoured my breast once more. He rubbed in circular motions, and white flames burned across my skin again. He slid his hand back, using his fingers to enter me. The intense sensation made my breath hitch.

My head rolled back, and I closed my eyes, overcome by emotions. I wrapped my fingers in his hair, pulling it hard, needing to release the tension. The friction increased as his hands did magical things to my body. If they could do this, anticipation thrummed through me over what came next. "Now. Please."

He removed his hand and situated himself between my legs. His tip touched right outside of me. He growled, "Let me know if it hurts." He propped himself on his elbows and kissed me.

I ran my hands down his back, his hard body primed and ready.

I bucked against him as he slowly entered me. Everything I'd heard said the first time hurt, but he thrust slowly and gently, each time only getting a little deeper than the last. My whole body jolted from our connection, and the cold spot warmed to piping hot, matching the intensity.

He groaned as he picked up the pace, slamming into me harder. "God, you feel good," he rasped as he kissed me again.

I dug my nails into his back as he slammed into me, making my insides shudder. I moaned and matched his pace, wanting him deeper.

I pushed him off me and onto his back. He was trying to take it easy, but something clawed inside me. I straddled him and slipped him inside me once more. He filled me even more, hitting exactly where I needed. I moved, pounding him inside me.

He groaned as his fingers grabbed my waist and bucked in rhythm.

Using the wall to steady myself, I felt my body tighten as something shifted inside me. I convulsed as an orgasm rocked my body, and Egan shook underneath me. We released at the same time, and something snapped between us. My vision went black.

CHAPTER SEVENTEEN

My eyes wouldn't open, and Egan's hands clutched my arms.

"Jade," he said with worry. "Jade." He gently rolled me off him and faced me. "Baby." His fingers touched my face as he turned me toward him.

I wanted to comfort him, but I didn't have control of my body. The white-hot flame surged inside me. It traveled to my center and poured into the cold spot. As the two conflicting emotions clashed, my body shivered.

"Dammit," Egan growled, grabbed the covers, and tucked them all around me.

But they didn't do any good. The two temperatures battled each other. More and more flames poured inside, filling the void like a glass, but it was a slow build. My heart raced, and my head pounded in sync.

My breathing became shallow, but my mind grew clearer. My thoughts processed faster than ever before.

As the flames filled the cup, energy exploded inside me. My skin tingled, and even my hair changed.

This had to be because we'd completed the bond. I could feel it taking hold.

"What did I do to you?" His words broke as he shook my shoulders. "Jade, wake up. Please."

Not being able to speak was a good thing just then. I'd have had a smart-ass reply. Being paralyzed was not high up on my list of things I wanted—I'd rather be awake and talking too—but that wasn't an option.

My heart rate increased as the magic took hold. My body grew stronger, and my hearing heightened. I could hear Egan's heartbeat and his lungs filling and contracting. A group of girls walked outside the dorm, talking about their weekend and how hungover they were. A bird chirped from miles away.

Egan moved away for a second, and I heard him messing with his phone. A ring on the other end pierced my ears. Right when I thought the voicemail would answer, a male's voice answered instead, "Hey, son."

"Dad, there's something wrong with Jade," Egan rasped. "She's not responding to me. I don't know what to do."

"What happened?" Concern laced Egan's dad's voice. "Is she hurt?"

"I ... I don't know."

His dad asked loudly, "How the hell do you not know if she's hurt? You can sniff out her wounds."

"She wasn't attacked. She's not hurt like that." Egan cleared his throat. "We solidified our bond, and right afterward, she crumpled against me."

If my body could move, I'd be hiding. He'd just informed his dad that we had sex and I'd passed out. I'd never even met the guy, and he already knew way too much about me. That would make meeting his parents very uncomfortable.

"Oh, son." His dad sighed. "You should've called me first so you and she were prepared."

"I did not want to have that conversation with you. Besides, it just kind of …" Egan trailed off, searching for the right word. "… happened."

"After the huge fight you had, I guess I should've expected it. But since you two went from spending barely any time together to completing the bond, she's going through her change faster."

"What do you mean?" Egan turned back to me. "You never told me there was a fast-track option."

"When two people fight it like you two did, fate intervenes. Fate knows what she's doing, and she'll ensure you complete the bond sooner rather than later." His dad chuckled. "I should've warned you, but I didn't think about it. It's been a while since anyone's gone through this, but since she was so resistant, your bond kicked in harder. She'll be fine."

With everything going on inside me, his explanation made perfect sense. The tingling was already dulling, and I felt like a stronger version of myself just lying there.

"Okay." Egan sounded relieved. "Does it hurt when they transform?"

"From what your mother said, it didn't hurt one bit. She explained it more as feeling invigorating and different. The adjustment to her dragon will be harder, though, since the change wasn't as gradual and was basically sprung on her. Just be calm and call me later. Remember, she was born with her soul knowing this would happen one day, so her body is prepared to embrace it."

I hadn't thought about what becoming a supernatural really meant, but the fact that my body had known this would happen one day resonated with me. Well, okay, that was a stretch. But after the last few days, very little didn't make at least some sense to me. My entire world had changed in the blink of an eye.

"I can't lose her," Egan replied dejectedly. "We were finally making things right. If I lose her now—"

"Son, stop. You aren't going to. She'll be alert in a few minutes. Call me in ten if she hasn't woken, and I'll be there as fast as possible."

His father's concern warmed me. That was what parents should give their child. No wonder Egan had grown into such an amazing man.

"Thanks, Dad." Egan touched my arm. "I'll let you know either way. Love you." He dropped the phone and kissed my cheek. "I'm so sorry. I didn't know this would happen. Had I known, I would've been stronger and made us wait so things would be easier on you."

The tension in my body lessened, and my eyes opened. My breath hitched. I'd never seen things so clearly before. I could easily read the books on the other side of the room, whereas their spines would normally be a blur. And the sunlight shining through my window seemed brighter. I turned my head to him. "Hey," I said, my voice breaking.

"Oh, thank God." His forehead touched mine, and he kissed my cheek. "Are you okay?"

"Yeah, I think so." I smiled at him and slowly sat up. I glanced around the room, and my head swam. "Just feel a little strange." I steadied myself with an arm as I wobbled.

"Did it hurt?" he asked, sitting up next to me. The covers fell from his chest, giving me an amazing view of his muscles, each one defined and lickable.

My body warmed at the sight. Something inside me snapped. "No. Not at all." I kissed him hungrily, wanting him again already.

He growled and pulled me close to him. This was different from before—more animalistic. He wasn't being gentle and was treating me more like an equal.

I reached down and took hold of him, need filling me again. His normal citrus smell turned spicy, and something inside me clawed more desperately than before. God, I didn't think it would be possible for him to smell even better.

His hands slipped between my legs again, but when he touched me, it felt more amazing—like I could feel more. His emotions slammed into mine, startling me. He felt so much for me that it almost took my breath away. We were completely smitten with each other.

You're so gorgeous. His words popped inside my mind. *And you're driving me insane.*

Startled, I pulled back. "What the hell just happened? You spoke inside my brain." Was I officially losing it?

"It's our mate bond." He grinned and rubbed my lip with his thumb. "Now that we've pretty much completed the bond, we can speak to each other through our minds, no matter the distance." He sucked on my bottom lip, and I gasped.

"Can you do that with others?" I wasn't sure how I felt about people being inside my brain. "Can you hear all my thoughts?"

"We can only do this with our mates. And your mind is projecting your thoughts at me. You'll have to learn how to block them and only let the ones you want me to hear trickle out." His fingers rubbed circles again. "I'm sure I'll also struggle since it's new for me too. Your dragon is calling out to mine."

"My dragon?" That had to be what I felt inside me. "You can sense her?"

"Yes. Can you not sense mine?"

Now that he'd mentioned it, maybe I could. There was such a strong connection between us now. "I think I can." I touched his chest, and both his skin and magic poured into me. It wasn't a jolt anymore but an exchange of power. The fact that we both needed to figure out our connection calmed me. I wasn't alone concerning everything.

He grabbed my waist and pulled me down, and I fell flat on the bed again. His lips were on my neck, and his teeth raked against my skin. He climbed on top of me, his fingers not missing a beat. My body spasmed as pleasure coursed through me.

I moved my hand, wanting to please him too. His lips landed on mine as a finger flicked my nipple.

He removed my hand, positioned himself between my legs, and slammed into me. My head hit the headboard, which, for some reason, didn't hurt and only intensified the pleasure. I raised my hands over my head to steady myself as I wrapped my legs around his waist.

Using the headboard as leverage, I moved in motion with him as he plunged deeper and deeper. He lowered his head, capturing my lips in a kiss, and used an arm to grab my waist, lifting me higher. Our emotions intertwined and brought me closer to the edge.

He groaned as his body spasmed from an orgasm, causing one to erupt through me too. He stilled on top of me, kissing my cheek.

Egan's phone buzzed, and he moaned. "I should get that." He opened it and texted a reply. "It's Dad making sure you're okay. I called him when you were out."

"I heard you." I looked at the message and at the time. "Shit, my class starts in thirty minutes, and I need to grab something to eat." I wanted to go another round with him, but I didn't want to fall behind in my studies.

"Then we better take care of you." He stood without a moment's hesitation and pulled his clothes back on.

I stood there for a moment, taking in the view. I couldn't believe how lucky I was to have him as my mate. That word didn't make me wince. Progress.

"Are we in a hurry or not?" He sat on the bed and put on his shoes.

"Yes." I snapped out of it and got ready. "We are."

We entered the Student Center, and the loud noises and bright sights overwhelmed me. I could hear every individual conversation, and the lights were so bright they were almost blinding.

"Hey, are you okay?" Egan asked and pulled me out of the way of the foot traffic.

I got ready to reply then realized it wasn't the best idea. I tried projecting my thoughts toward him. *It's so loud and bright in here.* I wanted to cover my ears and close my eyes, but that would attract unwanted attention. *It's probably stupid, but it caught me off guard.*

It's not stupid at all. He frowned. *I should've thought about it. Why don't you go outside, and I'll get you something to eat. We can sit on a bench.*

It was freezing outside, but I'd rather be cold than inside here. *Okay, thank you.* I reached into my back pocket and pulled out some cash. *Here.*

Uh ... no. He kissed me and walked off. *This is on me.*

His emotions mixed with mine, conveying how important it was for him to take care of me, so I didn't say anything. Had it been just a few hours ago, I would've pressured him into taking my money. It was crazy to think how much had changed. Granted, I'd refuse to let him take care of everything for me, but maybe I could let him have some small victories from time to time.

As I walked outside, I braced myself for the chill, but it didn't come. The air was cool, but my body still felt warm. Normally, I'd be freezing already, but I could easily stand out here all day without a problem. I'd been so caught up with Egan that I hadn't realized it on our walk over.

"Hey, you," Sadie said, heading over to me. Her light pink hair sparkled in the sunlight, and she looked casually stylish as usual. She wore dark jeans and a white flowy shirt. "How are you doing?"

"I'm okay." I wasn't sure what to tell her. Did I just proclaim that Egan and I had sex and our bond had been formed? It was great to see that my social awkwardness was firmly intact. That weakness would've been nice to lose during the transition.

Standing a few feet away, she sniffed the air. Her mouth dropped open, and her eyes widened. "Oh my God. You and Egan—"

"—had sex." Why did I chime in? I must have wanted to make this moment as awkward as possible.

"Well, yeah." She laughed. "But I was going to say you finally got your acts together."

That was a better way of putting it. My face felt like it was on fire, and I glanced at the ground. "Yeah, I can't believe he waited for me. He was way more patient than I deserved."

"He would've waited forever for you." She somehow smiled bigger. "I'm just excited that you all worked through it so fast. You figured it out faster than Donovan and I did."

"Really?" That was hard to believe. They were so perfect together. I couldn't imagine them any other way. "Are you two—" I paused and glanced around, making sure we were alone. "—mates too?"

"Yes, we are. It works similarly for us like it does for Egan's kind." She hugged me and then went still before pulling back. She tilted her head and squinted. "Or rather your kind. At first, I thought I was just smelling Egan, but that's you. How did he turn you?" she asked with an edge.

Of course, she'd ask that when he wasn't around. That was the secret he'd told me that no one outside of their race knew. "Uh ... he didn't, per se." I was brand spanking new to this and didn't want to start off by being the one with a big mouth. That wouldn't go over well with the other dragons.

The doors opened, and Egan walked out, carrying four biscuits and two cups of coffee. When his gaze landed on Sadie, he grimaced.

"What the hell is going on?" Sadie's eyes narrowed, and she crossed her arms. "What did you do to her? She's not herself anymore."

CHAPTER EIGHTEEN

Protectiveness surged through me. "Hey, don't talk to him like that." Sadie should know he would never do anything shady. I refused to let her imply he would.

Warmth radiated through our bond as Egan said, *It's fine. Let me talk to her. She's defending you in her own way.*

He walked over and handed me a biscuit and coffee. "It's not what you think." He winced and glanced around the courtyard. "Look, now isn't the best time to talk about this." He gestured to a group of students giving us strange looks as they walked past us.

Sadie stepped toward him, glaring. She wasn't giving the topic up. "Egan, she's different. Please tell me this isn't how you convinced her to stay with you."

"No, of course not." He flinched and stepped in front of me, blocking Sadie. "How could you think that?"

"Are you serious?" She pointed at me and sighed. "That's why. She's different from yesterday."

"I would never do anything against her will." He lowered his voice to barely above a whisper. "I told you the other day she would change when we completed the bond. This is what happens among my kind."

She sucked in a breath. "I had no clue you meant this."

This was the most uncomfortable situation I'd been in my entire life. My heart thawed toward her since she was sticking up for me, but I felt horrible for Egan. They were close, and I hated that I might've come between them. Keeping my mouth shut was extremely hard, but I understood why Egan wanted to handle it. This was a conversation more for them than for me. I got to be the bystander.

"Look, there's a lot about us you don't know." He took a deep breath like he was weighing each word, his attention on her. "And I haven't been at liberty to say, for many reasons. But things are changing. More of us will be rejoining society now."

"That's amazing news, but I wish you would've been more blunt about what we should expect. She's been around for a month, and it's just coming up. And yes, at one point, I didn't want you telling me things to protect yourself, but we're friends, and Tyler isn't part of the equation anymore." She motioned toward the dorms.

"There were many more reasons I couldn't share information with you beyond that." Egan sighed. "I had to protect my family."

"But you can trust us. We're all close, and you fought alongside me to take down Tyler. You know things about me that only our group knows. I get that you have your secrets, but something that affects us all is a huge deal."

"The keywords are 'fight alongside you.'" He inhaled sharply. "And I would do it all over again in a heartbeat. You're my best friends in the world, but my hands were tied until her. There is a lot to our history that no one realizes. You have to understand that she not only changed everything for me, but she also validated my whole reason for being here."

"It's hard to wrap my head around is all." Sadie shifted on her feet. "We knew you were full of secrets, but now I understand why you had no problems with Donovan being my mate when he was mostly human. You'd think supernaturals would remember that about dragons."

"We've been hiding for centuries." Egan leaned on his heels. "Like with all things, time has a way of erasing people's memories, and even then, we tried not to make it public knowledge.

"I am sorry you're hurt," he said sincerely. "That was never my intention, but a lot is at stake for my kind. We've stayed hidden for a reason."

"You're right." She exhaled shakily. "I'm being unreasonable, but I care about her too. This took me by surprise."

I glanced at my phone and frowned. "I hate to interrupt, but we need to head to class before we're late."

"Dammit," she grumbled. "I didn't get any breakfast."

"I can share half of this with you." I lifted the biscuit, hoping she'd say no. I kept my coffee securely in front of me. Even in friendship, I had to draw a line somewhere.

"Here." Egan handed Sadie one of his three biscuits. "Jade needs a meal after this morning."

Wow. He had to go there. First, his dad, and now Sadie. *Are you going to tell everyone we had sex? Should I be thankful you didn't say twice?*

He faced me, and his eyes glowed faintly as he smirked. *I was referring to the change, not being intimate.*

Yeah, I knew that, I lied, and a horrible stench hit my nose. I gagged. "What the hell is that smell?"

"I have no clue what you two were talking about." Sadie waved her free hand in front of her nose. "But I know you just told a huge lie."

"Wait ..." My stomach dropped. "Lying smells?"

Egan was smart enough to pretend he wasn't smiling. "Yeah, and the person's heartbeat increases, so you can hear and smell it from most everybody. There's only one person I've heard of who could lie without anyone knowing."

"Yup." Sadie visibly shook. "The man who I thought was my father for most of my life. He was a lying piece of shit."

How she felt about him was clear. "You knew every time I lied to you?" I cringed, trying to remember what I'd said.

"I liked smelling you lie when you'd deny your attraction to me." He winked. "And don't forget the time you lied to me about having a backpack."

Oh my God. No wonder it had looked like he'd smelled something bad. It had been my lie. Thankfully, I hadn't stunk.

"Let's go," Sadie said and gestured to Egan's coffee. "You aren't willing to give that up as well, are you?"

"Here you go." He handed her the drink, turned, and kissed me. *Just know I refuse to kiss and tell. I only called my dad because I thought something was wrong. I would never disrespect you like that even though those two times have been running through my mind constantly.*

Heat shot through my body. *We'll need a repeat performance and soon.*

"Also, people can smell arousal." Sadie wrinkled her nose. "And here I thought Roxy and Axel were bad."

"Does it smell spicy?" Maybe that was what I'd smelled when Egan and I had sex the second time.

"Yes, it does." He chuckled. He pulled me against him and kissed my lips one more time. "Now go. I'll grab some more breakfast and see you in Spanish class in an hour."

As I walked away, I could feel his eyes on me, and I licked my lips, enjoying his taste. At least, those were fewer calories than cinnamon rolls and way more delicious. I swayed my hips a bit more for his viewing pleasure.

Jade, he warned. *You won't be going to class if you keep doing that.*

A chuckle escaped before I could stop it.

"You look really happy." Sadie grinned, but her forehead lined with worry. "I'm glad, but how are you? I can't imagine how you're feeling."

"I'm actually really happy." It'd been so long, I'd almost forgotten what happiness felt like.

"I'm glad, but that's not what I meant." She kept her focus forward. "I meant, how are you feeling?"

We passed a few girls on the sidewalk, and I realized she was speaking in code. "A little out of sorts, but stronger than ever before." Staring into the woods, I could see each individual leaf a hundred feet away. No matter where I looked, it was like I was staring through a microscope. I blinked, but the strength of my vision didn't lessen.

"I bet." Sadie blew out a breath. "Donovan had a hard time too."

My body stiffened, and I was thankful no one was within hearing distance. "Donovan was human? Did he change after you completed the bond too?" I'd figured all of them had been born this way.

"Mostly human, but he had a little shifter in him." She adjusted her backpack on her shoulders. "Tyler had a vampire try to kill him and Axel. Roxy and I found them and bit them, initiating their transformation into a full wolf."

"Whoa. Is Tyler the one you thought was your father?" He sounded like someone my aunt would get along with.

"Yup, and he wanted me to be with someone else, so he tried to kill Donovan to force my hand." She rolled her eyes. "It was ridiculous. Needless to say, he wouldn't let it go. Then, I found out he wasn't my real dad. Tyler actually had my dad imprisoned. Last semester was a huge mess."

Boy, did it sound like it. "Is everything good now?"

"Yeah." She took a sip of her coffee. "It's been really good. Dad and I are getting to know each other, and Tyler is no longer a threat. Things are settling, and I must say I'm the happiest I've ever been too."

"Is your dad fae or shifter?" Her being a hybrid had piqued my curiosity. I wondered how common that was.

"He's fae." She looked skyward, deep in thought. "He's teaching me how to connect with that side of me and control it. Since there aren't many hybrids, I have to learn each side of me separately then figure out how to make each side work together. It's challenging but in a good way."

"Wow, I thought there would be more hybrids in the world."

"No." She shook her head. "We're a segregated bunch. Our friend group is unique. We're hoping to help bridge the gap between the races. We all may be different, but we have a lot in common. Hell, if the humans can do it, so can we."

As we approached the building, Sadie stopped me several feet away from everyone. She bit her bottom lip. "Egan's a great guy, and I'm ecstatic to see you two together, but I need to hear it from you. Did he tell you before you completed the bond?"

"Yes, he did." He'd told me in the heat of the moment, but he had tried to get me to slow down. "I made the choice, not him."

"Good." She nodded, and her shoulders relaxed. "Donovan didn't get that choice, and it's something I still feel guilty about to this day."

"Why?" She'd saved him. There was no reason for her to feel guilty.

"Like I said, he struggled at first," she said and headed to the door. "He wasn't thrilled with what I'd done, but he came around, thankfully. The problem with biting someone to change them is that less than one percent of people survive the change, and the ones who do have abnormalities like not being able to see or hear. What I did was risky, but him and Axel already being part animal prevented those issues from occurring. That's another reason I freaked out. Something could've happened to you."

"You did the right thing. And I'm perfectly fine. I appreciate your concern." I would've done the same thing had I been in her position. "And it obviously worked out for both of us."

"It did." But the smile left her face. "I got lucky, but I learned something that day. Everyone should be given the choice, and that's why it's important to me that he gave you that option."

"He's taken care of me since the moment we met," I assured her. "He tried to talk me out of doing it so fast."

"I'm not surprised. He's a true gentleman." She bumped her shoulder into mine. "I'm glad we're stuck with you. Now, we'd better get to class. It's about to start."

My classes passed in slow motion. Spanish felt like pure torture with Egan sitting so close yet still too far away. I couldn't pay attention while his scent and memories of this morning ran through my head. The spicy edge to his scent alerted me that he was struggling as well, which ramped me up even more. We were feeding off each other in very inappropriate ways.

As soon as class ended, Egan stood and carried both his and my backpacks. He took my hand, and I felt as if our souls were connected.

We walked in comfortable silence. Outside, I reached for my bag.

"I've got it," he said as he dodged my hand.

"You've got another class." I stepped closer to his side, enjoying how close he was. "Are you planning on taking two bags to class?"

"Nope." He kissed my cheek and winked. "I'm skipping class to spend more time with my love."

My heart soared at the word, but I didn't make a big deal out of it. It was a pet name, not a proclamation of his love for me. "You missed Friday too." I purposely left out the fact it had been due to my horrible attitude.

"So?" He wrapped his arm around my waist, managing to balance both bags on his shoulders. "It almost killed me to be away from you earlier. I need the rest of the day with you right next to me."

"At least, you changed clothes in that hour," I teased. "You wore your other clothes several days in a row."

"Don't remind me." He led me past the Student Center and straight to the women's dorm. "But I showered and trimmed." He rubbed the scruff on his chin. "And I need some alone time with you before we have to meet up with the others for lunch."

"Alone time?" The thought already had my body primed and ready. "I guess if I have to ..."

"Oh, you have to." His smile made him so damn breathtaking.

Just from this morning, I impossibly felt so much more for him. He was everything I'd ever wanted or needed. "Fine, but only because I don't want to hurt your feelings."

"It would hurt them, all right."

My cheeks hurt from smiling so much, but I was giddy. Nothing could bring me down from my high.

We rushed into the women's dorm and were in my room within seconds. He dropped the bags to the floor and grabbed my ass, lifting me into the air. I wrapped my legs around his waist as he carried me over to the bed.

His lips captured mine, and I moaned as our tongues tangled together. His fingers kneaded my ass before he lowered me gently onto the mattress and released his hold. I whimpered in desperation. I didn't want him to stop touching me.

Aggravated, I climbed to my feet and pushed him so he sat on the bed. I straddled him and rocked against him, feeling his hardness.

All of my senses were locked on him as he cupped my breast, rubbing my nipple through my shirt. I grabbed the hem of my shirt to pull it off me when I heard footsteps approaching our door.

Of all times, Vera had decided to come back now. Right as I pulled back to stand, the door opened.

"What the hell?" Vera gasped.

CHAPTER NINETEEN

My roommate had walked in on Egan and me, making my skin crawl. I'd never imagined anything like this would happen to me. Prior to coming here, I'd been determined to never get close to anyone, yet here I was, close to him both physically and emotionally.

I jumped to my feet and closed my eyes. "I'm so sorry. You've been gone, and you normally have class right now."

"Uh ..." She held her worn leather binder close to her heart. "Yeah, I have been." Her attention shifted to Egan, and she frowned. "I thought you two weren't together."

Wow, as if this could get even more uncomfortable. "We weren't." I glanced at Egan, at a loss as to what to say.

"But this weekend, I convinced her to give me a shot." Egan smiled adoringly at me. "I had to wear her down, but I'd do it all over again in a heartbeat."

"This weekend?" Vera scowled. "You've been together all weekend?"

She hated me eating in the room, so she must not be thrilled about sex. "We didn't fornicate on your side of the room."

Egan chuckled and tried to cover it up with a cough. *Fornicate?*

When I get uncomfortable, things just fall out of my mouth. Sarah hated when I did that, which would just make me more nervous, and I'd say even more outlandish things. She'd eventually avoided taking me out in public at all costs.

Like telling a guy, who was trying to buy their mate's schoolbooks, that she wouldn't have sex or provide blow jobs in the form of payment? he teased.

Yeah, that wasn't my finest moment. Finding him super attractive didn't help matters either. *But yes, my point exactly. And in all fairness, I didn't know we were soul mates. Here I thought you were a gentleman and wouldn't make fun of me.*

Oh, stop. He grabbed my waist and pulled me against his chest. *I'm just teasing.*

Vera cleared her throat. "That's such a relief," she spat. She was more pissed than I'd guessed.

"Look, this is my room too." I wasn't about to apologize for having my mate in my dorm. "I have a right to have people in here too." Things had gone well until now. We didn't talk much, and she kept to her side.

"Why don't you have sex in his room?" She marched over to her desk, opened the bottom drawer, and threw her grandmother's journal into it.

She was usually so careful with it, and her reaction caught me off guard. "Because my roommate wasn't around." I realized I'd never been to his room, but that wasn't completely strange. We'd become official not even twenty-four hours ago.

"Well, I'm back." She crossed her arms, giving me a wicked death glare. Her nerdy attitude was completely gone, replaced with one of a complete and utter bitch. "So he can leave. Now."

"Are you serious?" Her rage made no sense. Sure, I could see how she'd be a little upset over what she'd walked in on, but she was livid.

"Sadie and the others are probably at the Student Center." Egan stood and intertwined our fingers. "Let's go eat some lunch and give her time to get settled after being gone all weekend." *It's not worth upsetting her more than she already is.*

I wanted to stand my ground, but I'd learned to choose my battles. Hmm ... I was still considered a person, right? *Things* didn't seem appropriate. More questions for me to ponder. "Yeah, okay." I didn't want the rest of my year to be unpleasant, so I'd suck it up. *Give me a second?*

Of course. He kissed my cheek and let go of my hand. "I'll give you two a chance to talk and wait out in the hallway."

Vera stood in front of her desk, glaring at him the entire time he walked out the door. As soon as the door shut, she faced me. "That is not something I ever want to walk in on again."

"Look." I paused to collect myself and not react irrationally. "I'm sorry. Believe me when I say I'd rather you hadn't walked in on that either." In fact, I'd rather fall and skin my knee and have blood pouring all down my leg and into my shoe. Like legit, this was mortifying, and the way she was acting made it worse.

Her body remained tense, but she dropped her arms. "It just caught me off guard. The last time I tried talking to you about him, you ran out the door."

"I know." Ugh, I hadn't meant to hurt her feelings. "We have this connection that scared me."

"Really?" She lifted an eyebrow. "What kind of connection? Sexual?" She chuckled.

"Real funny." This was the most personable conversation we'd had. She either asked questions I didn't want to answer or had a nose buried in a book. "But it's more than that." Fated mates didn't even describe the magnitude of my feelings, but I couldn't use that term with her since she was human. "I'm drawn to him, and being with him makes me feel whole."

"Interesting." She tapped a finger on her bottom lip. "Well, that's amazing." Her words lacked enthusiasm.

"I'll get out of here so you can get settled in." Her less-than-thrilled reaction told me I needed to give her time to deal with whatever had happened this weekend. This reaction couldn't have been over her walking in on us. "Is everything okay? You left without a word, and your clothes were thrown everywhere."

"Yeah." She glanced at the door. "I wanted to take care of some things, but I couldn't get it finished." She shrugged. "I'll get it right next time."

"That sucks." I opened the door and glanced over my shoulder. "At least, you know what you're up against."

"Very true." She opened the drawer that held the leather book and turned her back to me.

She'd dismissed me, and that was perfectly okay with me. I rushed out the door and found two girls talking to Egan. I'd never noticed them before, but that wasn't saying much. I wasn't a social butterfly and usually avoided looking into people's eyes. I didn't want them to see I wanted to talk or was staring at them.

The girl with bleached blonde hair touched his arm. Egan moved to get her to drop her hand, but the hussy stepped with him, keeping her hand firmly in place.

Raw anger flowed through me. I'd never been this angry in my entire life. I marched over and removed her hand while purring, "Hey, baby."

His eyes lightened to liquid gold. "Hey, you." He kissed me right in front of the girls, helping me stake my claim.

"Oh." The other girl tossed her caramel hair over her shoulder. "I thought you were waiting on a friend. I didn't realize—"

"Now you do." A roar sounded inside me, startling me. The only plausible explanation was that the noise had come from my dragon.

"She's the only one for me." He pulled away and cupped my cheek. *Your eyes are glowing. Calm down.* But the corner of his mouth tilted up.

I'm sorry. I tried focusing on him and forgetting about the two girls, but I couldn't. *It's like I can't shut it down.*

Your dragon is going crazy. He hugged me, pulling me flush against his chest. *Between changing less than a day ago and the new mate bond, your animal side is a little more in control.*

Having his arms wrapped around me and breathing him in worked its magic. I buried my face into his chest.

Egan took my hand and tugged me toward the elevator. "You two have a good afternoon."

As I walked by them, I glared, not wanting to leave, and Egan wrapped an arm around me to help my legs move. His shoulders shook against my arm. He clearly enjoyed my jealous fit of rage. If I hadn't been so angry, I probably would've found it funny too.

A frown remained firmly locked in place as we entered the Student Center. Egan ushered me toward his friends, who had their usual two tables pushed together. Axel and Donovan sat on the end across from each other with their mates right next to them. Katherine sat next to Roxy, and Lillith sat next to Sadie.

Roxy grinned and said loudly, "Look who we've got here. I almost thought they wouldn't come."

"Do you not smell the amount of horniness pouring off them?" Lillith whispered loudly. "You think they would've taken care of that before joining us so we wouldn't all lose our appetites smelling that." She lifted her drink.

That was enough to snap me back to reality and forget those two girls. I jerked my head in their direction and wanted to disappear.

"We got her attention now." Roxy leaned back in her seat and nodded to Sadie. "So, Sadie informed us that you all"—she lifted one hand, made it a circle, then inserted her pointer finger into the hole.

Lillith took a sip of the blood hidden in her coffee mug. "Be careful which way you point the circle. I think if you turn the hand so the fingers are closer to a heart shape, it represents the anus."

"What?" Katherine choked. "Are you serious?"

I'd never been so damn embarrassed before, but if I hid, it would only encourage her.

"Roxy," Egan warned. *She enjoys making people feel uncomfort-*

able. I'm sorry. If it's any consolation, Sadie and I became friends first. She was part of the package deal.

"Just ignore them. She has to be making that up." Sadie didn't sound so sure. "Either way, I informed them that you completed the bond. I didn't call out sex specifically."

Donovan sighed and shook his head. "You know how Roxy's mind works. Are you really surprised?"

"So." Roxy waggled her eyebrows and took a huge bite of her pizza. "How many times have you all made it official?"

Axel groaned. "Leave her alone. If you scare her off, I'll have to hear Egan whine and cry about her again. It was brutal. Don't make me relive that."

Egan scowled at the vibrant redhead. "Let's go get something to eat so those two can calm down." He pointed right at Lillith then Roxy.

"Oh, stop." Sadie stood and snatched my arm. "Lillith, will you go sit by Katherine so Jade and Egan can sit next to each other?"

"Fine." She grabbed her drink and walked around us. "But only because they're new to their *relationship* and I don't want to hear them complain." She winked at me, letting me know she was kidding.

"Come sit next to me while Egan grabs your food." Sadie sat back in her place and patted the spot next to her. "I promise I'll make them behave." She stared pointedly at Roxy.

"I'll behave." Roxy pouted, but her hazel eyes were alight with mirth. "But only because I like her."

It finally sank in. I had an actual group of friends. For the first time in my life, I felt complete.

Before I realized it, it was Friday. I walked out of Spanish class and was heading to my dorm when the tingling feeling overtook me. The feeling had gotten so bad any time I wasn't around Egan; I felt like I was being watched even when I was in my dorm room at night.

Thankfully, I'd gotten a hold on projecting my thoughts quickly. I didn't want Egan to worry about me more than he already did.

It had to be paranoia just like when I first got here. The feeling had eased for a little while, but the past week had been almost unbearable. If Egan hadn't already missed so many classes, I would've asked him to walk me back to the dorm. That was something I would've refused a week ago, thinking it made me weak, but I was learning that asking for help wasn't a weakness.

Overcoming the urge to run, I walked briskly across campus. Within minutes, I made it to my room and shut and locked the door.

Vera and I hadn't argued since the Monday mishap, but our relationship was strained. She'd tried talking to me the other night again, but the topic had centered around Egan. Don't get me wrong, I loved talking and thinking about him, just not with her or anyone outside our friend group.

Luckily, I was acclimating to my dragon, but she was probably making my paranoia skyrocket. The sensations were intense, so I had to be reading into stuff that wasn't there.

Despite those thoughts, I marched over to the window and shut the blinds. Darkness or light, my vision never changed, but if someone was watching me, they couldn't see through the plastic.

Even with the blinds closed, that nagging feeling tugged on my subconscious. My skin crawled, and my dragon shifted uncomfortably inside me. Maybe I needed to talk to Egan after his class and tell him what was going on. It made me feel like I was going insane.

Trying to distract my racing mind, I pulled my phone from my pocket and opened Messenger. I'd avoided logging in for the past week, and I had ten new messages from Mom. She begged to know where I was and if I was okay. I had a feeling Sarah was pushing for a location.

I quickly tapped out a reply, telling her not to worry and that I was fine. I hadn't told her that I'd left to attend college. That would have narrowed down the possibilities of where to find me.

Once I was done messaging her, my focus landed on Vera's desk.

She'd been clutching her grandmother's journal more since she returned from wherever the hell she'd gone to. What could be so important in that thing? She rarely left it behind, but if the journal was here, maybe I could find out what was so special.

My dragon brushed across my mind, and the urge to look at it intensified. One quick look wouldn't be a big deal. If nothing seemed odd, she'd be none the wiser. But for her to be that attached to it, something special had to be involved.

I stood and slowly walked over to the desk, quiet as a mouse. She wasn't in the room, but it felt like she could easily catch me. Instead of questioning those feelings, I tiptoed over. As I touched the handle of the drawer, a bird cried outside my window.

My body stilled, and something crashed into the glass.

CHAPTER TWENTY

No way. A bird couldn't be trying to break through my window. That had to be a coincidence.

Another *kak* sounded, and the bird slammed into the window again. A faint crack in the window made my stomach drop.

Holy shit. A bird really was doing that. The shock was enough to drop the barrier I'd put up between Egan and me.

The bird hit the window again and again, and the glass fractured even more.

What's wrong? His concern was evident in his tone. *Are you okay?*

I'm not sure. I couldn't lie to him. I stood as snooping through Vera's desk had become way less of a priority. *A bird is trying to crash through the window of my dorm.*

I'll be there in a flash.

I was slightly relieved that he was on his way, but I wasn't out of the situation. I braced for the bird to hit again, but nothing happened.

Day by day, things seemed to get more bizarre.

When everything remained silent, I crept across the room toward my bed. I placed my knee on the mattress and leaned toward the blinds. I peeked through and came face to face with a falcon.

I screamed bloody murder and stumbled back as the door burst open. Egan raced into the room and pulled me against his chest.

"What's wrong?' He pushed me behind him. "I heard you scream."

"Uh ... no." I moved around him. "We can face the threat together, thank you." I liked that he wanted to protect me but hated that he thought I couldn't protect myself. I felt all confused inside. At the end of the day, I needed him to treat me as an equal, but that was a conversation for another time.

"Jade, what happened?" he asked with frustration.

"A bird slammed into my window over and over again. Then it just stopped." I rubbed my arms. "I peeked through the blinds, and a falcon was there just staring at me." It had to be the bird that had killed at least one of those girls, if not Amber too. "I think it's gone. I don't hear anything now."

He opened the blinds, and as I suspected, the falcon was no longer there. A deep, long crack marred the glass, proving I hadn't lost my mind.

"What were you doing when it happened?" He ran his finger along the crack. "Luckily, it's only on the outside and not broken inside, but it had to hit it hard to accomplish this."

"You're telling me." That bird had wanted in. "And I was over by Vera's desk. I ... wanted to check something out." That sounded much better than coming right out and saying I was snooping.

"I don't like this." Egan frowned. "My roommate is going home for the weekend. You can stay with me until the school fixes this window."

That thrilled me, but why hadn't he told me that sooner? Maybe he hadn't wanted me to stay with him. "No, it's fine. I don't want to impose." I tried to keep the hurt from my voice.

"Uh ... it's no imposition." His forehead wrinkled. "In fact, I kind of demand it. Ever since I learned about his leaving this morning, my thoughts have been consumed with us spending the whole weekend locked in my room. I'm thinking we order in so we don't have to leave."

"Now that sounds like a plan I can get behind." Then I remembered. "But I have to work nights at Haynes."

"What?" Egan's face fell. "No. Why don't you quit?"

"Excuse me?" I'd been letting him buy me lunches because he always ran off to get it while the girls talked to me, but I didn't want him to become my sugar daddy. "No, I need money to support myself."

"First off, you don't need to worry about money anymore. I'll take care of you."

"I don't want to be a mooch." The thought of relying on someone else for everything scared me. "I need some independence."

He flinched.

"Not independence like that." Damn, I really needed to work on my communication skills. "I don't want to ask for money if I need something."

"Yeah, I get that." He nodded, although his lips turned downward. "But that's not the main reason. Remember when I came into Haynes last Friday?"

"Oh, that's something I'll never forget." Amber had been all over him, and later, she'd wound up dead. I'd wanted to hurt her, but I never would have wished death on her. "I had to leave early, remember?"

"Yeah, I remember." He brushed my cheek. "But I haven't told you the real reason I showed up there."

"I'm all ears." Patience was not my best virtue.

"Give me a second." He chuckled. "Now that you know about us, I can tell you. We're tracking the falcon that's been attacking people."

"Yeah, that bird has lost its mind." I gestured to my window. "It had to be him."

"It was. I recognize the scent, but there's more to the story than that." He closed the blinds. "It's a falcon shifter."

"Wait ... are all birds shifters?" I hadn't considered the possibility that all animals were shifters.

"No. Only falcons and crows, but not every one of them is necessarily a shifter." He shrugged. "The others are true animals."

"So someone is using his animal form to attack and kill girls." A chill ran down my spine. "That's pretty morbid. What about animal control? They'll kill him if they find him."

"He shifts back into his human form, and no one is the wiser." He pointed back and forth between us. "Except for supernaturals like us."

That was still strange to hear. Being something other than human was taking a bit to get used to. Maybe because I hadn't shifted before. Then the memory of the woods settled over me. "Wait ... that day when you found me in the woods, running for my life, I could have sworn I heard someone chuckle as they chased me, but I thought I was losing my mind."

"It was the bird." Egan tensed. "He was after you. I don't know what would've happened if I hadn't found you when I did. But whoever it is was hanging around at Haynes. Their scent was all over the place. You can't go back there."

"First off, it's my choice." I tried to calm the annoyance he'd stirred up. "And second, I can't leave them high and dry. I did that last weekend. I have to put in a notice." If he was concerned for my safety, that was something completely different from wanting me not to work.

He hung his head. "Fine, but I'm going with you. I'll take a seat at the bar and keep out of sight as well as possible."

I crossed my arms and lifted my chin. "But if a girl touches you, I can't be held liable for my reaction."

"I'll make sure no one touches me." He kissed me, and the rest of my worries melted away.

"ARE you sure you don't want to call in?" Egan asked for the tenth time. He sat on his bed, watching me pull my work clothes on. My body was still warm from the sex we'd just had.

"I have to." His dorm room was the same as mine. It was obvious that both buildings had been built at the same time with the same layout. The only difference was that Egan's scent was everywhere, and his dark blue sheets smelled like heaven. I could easily get used to waking up with him every day. "Besides, you have Donovan and Sadie coming too."

At lunch, he'd asked them to join us in case we'd need backup. Apparently, Lillith and Axel would hang out in the back alley while Katherine and Roxy would wait out front in a car. They felt certain that whoever was hurting these girls either went to Haynes to stalk his prey or, even scarier, worked there.

A knock sounded on the door, and Donovan's and Sadie's scents hit my nose.

"You ready?" I faced him, arching an eyebrow.

"One second," he called and wrinkled his nose at me. He stood in his naked glory and grabbed his clothes from the floor.

I leaned back against the wall and enjoyed watching him dress.

Like what you see? He pulled up his pants as he thrust his ass out. He was so muscular it didn't jiggle.

Before mating with him, I wouldn't have believed he had this playful side. It came out in spurts, and he could make me laugh like never before. *Maybe. But instead of trying to make your ass jiggle ...* I trailed off while lifting my eyebrows suggestively.

Keep looking at me like that and you won't make it to work. He threatened good-naturedly. *And you won't be allowed to complain about it.*

My body was ready for another round. I didn't realize I'd be so sexually charged, but I couldn't get enough of him.

"Okay, I wish Roxy were around," Donovan grumbled. "I can smell them from out here."

Sadie giggled. "Leave them alone. I'm just happy Egan found someone so great."

A smile spread across my face.

Egan walked over to me and took my hand. He kissed me quickly and said, *I agree with her completely.* He opened the door, revealing Sadie and Donovan.

Sadie had on dressy black slacks and a baby-blue top that contrasted with her hair. Donovan wore his usual jeans and a black t-shirt. He had an arm wrapped around his mate.

"You two ready?" she asked.

"Yeah, I'm scheduled to start in fifteen minutes, so we'd better haul ass."

"Then we'd better go." Egan pulled his car keys out of his pocket, and we headed down to the first floor.

In the parking lot, I realized I'd never seen Egan's vehicle before, but when he led me to a new maroon Jeep, I wasn't surprised. The car fit him perfectly.

"Here you go." Egan opened the front passenger seat and helped me inside.

"Yo," Roxy called out as she, Axel, and the two vampires headed our way. "Are you not going to wait for us?"

"The whole point was to arrive separately in case anyone is watching." Sadie rolled her eyes. "So, no, we weren't planning on waiting on you."

"Fine." Roxy sighed and wrapped her arms around Lillith and Katherine. "They waited for me."

"Because we had to." Lillith shook her head. "At least, I won't be stuck with you once we get there. That would be a disaster."

I'd been surprised that Roxy and Axel wouldn't stay together, but Egan had explained that they were splitting up because of their pack link. That way, someone from their pack would be with each group and could easily communicate if something went down.

"We really need to go." I hated to be late. I'd promised Egan I would turn my notice in tonight since he felt like I was in danger there. I had no desire to relive that moment with the creepy bird shifter.

"Remember to blend in." Donovan glared at Roxy then Lillith. "Especially you two."

"I feel attacked," Roxy huffed.

Lillith pursed her lips. "You do realize they didn't put us together for a reason?"

"Are you surprised?" Katherine pulled at her navy blue top.

"Nope." Lillith pouted. "A very smart call on their part."

Axel sighed. "At least, I'll be with the accountable one."

"Hey." Roxy punched him in the arm. "I'm your mate and standing right here."

"Of course, I want you." He widened his eyes at Donovan. "Not her."

"Uh ... I'm right here too." Lillith placed a hand on her hip.

"Good luck, man." Donovan laughed and shut the door.

Soon, Egan pulled out of the parking spot, leaving the four of them behind. The entire ride to the steakhouse passed in silence. Whether anyone wanted to admit it, we were all on edge. My skin itched like something was going to happen, but my dragon couldn't sense that ... right?

When the restaurant appeared, I brushed off my anticipation to focus on the task at hand. The first order of business was clocking in and giving Ollie my notice. I just needed to go in and rip the Band-Aid off. Then I could begin searching for another job.

The four of us entered the building, and Betty was behind the desk.

"Hi. How many are in your party?" she asked, her eyes locked on Egan.

If I hadn't known better, I would've thought I was a wolf shifter. The urge to pee on Egan's leg was awfully strong. "Three, and please sit them in my section." I kissed Egan's lips and winked. "I'll come get your order soon." I turned and sashayed away, feeling his eyes focused on my ass.

I headed toward the back and caught Ollie marching to the back of the kitchen. He hated going back there. Odd.

"Hey, Ollie." I increased my pace. "Wait up."

He paused and turned to face me. "What's up? I'm in a hurry."

Well, okay then, I'd cut to the chase. "I wanted to let you know that this weekend is the last one I'll be working."

"Aw, really?" His shoulders sagged. "That's a damn shame. But at least we have you for this weekend." He spun back around and continued toward the back.

Okay, that was easy and strange. But hell, after that bird attack, I'd take it. I went to work and found Egan, Sadie, and Donovan seated in the back section of the restaurant.

I hurried over with my pad and pen. "What can I get you all?"

"Waters for all of us," Egan said, scanning the room. *He's here again.*

I hadn't caught the scent yet since my dragon side formed, so I had no clue what to look for. *Are the others here yet?*

Yeah. He touched my arm. *They're getting in position. They pulled up a few minutes ago.*

That made me feel a little better. I forced a smile and nodded. "I'll go get your drinks and come back for your order."

I walked to the drink station and was filling the waters when a server hurried over to me.

She glanced over her shoulder toward the kitchen. "For some reason, Ollie needs your help. He said it's about one of your table orders."

Ugh, I'd just taken over Chad's shift, and there was already an issue. "Okay, thanks. I'll go back there now." I placed the water on the table and rushed toward the back. The cooks were all busy with no sign of Ollie. I glanced toward the back door and saw him standing there with a phone in his hand.

I marched over. None of this made sense. If an order was wrong, he'd be with the cooks. I opened my mouth to say, "Hey," when he looked at me and blew powder in my face. The room began to spin, and my legs wobbled.

CHAPTER TWENTY-ONE

I tried connecting with Egan, but my head was swimming too much. My own thoughts were nearly unintelligible.

"Are you drunk on the job?" Ollie scoffed and wrapped an arm around my waist. "I can't believe the audacity."

My legs wouldn't hold my weight, and my body sagged against him like he was helping me. For anyone watching, his accusation looked believable. Everything inside me told me to push away, but his arm was tight around my waist.

Could Ollie be the falcon shifter? Surely not. But why else would he be doing this? Others had quit, and they hadn't wound up hurt the next day or weeks later.

"Guys, I have to take her home," Ollie told the cooks. "If anyone is looking for me, tell them I'll be back when I can."

The older cook nodded as he frowned. "Yeah, get her out of here. I don't need her puking back here. The last thing we need is the health department hearing about that."

Ollie opened the back door and tugged me outside. My feet couldn't move, tripping me. I was so out of it I couldn't even groan.

Something inside me screamed to yell for help or connect with Egan, but I couldn't function. I wasn't sure how I was even breathing.

The dusky sky hit my eyes as my gaze settled on a black sedan parked in the back. The driver's door opened, revealing the occupant. My stomach roiled when I saw her face.

It was Vera.

My own fucking roommate.

Why would she be here?

"Get her inside." She opened the back driver's side door, gesturing for Ollie to hurry. "Those other two will be here any second." She wore all black, making her words sound even more ominous.

I'd never felt so betrayed. We'd never been close, but this was cold. What had I ever done to make her want to hurt me? Had sex while she was out of town? What was worse was that she knew who Axel and Lillith were. That meant she'd been watching me. Could she be the reason I'd felt constantly watched?

"She's dead weight," he groaned and threw me over his shoulder.

My head hung, giving me a view of his scrawny ass. Definitely not the last sight I wanted to see before croaking. Maybe this was part of their torture.

"Hurry," she hissed as Ollie carried me over. As he tossed me in the car, Axel and Lillith rounded the corner.

Lillith's eyes widened, but then I landed in the car, and all I could see was the light tan leather of the seat and the tan floorboard.

"Get in the car!" Vera said loudly as she slammed the back door. Within seconds, the passenger door opened as they got in. There was a bang on the glass above my head, followed by the squealing of tires as Vera punched the gas.

"Dammit." She turned the car sharply. "We were supposed to be farther away before they realized she was gone."

"I'm sorry," Ollie huffed. "But I got her as soon as I could." He didn't sound thrilled.

Jade? Egan sounded half-crazed. *Are you okay?*

Ugh. My grunt was the only response I could manage, but it was better than what I could do a few minutes ago. *Veewwwaaa.* And I sounded like a toddler, but I considered that a huge win.

Your roommate? Horror pulsed through our bond. *She's with you. Is she okay?*

Great, now he thought we were both in danger. I didn't want to say anything in case it made things worse.

Don't worry, he reassured me. *We'll find you. I can follow our bond. It might just take a minute before I can get there, but I'm on my way.*

I didn't realize he could track the mate bond, but hell, I didn't know much. I hadn't been a supernatural long—not even a week.

"What are we going to do?" Anxiety wafted off Ollie. "They'll be hunting us now."

"Nothing changes." Vera sounded resolved. "Our plan is still intact."

"You're playing a dangerous game." Ollie sounded tense. "And you've got more people at risk than yourself."

"It doesn't matter what you think," she spat. "I'm the one who makes the call, or should I remind you why?"

That was enough to shut him up.

I wiggled my fingers, and my thoughts began to clear. Whatever they'd done to me was wearing off, but I had to be careful. I didn't need them knowing.

Silence descended as we traveled farther and farther away from the restaurant. I should've realized that Ollie's creepy behavior had something to do with this, and Vera had gotten way too upset about Egan and me the other day. All of these red flags, and I'd ignored them. I'd figured she'd been upset about something that she'd done that weekend, but maybe there was more to it than that.

Egan? I linked with him, hoping I was clear enough to understand. Thankfully, I sounded almost normal again. *Are you there?*

Yes. Are you okay?

I'm not sure how to answer that. I wasn't hurt, but I was far from okay. *Vera and Ollie kidnapped me.*

She helped kidnap you? He sounded surprised but not completely shocked. Regret flowed between us. *I picked up vibes from her, but I didn't think it would be something like this.* He paused. *What did they do to you? Lillith said it looked like you were paralyzed.*

That was the million-dollar question. *I have no clue. Ollie blew something into my face, and I went completely slack. I almost fell to the ground. He told the cooks I was drunk and he needed to take me home. Vera was out back waiting for us with the car.*

I had a bad feeling something would happen tonight. She has to be a witch, which makes sense given the leather journal we saw the other day. She used a spell on you. He growled through the bond. *We're looking for you, but it's hard since you're a moving target. Are you still on the road? Can you tell us anything about your surroundings?*

No, I can't. The car took a turn, and I adjusted my head ever so slightly. Ollie glanced back immediately, and I went completely still.

Please, God, don't let him realize I moved my head. He frowned but said nothing.

I can't risk trying to look around. I'm trying to look like the spell is still working. Add that to the list of things I never imagined I'd say. *But we're taking some sharp turns.*

That tells me you're heading out of downtown. He sounded so distraught. *When you get there, tell me anything you can see. Axel is right behind us. We're all heading that way.*

I hated that I hadn't listened to him. In hindsight, demanding to turn in my notice had been stupid. I'd thought he was being overly paranoid, though. He tended to get very protective, so I'd brushed it off as just that. Apparently, I needed to trust his instincts more and realize he wasn't trying to stifle me. *I'll let you know if I figure out anything.*

He sighed. *Please, be safe. I can't lose you.*

The words "I love you" almost projected into our bond, but I bit my tongue. I refused to tell him that for the first time in a situation like this. I had to make it out alive and tell him in person.

Time crept by, and I had no clue how long we'd been driving. Eventually, she turned again, and the car bounced as we crunched over gravel. We had to be approaching our destination.

We're slowing down. This would give him some indication of how far we'd traveled, which should aid them in their search for me. *I'll let you know what I can see when they get me out.*

"Do you think they're tracking her?" Ollie asked, almost scaring me.

The car had been silent for so long. I managed to clamp down my reaction, keeping up the act of not being able to control my body.

"No, the spell should block them," Vera said as the car came to a stop. "We should have a few hours before it wears off, so plenty of time."

"I hope you're right." Ollie exhaled and opened his door. "I'll bring her inside."

A few seconds later, the door opened, and Ollie placed his hands under my arm, tugging me toward him. I remained dead weight and took a deep, calming breath. If I moved, there was no telling what they would do.

He grunted as he dragged me toward him and turned me over so I was facing the roof. He leaned over, grasped my upper body, and threw me over his shoulder again. Before he could straighten, my head bounced against the top part of his ass. I squinted, trying to forget the up-close view I had of his ass cheeks.

"What's taking so long?" Vera sounded unhinged. "Get her in here now."

"I'm trying." He stood and hurried toward the log cabin.

As my body jarred, I took in as much of my surroundings as I could. *We're at an older log cabin. I can't get a good view of it from my position, but it looks like we're in the middle of the woods with no nearby neighbors.*

Of course you are. They'd make sure it wouldn't be easy to find, he said tensely. *We're fifteen to thirty minutes out. Now that you've stopped moving, I shouldn't make any more wrong turns.*

Hopefully, you'll get here before anything bad happens. I wanted to hug him and never let him go. *She thinks the spell will take another couple of hours to wear off. I don't know why she thinks that, but I won't question it.*

Okay, I'll let you know when we're close. His voice broke. *Just promise me you'll do whatever is necessary to survive.*

I'd been in survival mode for as long as I could remember. Even if I didn't have him to live for, I wouldn't just roll over. I'd done that too often before getting away from Sarah, and I wouldn't keel over and give up now. *I promise.*

The door to the cabin creaked open, and we entered the house. The thick scent of dust settled deep into my lungs, giving me the urge to cough. I swallowed it down, wanting to appear as out of it as possible.

"Set her on the couch," Vera commanded as she walked deeper into the room. Her shoes echoed against the old wooden floors. "Make sure I can see her eyes."

Ollie walked over to a dusty fabric couch and dropped me on it. A cloud of dust puffed all around me.

"Where the hell are we?" He coughed and wiped his nose. "Looks like no one has been here in years."

"Try decades." Vera chuckled as she hovered over me, sneering at me with disgust. "At least, she's awake. I was worried the spell would knock her out. Now I don't have to wait to tell her why she's here."

That would be great information to start with. I blinked, hoping it wouldn't make her suspicious.

"You see, I came here looking for the dragon." Vera wrinkled her nose. The nerdy girl was gone. Her hair cascaded down her shoulders, and her glasses were missing. "I'd heard about the dragon and his friends and how they were coming back to Kortright."

Why would she be after Egan? He was a good person and never treated people poorly.

"I'm sure you're wondering why." She tapped her head. "You may not be able to speak or react, but I know how a woman in love reacts. It's really rather easy." She took a few steps away and placed her hands behind her back. "The dragons hurt everyone who gets in their way and need to be stopped."

"Maybe we should get out of here." Ollie rubbed his fingers along his pants. "I have a bad feeling about this."

"Shut it, bird," Vera snapped. "You're being paranoid like always."

Ollie's mouth clamped shut, and anger flared in his eyes.

"You see, I had a feeling the dragon would meet his mate, so we watched him. Any girl who got close to him, we killed, hoping he'd fly back to his thunder so we could locate their secret living place." Vera rolled her eyes. "I thought it was you, but the way you shut him down made me think I'd completely misread the situation. That was until I walked in on you Monday."

That was why she'd been so angry. She realized she'd made a mistake and the girl she'd been looking for was right under her nose. It had nothing to do with catching us in the act.

"I had to be smart after acting crazy, so I planned to get you from Haynes." She clenched her jaw, looking damn scary. "I should've known the dragon and his little squad wouldn't let you go off alone. He must have tracked Ollie there the week before when we killed that server girl."

Amber died because she'd been all over Egan. Now I felt bad for being so angry at her.

"You must be wondering why I'm telling you this." She gave me a sad smile. "I want you to understand that I'm righting a wrong from so many years ago. That this is very unfortunate—you actually were a decent roommate—but there is something so much bigger at play."

Her words and actions suggested sympathy, but the feeling was missing. There was a coldness to her that told me that she enjoyed doing all of these bad things. That she felt they were just and righteous.

It was the same gleam I'd seen in Sarah's eyes, and a realization settled heavily on my chest. That was the look that would be in Sarah's eyes right before she'd give me the strongest beating. So I already knew what would happen next.

CHAPTER TWENTY-TWO

Vera would kill me soon. After the villains justify all of the reasons for their actions, they usually take action. So far, I was a means to an end, despite not being a horrible roommate.

A knife magically appeared in Vera's hand. "But most importantly, your death will not be in vain. Your death will mean something and will not go unfelt by your mate."

Mate.

Egan.

There was no way in hell I'd allow that to happen. I had too much to live for. Adrenaline coursed through me, and I welcomed it. There had to be a way out of this situation. My dragon surged inside.

"Isn't that what we all want?" The gleam in her eyes hardened. "To be loved and remembered?" She sneered as she raised the knife above her head and her gaze landed on my heart. "I'll make it quick, don't worry."

My dragon brushed against my brain, fueling my body. I didn't really know her yet, but I had a feeling we'd get more acquainted.

As Vera's hands slammed down, I kicked her in the stomach. She crashed against the wall.

Ollie froze and looked at Vera as she bounced off the wall. His mouth dropped, and his brows furrowed. "I thought you said—"

"I know what I said!" Vera screamed. Her breathing turned ragged as she glared at me. "How did you get the spell to wear off so quickly?"

Yeah, like I'd tell her that. I stood and lifted my chin. I'd fight them both. *How close are you?* With her witchy magic and Ollie transforming into a bird, I was at a disadvantage.

We're getting closer. Maybe ten minutes away. Egan's displeasure was clear. *Is something happening?*

Yeah, she tried to stab me. And I would kick the bitch's ass.

What? He growled, and the sound scared me. *Are you hurt?*

Okay, I should've maybe led into it more gently, but at least all his rage wasn't channeled toward me. *I'm fine, but get here as soon as you can.* I disconnected from him, needing to focus.

All of my years of martial arts had better pay off.

Vera sneered and threw the knife at me.

I ducked, and the knife passed over my head, the breeze hitting the top of my hair. I'd barely dodged it. I turned and found the knife lodged into the couch cushion, dust floating all around it.

"Get her!" Vera commanded Ollie.

Ollie moved immediately, stalking over to me. His gaze locked on my waist, making it obvious where he planned to attack.

He jumped, charging to sack me.

I turned to the side and kicked him in the chest. Usually, the impact would have thrown me slightly off-balance, but it was like I'd kicked a soccer ball instead of a guy who weighed twenty pounds more than me. Further proof of how much I'd changed.

As he landed on the ground, Vera raced across the room toward me, aiming for my face. My arms flew up, blocking her assault. I grabbed her shoulders and tossed her to the ground.

"Ugh," she groaned as she crumpled to the floor.

Arms wrapped around my arms, restraining them. I leaned

forward, causing Ollie to lose his balance and fall over my head. The hold on my arms lessened as he landed hard on his back.

I straightened and kicked him in the side, and he curled into a ball.

"You bitch," Vera spat, clambering to her feet. "I won't feel bad about this at all now."

Yeah, she hadn't before. Pleasure radiated off her. Now she'd be less rational and methodical, which would piss her off more. But I wasn't sure what a witch was capable of, so I didn't have a clue what to expect.

She ran over to the dirty plywood cabinets and pulled out a large steak knife.

What the hell was it with her and knives? I expected her to use magic, but she didn't seem inclined. Maybe she was trying to disarm me.

Instead of running at me, she walked slowly like she had a plan.

It was time for me to go on the offensive. I rushed at her, keeping focused on her. If I could break her leg, it would hinder her enough that I'd only need to focus on Ollie. Since she was holding a knife, I went with a kick.

Right before my foot connected with her knee, she swung the knife downward, jamming it into my calf. It sank so deep it hit bone.

She stumbled against the counter as blinding pain seared up my leg. I fell to the ground, and a thick, metallic scent hit my nose. The knife stayed lodged in my leg.

Jade, you're hurt. Egan's voice was low and raw. *I'm shifting to get to you faster.*

I'd opened the bond up because of the sheer pain. I wanted to respond, but I couldn't.

I grabbed the handle and yanked before I could think too much about it. Blood poured from my wound, soaking my pant leg, and dripped into my shoe. Dammit, this would make fighting more difficult for several reasons—the pain, and my feet might slip in the blood.

My blood coated my hands, and I dropped the knife.

"Did you really think you could escape?" Vera laughed maniacally. "You may be turning into a dragon, but you're not there yet. And there are two of us against your one. Hell, you don't even know how to use your dragon yet. I bet the shifter hasn't taught you because he wants to be the one to protect you, but it's only given me the advantage."

If there was any truth to her words, I'd be addressing that with Egan—if I made it out of this alive. He needed to teach me, not shelter me.

Vera crouched over me with a cruel smirk and grabbed the knife. She wiped the blood off the blade on her black jeans without flinching. "All it takes is the right kind of wound."

I had no choice but to fight. If I didn't, I'd be dead. I slumped my shoulders despite my dragon roaring in my ears. She didn't want me to appear weak. She wanted us to die as warriors, but I had no intention of dying. "So this is how it ends? You kill me, and then what? If Egan goes back to his thunder, he won't make it easy for you to follow him."

"Please," she scoffed. "You really are stupid. He should've taught you everything before letting you join our world." She looked down her nose at me.

"You're going to get us killed," Ollie groaned as he stood, clutching his side. "You're wasting time. There's no telling when that spell wore off. That dragon could be here any second."

"Shut up!" she screamed, her face turning red as she stared at him. "I tell you what to do, not the other way around."

He flinched but shut up. His hands shook with either rage or fear. Maybe a combination of both.

"She needs to understand how she will be the fall of her mate and his family." She squatted next to me and smiled as she watched the blood pour from my wound.

A puddle of blood now surrounded my leg. I was bleeding a lot. If my blood loss continued at this rate, I'd get lightheaded and pass out. I had to kick her ass before then.

"Since you're his fated mate, I can use any part of you to locate him," she said with giddiness. "Your hair, your fingernail, your blood. Anything. I can find him through you because of that connection."

My blood turned to ice. This was a whole lot harder than I'd realized. Here I'd thought if I died, he would be safe, but he wouldn't. "Then why didn't you take something of mine back at the dorm?" There didn't have to be any senseless killing.

"Because he purposely doesn't go back to his thunder that often. We've watched, and he hasn't gone back since the beginning of spring semester." She glared. "Dragons are smart. They know how to stay hidden. I need to give him motivation to go back and rally his troops. That way, I can locate them, and Ollie can do the rest."

"What's so important about that journal?" If I kept her talking, I could buy Egan time to get here.

"Ah, that old thing?" Her eyes lit with pure rage. "That weaves my tale of how the love of my life did me wrong. And includes my plan for revenge. Just a few choice spells that will wreak havoc on the dragons."

Her grandmother was the one who'd gotten hurt, and that journal had fueled enough anger in her granddaughter to get revenge. Maybe their whole family was messed up. Anger could only get someone so far.

The threat against my thunder made my dragon roar inside me, and I punched Vera in the jaw. The crunch of bone sounded like a little victory in my ear.

Falling back on her ass, she clutched her jaw and dropped the knife. "Yuuu bshhh." Tears poured down her face, but her eyes were raw with pain.

Her mouth was crooked, evidence that I'd broken her jaw. Hopefully, that would even out the playing field.

Ollie rolled over and climbed to his feet. His eyes lacked the malice of Vera's, but he was gearing up to fight me again.

I rose to my feet, putting my weight on the uninjured leg.

Fighting wouldn't come easy, but I couldn't lie down and die. I'd go out fighting.

He kicked my injured leg, and I fell back to the ground as nausea rolled through my stomach. I'd never been in so much pain in my life.

They circled me like I was the prey. Hell, I had to be honest.

I was their prey.

"Yu cud hv md this esy on yu," Vera growled. "Bt slw it isss."

"I don't like taking the easy way out. So, bring it on." If I appeared confident, maybe they'd hesitate.

Vera kicked me in the face. My head jerked back, and my neck popped.

I'm almost there. Egan linked; white-hot rage filled the bond. *Hang on, baby. Can you tell me what's going on and where you're injured?*

Hope sprung in my chest. He was close. I almost thought I wouldn't get out of this alive. *They're circling me. She stabbed me in the leg, all the way to the bone.*

All I had to do was make her put off killing me a little longer.

I rubbed my neck, trying to massage the pain away. "You'll never take them down. Egan will find you and kill you."

"Lts hooop sssooo." She leaned down and pressed the knife against my neck. A trickle of blood dripped down my neck and onto my white shirt.

That was all I needed—more blood loss.

A roar shook the cabin as the loud flapping of wings sounded outside.

"Holy shit!" Ollie yelled. "The dragon is here."

She turned her head to the side, shifting her arm. A bracelet I'd never noticed before appeared from underneath her long shirt sleeve. The old sterling silver band had seen better days, but the stone was the most interesting part. The stone was clear, reminding me of a quartz, but the black flecks inside looked like ash. A thick, sturdy clasp at its base prevented it from coming off easily.

My dragon caressed my brain, and I understood her for once. She was telling me that only something important would be locked up that tight.

I took a deep breath to calm my nerves as she dug the knife in deeper.

Ollie's voice grew high as he said, "We have to end this now and run."

"No, he wn't hut us as lnng ss we uus hr ss a shieeeld." Her eyes flicked to the door, which was all I needed. I sat up, snatched the hand that held the knife, and removed the weapon with my free one.

Vera jerked back, trying to pull from my grasp. My fingers curled around the bracelet, and I yanked it hard. The clasp broke.

"Nooo," she gasped, and her nails sank into my arm, tearing into my flesh. She clawed at me desperately, trying to get the bracelet back.

I hit her in the head with the butt of the knife, and she dropped.

Now my attention was on Ollie, who was staring at the door, not paying attention to his surroundings. I stood, clutching the knife and bracelet securely.

I had to put him down. I attempted to rush him, but my feet tripped over each other as my peripheral vision darkened and blurred. The blood loss was finally catching up to me. Ollie grabbed the wrist of my hand holding the knife and pressed his thumb against mine. The weapon fell to the floor. He spun me around so my back was against his stomach, and he placed his knife against my throat.

His breathing became labored, and something large slammed against the outside of the cabin. After another large ram, the walls crumbled as a dragon stepped through the debris.

Egan was here.

My eyes took in his gigantic form. He was as large as the cabin and had dark olive-green scales. His golden eyes were as bright as the sun as they zeroed in on Ollie and the knife at my neck.

He threw his head back and roared; flames spilled from his mouth.

No one had to be a dragon to understand the message: Let her go now.

"I can't." Ollie's hand shook as he dug the knife deeper into my neck.

Feeling blissfully numb, I sagged against Ollie's chest. My body grew heavy, and it was too hard to keep myself upright. It took every ounce of strength I had to keep my eyes open. *I don't know how much longer I can last.*

The dragon took several menacing steps toward us and opened his mouth, revealing his sharp, jagged teeth. *I'm getting you out of here.* He hissed, blowing hot smoke in our direction.

"Ddd it!" Vera screamed. "Kll hr nw!" Her voice was wild and crazed as she ran behind us.

Ollie dug the knife in deeper. This was the end.

Tears burned my eyes, and the most important words I'd ever said ran through my head. *I love you.*

DRAGON HEIR

THE HIDDEN KING TRILOGY

CHAPTER ONE

A few tears dripped down my cheeks as I stared at my fated mate in his angry dragon form. Smoke trickled from his nose, and his large, dark-olive-scaled body shook with rage. The cabin wall he'd barged through still rattled from the force. He was easily as wide as the cabin and extremely strong.

Ollie dug the knife in deeper against my neck. More blood poured from my wound, down my neck, and into my dark brown hair. Between the blood loss and the deep stab wound in my calf, my head swam. Knowing how to connect with my dragon would've come in handy, but it didn't matter.

I'd soon be dead.

Do not close your eyes, Egan said sternly. *Stay with me.* Fear permeated the bond.

I tried to force my eyes to stay open, but I was so damn tired. I had no clue why the falcon shifter was helping Vera, not that it would make a difference. Once Ollie slit my throat, keeping my eyes open wouldn't help. My eyelids fluttered as my dragon surged forward in a last-ditch effort to save us. She lent me her strength to tighten my hold on the bracelet I'd yanked off Vera. I muttered in barely a whisper, "Ollie, please. Stop. You don't have to do this."

The words slipped from my lips, even though it was a waste of energy.

Desperation slammed into me as Egan threw his head back, letting flames burst from his mouth. He charged toward me like he could prevent Ollie from finishing the job.

I closed my eyes, unable to watch Egan's reaction as I died. Even in death, that last look would haunt me.

I tensed, prepared to meet my end, when the knife clanked to the floor and Ollie's arm slackened. His body sagged, and I slipped from his arms. Too late, he reached for me like he realized what had happened. Unable to support my full weight, I sank toward the floor.

Egan dropped beside me, splitting the floor from his weight, and I landed on his neck instead of on the hard floor. I couldn't have survived another blow, so he'd bought me a little more time, but I wasn't sure I wanted it. The pain was all-consuming.

Car doors slammed shut outside, and Ollie sprang into action. He stumbled backward on his lanky legs, trying to get clear of us, his hands raised in surrender. His golden-brown hair stood almost straight up in fear.

"Do smthng!" Vera barked loudly despite her broken jaw and being so small. Her sable eyes were nearly black, and her stringy, caramel hair stuck to her face. "Kll hr!" she screamed barbarically.

Footsteps hit the ground as Sadie and the others ran straight to us through the completely destroyed wall. Arms slipped around my waist, and someone tugged me away from my mate. I wanted to yell and scream. I needed to be with him.

It's Sadie, Egan reassured me as he climbed back onto his feet, his attention locked on the falcon and the witch. *Let her take care of you while I handle them. I'll be right back.*

The comforting scent of musky vanilla hit my nose, confirming that it was her. They'd all come for me, and it meant more to me than I could ever say. I didn't see how I would come out of this alive.

Sadie was the next person I felt safe around. Since my dad's death, I hadn't felt secure and protected until I'd stumbled upon Egan and Sadie just over a month ago.

I smelled Donovan's and Axel's musky shifter scent as they rushed past me to fight alongside Egan. From where I sat, I watched Donovan grab Ollie by the throat and lift him into the air.

"Please don't," Ollie cried. "The witch was controlling me. I didn't have a choice but to hurt her."

"You expect me to believe that?" Donovan yelled, the vein between his brows popping. "Do you not realize how important she is to us?"

I startled at Donovan yelling, causing my leg to jerk, and I groaned in pain. I'd never experienced such agony before, not even after Aunt Sarah's worst beatings. Between the dizziness and nausea, I wasn't sure how I hadn't projectile-vomited yet.

"I'm telling the truth. Jade clawed the bracelet Vera was using to control me off the witch and told me to stop." Ollie pointed at me with a shaky finger. "Why else would I let her go, especially with you all charging at me?"

"Roxy, help me get her on the couch," Sadie said. Hands picked up my legs as Sadie adjusted her grip on my arms. "Lift her on the count of three. One ... two ... three." They picked me up, and I cried out in pain.

Just hold on a little longer, Egan pleaded as he hissed at the witch.

"Let's get you situated so we can check you over," Sadie said calmly, but the pain overwhelmed me, and my head grew light.

They slowly carried me over to the dirty old couch that had definitely seen better days. A cloud of dust covered me, tickling my nose.

"Shit," Roxy huffed and let go of my leg. "This isn't good."

Sadie's eyes landed on my leg, and she went still. "Lillith! Katherine!" Sadie shouted. "She's lost a lot of blood. We need your help." Worry filled her light blue eyes, and her rose-gold hair hung in her face as she stared down at me. Her usually sun-kissed skin appeared as pale as the vampires'.

The floor shook with each step Egan took as he charged after Vera. I really hoped he made her hurt like I was hurting. She enjoyed the pain she'd caused.

The crackling sound of fire hit my ears, and the smell of brimstone filled the cramped space. Normally, I would have lifted myself to check on him, but it was hard to even breathe.

"We have to move fast." Roxy ran her blood-coated hands through her red hair. Even with the scarlet color of her hair, the blood was noticeable. Her hazel eyes had lost their usual smart-ass sparkle.

"You kidnapped her back at the restaurant, right under our noses." Donovan sounded as scary as Egan. "Did you actually think we'd let you walk away?"

The witch had looked distraught when I'd taken the bracelet, and the clasp had been sturdy. Maybe Ollie was telling the truth. "Bracelet," I mumbled and tried to raise my hand, but I couldn't. My eyelids were too heavy to keep open.

I wanted to stay conscious, but the world was fading along with the pain. The reprieve, even for a little while, would be a godsend. I didn't want to fight the darkness anymore. Sounds began to fade as loud footsteps rushed over to me. The vampires' signature scent of cotton candy alerted me that one of our friends had neared the couch.

A hand turned my head toward the vampire hovering over me. Something warm and thick pressed against my lips and dripped into my mouth. I wanted to pull away, but then my taste buds went crazy. I sucked hard, pulling more of the substance in. It tasted like rocky road ice cream.

Within seconds, my body felt stronger, and the sharp throbbing in my leg receded. I opened my eyes and found Lillith's wrist against my mouth.

No way. She wasn't feeding me her blood.

I jerked back and wiped the excess blood from my mouth as it trickled from the wound on her wrist to the ground.

"What the hell?" They could've warned me first.

"You needed healing." Sadie brushed my hair out of my face.

"Vampire blood does wonders even if the thought is a little unappealing. You would have died otherwise."

Egan turned to me, his focus drifting from the witch. *Are you okay?*

Yeah, I assured him. "Her blood tastes good." That couldn't be normal. I sat up and lifted my pant leg. My wound had stopped bleeding and was already scabbing over. Considering how bad it had been only seconds ago, that was a miracle.

"Please," Ollie whispered. "I didn't want to hurt her."

Everything around me came back into focus. Killing Ollie would be a mistake if what he said was true. As long as we had the bracelet, we could control him and get whatever information we needed from him. But first things first.

"Thank you." I smiled at Lillith and climbed to my feet. Even though I felt immensely better, I still was a little woozy.

"You're not completely healed." Lillith looked paler than normal, and her jet-black hair and dark brown eyes surrounded by the dark red ring contrasted against her skin more than usual. Her all-black clothing added to the creepy effect. "So take it easy."

I linked with my mate. *We all know he's telling the truth.* I opened my hand, revealing the bracelet. The tarnished silver and strangely clear, quartz-like crystal with flecks of ash shone in the light. "We'd know if he was lying."

As I turned to Egan and Vera, the witch vanished into thin air. How the hell had she done that?

"She just disappeared." I pointed excitedly over to where she'd stood. Even though Egan had used his flames, nothing was on fire. He had to be able to channel it perfectly; otherwise, the cabin would've been up in a blaze.

Donovan dropped a purple-faced Ollie and scanned the room. "Where the hell did she go?"

Axel rushed to where she'd been and sniffed. "It's like she was never here. I don't smell a trail leading out the door."

A car started outside, and the tires squealed. I ran to the window and saw her speed down the gravel driveway.

Roxy ran to their car.

"Dammit," Axel grumbled and ran after his mate. Roxy jumped into the driver's seat, and Axel got into the passenger seat. She lurched the car into gear as she chased after the witch.

"Where is the witch going?" Donovan demanded as he turned back to Ollie.

The poor guy lifted his hands and averted his gaze to the ground. "I … I don't know. She didn't tell me anything."

"Why should we keep you alive?" Sadie asked in a calmer but deadlier voice.

For the first time, I saw the true supernatural side of her, and she was a force to be reckoned with.

"Look, I swear." Ollie looked at me. "She told me what to do and who to attack." He gestured at the bracelet in my hand. "The black ash is from my scorched feather. She performed a spell to control me. You can keep the bracelet until I can prove I'm trustworthy. Just please, let me live."

Only one thing could prove he was telling the truth. I held the bracelet and lifted my chin. "Ollie, pick up the knife."

"What?" he asked, but he bent down and picked it up. Fear filled his eyes as he held the handle firmly in his hand.

What are you doing? Egan asked as the smoke dissipated from his mouth.

Finding out if it's true. I lifted a brow, daring the falcon. "Cut your forearm until I say stop."

"Please don't." His voice shook as he obediently cut through his skin like it was a piece of paper. Blood poured from the wound, and he continued to press the blade down harder and harder.

No one would do that willingly. "Stop." I couldn't make him hurt himself too much.

"Thank God," he whimpered and dropped the knife.

Lillith marched over to the falcon shifter. "What was her end game? You have to know that much."

"She wants to find your thunder," I told Egan. She'd let me in on that secret.

"Yes." Ollie nodded. "At first, she had me attack random girls, hoping you would investigate and we could nab something of yours to track you. But we only got a few items that weren't really tied to you and couldn't provide the best locations. When she realized you weren't inclined to go home, she upped the game and had me kill girls she thought you were either interested in or who could be your potential mate."

"Like Amber." I walked over to Egan and leaned against him, brushing my fingers against his hard scales. "Either Ollie told her, or she thought you were dating her."

Egan leaned against my hand, and I felt a purring sound emanating from deep inside him.

"It was me." Ollie hung his head. "She commanded me to tell her anything I could get on him. Given how intimate Amber seemed with you, I thought we'd found something."

"So you killed her?" Even if he'd had to, he'd committed cold-blooded murder. I couldn't imagine the pain Amber must have gone through. "And all those other girls."

"Yes." Remorse poured off Ollie. "I hated it, and I'll never forgive myself, but I had no choice. Vera was convinced that if his mate or girlfriend was killed, he'd rush home to his thunder, and if we had the blood of a girl he was emotionally tied to, the locator spell would be that much stronger."

Katherine wrung her hands. "Anything you have a connection to would strengthen the spell."

Then it hit me and hard. I sucked in a breath and glanced at my leg. She'd wiped my blood on her jeans before she'd disappeared. "She has my blood."

We weren't safe. She could find us anywhere.

CHAPTER TWO

The room was silent as everyone took in my words. Vera having my blood was disconcerting.

"What do you mean she has your blood?" Katherine asked as she tugged on the ends of her long brown hair. Her matching-colored eyes, with red ringing the irises, looked at me.

"My leg wound." I lifted my leg and gestured to my black slacks. Blood had soaked into the material and still dripped into my already overfilled black dress shoes. "When she yanked out the knife she stabbed me with, she wiped my blood on her clothes. Can't she use that or anything else she might have collected from our dorm room to track me?" The supernatural world had so many rules and caveats. Being human had been a whole lot simpler.

We need to get you back to the dorms so you can rest. Egan was still tense from the fight.

That sounded like a good plan. I felt stronger, but I was still exhausted. At least, I could stand and hold my weight, but I was tempted to crawl onto that nasty couch and take a long nap. However, the witch was still out there, and we had to figure out what the hell to do with Ollie. Even if I could control him, I didn't want him leaving our sight.

"I wonder if Roxy and Axel caught up to the witch." I doubted they had. Vera had several minutes' head start, but the roads were free of traffic. Maybe they'd gotten lucky.

Sadie sighed. "They didn't catch up to her. They're actually on their way back. It's like she vanished again."

"Can a witch hide a whole car?" There was so much I had to learn, and after tonight, I needed to catch up.

Ollie shook his head. "She's powerful. She knows long-forgotten spells. It's the oddest thing. That's how she was able to trap me. I had no clue it was even possible."

"I wonder how she has so much knowledge." Lillith pursed her lips. "She must have a spell book."

The image of the leather notebook flashed in my mind. "I think I know how. She carries around a book she says was her grandmother's journal. Maybe it's her grandmother's spell book."

"You're right." Ollie rubbed his neck, still red from where Donovan had held him. "I've seen it too. It makes sense that she would keep it close, especially while using magic."

"Great, but how did she go undetected around us?" Donovan frowned and towered over Ollie and the others. "We should've smelled her."

"She knew who we were." Sadie rubbed her bottom lip with her thumb. "She probably used magic to conceal herself."

"That's why she was in our room so much." The more she was outside, moving around, the more magic she had to use to hide herself.

Can you get the car keys from Donovan? Egan shifted away from me. *I'd like to grab the spare clothes from the back and change into human form.*

"Donovan, can I get the keys?" I lifted my hands, ready for him to throw them. "Egan wants to shift back." I wanted him to as well. I'd never seen him in his dragon form before, and it tugged at me differently. I always felt safe around him, but in this form, I had no doubt he could protect me from anything.

That was why I needed to learn to control my dragon. Maybe tonight wouldn't have been so bad.

"Sure." He lobbed them gently at me, keeping his focus on Ollie.

The only reasons Ollie wasn't dead or injured were because the witch had been controlling him and we had the bracelet in our possession. Still, I didn't trust him either, so Donovan's wariness made it easier for me to leave with Egan. "Come on. I'll get your stuff out for you."

The others stayed behind as Egan and I went to his Jeep. I opened the trunk and found two bags.

Mine's the one on the left. He pointed one long claw in that direction. *Can you hand me the clothes? I'll go into the woods and shift back real fast.*

Happy to help, I placed them in his large dragon hands. He hurried off, nearly taking down a tree to go hide somewhere. As his huge body shrank, magic crackled in the air.

Needing a moment to myself, I leaned against the Jeep and waited for him to return. The night was catching up with me, and I couldn't believe I'd survived. To think I'd gone to work tonight at Haynes Steakhouse, believing Egan was being overly paranoid because of the killings popping up on campus, and I'd come close to the same fate. I hated that I hadn't respected his wishes that I just quit, but even if I had, Vera would've used Ollie to attack me, so maybe getting the kidnapping out of the way had been a blessing in disguise.

Either way, I had a feeling that wasn't the last we'd seen of her. She had something against the dragons—wait, against us. I was a dragon shifter too even if I hadn't shifted into a dragon yet.

Footsteps drew closer, and my sexy mate stepped out of the trees. He was so gorgeous he took my breath away.

He approached me, towering over me by a foot, which was saying something since I was almost six feet tall. He was built like an MMA fighter, and his loose, hunter-green t-shirt molded to his muscular chest and arms. His blue jeans clung to his ass and legs the way they should on a man. His longish blond hair was messy and not in his usual upward style, and his matching scruff was a tad longer than normal.

He pulled me against his hard chest and wrapped his arms around me tightly. "Are you okay?"

Emotions surged inside me, almost uncontrollably. His presence made moisture spring back into my eyes. "No, but I will be." That had been my motto growing up: Suck it up and survive.

"Honey, I'm so sorry." His voice cracked with emotion. "I'll never be able to forgive myself for you getting hurt because of me."

"No, you don't get to do that." I pulled back and stared into his golden eyes. "You did nothing wrong. You can't blame yourself for what that psychopath did. Believe me, if we did, I'd have so much to apologize for." My aunt hated me, and I'd never understood why. After moving in with her following my father's death, she'd completely controlled my mother and me. Even though she and my mother's relationship was unhealthy, my aunt had focused her hatred on me, but I'd rather she hurt me instead of my mother. When I'd told Egan all about my past, he'd listened without judgment. I'd never found someone like him before.

His face softened, and he blew out a breath. "You're right. It's just hard at times."

The sound of crunching gravel under tires and the purr of an engine filled the air as Roxy and Axel were heading our way. They were a few miles out, but with my supernatural ears, I could hear things from a greater distance away.

"Now isn't the time to discuss that." We had so much to do. I stood on my tiptoes and kissed him, enjoying his sweet taste and the feel of his soft lips. After living through this hell of a night, I needed this moment.

The car came into view, breaking the spell we'd fallen under. I glanced over my shoulder as Roxy and Axel got out of the car. Axel's deep-set frown wasn't his normal expression and made him seem intimidating with his buzzed dark hair and piercing brown eyes.

"No sign of her?" That was the only thing that look could mean.

"Not one." Roxy slammed the driver's door shut and pouted. "That's not fucking possible."

"Maybe you couldn't catch up," Egan suggested.

"There's no way in hell." Roxy crossed her arms and marched over to us. "I drove fast enough to catch up."

"She isn't lying." Axel shivered. "I thought we might die. She almost rolled the car trying to catch up to her before we hit the main road."

"Don't start with me." Roxy placed her hand on her hip and glared. "Your crying didn't help matters."

"I was not crying." Axel breathed rapidly. "I was yelling out of fear for our lives."

I'd never seen these two argue before. They were usually in sync, but stress had a way of bringing out the worst in people. "I'm sure it was the intensity of the moment. It's been a rough night for everyone."

Roxy's shoulders slumped. "You're right. It's been rougher for you than the rest of us. I just feel like a failure for letting her get away."

"Babe, you did everything possible." Axel wrapped an arm around her shoulders. "Believe me when I say that. I was right beside you in that car."

The corners of her mouth tipped upward, and a smile broke free. She wrinkled her nose. "I hate you. Just know that."

"The feeling's mutual." He winked and kissed her forehead. "Let's join the others."

The four of us stepped through the huge hole in the cabin wall. Ollie stood against the wall with Donovan watching his every move as if he might fly away.

"What's the plan?" Roxy asked. "And why is he still alive?"

"Apparently, the witch was controlling him." Lillith shrugged.

"Now Jade has the magic bracelet and made him cut himself." She gestured to his wound, still dripping blood.

"You totally should have had him cut his penis off." Roxy faced me. "That would've been a better test."

"Uh, no," Ollie said in a very high-pitched voice. "Please don't." He stared at me with pleading eyes.

He actually thought I would do it. Roxy sure enjoyed messing with people, and keeping a smile off my face took a lot of work. "She has a point."

He placed his hands on his chest. "Please, I'll do anything."

Now he'd made me feel bad, taking all the fun out of it. "No, I won't do that, even though I should after all the shit you pulled, willingly or not. You could've warned us."

"I couldn't," he whined. "She prevented me from telling anyone."

"Oh, come on," Lillith growled. "You could've written it on a piece of paper or done something to alert us."

I agreed, but lecturing him wouldn't do any good.

Egan tensed beside me, breathing rapidly. "You prick. I don't care if she was controlling you. It's taking every ounce of self-control I have not to pummel you."

"Look, I don't know much, but I want to find her, same as you." Ollie dropped his hands. "My cast can help. The more people searching for her, the faster we'll find her. One thing is certain: if you or Jade go to the thunder, she will track you using Jade's blood."

"Cast?" I asked.

"Yeah, a group of falcons is called a cast, like a wolf has a pack," Ollie answered.

"What? How?" Axel's brows furrowed. "If she has Jade's blood, how can she track Egan?"

"She was hoping his emotional tie to her would help us track him, but she wasn't certain." Ollie pointed at me. "But now they're fated mates, which means they share the same soul, and her blood can be used to track them both."

That sounded logical in a creepy way. *What do you think?* He wasn't lying, so he believed the words, even if they weren't true.

If there is a chance we might lead her to the thunder, we can't risk it, Egan said as he intertwined our fingers. *I can get someone to come here to help us find her.*

That sounded like a decent option. If they came to us, we wouldn't have to worry about leading her to them. *They'll have to be careful. She'll try to put a locator spell on them too, so whoever comes needs to stay until everything has settled.*

You're right. He squeezed my hand lovingly.

"As fun as this is, I want to get the hell out of here." This place would always be linked to my second worst memories of locations now, coming in right after my aunt's house. "Can we head out?"

"Of course." Sadie placed a hand on her heart. "I wouldn't want to be here longer than necessary either. Seeing you like that was horrible enough. But what are we going to do with him?" She nodded at Ollie.

"We'll bring him with us." Egan's tone held an edge. "There's no way we're letting him out of our sights. I'll stay with Jade in case the witch shows back up in their room, and either Axel or Donovan can stay with my roommate. Ollie can take one of their spots in their room."

The thought of Egan staying with me excited me way too much. I hadn't considered how I felt about staying in my dorm room alone after Vera had made it clear she wanted to kill me. "They may not be too thrilled with that." Egan had thrown the plan out there without verifying it with anyone.

"No, it's fine," Donovan agreed. "That's the best plan. We want him close by."

"All right, then." The decision had been made, and I was desperate to leave. "Let's go."

"Wait ... maybe I'm not okay with staying with a wolf shifter that would enjoy killing me." Ollie scoffed. "I don't know them. What if they hurt me?"

"We won't," Donovan spat. "Or are you calling us liars? Can you not smell a lie?"

"Fine." Ollie's shoulders sagged. "It's not like I have a choice. At least, I'll be on campus for my classes."

"He can ride back with us." Egan turned toward his Jeep.

As our group headed outside, a nagging feeling ran down my spine. I stopped in my tracks and spun around to face the woods.

CHAPTER THREE

The creepy feeling of someone watching overwhelmed me. But I scanned the woods and didn't see anything out of the ordinary.

Egan's hand tightened on mine as he linked with me. *Someone's out there.*

Yeah, but I don't see a damn thing. This night kept getting worse and worse. I'd figured it'd been Ollie watching me, but it couldn't have been just him. *Do you think it's Vera?*

No. He released my hand and walked a few steps toward the trees. *She'd be cloaked, so we wouldn't be able to sense her. It's something or someone else.*

The feeling vanished. That was so strange and unnerving. Could she have someone else tracking us? I hadn't considered more people could be involved. I turned to the car and realized everyone was tense. They'd felt it too.

How I wished I was only being paranoid.

"How many others are working for her?" I asked Ollie.

"I ... I don't know." He rubbed his hands together. "She was always alone around me. I thought I was the only one."

Dammit, he wasn't lying. He didn't have any helpful insight.

"Let's go." Egan unlocked the Jeep and waved us on. "Everyone get in. We'll be safer on campus."

That got us all moving.

Lillith, Katherine, Roxy, and Axel ran to the Honda as the rest of us rushed to Egan's Jeep. I climbed into the front passenger seat and felt bad when Sadie slid into the back seat, positioning herself between Ollie and Donovan. Under normal circumstances, I'd sit in back, but after Ollie had held a knife to my neck, I hated the thought of being around him.

I couldn't hold in a chuckle when Axel jumped into the driver's seat. Roxy pouted for a second before giving up and getting in the front passenger seat of the other car. Axel hadn't been kidding when he'd appeared less than thrilled about Roxy's driving. She was the type to act first and think about consequences later.

When the cars moved forward, my breathing hitched, revealing how upset I'd been. Now that I felt safer, my body sagged against the car door. "Shit, I'm getting blood all over the interior."

My shoe wasn't overflowing with blood anymore, but my pant leg was soaked, and blood coated my shoes.

Egan didn't even flinch. "Don't you dare worry about that. I can clean the car or buy a new one. I'm more worried about getting you clean and dry someplace safe."

Donovan chuckled from right behind me. "Besides, it's about time his car had blood spilled in it."

"Is this normal for you all?" I got that Sadie had contended with a man who'd lied about being her father, but I hadn't expected that all of them had experienced so much violence.

"It is, unfortunately." Sadie sighed. "I'd hoped that things would have calmed down, but it's obvious that's not happening."

"You don't have to be part of this." Egan glanced in the rearview mirror at her. "They're after my thunder, for God knows what reason. It doesn't have to affect any of you."

"Are you serious?" she asked, her nostrils flaring as she shot daggers at Egan. "You fought with us when you didn't have to. Did you think we wouldn't return the favor?"

"You still have your own pack to get settled." Egan's hands tightened on the steering wheel. "And you're getting to know your dad."

"Dude, come on." Donovan sounded as upset as Sadie. "There's no way we're not helping you figure this out. Besides, you may not be a wolf, but you and Jade are like pack to us. And wolves take care of their pack mates."

"You guys really are odd." Ollie leaned forward and looked at each one of us. "You do realize most races keep to themselves, but you have vampires, dragons, wolves, and fae all in the mix."

"Things are changing." Sadie arched an eyebrow at him. "More races are coming together. It'll take time, but we must realize that coming together as a community will make us stronger and better than isolating ourselves. When we come together, we can help each other with our resources."

"Or races can hold their resources as leverage over one another's heads." Ollie scoffed. "You saw what that witch did to me. I'm all about sticking to my own kind."

I couldn't blame him there. People survived by keeping their heads low and focusing on themselves. But the way Sadie had described the world she envisioned sounded pretty damn good. Hell, I hadn't been around them long, but if anyone could accomplish that vision, it was this group.

However, if Ollie and Sadie kept going down this road, it would turn into an argument, so I steered the conversation in a more productive direction. "How did the witch get to you?" That was one thing I'd been wondering since hearing his long-winded story. I opened the hand still clutching the bracelet and examined it. It was a gorgeous piece of jewelry and very authentic. The specks of ash were almost fluffy, confirming they had come from a feather.

"She found me here." He tilted his head. "Okay, not here but at Kortright, on the first day of second semester. I was flying in the woods, enjoying the freedom from my cast. My parents are a little intense. They're the oldest and viewed as the leaders of the cast."

I was all too familiar with overbearing adult figures. "They couldn't be that bad since they allowed you to go off to college." Aunt Sarah had been determined to keep me in her sights.

"I didn't have a choice." He sighed. "Family business and all. They're big-time lawyers who have never lost a case. They expect me to follow in their footsteps, so I chose this school since it's several hours away and doesn't get cold like in the north."

"So Vera caught you in the woods?" Egan turned onto the main road, heading back to campus.

"Not exactly." Ollie looked out his window, watching the trees fly by. "I got tired of flying around, so I stopped on a branch to rest and preen. She found me while I was preoccupied, and when my feather fell, she caught it. She must have been tracking me. I didn't realize the problem until I smelled fire. She burnt my feather right then and there and captured enough ash to put in the bracelet."

"Wait ... did you chase me that day?" Had he been in the woods, making me feel so damn threatened?

"Yes, she told me to scare you off." He scratched his nose. "I tried so hard not to, but I didn't have control over myself. I was a passenger inside my own body."

That description sounded horrible and put his experience into perspective. Too tired to hold my head up, I propped my head against the passenger door window and enjoyed the cool glass against my skin.

"How come we never saw you on campus?" Egan hadn't relaxed one bit. He focused on the road ahead, following behind Axel. "You say you're a student there."

"My classes are later in the afternoon." Ollie yawned. "I needed to work the evening shifts to cover my tuition and board since my parents weren't thrilled about me coming here."

Evenings and weekends were the best times for tips. That was one reason I'd requested the weekends when I'd applied at Haynes.

"Do you know anything else about the witch?" Sadie asked. "Even something that seems insignificant could lead us in the right direction?"

"No," he said with defeat. "I've got nothing. She only came around when she wanted me to ..." He cleared his throat. "... hurt someone and commanded me not to tell anyone about her, what she asked of me, and our connection. Other than that, she left me alone."

He'd been a victim just like me, but that didn't change the fact I needed time before I forgave him. Yes, Vera had controlled him, but he'd hurt me and others. Amber's face popped into my mind.

The Jeep descended into silence, and after a few moments, Egan relaxed enough to take my hand. Today felt like it would never end. So much shit had happened, and I was ready to sleep, hoping tomorrow would be better.

We pulled into Kortright's parking lot, and I sat upright in the car. As soon as the cars parked, we all jumped out.

I cringed at my clothes. "Uh ... I need to change. I don't want anyone to see me like this."

Lillith's skin wasn't as white as she approached us. She took a large sip from the cup in her hand. "We can go behind the buildings and up the stairwell."

"That's ideal since I plan on sneaking in too." Egan stood in front of the Jeep. "Let's get you inside. It's before midnight on a Friday night. Most everyone is still out partying."

Donovan walked over to Ollie and grabbed his arm. "We'll get falcon boy settled, and I'll move my stuff into your dorm."

"We'll come help you," Sadie said as Axel and Roxy followed behind Donovan too.

That left Egan, me, and the vampires behind.

"Let's go," Egan said as he took my hand, and our group walked behind the men's dorm to the women's.

Light and darkness might not affect my vision, but as we walked between the buildings and the woods that surrounded the campus, I searched the trees frantically for anything out of sorts. I didn't feel the tickle down my spine of someone watching me, but that didn't mean the witch wasn't near.

Do you sense something?

Egan slowed, following my gaze to the woods. *I don't.*

Thank God. *I just want to get inside and wash all this dry blood off me.*

We rushed up the stairs, and in my room, I almost cried with relief. Vera's side of the room remained untouched. Her Star Wars poster hung over her neatly made bed. Even her desk still had her college books sitting to one side.

That stupid feeling of being watched swarmed around me again. "I'm so tired of this feeling." Vera had to be doing this. "This is what I felt the other day before Ollie crashed into my window repeatedly."

"She must be using a spell." Egan rushed over to the desk and opened the drawers. "There has to be something here."

Lillith gestured to the ceiling. "She's astral projecting."

I looked up and saw a faint figure hovering in the air that looked like a ghost. The figure flew through the window outside, vanishing from the room.

"What the hell is astral projection?" They needed to remember to treat me like the supernatural newbie that I was.

"A witch can go into a dream-like state and project herself anywhere to watch over." Lillith shook her head and scowled. "It takes an extremely strong witch to do it, but that just confirms what we already know about her."

"This is ridiculous." This woman was stalking me. There was no telling how often she'd watched us. "How can we stop her?" If she could locate me, she could watch me wherever I went.

"Dad taught me a sigil when I was younger in case I ever needed it." Lillith turned around, looking for something. "I need something to write on the wall with."

"Oh, here." Katherine snatched the Sharpie from my desk and tossed it at the other vampire. "That should work."

The thought of messing up the dorm walls put me on edge, but

I'd rather pay to have it repainted than let that psycho bitch hover over me. I bit my tongue as Lillith went to work.

On each side of the window, she drew a symbol that looked like an A with the point to the right and a squiggly line underneath. She drew it on the back of the door too. "There. All entry points to the room are covered. As long as nothing happens to the symbol, you'll be protected."

Egan tensed. "We'll change the locks first thing in the morning."

"Now that sounds like a plan." Lillith yawned. "If you two are good, I'll head back to my dorm. The bed is calling my name after all that shit tonight."

"Same," Katherine agreed and hugged me. "I'm so glad you're okay. Tonight terrified us. We thought we might lose you."

This was awkward. I patted her shoulder and hoped my forced smile wasn't scary. "Thank you for being there for me."

"Always."

The vampires left the room, leaving Egan and me alone. I hurried to my closet and grabbed some pajamas to change into along with a towel. I needed a shower pronto.

I faced the door and came to a stop. Egan stood there, holding the door open.

"Uh ..." I wasn't sure what he planned to do. "Are you going somewhere?" Disappointment flared through me. I'd expected him to spend the night with me, but he'd obviously changed his mind.

"I'm going to the shower with you." He motioned toward the bathroom. "There's no way I'm letting you go in there with that witch looking for you."

"But it's the girls'—"

"I don't care," Egan said and placed a hand on the small of my back, took my towel and clothes, and led me into the hallway. "I can't handle you being alone in there. If anyone is in there, I'll wait outside in the hallway."

His concern for me made me fall for him even harder, which surprised me. I hadn't thought that was possible. "Fine."

The bathroom was completely empty, so Egan joined me inside. I was determined to hurry before someone caught us in here. I turned the water on and stripped, laying the clothes on the shower floor so they could soak. Getting the blood out of them would require some elbow grease. I walked out to grab my supplies, and my gaze landed on Egan. His pupils turned to slits as he took in my naked figure.

My breath caught as need surged through me. I'd almost died tonight, and the thought of him between my legs seemed way more important than taking a shower.

He must have felt the same way because he crossed the room and kissed me hard while his arms wrapped around my body.

I opened my mouth, allowing him access inside. His sweet taste made my head spin, and his hands cupped my ass cheeks. We lost sense of time as we devoured each other.

A door swung open, and I froze. Someone was heading in here, and there was nowhere Egan could hide.

CHAPTER FOUR

I took several steps away from Egan like that would improve the situation despite being completely naked. Now he probably looked like a creeper instead.

Roxy's and Sadie's musky scents hit me.

They rounded the corner of the small hallway, and Roxy wore a shit-eating smile. Glancing at Sadie, she gestured at Egan, then me. "See, I told you she'd be naked."

"She was covered in blood." Sadie lifted her right hand. "Of course she'd be naked."

"Oh, you know what I mean." Roxy sniffed loudly. "Arousal is in the air. I thought we might walk in on dangling bits. I was kinda hoping ..."

A low growl escaped me before I could hold the sound in, but my dragon surged forward at the thought of her seeing Egan naked. I'd taken a step toward Roxy when Egan's arm slid around my waist, pulling me to his chest.

His touch calmed me enough for my dragon to recede.

"She's kidding." Sadie smacked her best friend hard on the arm.

"You know you can't joke like that about someone's mate, especially when they're newly mated."

"You're right." Roxy's face turned serious for once. "I'm sorry. I'm just giving you a hard time, but now probably isn't the best time since you're still covered in your own crusted blood."

I realized I was standing stark naked in front of all three of them. "On that note." I pulled away from Egan and saw that I'd gotten some flaky blood on his shirt. Trying not to focus on that, I snatched my towel from his hand and wrapped it around my body. "I'm going to go get the blood out of my clothes and off me."

"You really think you can get the blood out of those clothes and shoes?" Sadie's brows furrowed. "With the amount of blood you lost, you probably can't soak them long enough to get them clean."

Unfortunately, I agreed with her, but I was low on money and didn't have a job. I needed to salvage them. "It's worth a shot."

"Look, we can get you another outfit tomorrow." Egan pushed a piece of my hair behind my ear. "There's no point in trying to save them."

He was right even if I didn't have the cash. "Fine." I wouldn't need that outfit since I wasn't working at the steakhouse anymore.

"Girls are trickling in." Roxy tapped her ear. "You need to get out of here before someone else catches you."

"You two are staying here with her, right?" Egan tensed, not thrilled about leaving. "That witch astral projected into the room right before we came here."

"Yeah, that's one reason we're here." Sadie winced and shook her head. "We've got to figure out who the hell she is and what we're up against."

"Later," Roxy said as she grabbed Egan's arm, tugging him to the door. "We'll protect her. Go hide in her room."

Egan put my pajamas down on a bench and glanced over his shoulder at me, his face drawn with concern. *If you feel anything odd, let me know. I don't care if I get in trouble for being here. I refuse to let anything happen to you. You've been through enough.*

I promise. After ignoring the danger of going to the steakhouse, alerting him to anything that felt off seemed more than fair. He hid it well, but tonight had taken a toll on him. *Now go.* I headed into the shower, picked up my soaking wet clothes and shoes, and threw them away. Everything inside me screamed to keep them, but I had a feeling I'd have to fight Egan and the girls if I tried.

Needing to get the blood off me, I stepped into the shower, letting the hot spray hit my entire body. No matter how many times I lathered, I still felt like I had blood all over me. I scrubbed myself hard.

Footsteps headed my way, and Roxy called out, "You okay in there? It's been a while."

"Yeah, sorry." I'd lost track of time, but I finally felt somewhat clean. I turned the water off and dried off with my towel. As I stepped back into the tile hallway, I turned left and stopped, noticing my reflection staring back at me in the mirror. My dark hair looked a touch darker when wet, but that was normal. Between the dark circles under my brown eyes and my abnormally pale skin, I looked like death walking. No wonder I didn't feel up to par.

"Are you okay?" Sadie stepped into the view, her eyes lined with worry. "Can I help you with anything?"

She had good intentions, but I hated when people looked at me like I was a charity case. That was the same expression everyone had worn at my dad's funeral, but I had to remind myself that Sadie would never intentionally make me feel that way.

Pushing down my prickly feelings, I inhaled sharply. "Yeah, sorry." They were probably eager to leave the bathroom. "Just out of it." I rushed into the open room with benches that everyone used to blow-dry their hair and put makeup on. I slipped into my pajamas and brushed my hair.

"Hey, I wasn't rushing you." Sadie sat on the bench beside me. "You were just back there a while, so I thought I'd check on you."

I paused from brushing my hair. "No, I know."

"Uh, speak for yourself." Roxy squinted at me with a cocky smirk.

"I'm all about rushing her. I don't want the scary dragon to come in here and eat us because he thinks we're messing with his mate."

Even though she was trying to make me smile, I couldn't. "Sorry, I'm not in the best frame of mind."

"You almost died tonight." Sadie sighed and rubbed my arm. "I've been severely injured before, and right when you think you're fine, you reach your breaking point. What you need is a good night's sleep in your mate's arms."

"Maybe something more than sleep." Roxy waggled her brows. "That would definitely put you in a better mood."

The thought was tempting, but I felt way too tired to do more than think about it. Maybe he could help me forget in the morning. I picked up my wet towel and headed to the door. "I'm calling it a night."

The two of them followed me out and walked me to my dorm. Inside, I found Egan already changed and lying on my bed. He had some crackers, Doritos, and two Cokes sat on my desk. When he saw me, he held out his arms for me.

My legs propelled me forward, and I climbed into bed beside him.

Egan nodded at Sadie and Roxy. "Thanks for keeping an eye on her."

"No problemo." Roxy winked at me. "She needs rest, and I need her back to her usual self."

"We all want that." My body grew numb. I laid my head on Egan's chest, listening to the steady heartbeat.

Sadie turned the lights off and closed the door. Within seconds, I drifted into a deep sleep.

The sun shone between the blinds, hitting my eyelids. My eyes fluttered open, and the last twelve hours flooded back. I searched for Egan, but he was nowhere in the room.

I linked to him, worried something had gone wrong. *Where are you?*

Dammit, I was hoping to get back before you woke up, Egan responded, sounding like his normal self. *I called my dad this morning to inform him of what happened last night. I didn't want to wake you, so I snuck out and got you a cup of coffee. I'm heading up the stairs and will be there in a second.*

Coffee sounded amazing, but the part of him telling his dad did not. The last thing I wanted was for his parents to disapprove of me. If they thought this was happening because of me, they might discourage Egan from being with me.

The door opened, and Egan stepped into the room. His hair was styled in its usual way, and he wore a clean, black, button-down shirt and blue jeans that left very little to the imagination. My body became alert, and I hadn't even taken a sip of coffee yet.

"Good morning." He shut the door, locked it, and put the drink on the desk next to the two Cokes we hadn't touched last night before kissing me quickly. "Are you feeling any better?"

"Mmhmm." I grabbed the back of his neck and pulled him down so his lips met mine again. *But I won't be if you stop doing this.*

Well, we can't have that, he replied as he slipped his tongue into my mouth. *I wouldn't be a good mate if I didn't oblige.*

My eyes stayed locked on him as he removed his shoes and slipped into bed. He pulled me into his arms, but that wasn't nearly close to enough.

Overcome with need, I slipped my hands under his shirt and traced his six-pack with my fingertips. His body shuddered, empowering me.

I sucked in a breath, enjoying the unique mixture of his citrus scent and sweet vanilla taste. He reminded me of happiness, which seemed altogether fitting.

Pulling back, I yanked the edges of his shirt up. *Off. Now.* I needed to feel his skin, and the clothes were an unnecessary barrier.

Maybe we should rest, he suggested and pulled away slightly. *You almost died last night.*

Which is exactly why I want to feel alive. I ripped the buttons from his shirt, slid the flaps open, and ran my hand across his body. *Please don't say no.*

I could never do that. His lips slammed back onto mine, and his desperation bled through the bond. He wanted this as badly as I did. We both needed the connection.

He trailed kisses down my neck, and his calloused hands brushed against my skin. His breathing picked up as his teeth grazed my skin. He wasn't being nearly as gentle with me this time around, and it turned me on even more.

I slipped my shirt off and tossed it on the floor. I hadn't worn a bra to bed, and his eyes landed on my breasts.

You're so fucking gorgeous, he growled and placed his mouth over my nipple. He bit gently and flicked his tongue. My body blazed.

Not missing a beat, he pushed down my pajama pants and touched between my legs. His fingers rubbed the perfect spot, hard and fast. He wasn't building up at a slow pace; he was desperate to please me ... desperate to claim me again.

One of my hands slid into his hair as I unbuttoned and unzipped his jeans with the other. I then shoved my hand inside his boxers and stroked him as he worked on me.

His breath hitched, and he nipped harder on my breast, creating pleasure instead of pain. My dragon roared inside me, but it didn't seem strange. She needed to connect with Egan's dragon the same way I needed to connect with Egan.

We touched and fondled each other, pushing each other closer and closer to the edge. Right when I almost fell off, Egan stopped and stood, pushing down his jeans and boxers and removing my bottoms.

He moved to slide between my legs, but I didn't want that. I pointed to the bed and linked with him. *Lie down. It's my turn.*

Whatever expression he saw, he didn't attempt to argue. Instead, he climbed into the center of the bed and sat against the headboard.

I took him in, enjoying the view of his skin and muscles. He was hard in all the right places, and my body was buzzing and ready.

In a flash, I straddled him, and when I grabbed him to slip inside, he caught my arm.

One second. He cupped my face and kissed me gently then moved his head to stare deep into my eyes. *I love you, Jade.*

My heart pounded hard, and not from the sexual chemistry between us. *Look, I know I said it last night, but don't feel obligated to say it back.* Besides my parents, I'd never said those words to anyone else.

You think that's why? His pupils turned to slits. *I've loved you since the moment I saw you on campus. You had my heart from that very first day and will have it for all eternity.*

The depth and sincerity of his words stole my breath. I'd always thought that feeling this way for someone would destroy me, but it made me stronger in so many ways. *I loved you then too, but I was too scared to acknowledge it.* All I'd done was stupidly try to run away.

I know. He kissed me and grinned. *But you needed space and time to catch up. When I was growing up, I spent my entire life knowing there was someone perfect out there for me. You didn't have that opportunity. I'd wait for you all over again because this is worth every ounce of hurt.*

My eyes burned with tears, and the need to mate with him was stronger than ever before. This time, when I guided him inside me, he didn't stop me. We looked into each other's eyes as he slowly entered me.

I rocked on top of him as he filled me entirely. I grabbed the cheap headboard for leverage as I moved faster and faster. His mouth found mine as we moved in time with each other. I slammed him inside me over and over as our bodies gave over to the friction.

Egan's feelings crashed into me like a dam breaking. I felt how much he loved me and the pleasure he felt while inside me. If I thought I'd known how much he cared about me, I'd been wrong. He loved me so much it hurt.

Wanting him to know I felt the same way, my dragon guided me into pushing my emotions toward him. Our breathing and pace increased as we fell over the edge, and an orgasm ripped through us and combined into one. The world shook as everything inside me contracted. I'd never felt pleasure like this before.

We stopped moving, locked in our position. I peppered his face with kisses, giving myself over to him completely.

Something burned between us, and I never wanted it to stop.

A loud knock sounded at the door. The scents were unfamiliar. They had almost a brimstone quality to them.

"Shit," he growled. "I wanted to talk to you before they got here."

"Who?" I asked as an uncomfortable expression flitted across his face. What the hell was going on?

CHAPTER FIVE

Another round of knocking pounded against the door. Whoever waited wasn't very patient.

I climbed to my feet and snatched my clothes off the floor. *Who's out there?*

When I called Dad this morning, he said he'd send a couple of dragons to us. Egan followed my lead and dressed quickly. *I wanted to tell you, but they got here quicker than I anticipated.*

A deep, commanding voice asked from the other side of the door, "Are you going to let us in?"

I glanced down at my clothes and cringed. Great, I was going to meet my very first dragon shifters, outside of Egan, in my pajamas. I wished I'd grabbed clothes from the closet instead of the floor.

Egan finished buttoning his jeans, hurried to the door, and opened it to reveal a gorgeous man and woman.

The man stood close to seven feet tall, only an inch shorter than Egan. He had a similar muscular build but, again, a smidgen smaller than my mate. That was where the similarities ended. The guy had hair long enough that he brushed it back from his face, along with a short beard. He tugged at his tight-fitting black shirt, his gray-green eyes narrowing in annoyance.

The girl was a foot shorter than the guy. She shook her head, her long vanilla-blonde hair brushing her shoulders. "Sleeping in, I see." Her long-sleeved, royal blue shirt hugged her athletic frame, emphasizing her cleavage. Her honey eyes scanned me as the corner of her mouth tipped upward like she found something about me amusing.

The way her face lit up when she looked at Egan, though, almost had me spitting with rage.

She rushed into the room and threw her arms around my mate. My dragon roared, but I pushed her down. My hands clenched into fists, and I forcibly held them at my sides. If I let go of an ounce of self-control, I'd grab the hussy by the hair and yank her off my mate.

My blood boiled at the familiarity between the two, but I reminded myself that Egan had given me no reason to doubt his loyalty. That didn't stop me from feeling self-conscious in my baggy, plaid pajamas next to her.

My mind raced to come up with a witty comment to her very rude remark. "Uh ... yeah." My awkwardness, which had started to disappear after I'd bonded with Egan, hit me full force. I hated that someone had the power to make me feel that way again, adding to my already heightened anger.

Egan returned the hug briefly before wrapping an arm around my waist and pulling me against his side. "She had a rough night. Cut her some slack." His tone was neither friendly nor cold.

"Of course." She chuckled awkwardly and waved a hand at me. "I wasn't thinking. Your parents filled me in on what happened to her. Poor girl couldn't even protect herself."

The overwhelming urge to slap the bitch clawed into me. My dragon wanted to put her in her place, but I didn't know how. I had no control over her, and the girl could kick my ass. Her coming here, looking gorgeous, hugging my mate, and insulting me within a minute of meeting me didn't help. Worse, his parents had told her everything.

On the positive side, I'd experienced feelings like these all my life, and even though the emotions were more intense, I'd learned to keep them in check. If I hadn't, I wouldn't have survived this long.

"Remember, she's only been a dragon for a week." Egan frowned and tightened his hold on my waist. "Jade, this is my friend from childhood, Mindy." He kissed my cheek and smiled proudly at me. "And this is my mate, Jade."

The amount of adoration in his eyes calmed my dragon down ... mostly.

"You're Ladon's son," the guy hovering in the doorway interjected. "It's nice to meet you." He bowed his head slightly.

"And you are?" Egan asked, arching a brow. "You're not from our ... home."

The sound of footsteps heading down the hall alerted us that humans were close by. By the way the man had tensed, he clearly wasn't comfortable here.

Based on what I'd learned, dragon shifters kept to their own race. Even though Egan had been around humans for a little over a semester, he still stood out—or he did to me. He was breathtakingly gorgeous and more of a gentleman than Dad. His slight accent drove me wild and added to his mysterious allure.

The two girls walked past my room, but when they spotted the guy standing at my door, they stopped in their tracks. Obviously, he had the same effect on them as Egan. The new guy didn't affect me like that, but that was because of Egan.

Without acknowledging the girls, the dragon said, "My name is Draco." He shook his head, oblivious to the girls. "But I live close by, and your dad asked me to come."

We needed to shut this conversation down since we had prying ears. If the dragons weren't used to censoring themselves, he could say something outlandish. *Why don't we go into the woods or somewhere discreet to have this conversation?* The dorm room wasn't big enough for three towering dragons and me, and I had a feeling Mindy would jump at the chance to sit next to Egan on my bed. I wasn't sure I had that much self-control.

Yeah, you're right. Egan lifted his chin. "Why don't you two head downstairs? We'll be there in a few minutes."

"You could come down with us while we wait on her." Mindy frowned. "I haven't seen you in a while, so it'd give us time to catch up."

This girl was pushing my buttons. If my dragon hadn't been up in arms, my human side would've been.

"You'll have plenty of time to catch up with us." Egan gestured to the door. "And I want to stay close to Jade. You two head on down."

Her mouth opened like she might say more, but she reconsidered. Her shoulders sagged in defeat as she turned to the door. "Okay. Don't be too long."

The door shut, leaving us alone in the room, and Egan's attention turned to me. His face wrinkled with concern. *Hey, are you okay? Your emotions were all over the place.*

Peachy. I'd meant to keep the sarcasm from my voice, but my disdain bled through. *I almost died last night. I'm still adjusting to my dragon. And now two strange dragons appeared at my front door.* And one of them had a predatory look reserved for Egan. She wanted to devour him and claim him as her own. *How did they know where to find us?*

I planned on telling you before they got here. He placed his forehead against mine. *Then you distracted me, but I still thought we'd have plenty of time before they arrived. Dad sounded concerned, but I didn't realize he was that worried. I told him to look for us here since I refuse to leave your side.*

His words eased some of my anxiety. *Your dad doesn't want you hurt.* And neither did I. I was thankful they'd sent backup. *But Mindy seems to know you very well.* I hated acting this way, but I needed to know. *Did you two date before me?*

What? He lifted his head and stared into my eyes. *God, no.*

There's been no one other than you—ever. I never had the desire to be with anyone else.

But the way she talks to you and looks at you ... Ugh, I felt downright stupid, but I had to be honest with him. *It's like she's very familiar with you.*

We grew up together, and our entire thunder is close. He took my hand and rubbed his thumb along my skin. Some of his anxiety and discomfort floated off him and into me. He sucked in a breath. *Before we realized the severity of our situation, our thunder arranged mateships. When she was born, my parents and her family arranged for us to be together. But when the leaders determined that our numbers were getting too low, they agreed I should try to find my mate and reenter the human world to reintegrate into society. We weren't sure if our fated mates were still out there since we'd been in hiding for so long, but we had to try since our race is dying off. Her parents agreed, effectively terminating the agreement right before I attended Kortright last semester.*

That's why she has that look in her eye. All her life, she'd grown up thinking Egan was hers. Great. *Of course, your parents sent her here right after I put you in danger.* Probably to show Egan how I didn't belong in his world. Here I thought we could get through anything, but his parents' attempt to influence our relationship wasn't a good sign.

You think that's why? Egan's eyes glowed bright yellow. *She's here because she helps younger dragons connect with their animal. They thought she could help you get control faster.*

Are you sure about that? I'd learned in our short time together that Egan thought the best of people. That was one of the traits I loved most about him, but I tended to be more cynical. Our conflicting viewpoints were likely a product of our upbringings, though. *Maybe they hope you two will reconnect.*

Baby, no. Egan kissed me gently. *They're ecstatic that I found you. Besides, I'm the reason you got injured last night, not the other way around. The witch wants to find my thunder and wants to use you to accomplish that. They sent Draco here to protect you while I'm in class and to keep watch at night in case the witch shows up. They can't wait to meet you, I promise. I didn't even think about Mindy, or I would've told you sooner, but it seems like a lifetime ago.*

I'm being stupid, aren't I? Maybe my dragon had more influence than I realized. *It's just ...*

Not stupid at all. His eyes turned to slits as he grinned. *It's natural for us to be protective of our mates, and I won't lie.* His lips touched mine, and his tongue slipped inside my mouth. *It's hot. But it's my job to ensure you don't ever feel that way again.*

Getting lost in his kisses was so easy. My hands wrapped around his neck, and I fisted his hair. He groaned and pulled me closer. His hands slipped under my pants and grabbed my ass, and my body warmed again.

In my mind, there is, and will only ever be you. His words were a promise. *You hold my heart captive, and I love that you do.*

All of my anger and jealousy disappeared as I opened myself up to him. Our minds connected, and my breathing increased. We should stop this. If Egan's parents found out we kept them waiting and why, I wouldn't ever be able to meet them. They'd sent us help, so we needed to figure out our next move.

I stepped back, removing my lips from his. "We'd better get down there. I have a feeling Mindy won't wait long before coming back up here."

"That's true." He licked his lips. "But we will continue this again soon. And when I say soon, I mean like within the hour."

"Maybe, if you behave." I winked at him, enjoying our time alone.

"I love you," he said.

A smile spread across my face. "I love you too."

Forcing my attention to my closet, I pulled out some jeans and an eggplant-colored sweater and changed. Right before walking out the door, I put the broken bracelet in my pocket to keep it close. I didn't want Ollie stealing it from us. He seemed honest, but I didn't want to underestimate him.

In the main lobby, we found Mindy pacing in front of the double doors. She scowled at Egan's and my joined hands.

Annoyance flared inside me. That hadn't taken long.

Egan squeezed my hand lovingly. *It may take her a minute to adjust, but you have nothing to worry about.*

I hadn't considered that she'd probably had her entire life planned out with Egan as her mate, and that had changed in the blink of an eye. Maybe I should cut her some slack.

Draco was leaning against the front desk with his arms crossed and pushed off to follow us out the door.

"Where are we going?" Mindy asked as she walked on Egan's other side.

"Let's go to the woods." Egan turned toward the large brick library. "We'll have more privacy there."

Humans stayed away from the woods, especially with all of the recent deaths. The university discouraged anyone from going out there alone and strongly recommended that groups stay away. They wanted to ensure they weren't liable for anything that might happen to their students.

We walked past the building and the picnic benches and entered the tree line. The pathway narrowed, and Egan quickened our pace so that Draco and Mindy fell behind. We walked a mile deeper before stopping. The sound of scurrying animals was the only noise we heard. We were alone.

Egan cut to the chase. "I expected someone from my own thunder to come here."

"I come from a line of strong fighters and served as our king's protector." Draco didn't sound boastful but rather matter-of-fact. "With the attacks and the witch trying to find your thunder, your parents reached out to thunders across America. It seemed fitting that someone from my family would volunteer to help serve and protect."

"You have a king?" Egan hadn't mentioned the hierarchy, a concept that was foreign to me.

"We did until the royalty went into hiding," Mindy interjected, refusing to be left out.

"If you're the best fighter we have, then that's fine," Egan said as he looked at me. "All I care about is making sure she isn't placed in harm's way again."

Draco nodded curtly. "My goal is that none of us are. We don't need any of us getting injured or tortured into revealing the location of our thunders. That would cause problems for us all."

A branch broke a few yards away, and our group fell silent. Something was near, and I didn't recognize their scent.

CHAPTER SIX

The four of us stood still as we listened. At least four people were closing in on us, and they had the same musky smell as Sadie and other wolves. They were wolf shifters.

Their scent grew stronger although they made no other sounds. They knew how to stay quiet, which would have eliminated them from being human if their smell hadn't tipped me off.

Stay behind me. Egan stepped in front of me to protect me. *There are only four wolf shifters. If they're aggressive, Draco, Mindy, and I will take them out.*

Of course, I wasn't part of that equation. Needing protection was really pissing me off. I'd always relied on myself; then this whole new world had made me feel like that was impossible. But rushing in would only get me hurt and Egan too as he tried to protect me. *I can help, though.*

I know you can. He spoke slowly, weighing his words. *But you almost died not even twenty-four hours ago, and you and your dragon aren't connected yet. These are wolf shifters, and they won't hesitate to use their animal.*

I took deep, steadying breaths. He wasn't being a dick. In fact, he was right. No matter how strong I was in human form, I wasn't supernaturally strong ... yet. That didn't make it any easier, but I'd get there. *Fine, but if anything happens to you, I can't sit back and do nothing*. Just like he wanted nothing to happen to me, I couldn't watch him get hurt.

We'll be fine. Egan reached behind and touched my arm. *When I fought alongside Sadie and the others, I took out twice as many as they did. This should be easy*.

I bit my tongue, not wanting to distract him, but arrogance like that usually didn't play in your favor. That was one reason I managed to kick the guys' asses in martial arts. They thought they could beat me easily.

Mindy scowled at us but was smart enough to keep her mouth shut.

"Who's there?" Draco called out, his voice low and damn scary. "Show yourself, and I won't hurt you."

"Like hell, we won't." Mindy rolled her eyes and spoke loudly like she wanted all the attention on her. "Unless they brought me cake, I'm gonna kick their asses for just sneaking up on us. They have no clue we have as good of a sense of smell as they do."

I wondered if most dragons were this arrogant and if Egan was the exception. Either way, Mindy's attitude wore on my nerves.

"If I were you, I wouldn't be so cocky," a deep, growly voice said from only a couple feet away, but he remained hidden in the trees. "You don't know what you're up against."

Something in his words didn't sit well with me. He didn't sound surprised that we were aware of his presence. *Something's off*. My gut rarely led me astray, and it was yelling at me to run. But we were past the point of escape, especially if they had something up their sleeve.

"Oh, please." Mindy giggled and looked at Egan. "Can you believe these guys?"

Four men stepped into view. They were shorter than our little thunder, except for me—they were about my height. They all were shirtless with defined muscles. They didn't look nearly as strong as

Egan and Draco, but they could hold their own. The one with dark auburn hair had a wolf tattoo on his upper right arm.

Gesturing to the tattoo and lifting a brow, I said before I could clamp my mouth shut, "Is that to remind you you're a wolf?"

The taller of the four bared his teeth, his dark eyes locked on me. "Do you think you're funny?" The wind picked up, blowing through Dickwad's shaggy bluish-black hair.

Okay, maybe I came off as arrogant too. "No, it's just ..."

Egan tensed and cleared his throat. "What do you want?" He lifted his chin. "Weren't you part of Tyler's pack?"

The one who pretended to be Sadie's dad? My inner alarm rang louder.

Yes, Egan said, his voice strained. *They left when the new alpha took his spot.*

"Ah ... you remember." Dickwad wrinkled his nose in disgust. "I remember you too. You killed my brother that night you stormed our pack."

Revenge was very dangerous and made people desperate. They'd go to any lengths necessary to achieve it.

"I only did what I had to do," Egan said with regret. "I didn't enjoy harming anyone."

"I can't say the same for myself." Dickwad smirked, and his eyes darkened. "Hurting you and the girl you're protecting will bring me immense joy."

"You really think you can take on four dragons?" Draco closed some of the distance between us, positioning himself to protect all of us.

Four was a stretch seeing as I couldn't connect with mine.

"Oh, yeah." Dickwad chuckled as he and the auburn-haired man removed their hands from behind their backs, revealing the chained rope they each had balled in their hands. The other two shifters, who looked like twins, bent down and pulled out two tranquilizer guns from the trees they'd stepped from moments ago. The only difference between the two was that one was an inch taller than the other.

They'd obviously come prepared, but they only had two of each item. They hadn't expected to find four of us. Hopefully, that would swing things in our favor, seeing as we didn't have any weapons of our own.

"I'll give you one chance to come forward willingly. We can do this the nice way or the more challenging way." He glanced from Egan to the other two. "Honestly, I'm hoping you choose the challenging way, but I was asked to give you the option."

"You were asked?" That sounded like he wasn't the one calling the shots. This had to be related to the witch.

He ignored my question like I hadn't spoken and released one end of the rope, letting it fall to the ground. I realized it wasn't a rope at all but a fishnet that when held together looked like a garrote.

"You expect a gun and thin rope to work against us?" Mindy flipped her hair over her shoulder. "I mean ..."

"Oh, it'll work all right, but I don't give a damn whether you believe it," Dickwad snarled at her. "You'll soon see what it's capable of." He motioned for the other three men to step closer. "Silence will equate to resistance, so don't think you've got the upper hand."

"Do you really think we'd offer ourselves up to you?" Draco straightened his shoulders, emphasizing the size of his chest. "Don't insult us. Just move on to the action."

He rushed forward and punched the leader in the jaw. Dickwad stumbled back a few steps before stopping. He rubbed his jaw and growled at the dragon warrior.

The other three wolf shifters sprang into action. The taller twin pointed the dart gun at me. Egan charged at him, and his shirt ripped as his dark olive wings sprouted from his back. He spread his wings, shielding me from the guy's view.

I'd expected him to shift into his complete dragon form, but he didn't. He was half-beast, half-man, and it blew my mind. I hadn't known that was possible.

He linked. *Duck.*

Refocusing on the threat, I dropped to the ground. The tranquilizer dart buzzed over my head, narrowly missing me.

Egan sacked the guy, and they tumbled to the forest floor. The auburn-haired guy sprang into action, slipping the fishnet wire around my mate's neck.

Oh, hell no. No one hurt my mate.

I jumped to my feet and ran to Egan's aid. Draco was still fighting Dickwad, and Mindy had vanished, so I was Egan's only hope.

I'd only taken a few steps when the guy with the other tranquilizer pointed the gun at me again. I knew I had to do something before he fired. At this close range, it would be a miracle if he missed.

Time slowed as I watched the shorter twin pull the trigger. I couldn't reach Egan to help him get out of the wire since I couldn't connect with my dragon, making me that much slower than everyone else here.

Something solid slammed into my side, knocking me to the ground. I spun around, ready to attack the assailant, when Draco's face came into view. His jaw was clenched, and he quickly scanned me for injuries.

"I'm fine." I turned to Egan. "But he's not."

The auburn-haired guy tightened the metal fishnet around Egan's throat, and my mate's face turned red.

"Dammit," Draco hissed and stumbled back, his clothes ripping. Navy blue scales covered his body as he grew larger, shifting from man to complete beast. He threw his head back and roared.

Under normal circumstances, this would not be ideal. We weren't that deep in the woods, but our lives hung in the balance.

"Shoot him!" Dickwad yelled as he focused on Draco. "We need to knock him out."

I stumbled to my feet and noticed that the shorter twin who had been aiming at me was transfixed by Draco's full-body shift. His mouth hung open.

This might be my only chance to knock one of them out. I hunkered close to the ground, staying low and quiet. As long as I didn't make any loud noises, maybe he'd stay focused elsewhere.

My hand hit my jeans pocket, and my fingertips brushed against the outline of the bracelet. Shit, I'd forgotten all about it. If it worked, I could get us some reinforcements.

I placed my hand firmly over the bracelet in my pocket. I wasn't sure I could mind link with jewelry, so I spoke very low. "Ollie, we need you here now. Bring the wolves and vampires with you."

"The girl," Dickwad grunted.

The shorter twin with the gun pivoted toward me and fired, but Draco crashed between us, causing the dart to bounce off his scales like he was bulletproof.

"What the—" the guy started, but Draco bit the guy's arm and jerked his head, throwing the wolf shifter several yards away.

I ran behind Draco, intent on getting to Egan. I couldn't let anything happen to him. *I'm coming,* I promised into our bond as I raced toward him.

Mindy hid behind a tree several feet away. She ran away, abandoning us to danger. That seemed fitting since she'd only come here for her own motives. The bitch had arrived here and tried to lay claim to a mated dragon. From what I'd seen of the supernatural world, mates were treasured across all races.

Egan linked, but his voice was weak, even internally. *No, stay back.*

If he thought that would discourage me, it did the opposite. He was fading fast, and I had to get to him. Draco was already fighting off the other two idiots, which hopefully meant I had the advantage against the auburn-haired guy beating up on Egan.

He had Egan in front of him as he leaned back against the tree for leverage. Egan's wings weren't any help against the way the guy had positioned himself behind him.

I had two options. I could either go under Egan's wings or around them. Around would take much longer but would be more effective. But when Egan's eyes rolled back into his head, that made my decision.

I couldn't let him pass out. If he did, the others would have leverage over us.

Trying not to overthink the situation, I pushed my legs as fast as they would go. I couldn't risk freezing and him getting hurt or worse. *Spread your legs.* I hoped he was conscious enough to do it.

Thankfully, his legs moved a few inches apart, but they shook. It wasn't much, but I'd make do. *Lift up as high as you can when I say go.* I said a little prayer, hoping what I was about to do wasn't stupid. I could wind up hurting him really badly instead of the dumbass behind him.

When I was only a few feet away, I yelled, *Go!*

Egan moved upward, barely, and I kicked right between his legs. I dropped down as my foot went forward, angling to hit the auburn-haired guy in the nuts. I didn't give a damn if it was a cheap shot as long as he released Egan.

"Aaagh," the auburn-haired guy groaned as he dropped the rope to cup his family jewels with both hands.

My mate fell to his knees, taking deep breaths as he rubbed the red marks cutting into his skin.

I snatched the net from the ground, ready to return the favor to the douchebag who had hurt my mate. I approached him slowly, wanting him to anticipate the moment.

He tried to stand but fell back to the ground. His face turned red from the pain, and he leaned over as his stomach heaved. Any other time, I would've laughed, but we were still in a huge fight we possibly couldn't win.

I hoped the asshole did puke so I could kick him in it. He deserved to wallow in his own waste for their unjustified attack against us.

Each step I took, he countered by stepping backward, but in his current state, I was much faster. I released one end, letting the wire net dangle from my fingers, careful not to let the thin wire cut into my skin.

"Jade, watch out!" Egan yelled hoarsely.

CHAPTER SEVEN

Heart pumping faster at the panic in Egan's voice, I jerked my head to the right as Dickwad lunged at me. His eyes narrowed. He clutched the end of the net and swung it over his head like a lasso.

Great, I was going up against the Lone Ranger. It was fitting since we were in the small Southern town of Hidden Ridge, Tennessee.

All I wanted or needed was for this thing to be over.

Draco was locked in combat with the twins. The taller one kept pointing the gun at him without pulling the trigger like he was playing chess. He was being more strategic than his shorter counterpart, who had turned his focus on me.

Getting me out of a net would be much easier than trying to protect me while I was knocked out. I dropped to the ground, but the shifter was too damn fast.

"No!" Egan screamed as Dickwad countered my attack. He released one end of the rope so the net spread out around my body.

The wire cut into my skin, and I cried out in pain. It felt like something was flowing through my blood. My skin wasn't burning;

rather, it felt like the magic was inside me. But with each jerk, the wire cut deeper, increasing my pain. My breathing turned shallow, and my eyes watered.

A huge cocky grin filled Dickwad's face as he faced Egan. "Your mate's dragon is getting fried as we speak."

No, the wolf shifter was goading my mate to make him reckless. *Don't listen to him. I'm fine.* I held my whimpers in, refusing to give the enemy any more pleasure in my capture and trying to prevent Egan from freaking out. The nasty sulfuric stench of a lie, though, wafted around me.

Are you lying to me? Egan's pupils turned to slits, but the raw skin around his neck hadn't healed. *I can feel your pain through our bond.*

That had to be why the auburn-haired guy had tightened the wire around Egan's neck: not only to cut off his oxygen and leave him impaired but also to inflict a grievous injury that hurt the dragon.

Rage coursed through me, and I welcomed anything that would distract me from my pain.

Egan stood on wobbly legs as he gathered his bearings. He took deep, rapid breaths to speed up his recovery. Even if the wire didn't have a magical effect on us, an injury like that would take more than a few minutes to heal. If he attacked now, he'd only get hurt worse. *You need to recover. Don't do anything hasty.* I tried to make him listen to reason.

There's no way in hell I'm doing nothing. I can't let you stand there in pain. He stumbled toward the leader. "Let her go. Now."

"Or what?" Dickwad chuckled. "You can barely stand."

If Egan wouldn't act rationally, I'd do what I had to do. "Yet you're standing close to me." I tried to anger him. "You're so brave. A real alpha-type leader." Disdain dripped from each word.

"What did you say?" Dickwad turned to me, his nostrils flaring.

I'd hit the nerve I'd been aiming for, but maybe I wasn't behaving super logically either. Egan and I were determined to take the brunt of Dickwad's wrath to protect each other.

A loud *kak* sounded, alerting me that Ollie was on his way. I'd been worried that the bracelet wouldn't work, but this was a testament to the witch's power. At least, her magic was working in our favor.

I yanked on the thin wire net, trying to get out, but I couldn't tell the top from the bottom. It reminded me of the day at the beach when I'd come so close to drowning. Dad and I had been out in the ocean, jumping waves. He'd held my hand as a large wave had crashed against us, and then a riptide sucked me away from him, pulling me into deep waters where I couldn't tell which way was up. My lungs had screamed for air, and even at the young age of eight, I'd known there was no way I would survive.

Then a strong arm had wrapped around my waist and pulled me to the surface. A boy no more than a year older than me had saved me. I often thought back on that time, sometimes with longing. Not only had it been the last day I'd spent with my father alive and a mom who was functional, but I'd also found someone I clicked with. I'd never found that again—until Egan.

His name brought me back to the present, and I watched my mate attempt to shift into his dragon form, but it was like his dragon couldn't surface.

"Wow, I hadn't expected for it to work so well." The asshole chuckled as he leaned back on his heels, watching my mate struggle. The way he took so much pleasure in watching us suffer spoke volumes about the kind of person he was. "It's entertaining to witness the supposedly strongest shifter fail. Maybe that's the real reason you hid all these years. You couldn't hack it living among other supernaturals."

"Or maybe they had to get away from the stupidity of arrogant jerks like you. After all, your breed likes to sniff each other's buttholes to pass the time."

His jaw clenched. "Say it again. I dare you."

Really? He wanted me to say it again. "You like to smell butt—"

The guy dropped the net and charged at me.

Dammit, Jade. Egan tried rushing toward me, but he was moving slower than me, which revealed how beaten he was.

Dickwad punched me in the jaw, and my head snapped back. My entire body sagged to the ground. Pain coursed inside me and down my jaw.

"You stupid bitch!" the guy yelled as he drew his foot back.

Right before his foot could connect with my side, Egan slid in front of me, blocking the blow. As his back touched my front, the net's magic sprung forward, and Egan twitched in pain.

Egan! I yelled through our bond like he couldn't hear me otherwise. I yanked and pulled at the wire. It sliced into my skin as I desperately tried to get free. I tried scooting back so the net wouldn't touch him, but my body refused to budge.

"Look how pathetic the two of you are." Dickwad laughed loudly, pacing in front of us, and pulled a knife from his hip. "When the wire breaks the skin, a spell enters your bloodstream for the next several hours. It weakens your dragon and makes you easy to hurt or ..." His face contorted into a smirk. "... kill." He shrugged like either option was no big deal.

The breeze carried in our wolf shifter friends' scent, giving me a second wind. They were on their way, and we needed all the help we could get. I kept my face a mask of indifference, not wanting to give away that backup was arriving.

Within seconds, his nose wrinkled as he smelled the oncoming threat.

"We've got more arriving!" Dickwad shouted and turned to the taller twin fighting Draco, and then he glanced over at the auburn-haired guy as he climbed to his feet. The shorter twin remained crumpled on the ground several yards away.

Draco roared as he yanked the gun from the shifter's hands then dropped it. He lifted one enormous foot and smashed the gun into pieces.

"No!" the twin yelled.

The warrior dragon squared up to Dickwad, who was only a few feet away from Egan and me.

Dickwad's eyes locked on the center of Egan's chest. Desperation took hold, and he charged at us.

Egan groaned as I felt him tug at the connection flowing between us.

I'm sorry, but I need to shift. He tugged on our bond harder. *He'll kill us before Sadie and the others get here, and with my dragon in such a weakened state, I need to borrow magic from you.*

Take what you need. I would never turn him down if he was doing it to protect himself. *You never have to ask.* I couldn't handle losing him. He meant way too much to me.

He funneled more and more power from me, but his body didn't shift any more than it already had. His wings spread out, shielding me from the leader's view, but he was sputtering.

I glanced below his wing to see what was going on. The guy was way too close for comfort. *Egan! Move!*

The words must have resonated with him because his head jerked upward, and he turned, wrapping his arms and wings around me. He rolled us out of the way just in time.

Dickwad croaked as he swung the knife, but the weapon caught nothing but air, and he stumbled.

Paws pounded the ground as Sadie and the others reached us. A black wolf ran between two trees, heading straight for us. A light-pink-furred wolf, a vibrant red one, and a dark brown wolf ran right behind the black one, who had to be Donovan.

They'd arrived in the nick of time.

Smoke trickled from Draco's nose as he roared. He flapped his wings, rising into the air, and he flew over Egan and me. He used his feet to claw into Dickwad's shoulders and wedge his talons between his shoulder blades.

Donovan ran past us and charged at the auburn-haired guy, who was picking up the second net from the ground.

The shifter lifted the net to catch the wolf, but Donovan jumped, lunging for the guy's neck. Donovan's teeth sank into the shifter's throat, and he ripped it out.

My stomach roiled, and vomit surged up my throat as blood, tissue, and skin flung in every direction.

A sweet scent arrived as Lillith and Katherine joined us.

"Egan, move." Lillith pushed my mate out of the way and searched for the end of the rope. She found it in seconds.

"Be careful." I swallowed the rising bile and turned away from the fight. The wolves and Draco were fighting, and we had the advantage now. The scent of blood didn't help my queasy stomach, so I focused on Egan's and the vampires' scents. "The wire is spelled, and I'm not sure if it's limited to dragons." Lumping myself in that category was still strange. Maybe when I finally shifted, it wouldn't feel so foreign.

"Got it," Lillith said as she worked diligently on the net.

Katherine stood protectively in front of us, keeping an eye on the fighting. "The fight's almost done, so we're in the clear."

Ollie flew down and landed beside me. He pecked at the wire, creating a small hole in the net.

"Holy shit." Lillith stopped and watched him with fascination. "No wonder you could peck through eyes and people's throats."

My stomach convulsed, and there was no holding it back anymore. The vivid images of the guy's throat, Amber's neck, and the poor girl's eyes flashed through my mind, and I lost it.

I turned my head away at the last second, and my stomach emptied all over the ground. Luckily, I didn't have much in it, so it was mostly bile.

Egan turned to me, concern in his eyes. "We need to get her back to the dorm."

I wiped my mouth with the back of my hand, and the wires cut into my lips. The stinging took hold again from the fresh wound.

Ignoring my pain and upset stomach, I noticed that Ollie had already pecked a decent-sized hole through the net. I gently pulled the wire toward me, and Egan shifted beside me, helping me move the wire around my body.

"Be careful," I reminded him even though we were moving methodically.

We both knew what happened when our skin got nicked. Within minutes, I climbed out of the hole as Sadie and her pack rushed into the tree line.

"Is everything okay?" I scanned the area for another threat, but I didn't hear or smell anything. The taller twin, Dickwad, and the auburn-haired wolf lay dead on the ground.

"They're going to shift back into human form," Katherine explained as she turned to the shifter who'd gotten knocked out first. "These guys are from Tyler's old pack."

"Yeah, I know." Egan sighed and pulled me into his arms. "They left that night right after the fight and before the new alpha had time to step up."

My stomach rolled again, and I closed my eyes. I buried my face into his strong chest and breathed in his unique scent to block out the blood.

"Thank God you came to help." Mindy's high-pitched voice was irritating. "Here, Draco. I rushed to get you your change of clothes when I saw you shift. I figured they would come in handy."

Was that really how she was going to justify hiding and letting the three of us risk our lives? I pulled back as Draco took his clothes and rushed into the woods like Sadie and the others had.

I made a huge mistake by pulling back because I again saw the dead bodies and blood all over the ground. Egan pulled me back into his warm, safe embrace.

"That one's alive," Egan said. "Let's take him farther into the woods and find out everything he knows."

That was when the realization sank in. We were at war, and we didn't know who we were up against. We needed answers, but if I was struggling with what I saw here, I might not be able to stomach what came next.

CHAPTER EIGHT

Egan's arms remained securely wrapped around me, but I needed to pull away to provide the illusion of strength. No one else here was having this issue. I nuzzled my head against his hard pecs. "Being a newbie sucks."

His shoulders shook with laughter. "Should I be offended? You are in my arms."

"God, no." I was so glad my head was still buried. My cheeks burned, and if Lillith saw, she'd make things worse. "It's just the gore surrounding us."

"I wouldn't say 'no issue,'" Katherine said gently. "None of us enjoy looking at it."

"Yeah, but I'm the only one who puked." It served me right for wishing the one guy would puke. Maybe karma was real.

"It's good to see your fated mate is so strong and durable," Mindy said with a chuckle. "Not everyone is programmed to be part of this life."

Oh, hell no.

Anger burned my blood worse than whatever magic coursed

through it. I stepped from Egan's protective embrace and stared the bitch down. "Oh, I'm sorry, is running off and hiding the right way?" I'd considered talking to Egan about what Mindy had pulled to see how he thought we should handle her abandoning us, but she'd helped me make that decision all by my lonesome.

"What?" Mindy's laughter turned high-pitched and nervous.

Lillith popped her hip and stared the gorgeous dragon shifter down. "You're sticking with the clueless act? We all saw you hiding over there when we rushed here to fight." Lillith pointed to a section of trees I'd seen her hiding in just minutes ago.

"You do realize the wolves would've found you." Katherine tilted her head, looking unimpressed. "They could smell you, just like the rest of us."

"There's a good reason for it." She crossed her arms, obviously displeased by the vampires calling her out. She stomped and whined, "Who the hell are these people, Egan? They can't just come here and accuse me like this."

"They're Jade's and my friends." Egan wrapped an arm around my waist, but a small, disappointed frown marred his face. "You know, the kind that would risk their lives to protect the people they love."

"Egan, if you had been in real danger—"

"I was, and so was Jade." He lifted his chin, looking down his nose at her. "You're supposed to protect the people in your thunder, and you abandoned us."

"She's not even ..." She took a deep breath and closed her eyes for a second. Then her bottom lip quivered, but there was no remorse on her face or in her voice as she said, "You're right. I'm sorry. You know I'm not trained for battle; I'm more of a teacher. I froze."

"You did a whole lot more than freeze," Roxy said as Sadie and their mates stepped into the pathway. "You ran. Who the hell are you and the other dragon anyway?"

"The more proper question is: Who are all of you?" Mindy

surveyed our friends and fluffed her hair. "Besides, I'm Egan's ... close friend." She gazed at my mate possessively, and my dragon roared.

At least, my dragon and I were on the same page about her.

"Close friend?" Sadie asked slowly. "What does she mean by that?"

"We're from the same thunder." Egan stiffened. *I'm so sorry. I never dreamed she'd act this way.*

It's not your fault. He wasn't responsible for her actions, but I'd be putting her in her place soon.

"Oh, we're more than that." She smiled sweetly at him. "I'm sure he hasn't told you—"

Scratch that. I'd be putting her in her place right now. "When you were born, your parents agreed to an arranged mateship that is now over." I wouldn't let this girl think she had a chance with my mate or that he might be hiding their arrangement from me. "Yeah, he told me." I returned her sweet smile, batting my lashes.

Roxy walked over to stand beside me. Staring straight at the girl, she said with disgust clear in her voice, "I'm betting since she knows all about you and that we were the ones fighting beside them, not hiding, that should put things in perspective. If it isn't obvious that you're a lot less important than you think you are, we'll have to add *stupid* to your ever-growing list of attributes."

The fact I'd found people who had my back, no matter what, dumbfounded me. I would never trade them for anything, even for a group of asshole dragons.

Something unreadable crossed Mindy's face as she waited for Egan to step in, but he didn't help her. After a few moments, she scratched the back of her neck and waved her hand. "You're right. I'm coming off like a bitch." She licked her bottom lip and smiled brightly. "I'm sorry. I was overwhelmed. I'm glad Egan has found such good friends who have his back."

"Unlike some people here," Lillith said lowly but loud enough for Mindy to hear. She turned her back to the dragon and glanced at us. "Is everyone okay?"

"Yeah." Donovan nodded and took Sadie's hand. "I can't get over that they were from Tyler's pack."

"I don't know why they'd be working with the witch." Sadie shook her head like she was trying to make sense of it. "As far as I know, they have nothing against dragons."

"I wouldn't be so sure." Egan's shoulders sagged. "Apparently, I killed the dark-haired guy's brother, so maybe it was revenge."

"Maybe." Axel shrugged. "But guys like them just want something to fight against. They don't care what as long as it gains them an advantage."

"Aw, my mate is so smart sometimes." Roxy walked over and kissed his lips.

"Sometimes?" Axel arched an eyebrow. "Just sometimes?"

"You're making this awkward for everyone." She grimaced as her hazel eyes lightened with humor.

"Ugh," the shorter twin groaned from a few yards away.

Draco reappeared from the woods, his hair a little wild, adding to his allure. He nodded at our wolf shifter friends and vampires. "I'm glad you came to help. I was getting worried until you came to our assistance." His accent was a tad thicker than Mindy's and Egan's.

"Hey, you were protecting our friends, so we should be thanking you," Sadie said, her eyes on the twin as he stirred. "Why don't we all catch up and get him situated?"

"Sounds like an excellent idea." Draco marched over to the enemy wolf, picked him up, and threw him over his shoulder like the guy weighed nothing.

Egan linked as he brushed my arm with his hand. *Why don't you head back to the dorm room? I can get Katherine to go back with you.*

Katherine was the only one nice enough not to argue. None of the other girls would willingly walk away, meaning I wouldn't either. Sure, my stomach might not be as strong as theirs, but I'd get there. *No.* I almost said I was fine then remembered he'd smell my lie. I didn't need to give him more ammunition to try to make me leave. *I want to stay here with you. Others may attack.*

Which is more reason for you to go. He kissed my forehead. *Seeing you hurt like that ...*

Remember, you won't be able to shift back into a dragon for a while. I gestured to his wings, now held close to his body. *You aren't at full capacity either. Besides, what if they attack me back at the dorm while you all are preoccupied?* That line of reasoning was difficult for him to argue against.

You're right. He tensed beside me. *You're in danger either way. At least, with you here, I can make sure you're okay.*

I felt bad. I hadn't meant to stress him, but my gut told me to stay next to him where I belonged.

Draco marched off into the woods, without looking to see if we were following. He expected to be obeyed.

"Well, okay then." Roxy snorted and walked deeper into the woods.

I followed close behind, eager to get away from the three dead bodies, and almost ran into Roxy, who'd stopped abruptly. She spun around, wearing a huge smirk on her face, and stared right at someone behind me. "Where do you think you're going?"

As I spun around, my gaze landed on Mindy.

Mindy stilled and huffed. "Uh, with all of you."

"Don't you know that the person who hides has to clean up the mess?" Roxy gestured to the three bodies across the pathway. "We don't need innocent humans passing through here and seeing this. I know you're a dragon and don't understand how this works, but suspicion is *no bueno* for us."

Mindy's mouth dropped. "But ..."

"Great. So glad you agree." Lillith crossed her arms, staring the girl down. "Unless you don't want to be a team player."

"No ..." She straightened her shoulders. "I ..."

"It would be appreciated." Egan took my hand and tugged me toward Draco. "Besides, we all need to be there to talk to the wolf shifter."

"Fine," she growled, unhappy with her assignment.

I glanced up in the trees and found Ollie perched, watching us. "Will you alert us if Mindy is in trouble?" Even if I didn't care about her, I didn't wish death on her. Maybe today would be the wake-up call she needed.

The bird *kakked* back and bobbed his head up and down.

I couldn't complain about anything he'd done so far, but he could be playing along to disarm me. I shouldn't let my guard down and leave the bracelet where he could get to it easily.

As we walked deeper into the woods, Egan told both groups why the dragons were here and caught Draco up on all of the craziness of life the last month or so. Reliving all the deaths and my own near-death experience wasn't fun, but I forced myself to push past it.

We were a few miles farther from campus and in an area humans didn't frequent. I had to give it to this group, they really went out of their way to ensure their existence remained a secret.

Draco dropped the shifter and stood menacingly in front of him. We didn't have anything to tie him with, so the guys formed a circle around him, making sure there was no way he could get away.

The girls surrounded the guys, so if he escaped the first wall, he'd have to get through us next. We couldn't afford him getting away until we got information out of him.

Stay close to me. Egan linked as he stepped back, his back brushing against my chest. *And warn me if you sense something strange.*

"Hey." Draco slapped the twin in the face. "Wake up."

"Dad?" The shifter groaned, his eyes fluttering open. After a second, he stiffened and sat up straight. He turned his head one way then the other, taking in our group of nine. "Where the hell am I?" No one answered, and his expression changed from one of confusion to immense pain. "Where's my brother?" he yelled.

I hadn't expected to enjoy this interrogation, but watching him realize his brother was dead tugged at my heartstrings. I understood each emotion that flashed across his face because I'd lived through the same thing when I'd found out my dad had died. That day, I hadn't just lost him but my mom too.

"You attacked us," Draco rasped. "Did you expect us not to protect ourselves?"

"No." He shook his head hard. "This can't be real. We were told this would be easy."

"Someone lied." Egan leaned toward him. "And left out important pieces of information."

"We watched the other dorm and knew the wolves weren't out." He chewed on his bottom lip. "We thought it'd be just you and her. We were told to attack before more dragons arrived."

"You obviously underestimated how long it would take them to arrive." Sadie stepped between Donovan and Axel. "Why are you after them?"

"Do you think I'd tell you?" he spat and snarled. "You killed my entire family."

"If your family had been on the right side, they'd be alive." Sadie's light blue eyes glowed. "You sided with a man who killed anything that got between him and what he thought he was entitled to rule."

"Who decides which side is wrong and right?" The twin's face turned pink. "You?" He laughed hard. "And you think you're better than Tyler?"

The gravity of the situation hit me—this was Sadie's fight, and everyone was letting her take the lead. This person was tied to the pack she'd been raised in. This guy hated us because of our alliance with her.

"I never claimed to be better." She kept her gaze locked on him, the alpha wolf inside her rising. "But I'm not a dictator who hurts others. No person should rule over the entire supernatural race. No one can make the best decisions for all. You have to see that?"

"Maybe." The guy lifted his chin defiantly. "But I don't give a shit," he spat. "I'll always side with those who want to hurt you and anyone close to you. I only want to pay the same respect you did to me and my family."

My worst fears were confirmed. This wouldn't be easy. He wouldn't spill his guts and plead for us to spare him. He would fight us tooth and nail.

Sadie lifted a hand, a pink glow filling her palm.

Knowing what came next, I closed my eyes instinctively.

CHAPTER NINE

I'd expected the twin to yell or cry, so when I only heard animals scurrying around, I was caught off guard. The twin should have been screaming for his life.

I opened my eyes slowly, afraid of what I might find.

Sadie stood in the same pose. The breeze ruffled her rose-gold hair, and her fae magic pooled on her palm. Her magic was the same color as her hair, which made sense now that I thought about it. I usually thought of her as just a wolf, but with her fae half in action, she was mesmerizing.

"Go ahead," the twin sneered. "Hurt me."

Maybe she was building up his anticipation. *Why is she waiting?* I'd rather get this over with than draw it out. I hated the thought of torturing someone, but maybe this was how things worked in their world.

She's at war with herself. Egan reached behind him and brushed his fingers along my arm. *She doesn't like the thought of hurting someone.*

"Do it," the twin screamed, as if desperate for the pain. "Hurt me."

I understood his plea. He'd lost his twin brother. Physical pain would numb the emotional toil tormenting him.

"No." Sadie lowered her hand and inhaled sharply. "I won't do it."

"We need answers," Draco said, his brows furrowed. "If you won't, I will."

"I understand, but if we want to be different from our enemies, we must act differently." Sadie bit her bottom lip and looked at her mate.

Donovan placed a hand on her shoulder and said, "If my mate doesn't think this is right, it's not."

My respect for her increased. She'd made a hard call. "Even if we tortured him, he might not tell us anything." I had a feeling he'd rather die and join the rest of his family in Hell than help us.

"Besides, it's not like we can let him go or hold him captive." We were at a university and couldn't keep taking hostages. Someone would get suspicious. We were already reassigning rooms because of Ollie.

"You're right." Egan pursed his lips. "And we're too much at risk already by staying here. Vera and the others aren't slowing down their attacks, despite humans being around."

"Unfortunately, going back to our thunder isn't an option either." Draco rubbed his hands together. "Not while they can track you two."

I felt horrible since my blood was causing the issue.

Guilt is wafting off you like a broken dam. Egan angled toward me. *There's no reason for you to feel guilty.*

That was what people said to loved ones even when they were to blame. I hadn't chosen to feel guilty, but I couldn't hide the truth. "I'm sorry I've made this whole situation worse."

"You have not." Katherine shook her head. "If anything, you got dragged into this because of us."

None of them looked at me with resentment, which shocked me. They should have been angry at me like I was at myself.

Sadie pressed her lips together. "This would still be happening if you weren't in the picture. The witch would've found another way. You are not responsible."

"Aw, how touching." The twin's mouth twisted into a nasty grin. "Even if they're right, it doesn't matter. You're mated to the only dragon anyone knows about, and between the group that's desperate to find the thunders and the ones who joined them because of what you did to our true alpha and our families, you're all going to die. Every single one of you. And I hope you suffer until your dying breath." He laughed maniacally.

A chill racked my body. This wasn't normal. People shouldn't cherish the thought of others dying, especially tragically. The more I learned about these people who were loyal to a sadistic leader, the clearer it became that they were monsters in every sense of the word.

"You're right. We can't stay here. We could always go back home." Lillith rubbed her hands together. "We'll be out of the way there."

"No, they'll find Mom's pack and your nest. We can't have that. We have to protect them too." Sadie glanced at her pack members as they mind linked together.

I'd learned that wolves could mind link with their entire pack, whereas dragons could only link with their fated mates. Egan had explained that for each strength a race had, it came with a weakness. They believed that because dragons were stronger, they couldn't connect with the entire thunder. Whereas wolves might be weaker, but connecting with their pack gave them an edge. Nature had found a way to balance the races and put them on equal footing.

"We go back to our home." Donovan nodded as the four of them had come to an agreement. "Everyone already knows where we live, and we have a decent-sized pack that will protect us when they do come to hunt us down."

Having a pack helping us sounded amazing, but that also meant more people could get hurt. How many deaths would I have to witness over the next weeks, months, or even years? I had a feeling I didn't want to know the answer.

"What about the humans?" Hopefully, there weren't too many close by. The thought of innocent people, who knew nothing about our war, getting pulled into the conflict seemed unjustly cruel. It was one thing to know what you were up against, but to be clueless ... that didn't seem right.

"Most packs live out in supernatural suburbs," Roxy informed. "There aren't any humans within miles of our pack neighborhood."

Egan faced them. "Are you sure? That would put your entire pack in danger."

"Egan," Sadie said gently, "you, Jade, Lillith, and Katherine are part of our pack as much as any of those wolf shifters. The vampires and you fought right beside us. It'll be nice to return the favor."

"Nice?" Axel wrinkled his nose. "I wouldn't use that word, but everyone is coming. We protect our own."

For me to be lumped in as part of their family broke the last remaining walls that had been partially standing inside. These people had torn down every self-defense mechanism I'd put in place over the years in less than two months.

"What are you going to do with me?" The twin rubbed the back of his neck. "Kill me?" His words sounded hopeful.

I'd been there once or twice. I wasn't sure if I'd been too much of a coward or too strong to kill myself. Maybe somewhere between the two. But if I'd thought someone had been willing to kill me, I would've begged them to do it in an instant.

Sadie smirked. "Worse. You're coming with us."

"What?" His mouth dropped. "You've got to be kidding me."

"Does that look like the face of someone who's joking?" Roxy asked, reaching around Sadie and waving her hand in front of her face. "I can't see it, but I'm sure it's her normal 'I mean business' face. You know, the one where her mouth is set and her eyes are narrowed as she stares you down."

I looked at Sadie's face and had to say Roxy had the description locked tight. "Yeah, that's the face."

"See." Roxy patted herself on the chest. "I know my bestie's signature look."

"I'm hoping I am welcomed to tag along too?" Draco crossed his arms, making his chest look mammoth. "I need to stay close to those two. I promised Egan's dad."

"Of course." Donovan gestured to the twin. "You protected Egan and Jade, so you're officially welcome."

"Good." He nodded. "If we're going to get going, we better move before it gets much later. The fewer people who see, the better."

"There's a spot through the woods we can pick you up at so we don't have to worry about students seeing him at the university." Lillith pointed northwest. "It's the same place we used when we escaped from the university last semester."

Axel frowned. "How come I don't remember that?"

"Because you and Donovan were almost drained by a vampire, and Sadie and I bit you, saving your lives." Roxy lifted a brow. "You weren't very coherent."

"I hate to bring this up, but Ollie and Mindy need to go too." Egan glanced at me from the corner of his eye.

The fact he wanted her to come with us irritated the hell out of me. "Why? She didn't even help us fight."

"She's right," Lillith said. "We wouldn't be missing much by leaving her behind."

"Dad sent her to help Jade connect with her dragon." Egan lifted a hand in surrender. "It's not that I want her with us, but if she can help Jade embrace her dragon like she does with the younger dragons in surrounding thunders, she'd be an asset."

"I'll keep an eye on her," Draco reassured the others. "I'll make sure she doesn't pull something like that again."

"Then we better get going." Sadie looked at Draco. "Do you need to get your car?"

"No, we flew here." Draco grabbed the wolf shifter's arms. "We'll need a ride or directions to your place."

"We have a van," Katherine offered. "You can ride with us."

Lillith pointed at Draco and the twin. "Why don't you take these two, along with Ollie and Dragon Girl, over to the pickup location, and I'll bring the van over."

"Sounds like a plan." Katherine took off back toward Mindy and the falcon with Draco following right behind, dragging the twin along.

"Please, just kill me," the twin begged as he tried to plant his feet. "I might as well be dead. She'll try even harder to find you with me in tow."

"She?" Draco arched an eyebrow. "Who is she?"

The twin smirked and shrugged.

He was baiting us.

Lilith waved him off. "He's trying to distract us, which means he's stalling. We need to get out of these woods. He probably means the witch anyway."

"You're right. And either way, *she* will attack us," Draco growled as he spun around, throwing the shifter over his shoulder. "And good, the more people she sends our way, the more information we can get from them and see what kind of numbers we're up against."

"No!" the guy screamed and hit the dragon's back futilely. "Stop."

Come on. Egan touched my arm as we made our way to one of the school buildings. *Let's get our stuff and get out of here.*

I noticed that he was leading me away from the dead bodies, but I didn't put up a fight. I'd seen enough death to last a lifetime and watching Draco kill the twin was something I'd rather not witness. Instead, I followed behind, enjoying the touch of his skin.

I WAS PACKED and sitting on the edge of my bed in the dorm room, waiting on the others to gather everything they needed. I'd packed up my entire life in less than ten minutes. It should have bothered me, but in these types of situations, it was ideal. Except it would've been nice to have had something to preoccupy me longer. Sadie's aunt, Naida, stood in the center of the room, going through all of the witch's items.

"Where have you been?" I hadn't spent much time with her, and she hadn't been a huge fan of mine at the beginning. Ever since Egan and I had cemented our bond, she'd vanished. According to Egan, that wasn't very strange for her.

Apparently, she and Sadie had stumbled across each other last semester at Kortright. That seemed to happen a lot at this university.

"My kingdom is having issues with my eldest brother coming back." She pushed her teal hair over her shoulder, and her matching eyes found me. Her hair contrasted against her golden-pink skin, and her white shirt emphasized her beauty.

"Sadie's dad?" If memory served me right, Tyler had hidden him for over eighteen years in a basement or hidden room.

"Yes." She took a few steps closer to me.

She was the same height as me when I was sitting. I hadn't realized how petite she was until now. "From what I've heard, I thought your people loved him."

"They did and do," she said as she sat at Vera's desk. She opened the drawers and dug inside.

Wow, getting information from her was difficult, but sitting with her in silence was more uncomfortable. "What's the problem?" I hated when people created small talk, but in all fairness, I wanted to get to know her better.

She huffed and paused her snooping. "My younger brother was sworn in as king since we all believed Rook was dead. But, by fae rules, Rook was destined to ascend the throne."

That could be problematic. "Does Rook want it?"

"No, he never did. But fae are sticklers for rules." Naida shrugged, appearing almost human.

I probably wasn't helping, but I hated the look on her face. "It sounds like you dodged a bullet and that fate intervened by allowing your other brother to take the crown."

She glanced at the ceiling and rubbed her chin. "I hadn't thought of it like that, but you could be right. Maybe you are meant for this world after all."

That was a huge compliment coming from her. Maybe she was warming up to me. Maybe.

Egan's voice popped inside my head. *I'm on my way to get your things. Everyone else is loading up the cars.*

I can meet you out there. I didn't want him to think he had to carry my stuff too. I loved that he was thoughtful, but I didn't want to become a nuisance.

No, please. Not after what we just went through, he begged.

He'd shifted back to fully human not that long ago. I couldn't fault him for being nervous.

"I take it he's on the way?" Naida asked.

"Yeah, how did you know?"

"You broke out into a huge smile. Sadie does that too." Naida shut the drawer and stood. "I am glad that Egan found you. He's a good guy and needs someone beside him for what comes next."

That sounded ominous. "What do you mean?"

The door opened, and Egan stepped inside, he focused on the one bag next to me. His brows furrowed. "Is that all?"

"Yup." One reason why I stressed when outfits got ruined. "Naida, are you packed up too?"

"I don't have much here either." She headed to the door, passing my mate. "I don't need to ride with you all. Let me settle some things, and I'll meet you there."

"Sounds like a plan." Egan placed the strap of my bag over his shoulder. "Call us if you need anything."

She walked out the door, and I glared at my mate. "They could hurt her too."

"Yes, but she can teleport, so she's not at any risk. Plus, she just came back from the Fae Realm, so her powers will be fully charged," he explained. "Now, let's go. The vampires, Ollie, and Mindy are en route. Draco and Sadie's pack are waiting for us at the vehicles."

"Mindy didn't demand to ride with us?" I figured that girl would've refused to leave Egan's side.

"She didn't have much of a choice."

We left the dorm and headed toward Egan's car. I almost asked about my car, but it had been acting up, and I didn't want to risk it breaking down on the road. I already knew how the conversation would play out.

Something cold brushed against my arm. I jerked to the side, looking for whatever it was.

CHAPTER TEN

The chill sank into my bones, but no one was beside me. I stopped in my tracks.

What's wrong? Egan stopped and scanned our surroundings.

I ... I don't know. It still felt like something was hovering over me. The icy coldness wasn't overwhelming like before as I felt a chill on only one side.

Maybe it was my imagination, so I walked a few steps forward, and the chill faded away until it rushed to catch back up. *There's something cold beside me, but I can't see anything.*

He pulled me to his other side and hissed, *That witch is projecting again. There's a faint outline that's harder to see in the sunlight.*

The day just kept getting better and better. But if she could track us and we weren't protected by the sigil, it made sense that she'd be here. For all we knew, she'd watched the entire fight in the woods. "Let's go." Standing here with her hovering over us did not sound appealing in the least, and in a car, we'd be constantly moving.

"We need to move. The witch is here, watching us again." Egan informed the others as he pulled his keys from his pocket and hurried to his Jeep.

"No time like the present," Roxy said and climbed into the backseat of the Honda, next to her mate.

Donovan got behind the wheel with Sadie sitting in the front next to him.

Rushing to Egan's Jeep, I planned on sitting in the back passenger seat since Draco was so large, but he beat me to the punch, leaving the front passenger seat open. I wasn't in the mood to argue since I wanted to get the hell out of there.

As I slipped into the car, the chill of the witch overcame me again.

She had to be trying to antagonize me. Following my gut, I smacked the cold spot next to me and watched the hovering figure dissipate. I smiled, but my victory was short-lived.

The apparition reappeared beside me.

Here I thought I'd figured out something on my own. I should've known better.

Egan slammed the driver's side door closed, put the key in the ignition, and spun out of the parking spot, leaving the witch behind.

I'd expected her to catch up to us, but warmth returned. "That's weird. She's gone."

The warrior dragon threw his legs on the bench and lay back against the car door. "She doesn't want to spread her magic too thin and will wait until later to come looking for us."

"It's wise that we're heading to Donovan and Sadie's pack instead of Titan's or Cassius's mansion." Egan caught up to Donovan, and his body relaxed a little.

"Who are they?" Sometimes, they forgot I didn't know all the players involved.

"Titan is Sadie's mom's mate." Egan paused, grinning. "I've never said it quite like that before, and it's kind of a mouthful."

"You do realize a human would've said stepdad, right?" I teased.

"True, but there aren't any humans in the car." He winked. *Not after we claimed each other.*

My body warmed at the meaning behind his words. Images of his naked body flashed into my mind, and I squirmed uncomfortably in my seat. It would have been nice if Draco hadn't been in the car.

Draco cleared his throat loudly in the backseat, letting me know he could smell my arousal.

For the first time, being a witch didn't sound so unappealing. Maybe I could turn invisible and never have to face Draco again. I wasn't sure if I could come back from that with him.

Egan's shoulders shook with laughter. *Don't be embarrassed.* He took my hand, leaving one hand on the steering wheel. *All mated shifters get like that. In fact, I can't wait until I get you alone again. After seeing you hurt, confirming our mate bond again would bring me comfort.*

From what you've all said, it only takes one time to complete the bond. If he was going to make light of my embarrassment, I'd give him hell another way. *So if that's the only reason you want to do that, you don't need to feel pressured or worried.*

You know that's not why I want to do it. His golden eyes lightened, and his pupils turned to slits as his dragon peeked through. *I just love—*

"How long have you two been mated?" Draco asked loudly to get our attention on him and off each other. Now Egan smelled spicy with his sexually charged thoughts. Was that better or worse for me?

"About a week." Egan squeezed my hand as his focus returned to the road ahead.

"So, very new." Draco yawned.

"Are you okay," I asked, directing the conversation away from Egan and me. "You sound awfully tired."

"Between the fight and flying to meet you early this morning while the night sky hid Mindy and me, it's already been a long day. I had to leave my thunder, meet Mindy a few miles away from your thunder, then fly the rest of the way here."

"My parents and I appreciate you coming here." Egan glanced in the rearview mirror at him. "We have over two hours left on the road if you want to take a nap."

"Yeah, I may take you up on it. Once we get there, I'll have to get familiar with the area. I'll keep watch on the first night."

He made it clear that his priority was to protect us. Egan's parents had picked a good one to send our way. *He seems sincere.*

It's interesting that my parents sent someone from another thunder, though. A small group of representatives get together a few nights every year at a secret location only they know about, but other than that, I didn't think they talked to each other much.

You have a way to communicate with each other, though, right? In case a thunder is attacked or the king is in danger? They had to have a plan in case something went horribly wrong.

Egan placed his hand on my thigh. *Yeah, they have a cell phone they keep for emergencies. I just didn't expect them to use it.*

With the witch looking for an entire thunder, if not all of them, the entire race is at risk. Do you have any idea why someone wants to find you all?

We were forced into hiding because we were being killed off by the Fae Dragon King. Egan frowned, and the knuckles around the steering wheel turned white. *Dragons are originally from Fae. Hell, some dragons still live there. Dragons are viewed as the strongest race, and a group of people thought that by controlling us, they could control all the races.*

It always came down to power. *If dragons are originally from Fae, why are you on Earth? Not that I'm complaining.* The thought of never meeting Egan broke my heart.

Honestly, the story is a little gray since we've been here for centuries, but it had something to do with the youngest brother claiming he should be king because the eldest brother wasn't fit to rule. The details are unclear, but the older brother left Fae to give his brother the crown, and many dragons followed him to Earth.

I was missing an important piece of the story. *Why would them coming to Earth negate the claim?*

Because Fae creatures lose their magic the longer they're here on Earth. The eldest brother sacrificed his power to get out of his brother's way.

But dragons are powerful. That had to have pissed the younger brother off. *You guys don't seem low on power.*

From what my father told me, we've evolved over time to become as strong as we were in Fae. At first, when we settled here permanently, we were really weak. After only a few decades, our magic adapted, mostly because our fated mates were human, binding our magic here instead of Fae.

I placed my hand on top of his. *How is that possible? You would've had fated mates back in Fae too, right?* The thought of him having another potential match didn't sit well with me.

In Fae, we didn't have fated mates like here, and a dragon can easily live for thousands of years. In a way, finding out we had fated mates confirmed we were meant to be in this world.

All of that information was a lot to take in at once. That was one thing I'd learned about the supernatural world. It was large, fast-moving, and there were so many things at play my head was constantly spinning. As a human, life had been simpler. All I'd needed to do was focus on surviving and staying invisible. Being invisible wasn't really an option now.

One question had been tugging at the back of my mind. *Mindy mentioned your king may be dead. Is that true?*

None of us know. The royal family went into hiding to prevent other races from trying to gain leverage of us and control our kind. Only a few knew the location. Over time, we all lost track, so the rumor is they're dead, but it hasn't been confirmed. I think the royal family is out there somewhere.

It was tragic that they'd had to hide away their royal family. *So your people were attacked and hid?*

Egan's eyes narrowed to slits. *Yes. You see, we left Fae because of politics. The last thing we wanted was to get involved with it here. The dragons that were captured were killed because they refused to work for the Fae Dragon King and couldn't tell them where our king was. Eventually, the fae dragons started kidnapping people they thought could be dragon mates to use them as leverage.*

What? They kidnapped innocent humans. *How do they determine who's a potential mate?*

Egan sighed. *If they thought a dragon looked too long at someone or seemed overly interested. Really, it was guesswork, and many people got hurt out of desperation. That's when we decided to close ourselves off and hide until our population dwindled to alarming numbers.*

You were successful on all accounts, then. Despite all of the shit we'd been through, I wouldn't change us meeting. I'd never felt so happy, even when my dad was alive. I leaned over and kissed Egan's cheek. *I'm glad you got to be the test case. I don't know what I'd do if I never found you.*

He turned and kissed me quickly. *I always felt a tug to leave the thunder. Now I know it was you. I would've found a way to leave. Your pull was too strong.*

A low snore sounded from the backseat, ruining the moment. We chuckled, and I leaned back in my seat. The rest of the ride passed in amicable silence.

DONOVAN PULLED off from the interstate right outside of Nashville. I didn't know why, but I hadn't expected them to live near a bustling city. However, we were on the outskirts, so the idea wasn't unfathomable.

I kept anticipating the cold brush warning me of the witch's return, but I'd only felt Egan's comforting presence the entire ride. I enjoyed the reprieve but knew she'd make her presence known eventually.

We pulled onto a gravel road far from civilization, which wasn't surprising since most packs wanted to stay off the humans' radar. We drove through the woods, and a few miles in, a quaint neighborhood came into view.

The dwellings looked like standard middle-income homes with the typical vinyl siding and a uniform feel of grays, yellows, and blues.

Draco leaned forward between the front seats. "This is their pack home?"

"Yeah." Egan pulled onto a paved road and followed Donovan through the subdivision.

People were out in their yards, waving to the shifters as they drove by. A few children even chased after their cars, thrilled to see the four of them.

I chuckled. "They're like celebrities."

"It's a fair assessment." Egan waved at a few people. "Donovan and Sadie are the pack alpha and alpha mate, with Axel and Roxy as the beta and beta mate. Tyler drove this whole pack into the ground, and they were the ones who saved them."

The pack probably viewed them as their saviors. That was a lot more amazing than being an actual celebrity.

We pulled up to two corner-lot houses across from each other, surrounded by trees, at the end of the road. Lillith's van sat in the driveway of the sky-blue house beside the one Donovan pulled into. She, Katherine, and Ollie stood outside near the woods, searching for something in the trees, their bodies rigid. Lilith rushed over to us.

I threw open the car door, and Egan was beside me in a flash.

Something had to be very wrong. Then I realized Mindy was nowhere to be found. "Where's Mindy? Is everything okay?"

Lillith glared at Egan and growled, "We have a fucking problem here."

CHAPTER ELEVEN

Sadie and the others hurried over to us.

Roxy asked, "I'm assuming the problem centers around a certain blonde dragon shifter who is missing and has already caused a lot of drama?"

Katherine grimaced. "The very one."

"What did she do?" Egan asked,

I understand why Dad sent her, but I wish he would've sent someone less skilled. If she's just going to cause problems, it'd be better if she wasn't around.

From the first moment I'd seen Egan, I could tell he was smart, but I'd been worried he'd been blinded by Mindy's antics. That statement, though, eased my concern. *It's not your fault. You didn't make the call, and I'm sure your father had no clue either.*

"This shouldn't surprise you, but she hasn't made the best first impression, so I was keeping an eye on her." Lillith's nostrils flared. "I asked her to help carry our stuff into the house. Well, about five minutes ago, I started looking for her, and we can't find her anywhere. There's no telling how long she's been gone."

"Where would she run off to?" Sadie's brows furrowed. "She doesn't know anyone here."

"I know, and the entire way here, she made it clear she wasn't thrilled about staying with a wolf pack." Lillith sighed. "I thought she would help with unpacking. I mean, that's not scary or threatening. She must have left while we were preoccupied, but I'm a little worried about how she disappeared. Do you think she went back to the thunder?"

Even though I would love for her ass to be gone, the witch could track Mindy back to the thunder. "Surely she wouldn't." If Egan's family got hurt, I'd feel responsible.

Ollie put his hands in his jeans pockets. "Maybe she's walking around the neighborhood. We were just jammed inside a van for a couple of hours."

Axel shook his head. "We didn't pass her on the way in. She's gone or out in the woods."

"Let's see if we can find her." Maybe she wanted to get away for a few minutes. I wouldn't blame her if she did, but she should've given them a heads-up.

"Do you want me to take to the sky?" Ollie gestured to the house. "I can shift and help search for her."

"That'd be great." Donovan took off toward the light blue house Lillith's van was parked in front of. He sniffed and waved for us to follow. "Come on, it smells like she headed into the woods."

At least, her scent was still on the ground. Maybe that meant she was close by.

We followed after him, and her cinnamon-brimstone smell surrounded me. Even though my senses had improved after Egan and I had completed our bond, they kept getting stronger and stronger the more I used them. I was glad they were improving gradually because they'd overwhelmed me at first.

Sadie caught up with her mate, and they took the lead. Even though dragons had an excellent sense of smell, the wolves had the clear advantage, so it was smart for them to go first.

Wings flapped overhead as Ollie caught up to us high in the sky.

Hopefully, one day, I could fly like that, even if only at night, hidden by the darkness.

Are you okay? I asked Egan. It rubbed me the wrong way that I felt inclined to ask him that, but I had to remember they were childhood friends.

He intertwined our fingers, and annoyance flowed through our bond. *Yeah, I'm fine. She pulled stuff like this all the time growing up. Back in the day, she liked sneaking away and testing boundaries from time to time. Hordes of people out looking for her made her day.*

That didn't surprise me. She was still territorial over Egan despite our bond, which fit that description. *You aren't worried?*

Not really. Egan shrugged. *But she should've told Lillith and the others instead of running off like that. I don't blame them for worrying.*

The woods grew thicker, and a few squirrels ran by, oblivious to us. The animals were acting normal, suggesting nothing horrible had happened. Granted, even when the wolves had attacked us, the animals had acted the same way, so maybe that wasn't the best indicator.

The thickening trees gave ample shade from the sun high in the sky. I could see why the pack had picked this area to live in. It would be a nice place to run and hunt in their animal form. Though it was February, warmth surrounded us, making this feel more like a hike instead of a search party.

Sadie turned left, keeping close on the scent. "It smells like we're getting close."

After a few steps, a loud cry sounded as if someone were in pain. Panic pulsed through me. It sounded like Mindy.

Without thinking twice, I took off heading in that direction. I ran so fast I caught up with Sadie and Donovan.

"Jade!" Draco yelled after me. "Stay behind me."

If he thought I would stop and wait for him, he'd learn otherwise. Even if I didn't like the girl, I didn't wish her harm.

The trees parted, revealing a large clearing with Mindy standing in the center. Her back faced us, and her shoulders heaved. Her shirt was ripped at her right shoulder, exposing a deep wound as if someone had stabbed her. Blood oozed from the wound and trickled down her arm.

Egan pushed between Sadie and Donovan and ran over to her, his face full of concern. "What happened?"

My jealousy raged, but I pushed it down. I had no reason to feel that way. We'd completed our bond, and they were friends. Of course, he cared that she was injured. But despite my rational thinking, a little anger still flared.

"I was scoping out the area for a place for Jade and me to train." She turned to me, wincing. "And I got attacked."

"Who attacked you?" That made no sense, but I couldn't deny her wound was real. I tapped into my senses but found nothing.

"It had to be the witch." Mindy leaned against Egan. "She had caramel hair and sable eyes and was asking where our thunder is."

That sounded like my former roommate, but she'd found us fast—before the rest of us had gotten here. "How the hell did she know where to find us?"

"She did see us packed up when we were leaving," Egan said as he touched Mindy's shoulder, examining her wound. "She probably guessed this is where we were rushing off to since we were leaving with the wolf shifters."

Lillith rubbed a hand down her face. "She's smart. She would've been watching in the shadows, waiting to strike."

"Where did she go?" Draco stood between Egan and me protectively. "Maybe we can find her."

"She attacked me, and just as I went to retaliate, she vanished." Mindy placed her head on my mate's shoulder.

I couldn't hold back the rage. It was one thing for her to be hurt and us paying more attention to her, but she was totally using this to touch my mate. My hands fisted, and I took a deep breath, trying to keep a level head. "That's what happened at the cabin," I said, forcing the words through clamped teeth.

Yup, ignoring her proximity to my mate wasn't happening.

Egan pried himself away from her and took a few steps away. "We need to get you back and clean your wound."

"Yeah, okay." She pouted and countered his movement, trying to get close to him again.

Roxy snagged her uninjured arm, keeping her from my mate. "It's a good thing the wound is superficial."

If I hadn't loved the spunky redhead before, I did now. She might love giving people shit, but she was as loyal as they came.

"Ow!" Mindy sniffled. "Even if it's my good arm, it still pulls on the other shoulder."

"Good thing you have shifter healing speed. You'll be back to normal in a few hours," Lillith said, calling her out on the way she was acting worse than it was.

I'm sorry she tried taking advantage of the situation. I won't let it happen again. Egan took my hand, pulling me close to his side.

With him away from her and next to me, my dragon relaxed. "Let's head back and get settled."

I realized I wouldn't be heading back to Kortright any time soon. I'd worked so hard to go to college, and not even a semester in, I was getting pulled out. Worst of all, I had no one to blame but myself.

Hey, what's wrong? Egan asked as we headed back toward the houses.

Just realized we're probably taking the rest of the semester off. Would they let me come back next semester since I was a scholarship kid? I doubted it, but if we went back, someone might get hurt, especially if Vera continued to hunt me.

This happened last semester too. Egan frowned. *Unfortunately, our life is a little chaotic. Once we get rid of this threat, things should calm down.* I sensed his guilt.

I hated that I'd made him feel that way. That hadn't been my intention. *I wouldn't change a thing if I had the chance.* I looked into his eyes, wanting him to know I meant what I said.

He kissed my forehead. *Good, because I could never let you go.*

"And we get to see new mates drool all over each other again," Lillith complained behind us.

"You're just jealous," Katherine teased.

"I am. Why can't vampires have mates?" she asked dejectedly.

The entire way home, Lillith and Katherine talked about us like we weren't even there.

Egan brought the last of our bags into our room and placed them on the floor. "Mindy gave up and headed back to the house with the vampires."

We were staying in an upstairs bedroom of Sadie and Donovan's three-bedroom house. Mindy had tried staying with us, but Egan and Draco had thought it was best if the warrior stayed with us instead of the teacher. Mindy had said she'd been the last one to get hurt, but Lillith had pointed out that it was because she'd gone off into the woods alone. So she was staying with the vampires and Ollie in the blue house on the corner. Roxy and Axel got to keep their home to themselves.

Lilith had drawn the sigils at every exit in all our houses to protect us from the witch's prying eyes. As long as we stayed indoors, we'd be relatively safe.

Draco was staying in the room across the hall from us with Sadie and Donovan staying in their bedroom downstairs. Our room felt homey and was at least three times the size of the one I had back at Sarah's.

The walls were light beige, and a set of windows overlooked the woods. A large, king-sized bed sat in the center, covered in light gray sheets and a dark gray comforter and pillows. The headboard, end tables, and chest of drawers were a light wood color that looked almost white. The large closet across from the windows could easily hold four times the amount of clothes I had.

Right across from the bed was the entryway to our own bathroom, and I could see an all-glass stand-up shower from there. The white tile looked clean, like no one had ever walked in it before.

"Hey." Egan wrapped his arms around me, turning me to face him. "You're somewhere else."

"No, I'm here." I enjoyed his warmth. "It's been a very long day, and it's not even dinner time yet."

"That I understand." He kissed my lips.

My hands fisted his hair, and I pulled him lower to deepen the kiss. Even though we'd had sex earlier this morning, it felt like it had been days ago. I slipped my hand under his shirt and ran my hands along his chest. His defined pecs had my body purring.

He leaned over me, laying me flat on the bed as his mouth worked my lips. My dragon roared for more, and I almost came unglued.

His mouth trailed down my neck as his hand cupped my breast, pinching my nipple between his fingers. A moan escaped me as he sucked on my neck.

Desperate to feel him, I unbuttoned his pants and pushed them, along with his underwear, down. I stroked him, and he groaned against my skin.

Jade. His voice sounded like a song. He pulled me upward and removed my shirt and bra, and his mouth immediately began going to work on me. I wiggled my hands between us, and I removed my jeans and panties, desperate to feel him inside me.

He positioned himself between my legs, but I wanted to try something else. I pushed against his chest, and he rose, confusion in his eyes.

"You don't have your shirt off," I said, my voice raspy.

"Oh, okay." He stood and removed his shirt from his body.

My eyes devoured every single inch of him. His body was hard in all the ways a woman wanted and in every way that counted. I flipped over and crawled to the pillows.

His pupils turned to slits as he watched me from behind. *What are you doing?*

Trying a new position.

He moved toward me and climbed behind me.

Never in a million years would I have dreamed that his touch would turn me on this much. He rubbed himself against me, getting into position.

He slowly entered me, going deeper than ever before. He asked, *Are you okay?*

Yes.

He filled me completely, hitting my spot perfectly. I moved underneath him, and he sped up his thrusting. My head grew dizzy as he pounded into me.

A moan left me that was way too loud, but I didn't give a damn. I opened our bond, letting him feel everything I did.

Whatever had him worried was gone, and the friction set my body on fire.

Our bodies moved as one, and we teetered close to the edge. I closed my eyes, enjoying each touch, each stroke, each feel. He leaned forward and bit the side of my neck. An orgasm rocked through us at the same time.

He rolled off me and gathered me into his arms. *I love you,* he whispered in my brain.

I laid my head against his sweaty chest, listening to his heartbeat. *I love you too.* I felt safe and secure there and drifted off to sleep.

The next morning, Egan and I entered the kitchen. Draco, Sadie, Donovan, Axel, and Roxy were already there. Sadie stood in front of the black stove, putting the last of the bacon on a large white plate. She walked past the light beige cabinets to the island where Roxy and Axel sat on high-backed chairs.

Roxy snatched a plate on the end and piled it full of bacon and pancakes. She pointed to the other wolf shifters and me. "You better get your food before the male dragons get theirs. If you wait, there won't be anything left."

If Draco ate like Egan did, that was true. We'd missed dinner last night, and after the others had gone to bed, we'd eaten leftovers. Egan had eaten everything I hadn't touched.

"Grab what you're going to eat," Draco said, gesturing to us. "We need to talk about something important."

Conversations that started like that were usually the very ones I didn't want to have.

CHAPTER TWELVE

Keeping calm, I took a plate and selected a few pancakes and a handful of bacon to place on it. I'd noticed that my appetite increased the stronger my dragon became. "Is something wrong?"

Sadie filled her own plate while frowning. "I think the better question is: Which problem do you want to discuss?"

"Fair point." Draco had many options to choose from: the dying dragon race, a witch hunting us down, a jealous dragon shifter desiring my mate, a falcon shifter that had tried to kill me. I had to stop. The list could go on for a while. I poured a cup of coffee then took a seat at their large round table fit for eight.

Draco licked his lips as he watched Donovan, Axel, and Roxy fill their plates with food. "I'd like to discuss Jade's training."

"My training? Why?" Connecting with my dragon was my first priority. The sooner I could bridge the gap between us, the less of a liability I'd be. Maybe I could help out in a fight instead of getting beat to a bloody pulp.

Draco stood and walked over to the food. "Mindy was attacked while scouring the area."

"Hey!" Roxy grabbed a butter knife from on top of the tub of butter and lifted it at the dragon. "Don't make me hurt you. We get our food first."

Draco's eyebrows shot up comically. "You're kidding."

"No, man." Axel put more bacon on Roxy's plate. "She's not. The best thing to do is wait. The one time Egan got food first, she almost attacked him."

Egan winked at me and chuckled. "True story. She better be glad I'm a gentleman, or it could've gotten ugly."

"Whatever, Egan. At the time, I was your favorite." Roxy eyed the food one more time and glanced at her plate. "I guess that's enough."

Yeah, I didn't believe that for a minute. If anything, Sadie had been his favorite. I'd been jealous of their relationship, although I hated to admit it now. It was not my proudest moment. I'd been pushing him away, and Sadie was his best friend. Of course, he would talk to her.

"In other words, all dragons are allowed to eat now." Donovan rolled his eyes and joined me at the table. "If it wasn't for Sadie, we wouldn't be as tolerant of you."

"Dude, she's my mate." Axel sat next to his best friend. "You'd still have to tolerate her since I'm stuck with her." An evil grin flitted across his face as he watched the redhead's reaction.

"Stuck with me?" She dropped her plate, and it clanged on the table. "Is that what you want to call it? I'll show you stuck with me tonight."

Axel's eyes twinkled with mirth. "Am I in trouble? Will you have to teach me—"

"Oh, dear God." Donovan closed his eyes and cringed. "Please do not talk dirty in front of us. I've told you how uncomfortable it makes everyone."

Sadie laughed, sliding between Donovan and me, and scolded, "You know, reacting like that only encourages them."

I smiled so big my cheeks hurt. Despite all the shit we were going through, this group could make me forget about it for a few minutes.

You're breathtaking when you smile like that. Egan slipped onto the seat next to me and placed his hand on my leg. His plate was overflowing with pancakes and bacon.

Sadie had cooked at least five pounds of bacon, and that was a conservative estimate. The salty smell was as intoxicating as the taste. I took a bite and almost moaned. *You're not too bad yourself.*

"Um ..." Draco sat next to Egan like he was afraid to get near Roxy. "I hate to change the subject." The smell of his lie hit us hard.

Roxy gagged and waved her hand in front of her nose. "No lying while eating. That's the ultimate sin."

"Sorry." He cringed. "I was trying to be polite, but I would like to pivot away from this conversation, especially since I want to talk about something serious."

"I'm on board with that suggestion. Please, proceed." Donovan stabbed a pancake and devoured it.

"Like I was saying ..." Draco lifted a hand. "I don't think it's wise for you and Mindy to go off like that on your own. We need to stay close in case something happens."

Egan tensed. "You're right. The sigils don't work outside."

I wouldn't let them take this away from me. "I need to train. I need to be able to protect myself."

"It's an easy solution." Draco tapped his chest. "I'll go with you."

Egan nodded. "And me."

"No." I didn't want to hurt his feelings, but that wasn't a smart idea. "I can't concentrate with you around."

My mate started. "How?"

"Oh, bless his heart." Roxy blew out a breath. "What she's tactfully saying is that Mindy will be salivating all over you the entire time, and the training sessions won't be very productive."

Okay, obviously I wasn't being as coy as I'd hoped.

Egan's focus pivoted to me, and he asked, "Is that true? Is that the only reason you don't want me there?"

There was no way out of this, and the truth would come out one way or another. "Yes, but it's not your fault." I hated that I sounded so insecure.

She means nothing to me. I need you to know that. Egan tightened his hand on my leg like that would reassure me.

You grew up with her. Of course, she means something, but I know she's not a threat. Still, it bothers me that she doesn't respect our relationship. Saying it out loud made me realize that was the problem. I understood how she would be smitten with him—hell, I was too—but her blatant disregard of me was too much.

You're right. I'll talk to her. More guilt wafted from him.

That pissed me off even more. He wasn't encouraging her in the least, but she kept persisting. He had nothing to feel bad about. Either way, he didn't need to handle this problem. *No, I'll talk to her. This is between her and me anyway.*

Sadie cleared her throat, aware that Egan and I were talking through our mind link. "Our entire pack is at your disposal. I can ask a few of our strongest to watch over them too. They can look out from the tree line so they don't interfere with the session. That way, if something happens, they can link with the entire pack, and you'll have backup quickly."

"That would work," Draco agreed.

Someone knocked on the front door before opening it. The smell of Mindy and Ollie hit me hard.

"Someone is making themselves feel at home," Roxy grumbled through a mouthful of food.

The two of them joined us in the kitchen, Mindy's eyes glued on Egan. She wore a skintight, light orange shirt that emphasized her breasts along with tight jeans. "Hey. I didn't realize we were having breakfast here."

"We weren't," Roxy said bluntly. "Sadie cooked for everyone in her house, and Axel and I showed up in time to get in."

Sadie smiled. "I can make more if you two haven't eaten."

Mindy chuckled nervously. "No, we ate before coming here."

Ollie ran his fingers through his thin hair, making it look like a nest. His scrawny frame looked awkward in its oversized black shirt and baggy sweatpants. He had to be wearing borrowed clothes. "Sorry to barge in."

"The front door was unlocked." Mindy fluffed her hair. "I figured it'd be okay with it being a pack neighborhood and all."

I'd hoped to enjoy breakfast before seeing her, but fate had other plans. I finished my pancake and set my fork down.

"Good, you're almost done." Mindy stepped backward awkwardly. "Are you ready to train?"

"Yes." I needed to connect with my dragon soon so she'd leave. We'd have to find a way to get her back to the thunder safely.

Draco finished the bacon on his plate. "We were just discussing that. I was telling the others that I don't think it's safe for you and her to go into the woods alone, so some wolves and I will be joining you."

"You can't come," Mindy said hastily.

Egan shifted in his seat. "Why not? After the witch attacked you, it makes sense to have protection."

Mindy inhaled sharply. "Since Jade is older and I haven't worked with a changed dragon before, I'm worried that other dragons could influence her own. She wasn't born with her dragon, so she's not as acclimated to it as most of the students I teach."

"Then we can have more wolves around instead, and you two can train in the clearing at the other end of the neighborhood, right behind some houses. It isn't isolated like the other location." Sadie tried to sound upbeat, but it fell a little flat.

"Fine." Mindy didn't seem thrilled, but she didn't argue. "But no dragons lurking nearby. Are you ready to go?"

"Sure." I didn't want to spend any time with her, but if this would help me, I could deal. I drained the rest of my coffee, needing the caffeine to get through the morning. Egan and I had reconnected several times throughout the night, so I was a little groggy, but I'd gladly sacrifice my sleep again.

"If anything seems odd, let me know." Egan kissed me. *And that goes for her too.*

I love you. And to think I'd stupidly fought our connection. *I'll let you know immediately if something is off.*

Donovan stood and finished his orange juice. After kissing Sadie, he waved for Mindy and me to follow him. "I'll take you to the clearing Sadie was talking about and introduce you to the wolves that will keep an eye on you. I need to check on someone down there anyway."

The three of us headed out the front door and walked through the neighborhood in silence. I didn't know Donovan that well, and he wasn't the most talkative person I'd ever met. He wasn't stand-offish, per se, but he was hard to read at times, unless it was regarding Sadie. The love he felt for her was evident in every way.

Even though I had a lot to say to Mindy, I hoped the training would give us time to bond, and maybe she'd back off without me needing to address it. I didn't want there to be any awkwardness between us, especially since we were part of the same thunder. If she was in love with Egan, it would be hard to see him with someone else, so maybe she needed time. At least, that was what I kept telling myself when it came to her.

The walk through the neighborhood was nice. The sun was high in a cloudless sky. The cool breeze felt pleasant on my hot shifter skin. After walking past fifty houses, we reached a large section of open space between several homes and the trees.

Three men stood in front of the curb that led to the clearing, and Donovan nodded as we approached. All three of them looked a few years older than us, probably in their mid-twenties.

The tallest one, who stood on the far left, rubbed his cleft chin. His short, tawny hair contrasted against his light olive skin, giving him a glow. Despite the chill, he wore a sleeveless white shirt that revealed his muscular arms. "Are these the two we need to watch?"

"Yeah, and if the witch or anyone else shows up, let me know." Donovan glanced at me. "You going to be okay?"

I tried to sound confident as I said, "I'll be fine."

"Let's get to work." Mindy marched over to the clearing without waiting.

I hurried to catch up, not wanting her to think I already couldn't hack it. I glanced over my shoulder, but the three guys were already gone. When Donovan had said they'd keep out of sight, he'd meant it. If it hadn't been for their faint scent in the air, I wouldn't have known they were around.

"First, we need to get you to connect with your dragon. Then we can try to access your power." Mindy tossed her hair over her shoulder and lifted her chin.

"Sounds great." I was willing to do whatever it took to embrace my new life. "So how do we begin?"

"Have you ever really tried intertwining yourself with your dragon?"

"I'm guessing no since I'm not sure what that means." I'd only ever felt my dragon when she was angry.

"Oh God." She blew out her breath in disgust. "I'll have to go super basic with you."

"Yes." I couldn't keep my annoyance from slipping through. "I've only been part dragon for a week now."

She waved her hand at me. "That's part of the problem. You think of yourself as part human and part dragon."

"That's wrong?" I'd seen Egan and Draco shift. When they were dragons, they were pure beasts. I wasn't sure how else to consider it.

"Of course it's wrong," she said condescendingly. "You aren't half and half. Your human and dragon sides are one and the same. You can't think of them as separate beings."

"So I think of myself as both?" That seemed strange because, in my mind, I considered them completely separate.

She crossed her arms and looked at the sky. "You'll see what I mean. Just try connecting with your dragon."

"How?" If she was a teacher; shouldn't she provide more guidance?

"That's not something I can help with." She held her arms

outward. “We all connect with our dragons differently. You just have to figure it out.”

All right, that wasn’t very helpful. I took a deep breath to calm myself and closed my eyes, but I didn’t sense anything inside me.

I searched deep within myself, and after God knew how long, something flickered inside—a warmth that I latched on to and tugged.

As soon as I did, a raging inferno slammed into me. I tried crying out for help but couldn’t.

CHAPTER THIRTEEN

The flames flicked throughout my body like never before. It had gone from nothing to a fiery temperature within seconds, terrifying me. I was out of control, and I wasn't sure how the hell to calm down.

"Are you okay?" Mindy asked, sounding genuinely concerned.

Unable to verbalize anything, I jerked my head from side to side helplessly.

She touched my arm and yanked her hand back. "You're hot. You must have found your dragon, and she's overtaking you. Push it down and away. Don't let her get the upper hand."

I wanted to yell, "How the hell am I supposed to do that?" But I couldn't do anything.

Egan's voice popped into my head. *Jade, are you under attack?*

Great, I didn't want him to be worried about me. I had enough on my plate without stressing over him. *I'm struggling to connect with my dragon, but I'm fine.* At least, I hoped I was.

"Get a handle on her," Mindy said with urgency.

Trying to push everything from my mind, I concentrated on the flames. I shut down the link between Egan and me, not needing any distractions. Knowing him, he'd be rushing to me right now, but I'd address that after I got control over my dragon. He couldn't see me struggling.

I tried to center myself. I'd learned in martial arts that letting your fear take hold meant you couldn't think or act rationally and your fear could take on a life of its own. I wanted to latch on to the flames instead of squash them, but maybe my dragon was trying to tempt me.

Maybe Mindy was right—I shouldn't consider each part as separate, but that was exactly what they felt like.

Ignoring the urge to embrace the flames, I continued to breathe in a steady rhythm, and after several long minutes, the fire receded. I wasn't safe yet. The flames could erupt again without much effort.

Mindy touched my arm again. "You're cooling down."

Her stating the obvious irritated me, but at least, she was concerned about me, and I didn't want to ruin the moment.

"Uh-huh." That was all I could manage since I was still focused on keeping my breathing and heartbeat steady.

"Good, keep doing that."

Her command irritated me, but I couldn't let her get to me.

The flames didn't appear to be a threat anymore, so I opened my eyes and found Mindy staring toward the neighborhood.

I turned and found Egan running toward me with Draco right behind.

Egan's eyes glowed bright, especially against his dark gray shirt, and his pupils were slits. He raced directly to me and placed his hands on my shoulders, scanning me from head to toe. "Are you hurt?"

Mindy placed a hand on her hip. "Don't be so dramatic. She lost control, that's all."

"She was scared," Egan bit out without looking at her. He cupped my face and lowered his forehead against mine. His breath hit my face, which surprisingly didn't smell like bacon.

"I'm fine." I shut my eyes, enjoying his touch. I always found comfort in him.

Draco stepped next to me and asked, "What happened?"

"She was trying to connect with her dragon, and it didn't go over well," Mindy answered for me. "But she's fine. She got it under control ... eventually."

The way she'd worded that got under my skin. It was like she was slighting me, but hell, I'd failed miserably and probably deserved it.

"She hasn't been a dragon long." Egan took a deep breath like he was smelling me. "She's the youngest one you've ever trained. You should probably take that into consideration."

"I'm sorry. I've never trained a former human before. The last instructor who trained a former human is dead, so no trainer alive has that experience. And from the sounds of it, your mother didn't struggle like Jade." She huffed.

Now that the adrenaline had left my body, my legs felt weak, but I didn't want Egan to know, so I forced myself to stand strong. "It's fine. She and I can figure this out together." I didn't need Egan discouraging her and causing her not to want to help me.

He frowned. "But—"

"I'll be fine." I kissed his lips and forced a smile. "Thank you for checking on me." It shocked me at times how much he cared about me. He was the kindest and most handsome man I'd ever met. I couldn't believe he was all mine.

"I will never not check on you," he breathed, his eyes penetrating my soul.

"Good." I kissed him again, not ready for him to go. *I love you.*

"I love you too." He said the words out loud for everyone to hear. "I think that's enough for today. Let's get you home."

"No, I want to try again." I had to get a handle on my dragon in order to feel stronger and more secure. I could also be a stronger force against the witch instead of a liability. "I mean if Mindy is okay with it."

"Sure, we've only been out here thirty minutes," Mindy said, digging at my failure even more.

Egan frowned, not happy with my decision. *You're tired. I feel it through our bond.*

I couldn't lie to him even if I wanted to. *I'll be fine. I'll rest for a few minutes, but I really want to try one more time, if I can find my strength.*

Jade—

I'm not asking for permission. I loved him wholeheartedly, and I understood that he was coming from a place of love and concern, but it was my decision, not his.

His shoulders shook with quiet laughter. *I understand how Donovan and Axel feel with strong-willed mates. I always thought they were overbearing, but it's easy to do when someone means so much to you.*

I reminded myself that he wasn't trying to control me. I'd lived with a controlling, manipulative aunt who'd acted, not out of concern but a desire for power. I'd promised myself when I'd run away from Sarah that no one would ever make decisions for me again.

"Fine." He took a step back and looked at Draco. "But we stay here."

"No, not happening," Mindy interjected loudly. "She almost lost complete control with only my dragon near. We can't chance having any more nearby."

"I'll be okay," I reassured him again. I understood why he didn't want to leave. If he'd felt even a smidgen of the fear that had overtaken me, I couldn't blame him one bit. But I couldn't let fear dictate my life.

"Are you sure that our presence would cause a problem?" Draco questioned, sounding skeptical.

"Look, I'm not sure." Mindy straightened her shoulders and grimaced, probably from her injury. "But the fewer variables, the better."

"She's right. I'll let you know if I need you. I promise." And if I lost control again, I didn't want Egan to see. He was upset enough just knowing I'd struggled.

"Be careful." He brushed his knuckles against my cheek and headed back toward the house.

Mindy scoffed. "Let's hope you can at least connect with your dragon for a second."

Yeah, I hoped so too.

When Egan was out of sight, I searched for her again, but I couldn't find a spark. All I felt was cold. Only a day into training, and I was already failing.

THE NEXT WEEK passed in a blur. Every morning, Mindy and I would train, but I was making less and less progress. I couldn't even find my dragon anymore.

I almost talked to Egan about it, but he was my safe space. When I was with him, the bad faded away, and I didn't want to lose that. Mindy was helping me despite her desire for Egan, but her frustration was deepening my depression.

"Here's some food." Egan placed a plate of biscuits, sausage, and eggs in front of me, along with a large steaming cup of coffee. "Do you need anything else?"

"No." My appetite had been nonexistent lately, despite things being great with Egan.

"You need to eat up," Egan encouraged as Mindy entered the kitchen with Ollie right behind. "You have training again all morning."

Ever since that first morning, Mindy and Ollie had always come over to eat with us.

"Yeah, like that'll help her," Mindy snickered.

"Isn't the student a reflection of the teacher?" Roxy asked, banging her shoulder into Mindy as she walked by. "And you sound like you're enjoying her struggle." She slid into the seat next to mine, staring the dragon down.

Surprisingly, the dragon didn't respond, but not even Roxy standing up for me could make me feel better. I couldn't do a damn thing right, and I was failing Egan.

Egan's shoulders tensed. "Mindy, I'd like to have a word with you."

"Of course." She batted her eyes at him. "Right now?"

"Now." He walked past her into the living room.

He hadn't been around her any more than he had to be, but my jealousy simmered below the surface. Why did he want to talk to her? Maybe he'd realized she was a better dragon than me.

My heart pounded as the two of them walked out the front door. I was being completely irrational, but I couldn't stand not knowing what they were talking about. I stood from the table and glanced at the people in the kitchen. "Uh ..." I almost lied but caught myself in time. They could guess what I was about to do, but I didn't need to flaunt it. "I need to go do something."

"Yeah, girl, you do." Roxy nodded. "That bitch wants your man."

Sadie glared at her best friend and said, "You know he—"

"Just let her do what she needs to do." Donovan smiled at me with understanding, his dark blue eyes lightening. "You've never had to struggle with feeling insecure about connecting with your animal," he gently reminded his mate.

"You're right." Sadie motioned to the door. "You'll feel better if you listen anyway."

Axel winked. "Your secret is safe with us."

Ollie was the only one who hadn't given me their blessing even though I hadn't been asking for it.

"Hey, you can tell me what to do." He gestured to the bracelet in my jeans pocket. "You have insurance."

Not wanting to waste any more time, I hurried into the living room and placed my ear to the front door. Discretion was pointless since everyone already knew what I was doing.

"You're discouraging her," Egan said with malice. "I thought you were better than that."

Mindy replied in a softer, almost girly voice, "Look, she's struggling. Maybe she's not the right mate for you."

"You've got to be kidding." Egan sounded shocked. "She's my fated mate."

"Sometimes, fate gets it wrong. Why should humans be our mates? We're strong and aren't liabilities like them ... like *her*. We can go back to the arrangement our parents made."

My anger burned inside. She was trying to talk my mate out of being with me. We might not be friends, but I thought we'd established a civil relationship. Obviously, I'd been wrong, and she only wanted to appease me to make a play at Egan.

His words were strong and final as he said, "All I want is her. If you think there is an ounce of me who contemplates the thought of you, there is not. She is the most important person in my life, and I'll give up anyone or anything that tries to come between us."

"You can't be serious." Her voice shook. "She's weak, Egan. You need someone strong beside you, especially for what's ahead."

"I'm strongest with her next to me, and you need to realize that helping her is the only way to salvage any type of friendship between us."

Tears burned in my eyes that he'd stood up for me. I couldn't believe I'd doubted him for a second.

His footsteps headed back to the house.

Dammit, I needed to get away from the door. I didn't want to see Mindy's enjoyment if she caught me eavesdropping. I rushed back into the kitchen.

Right as I slid into my seat, Egan entered the room. Everyone stared at him, and he paused beside me.

Roxy arched an eyebrow. "I take it things didn't go well outside."

"No, things did not." Egan kissed my forehead and pointed to my food. "And you haven't eaten anything."

"I'm not hungry." Especially not after overhearing Mindy's desperate pleas.

"Good." Mindy appeared in the threshold, avoiding Egan's gaze. "Let's go train."

"Maybe I should go with you." Draco stood and took a step toward the front door.

"We've already gone through this. It needs to be just her and me." She waved me on. "Let's get a move on. "

Gladly. I didn't want her anywhere near my mate. I kissed Egan's lips for longer than necessary. Maybe I was being petty, but I was reinforcing my claim on him. Stupid harlot.

Egan wrapped an arm around my waist and kissed me deeper. *It's sexy that you want her to see us together and stake your claim, especially after what you heard out there.*

I stiffened. *You knew I was listening?*

He kissed my nose. *I'd be upset if you hadn't been, but let me know if she does anything funny. I love you.*

I love you too. I turned to find Mindy watching us with a frown on her face.

When I'd caught her, she quickly smoothed her face like that would fool me. She marched to the door, and I grabbed my bag with an extra change of clothes I was certain I wouldn't need and followed closely behind.

As we stepped into the clearing, Mindy crossed her arms and stared me down.

I wasn't sure what she wanted me to do, so I stood there and stared back. Anger bubbled, but I held it at bay. Connecting with my dragon was more important than how I felt about her.

She rolled her eyes and waved her hand. "Go for it. Try to reach her."

The urge to slap her flitted through me, but I closed my eyes to center myself. Getting upset would distract me from the task at hand. I didn't know how long I stood there, but all I found was the same coldness from the past few days.

"I really hope you start doing better, for Egan's sake," Mindy said hatefully.

"What are you talking about?" I hadn't expected for her to come right out and say something like this to me, but I guessed after Egan's rejection, she wanted to give me a go.

"Do you really think a strong dragon like him needs a weak-ass dragon—" She sneered. "Let's be real, you're really just a human since you can't even feel your dragon anymore. Do you think our thunder will accept a weakling like you?"

Anger flared inside me, and the flames that had been dormant for days spurred to life. "I'm going to connect with my dragon if it's the last thing I do." I gritted my teeth, and my breathing increased.

Her eyes widened. "You're losing control again. You need to calm the flames within."

Shit, here I was, regressing even more, but my anger grew, and there was no reining it in.

Egan stepped from the trees, glaring at her, and growled, "What the fuck did you say to her?"

CHAPTER FOURTEEN

The animosity flowing off Egan pulled my attention from within and onto him. Egan had cursed? The flames dimmed as my anger tempered to a worried state for my mate. I'd never seen him act this way, so something had to be horribly wrong.

"What are you doing here?" Mindy whispered with dread.

I must have missed something. I scanned the clearing to determine what happened.

Egan marched over and took my hand as he stared Mindy down. He sneered, his expression morphing into one of pure rage. "Curious about your methods. You see, I had an interesting conversation with Mom yesterday while you two were training. Between that and your antics this morning, I wondered why you were adamant not to have me or Draco near."

"I told you why." Mindy's shrill voice hurt my ears. "We didn't need any distractions." Her cheeks turned pink, either from embarrassment or anger.

"The fact that you're telling the truth speaks volumes. You didn't want any distractions. Distractions from you sabotaging my mate from connecting with her animal. How could you do that to her?"

Smoke trickled from his flared nostrils, and he protectively stepped in front of me.

All of the dots connected. "Wait. You haven't been helping me?" I shouldn't have been shocked, but I was.

"I—" Mindy's mouth dropped like she wasn't sure what to say.

"All this time, you're the reason I was struggling. You made me feel like a failure." Rage coursed through me at the betrayal. My heart pounded, and my breathing turned ragged.

"You have to understand it's nothing personal. I'm just the better fit for Egan." Mindy lifted her hands as if in surrender, though her words declared war.

"Nothing personal?" She was crazier than I'd ever imagined. "That's the very definition of personal. He's my mate."

"Of course, someone like *you* wouldn't understand."

"What? Someone who isn't delusional?" And I'd thought the human world was cruel. She was on the same level as my aunt.

She waved a hand at me. "You're just a broken girl who somehow got mated to the strongest dragon in the world."

"Okay, you've said more than enough," Egan hissed and tried blocking me from her view.

"Yeah, protect her since she can't defend herself." Mindy's eyes narrowed as she sidestepped to look at me. "You're lucky he's standing between us."

"First off, no one cares or wants to hear your opinion." Egan's body quivered with unbridled anger. "Secondly, she's stronger than you have ever been. What kind of dragon runs and hides when her own kind is under attack?"

Mindy straightened her shoulders. "Please, like you were even at risk. Maybe if you hadn't run off to some stupid college, we'd be mated and the attack never would've happened."

Egan rasped, "Jade was made for me, and I refuse to contemplate a life without her. You need to get that through your brain."

Mindy lifted her chin in defiance. "It's a good thing you're handsome since you're obviously not very smart."

Did she think it was okay to say stuff like that? Flames flickered throughout my body at her audacity. "You made me think I was broken and that the thunder wouldn't accept me. Now you're going so far as to insult me and my mate."

"They shouldn't accept you," she smirked. "I should be with him. He needs someone strong."

The bitch was about to see strong. "You don't get to decide. He does." I let go of Egan's hand and walked around him. I refused to let him protect me. If this girl thought I was weak, I'd prove her wrong. "And he chose me. He's told you that repeatedly, so I'm thinking you're the one who's dumb."

"You can't talk to me that way, you stupid—"

I punched her right in the jaw. A loud crunch sounded as her head jerked to the side, and she collapsed.

The raging inferno inside me prevented me from doing anything else as it took on a life of its own. Arms wrapped around me and turned me toward a strong chest. My mate's face grew concerned as he watched me.

"We need to focus on you. You will lose control if we don't fix the problems she's caused." Egan's fingers brushed my cheek, but the usual comfort it provided was missing.

My dragon was angry and refused to not be heard, even with Egan trying to soothe us.

Footsteps pounded, and Draco said, "Get her away from here. I'll handle Mindy."

I wanted to finish the bitch, because breaking her jaw hadn't been enough, but I needed to take care of myself.

"Fine." He sighed. "But my conversation with her isn't over. She went too damn far."

I forced the next words through my thoughts, even though I didn't want to, but I refused to be that girl. I could work on myself while he did what he needed to. *If you need to talk to her—*

You will always be my first and most important priority. I'm just livid she did this to you. He scooped me up in his arms and took off toward the woods, barely jarring me.

I hadn't realized I couldn't walk until he'd picked me up. Every ounce of my self-control was consumed with trying not to implode. The more my anger festered, the more out of control it got.

He ran so fast my hair whipped around my face, and the air felt amazing. Between that and his touch, the flames receded slightly.

I'm going to put you down. I think this place will work.

He placed me gently on the ground, but I kept my eyes closed, staying in his embrace. The flames grew hotter without the breeze. *I ... I don't know what to do.* I tried pushing the dragon back like Mindy had told me, but it only enraged her more. She didn't relent, and I found myself retreating instead.

Those flames, you need to grab on to them, Egan said soothingly.

But they're so hot. I didn't feel the tug to connect with them like I had on my first day of training. *They'll burn me.*

No, they won't, Egan growled, annoyance wafting off him.

He'd never treated me like this, and it hurt. Out of all the times, now was when he'd be disappointed. *Okay, I'll try. Just be patient with me.*

Oh, baby, I am. I'm not upset with you. I'm angry with Mindy. She's been pushing you to this point all week, and I should've known. He kissed my forehead. *But I need you to trust me and grasp the flames. Don't hide or fight them. Your dragon is pissed because she's been trying to connect with you and you've rejected her.*

That was why she'd gone cold and I couldn't find her. She'd been hurt.

Pushing away my terror, I steadied myself and opened myself up to the flames. The flames licked against my mind, challenging me, but I held steady. After God knew how long, the urge to connect with the flames overcame me again.

I didn't hesitate. I should've trusted my instincts from the very beginning.

My dragon pushed forward, and I winced, ready for the pain, but the contact didn't hurt. She melded with me, and I stepped from Egan's arms and looked at the world around me. I thought my vision had been crystal clear after we'd bonded, but now I saw colors I'd never seen before. I had no clue what to consider them, but they were breathtaking.

As our minds blended together, immense power shot through me. My skin prickled as my body began to expand. I hadn't considered the possibility of shifting, and I pulled back from my dragon. She hissed and locked on more tightly.

You need to shift, Egan said reassuringly. *It's the best way to connect with your dragon half. Don't hold back. Let her take hold.*

Okay, I was willing to try. I didn't feel as overwhelmed now but rather more unsure of the unknown.

Here, take this. If I shifted, I didn't want to lose the broken bracelet we needed to keep a leash on Ollie. My hands shook as I pulled it out and placed it in Egan's pocket.

He nodded. *I'll take care of it. Just connect with her.*

She clamped tighter, and my bones shifted, but thankfully, it didn't hurt. Egan and Draco had made it look so easy, so natural, and now I understood why. My bones weren't breaking but rather moving and changing. Something sprouted from my back, ripping my clothes. Large boney wings stretched out.

I watched as my skin changed into olive scales a few shades lighter than Egan's. I was at least twice as tall and took up a quarter of the large clearing.

Egan stepped in front of me, smiling tenderly. *You're just as gorgeous in your dragon form as you are in your other one.*

His words did something to the beast inside, and a soft purr escaped. She'd been worried he wouldn't approve of her.

It surprised me that I understood her emotions, thoughts, and needs perfectly, even though she was a beast. She was part of me, not an entirely separate entity.

I'll be right back, Egan said and rushed toward a section of woods. *I'm going to strip down and shift with you.*

Just as I was about to ask why he didn't strip down here, a branch broke a few steps away. I turned, realizing we weren't alone; the musky scent told me wolf shifters were near.

It had to be the three shifters Donovan had instructed to watch us. I felt better knowing we had backup. The witch had been silent for a week, but she'd eventually grow tired of waiting.

The three wolves peeked through the tree branches, taking in my animal form.

It dawned on me that they'd probably seen me naked. *Please tell me they didn't see anything when I shifted.*

Maybe, but if they did, it wasn't for long. Egan stepped out from the woods in all his naked glory. His body began to change right before my eyes. *They're shifters, so nudity is nothing new to them. Don't be embarrassed. I just didn't want to destroy my clothes since I don't have a spare outfit.*

That was kind of sad. It would have been nice to see him naked for a while. It startled me that I enjoyed watching my mate shift into his dragon. Watching the change was intoxicating.

The beast within me was excited. This was the first time they'd meet. *I'm hearing you say that you have no problem with other men seeing me naked.*

His wings sprouted, and his pupils turned to slits. He growled deeply, *I did not say that, but there are times when that may happen, even if I'd rather it not. You don't want me to be jealous and rip our friends' heads off, do you?*

I felt truly free and strong. I teased, *Maybe. It might make me feel special.*

Don't tempt me, Jade. His dragon stepped toward me, his face caressing the side of mine.

Please tell me we can fly. The urge to take to the air and have the wind underneath me dug into me. I'd been jealous of Ollie as I'd watched him fly the other day, and I was finally in a position to experience it.

It's daytime, so we have to be careful. Only a quick, low spin around the neighborhood; then we come back here. If you want to do a longer flight, we'll need to do it at night. Egan stepped back and spread his wings, about to take to the air.

Deal. I realized was clueless. *Uh ... do I just flap and it works?*

Don't overthink it. Let your dragon handle that part. His body lifted into the air.

That sounded easier said than done, but he hadn't led me astray. I looked skyward, and my dragon took charge. My wings moved slowly at first, hovering me off the ground. Then they moved stronger and stronger, and soon I was higher than the trees.

Egan took off toward Sadie and Donovan's home, and as we flew over the neighborhood, a few kids pointed at us and waved.

Flying as a dragon felt as natural as walking. I twirled around, enjoying the surrounding freedom.

Lillith, Katherine, and Ollie were outside, sitting in the sunlight outside the homes we were staying at. They all smiled as they watched Egan and me move in rhythm with each other, flying around and playing.

My dragon was happy and at peace, almost purring. All too soon, Egan led us back to the clearing, our time in the air done. Tonight, I'd be begging him to go out again.

Right as we descended into the clearing, something cold and sinister brushed against me. My body tensed, and I spun around, looking for the apparition.

Of course, now would be when the witch returned. She disappeared for a while, probably wanting us to lower our guard. It had worked since she'd been the furthest thing from my mind. *Egan, the witch.*

Where? He surveyed the area for her in physical form.

No, she's projecting. I flew higher to get a better vantage, but I saw nothing out of sorts. Maybe my mind was playing tricks on me.

Let's land and shift back. We need to get back to the house where we'll be protected. He flew down to the ground and shifted back into his human form.

When I landed, I took a deep breath, unsure how to initiate the change back to two legs. My dragon was still stuck in my mind, so I did the only thing I could think of: I asked her, *Please, help me shift back.*

Instead of fighting me, she withdrew inwardly. The more she pulled away, the smaller my body became. Back on two legs, I ran toward the trees to hide. I'd forgotten that I didn't have any clothes handy.

Fully dressed, Egan stepped into the clearing. *I'll go ask a wolf near the training grounds to get your bag and bring it to me.*

Draco appeared through the branches, looking frantic. He carried the bag I'd stashed nearby for when I shifted. He handed it to Egan. "Here, get her dressed quickly. We have a problem."

Great, I had a feeling I knew exactly who, or rather what it was.

CHAPTER FIFTEEN

"Let me take a wild guess; Mindy is involved," Egan said, clutching the bag, and turned to me.

We were thinking along the same lines. The wolves' scent was getting closer, and I wrapped my arms around myself. I doubted they were as close as it felt, but with my stronger nose, it smelled like they were right on top of me. I was tempted to cover my private parts with leaves.

"Yes, but are you surprised?" The maliciousness dripping from Draco's words shocked me.

I hadn't spent much time with him since I was either training or exhausted from training, but like Ollie, he didn't say much. I figured it was due to their natures, but not being part of the core group didn't help. Even though Sadie and the others always included Draco, I was sure he felt on the outskirts of their close bonds.

That was the thing with this group. They were fiercely loyal and protected the ones they cared about.

Maybe if I tried pulling Draco in more and talking, we'd get to know him better. After all, he was here, risking his life for us. I'd been depressed about my dragon, and Egan had been working hard to keep that darkness from swallowing me whole. I could make more of an effort with Draco now.

"No, not at all," Egan said curtly. "She's probably trying to scare us so I won't stay mad at her."

Even if you don't stay pissed at her, I will. I couldn't easily forgive her deception. Not only had she tried to hurt me, but she'd also made me look like I couldn't adapt to this world and connect with my dragon. Every show of concern had been to hide her true intent.

I'm beyond pissed. She's lost my trust and my friendship. If I could kick her out of our thunder, I would. Egan hurried over to me, and when he saw me in all my naked glory, he stopped. The anger wafting through our bond dissipated, and the spicy scent of his arousal surrounded me.

It was true what they said: guys had a one-track mind.

My body responded in earnest, calling me out on my hypocrisy. Even though we'd had sex before breakfast, I could easily have gone another round or three with him. Hell, who was I kidding? I could spend days locked in a room with him and never get tired of his hard, sexy body.

A shifter coughed uncomfortably, reminding us that we weren't alone.

If I could have told them to scram, I would have without any hesitation, but we had the witch and Mindy to contend with. *Rain check?*

Only because I don't want to disrespect you like this with all these people around. He wrapped an arm around my waist and set the bag on the ground next to me. A low growl emanated from his chest as he kissed my lips.

You're about to make me beg you to give them a show. His sweet taste filled my mouth, warming my body more. I deepened our kiss, my hormones taking hold.

Egan obliged before groaning as he pulled back and glanced at his crotch. *You're making this really uncomfortable for me.*

His naughty side made him even more attractive. I never would've guessed until the past few weeks together. I loved that he was only like this with me. I rubbed my hand over him and waggled my eyebrows. *We can't have that. I could help you out.*

He kissed me and grabbed my hand, holding it still. He placed the bracelet in my palm and nipped my lip then stepped back. *I'm doing this because I love you.* He checked me out again, his golden eyes glowing brighter. He was struggling to leave me, and I loved it. *Hurry and get dressed before I change my mind or go crazy with so many guys standing this close to you while you're naked.*

I sighed loudly, letting him know I didn't approve of his decision. I quickly got dressed, put the bracelet back inside my jeans pocket, and headed to where he and Draco waited.

The warrior dragon ran his foot over the grass, averting his gaze from me. He scratched the back of his neck and rolled his shoulders, still uncomfortable. The best way to pretend that Egan and I hadn't almost mauled each other in front of him and the wolves was to steer the conversation in a safer direction. "What did Mindy do?"

"After a few minutes, she ran after you two." Draco surveyed the woods like he expected her to pop up. "But when I chased after her, I couldn't find her."

"Let's hunt her scent." Egan took off toward the other clearing, on a mission.

"That's what I'm trying to tell you," Draco said, causing Egan to stop and return. "She and her scent vanished, and I was only a few steps behind her"

The memory of the cold chill against my arm flitted through my mind. I'd been sure the witch had been watching us, but after Mindy had just vanished, I worried that the two might be connected. Surely she wouldn't let the witch take her to get Egan to focus on her?

"Dammit. We don't need her doing something stupid." Egan faced the watching wolves. "Can you let Sadie and Donovan know that Mindy is missing and we need help tracking her down?"

"Of course," the taller one said. "We'll shift and circle back." The guy disappeared into the trees, and within seconds, I heard three sets of paws hitting the ground, heading back to the houses.

Flames flicked against my mind, and I partially opened myself to them. My dragon surged forward, loaning me her hearing and eyesight. As I scanned the woods, I could see birds flying and a squirrel running from branch to branch, but I didn't see anything larger than that. "Egan, I felt that cold presence in the air. And now this."

"Let's not jump to conclusions. Let's head back to the house. Maybe she went there to throw Draco off her trail," Egan said and placed his hand on the small of my back, urging me forward.

"I hope that's what she did." Draco didn't sound convinced. "Otherwise, this could be really bad."

Egan sighed. "Let's search before we focus on any other scenarios."

The three of us hurried through the neighborhood, and at our section of houses, Lillith, Katherine, and Ollie were still sitting in front of the light blue house. They waved us over.

Ollie pursed his lips and crossed his arms as he sat back in the seat, giving us a wide berth. The only person he talked to was Mindy, making us more wary of him.

Katherine beamed at me. "We saw you up there flying with Egan. We knew you could do it!"

They were so proud I would've thought they'd accomplished something instead of me. "It was pretty amazing." Despite the potentially dire situation, I couldn't help grinning. I had no doubt that the memory would be one of my favorites.

My happiness was short-lived when Ollie's brows furrowed and he asked, "Where's Mindy?"

Lilith shrugged. "Who cares? She'd only ruin the moment."

I winced. Mindy had tried to make sure that moment never happened, which was way worse.

"That's not a good look. What happened?" Lillith glanced from me to Egan to Draco. When no one responded, she placed her hands on her hips. "I'm assuming a certain blonde, green-eyed monster did something unpleasant."

"Green eyes?" Draco's face wrinkled with confusion. "She doesn't have—"

"It's a saying." Poor guy. They couldn't talk like that around him. He'd only been in our world a week. "*Green-eyed* means jealous."

"Which she clearly is." Lillith narrowed her eyes, daring him to disagree with her.

Katherine patted her friend's shoulder. "I don't think he's disagreeing with you."

"Has she come back here?" Egan nibbled his bottom lip.

Lillith shook her head. "No. Was she supposed to? I thought she was down there with Jade."

The front door to Sadie's house opened, and she and Donovan walked outside with Axel and Roxy right behind.

"I heard the bitch is gone." Roxy's hazel eyes were alight with glee. "I gotta say, I never thought her ass would leave."

"Damn, Roxy." Donovan grimaced. "Tell us how you really feel, why don't you?"

"Oh, I thought I'd made it pretty clear." She lifted a brow, staring him down. "Do you need it spelled out more?"

"You two, stop it." Sadie rolled her eyes and faced us. "Over twenty wolves are searching for Mindy as we speak. No one can find her. It's like she disappeared."

Draco rubbed his forehead. "That's what happened to me too. I was hoping you all could pick up on her scent."

"When we were up in the air, I felt a coldness press against me like back at the dorm when the witch was watching us, and for Mindy to disappear moments before we landed is too suspicious." The witch must have done something to her.

"If you felt a coldness, that means the witch was astral projecting. She couldn't do anything in that state, could she?" Axel ran a hand over his buzzed hair.

Ollie stood and stepped closer, putting his hands in his pockets. "She has strong magic like the powder she gave me to knock Jade out.

There's no telling who's working for her. She could've given her something to take her without a trace."

Ugh, this was just lovely. "What do we do? Do you know where the witch is staying?"

"No." Ollie wrung his hands. "Like I said before, she told me as little as possible. I have no clue where she could've taken her."

"We should've known it was too quiet." Lillith scowled. "Instead, we played right into her hand."

Sadie paced. "If witchcraft hid them, we couldn't have done much. We wouldn't have been able to see her regardless."

"How do we find her?" The longer she was with the witch, the likelier she'd get hurt or give up the thunder.

Roxy crossed her arms. "You really want to find her? I say good riddance."

Maybe Mindy deserved that, but their thunder didn't. "She is someone's daughter and a member of Egan's—" My dragon growled, not happy with me. "My thunder. She's obviously an important teacher there for them to have sent her to help me, and she knows the location of the thunder. Do you think the witch will just give up on Mindy telling her where to find everyone?"

Egan pulled me against his chest and wrapped me in his warm embrace. *I've always known you're an amazing person, but the way you're putting the thunder before the shit she's done to us proves it.*

It isn't easy. I could be honest with him, but if I let Roxy in on that, she'd stir the beast inside. It was enough for her that Mindy had screwed me over.

"Fine, be the bigger person." Roxy stomped her feet dramatically. "And you're right. She'd give up that thunder in a heartbeat."

Sadie's eyes widened at her friend. "Let's hope not. Sometimes, it's best to think before you say whatever pops into your mind."

"Girl, sometimes I don't even know what's going to come out." Roxy waved her hand in front of her mouth. "We're sometimes shocked at the same time, but damn, I always agree with the words."

Lillith snorted. "That's a good thing since you said them."

Roxy nodded. "Fair point. It might get awkward if I didn't."

"Okay." Donovan clapped his hands. "Mindy is with the witch. We need to figure out how the hell to find her."

"The problem is the witch will see us coming since she can keep an eye on those two." Draco pointed at Egan and me.

"I have a suggestion," Ollie said hesitantly.

Lillith tapped her foot. "Which would be?"

"A witch lives an hour away from my cast." He rocked on his heels. "We helped her hide from hunters, and she owes us. She should be able to block the locator spell and maybe find Mindy, though I doubt that will work. But we could try."

The idea of Vera not being able to find us sounded promising. *What are your thoughts?*

I'm not sure, but you have the bracelet. If we could stop Vera from watching our every move whenever we aren't protected, it would take away her advantage. If we can't find Mindy, we may need to go back to the thunder and help them evacuate in case Mindy breaks and tells her their location. Egan sounded stressed, but there was so much at stake.

I brushed my fingers against the bracelet and stared the falcon shifter down. "Is this a trick?" He'd been outside too, so if the witch had gotten to Mindy, she could've gotten to him as well.

"No, I swear." He lifted a hand. "This is me trying to prove my loyalty to you."

"Where is this place?" Draco asked.

"It's in South Georgia." Ollie gestured to the sky. "Only a couple hours' flight or over a ten-hour car drive."

Egan intertwined our fingers and headed toward the house. "We leave at sunset."

"Okay." Ollie headed into the blue house.

I couldn't shake the feeling that something was off, but Ollie couldn't lie to me while I had the bracelet ... unless the witch had figured out another way to control him superseding the power over the bracelet.

CHAPTER SIXTEEN

We entered our bedroom in Sadie and Donovan's house, and Egan sat on the bed, putting his head in his hands.

"Hey." I shut the door and kneeled in front of him, placing my elbows on his knees. "We'll find her." I pushed down the annoyance building inside me to keep a level head. For the second time today, I reminded myself that he and Mindy had grown up together. It was normal that he'd be upset.

"That's not what this is about." Egan rubbed a hand down his face and dropped his hands on top of me. "Not only are you in danger, but our entire thunder is too. I won't lie; I don't want Mindy hurt, but she keeps putting people at risk. She should've known better than to run off like that."

"Of course you don't want her hurt. Neither do I." Although I wouldn't object to smacking her around some more, but I'd gotten a solid punch in that should've made my point with her. If not, I could always punch her again. I'd come to terms that I'd be stuck with her since we were like family. "We'll get through this." We didn't have any other option.

He placed his hands on my waist and picked me up so I straddled him. My legs could barely wrap around him, that was how muscular he was.

Gently, he cupped my cheek. "If anything were to happen to you, I don't know what I'd do. Being my mate has already put you in harm's way twice within two months. The first time with your roommate, and the second with Mindy."

His guilt ran clearly between us. It infuriated me that he blamed himself. "This is not your fault. You never asked for that to happen, and I wouldn't change what we have for the world. Would you?"

His face softened as he stared deep into my eyes. "No. I could never give you up, even if that makes me extremely selfish."

I kissed him and poured all my love for him into our bond, wanting him to feel the sincerity of my words. *I've never been this happy, and there are no take-backs.* The truth of my words sank into him. The only time I'd come close to being this happy was that day at the beach with the boy so many years ago, but even that paled in comparison.

His tongue slipped inside my mouth as his hand circled my neck. *The thought of us ever being apart terrifies me.*

Good. I breathed in his citrus scent as his fingers dug into my hip, turning me on. *There's no way I'd let you leave.*

A groan escaped him, and I ground against him. I would never get enough of him. His tongue stroked mine, feeling like velvet and turning me into mush in his arms.

Sadie and the others were still outside talking, leaving us alone in the house for once. I hadn't planned on taking advantage of the time, but now it was the only thing on my mind.

I pulled away from his mouth and kissed down his neck. When I got to the spot where I could feel his pulse against my tongue, I bit ever so gently.

He shook underneath me and purred in satisfaction. He turned his neck, giving me more access.

Leaning back, I lifted his shirt and pulled it over his head. I tossed it over my shoulder and placed my palms on his pecs. His muscles constricted underneath them as his hands grabbed my ass, pushing me harder against him.

Even through our clothing, the friction had started to build. My teeth scratched across his skin, and Egan rolled me onto my back. My body was trapped under his as his mouth peppered kisses toward my chest. He lifted my shirt and unfastened my bra, then placed his lips on my nipple.

My body arched, needing more of his touch, of his body, of everything. I unbuttoned his jeans and slid my hand inside his boxers. I ran my hand along him.

Dammit, Jade. You're driving me crazy. I was going to take it slow. He undressed me, dragging my panties off. His hand slid between my legs as his other one pushed his pants and boxers down.

Next time, I panted without any shame.

He grabbed my waist and tugged me so my ass was right on the edge of the bed. *Fine.* He moved between my legs and thrust inside me.

This time, he wasn't gentle at all, and I loved it. I moaned loudly as he clutched my ankle, lifting my legs higher so he thrust even deeper. His other hand slipped between my legs and rubbed.

Each movement went deeper than the last, slamming into the perfect spot. My body was already primed for him.

His fingers rubbed harder as he increased his pace. I clutched the sheets.

My breath caught as the pleasure built, and soon Egan and I were falling over the edge. He jerked as he finished inside me, and my body quivered from all of the sensations. He lay beside me and pulled me into his naked, sweaty arms.

There was no place I'd rather be.

My eyes grew heavy from the weight of everything that had happened today, and I dozed off.

I WOKE up alone in bed. The void hit me, and I glanced around the room. I was in the center of the bed, completely covered. *Egan?*

Hey, I'm downstairs. He linked. *I'm sorry, I didn't mean to stay down here so long. Draco knocked a little while ago and wanted to talk before leaving.*

You should've woken me. I climbed out of bed and snatched my clothes from the floor. I quickly dressed to join whatever conversation they were having. The room was already darkening, telling me it was later than I'd expected. It was close to sunset, so we'd be heading out soon.

I'm sorry. You were sleeping so good, and after the rough start, I thought a little rest would help with the long night ahead.

I couldn't get too upset at that logic. *I'm on my way.*

I opened the door and heard Draco's voice as clearly as if I were in the same room as him. I hurried down the stairs.

"I understand that her bracelet can control Ollie, but we can't go in there blind," Draco said.

"If you drive, we can go with you," Sadie suggested.

Egan sighed. "We can't chance that timeline. It'll take five times as long. Our thunder could be compromised in that time."

"Speaking of which, did you let them know what's going on?" Donovan asked.

When I stepped into the kitchen, Egan turned to me and patted his lap. He answered the others, his eyes staying on me, "Yes, and they're preparing in case they have to evacuate."

Everyone except Ollie was in the kitchen, sitting around the table, and there wasn't a vacant chair. I guessed that was why he'd gestured for me to come to him, and I'd take any opportunity to be close to him.

"What's the plan? There's no telling if or when Mindy could break. We wouldn't know until the witch attacked." I didn't know how big the thunder was, but if they'd been hiding for centuries, I assumed it was a decent size despite their dwindling numbers. I sat in his lap, and he wrapped his arms around me.

"Hopefully, she can hold out for a day. If we can't locate her, then we relocate the thunder and hope no one else gets taken. There's only a handful of people who know where all the other thunders are located, so the majority of the race should be safe. It's just our thunder at risk."

"All it takes is the witch finding one person who can lead her to them all." Draco pinched the bridge of his nose. "We might need reinforcements."

"Not for this." Egan shook his head. "The rest of your family should stay close unless we know, without a doubt, we're at risk."

Lillith lifted a brow. "There is absolutely no question where your thunder will go. You guys will come and stay in the mountains."

Egan tensed. "I'd hate to put your family out like that again."

"Stop it." Sadie pointed a finger at him. "You helped us, so of course Titan's pack will make room for you."

"And we have a huge-ass mansion with plenty of bedrooms that can hold at least twenty, if not more," Lillith added.

"Including all the woods in between," Katherine piped in.

"Hell, I'm down just for Julie's cooking. Katherine, your mom can cook. I miss it." Roxy rubbed her stomach.

Axel frowned. "She even talks about it during sex."

"Dude, really?" Donovan plugged his ears. "I don't want to know that kind of stuff. You used to be more couth until you mated with Roxy."

Roxy waved her hand. "Oh, please. That's bullshit, and you know it."

Donovan growled, "Okay, maybe a stretch, but not this bad."

Moments like these made it seem like the world wasn't so bad. I enjoyed listening to their back and forth.

A knock at the door interrupted the moment.

"I wonder who that could be?" Roxy deadpanned.

Donovan glowered at her.

"I'll go get it. Ollie is uncomfortable enough as it is without us making him stay out there longer than necessary." Katherine chuckled as she stood and hurried to the front door.

"Hey, at least he knocks." I gestured to Roxy. "You should be thankful for that."

"True. Mindy busted in like she owned the joint." Roxy pursed her lips.

"Just remember that the nest and Mom's pack is where you're going if needed," Sadie said discreetly to Egan as the front door opened. "You did so much for us, and we want to return the favor. Mom said she'll be pissed if you go somewhere else."

Why can't we bring them here? They were all on the same page, so I had to be missing something.

Because the nest and Sadie's mom's pack is still hidden compared to here. Everyone pretty much knows about this place, but only a handful of people know where Cassius and Titan live. We'd be safer there.

Ollie entered the kitchen with a gray bag on his shoulder, Katherine following right behind. From the doorway, he glanced at everyone sitting around the table. "Are you guys ready? I told the witch, Trixie, we'd get there around midnight. Her magic is strongest then, apparently."

"Sounds like a plan." As long as Trixie could block Vera from finding Egan or me, that was all that mattered. I only hoped she could locate Mindy too, but I had a feeling that was a stretch.

"Let's get going then," he said, rocking on his feet.

Egan huffed as I stood. There was no point in avoiding the inevitable.

"Would one of you mind carrying my bag for me?" He winced. "It's impossible for me to do it in my falcon form."

"Sure, I can." I took the bag and turned to Egan. "We should pack some things too." I didn't want to be stuck in my birthday suit down there.

"Already did." Egan gestured to a black bag on the floor by the door. "Draco put his stuff in there too."

"Well, okay then." I had to get used to bringing a backup outfit. I'd never had to worry about it before, but if I didn't get my head on straight, I'd get stuck in a very uncomfortable situation.

Egan, Ollie, and I headed toward the back door.

"Call us if you need anything," Sadie said, her forehead creasing.

The four of us went into the woods behind the house and stripped down to shift. This was only my second time, and my heart pounded. What if I couldn't do it again?

I closed my eyes, seeking the flames inside. Thankfully, they blazed in response to my nonverbal request. My dragon appeared, and all of my anxiety faded.

My body expanded as my wings ripped from my back. My vision became clearer, and the trees appeared to become smaller as my larger size took over. I stepped into the opening between the woods and Sadie's home and found Draco and Egan waiting for me.

Oh, snap, I almost forgot. I spun around and grabbed Ollie's bag with a talon. A *kakking* caught my attention as Ollie took to the sky.

It was time to go.

Draco took off, leaving Egan and me behind.

You ready? Egan asked.

Yes. My wings moved on their own. My beast instinctively knew how to take over. My body lifted skyward, and Egan stayed right next to me. Within minutes, we were flying high.

I glanced down, watching the world grow smaller underneath me. I'd always thought flying in an airplane was amazing, but nothing compared to this. The wind blew under my wings, and the cool night sky caressed my skin. I'd never experienced anything like this before.

Egan chuckled. *You're purring.*

Being here like this, with you by my side, I feel completely content. I probably sounded like an ass with all the shit we were going through.

No, I understand. Having you here next to me fulfills me in a way I didn't know I was lacking. It's okay to be content despite bad things happening. Otherwise, no one would ever be happy. He flew closer to me reassuringly.

He was right. If we let the bad outweigh the good, there would be no smiles or laughter. Just because I was enjoying the moment didn't mean I wasn't worried about what happened next. I would enjoy the next few hours.

We were flying high and covering ground quickly. When the moon began to peak, Ollie started his descent.

As we prepared to land, I realized we were in a thick section of woods. The location was more remote than Sadie's pack house.

We followed Ollie to a small cottage in the center of a flattened area. The house was fifty miles away from anything. A faint light flickered in a window, and when we were several hundred yards away, a thin, short, older lady came into view. Her eyes were locked on me, and an evil smile crossed her face. She lifted her hand, and light reflected off her face. Something dark permeated from deep within her.

Maybe Draco had been right. Ollie could have led us straight into a trap.

CHAPTER SEVENTEEN

I hated asking, but the witch made my skin crawl. We were only about a hundred yards away from her and descending quickly. With every inch I got closer to her, my internal warning clamored louder. *Should we go back?*

We don't have much of a choice. Egan sounded resolved and not as panicked as me. *Shifters generally feel uncomfortable around witches and their magic. The witches use the magic of the nature that we're in touch with. Since we can feel the disturbance that they create, it kind of goes against our very nature. But stay close to Draco and me in case something happens. I don't sense anyone else around, so I think we're okay.*

My dragon surged forward, tapping into our surroundings. I didn't detect any worrisome smells or sounds, confirming what Egan had said. I had to get used to being part animal since the extra-sensitive senses came in handy.

We landed, and the light illuminating her face dimmed as she stepped toward us. Her charcoal eyes took in our dragon forms, and she smirked. "I never thought I'd see one dragon in my lifetime, yet here three of you stand. Your race has hidden for so long, we all thought you'd gone extinct here on Earth."

She gestured to the woods behind us, and a few wisps of her silver hair fell from the bun teetering on top of her head. "Please, shift back into human form so we can speak."

Some of my anxiety calmed since she didn't seem so creepy now.

Egan stepped backward to the woods, not willing to turn his back on the witch. *Change right next to me,* he commanded, which annoyed me.

Fine, I will this time. But next time, why don't you ask? Maybe he was being protective, but that didn't mean he could treat me like that. I demanded respect, even when it was hard to give.

Now's not the time. Egan jerked his head toward the woods. *I'm trying to keep you safe, so be rational.*

The worst thing he could have done was tell me to be rational; every fiber of my being wanted to do the complete opposite out of spite. This new protective alpha male attitude better change fast. I did what any woman would have done to prove something to herself. I dropped Ollie's bag next to some trees so he could shift back without me having to see his dangly bits and stomped off to a section of woods farther away from Egan.

Of course, I hadn't thought that through, and the ground shook under each pounding footstep. At least, that drove the point home.

Where are you going? he asked in exasperation.

Away from you. I lifted my head high.

Good luck with that, Egan said with a chuckle.

Oh, I'd show him funny, but then I paused. Dammit, he had my clothes. I needed to change next to him, and it infuriated me. I had a problem doing what someone told me to.

Mustering up some dignity, I straightened my back and folded my wings to appear more rigid. I marched over to Egan and took the bag off the forest floor. If the situation hadn't been dire, I would've run off with them, but I had to be somewhat mature.

Even in dragon form, I could see Egan's shit-eating smile as he watched me head to the area he wanted me to change in. If I could have flipped him off, I would've.

I walked behind a section of trees and closed my eyes, pushing away all of the negativity. This was only my second shift back to human, so I wanted to concentrate. Like the previous time, my dragon released its hold on me without much of a struggle. My body began to change back to human just as Egan joined me.

Back in human form, I took my clothes from the bag and changed, ignoring my now naked mate beside me as he put on his jeans. I was still unhappy with him.

As I placed the bracelet in my pocket and moved to walk past him, he wrapped an arm around me and pulled me toward his naked chest. Thankfully, he had his jeans back on or things might have gotten out of hand.

I'm sorry for treating you like that. The witch is making me nervous, and I needed you next to me to keep me from losing my mind. He kissed me and let me go.

Unfortunately, my traitorous heart had already forgiven him. I wanted to stay upset a little longer, but that wasn't happening. *I understand, but no more macho asshole. Okay?*

He slipped his shirt on, his stomach muscles bunching, and a bit of drool collected in the corner of my mouth. He was so damn hot and all mine, the combination impossibly appealing.

Picking up the bag, he held my hand as we moved toward the witch. *I promise.*

When we stepped out of the woods, he released his hold on me. *Give me one second.*

He took off toward where Draco had gone and tossed the bag behind the large tree where the warrior dragon was waiting. In a flash, Egan was beside me again.

We returned to the witch and found Ollie standing next to her, waiting on us.

Needing to make sure I could still control Ollie, I fingered the bracelet in my pocket and spoke low so only Egan and Draco could hear. "Hug the witch and kiss her cheek."

Immediately, Ollie turned to the witch, pulled her into a tight embrace, and kissed her cheek.

The older lady's eyes widened, and she jerked away from him, wiping the slobber from her face. "What—"

I bit the inside of my cheek to stop myself from bursting into laughter.

Ollie swallowed loudly as he glared at me. "Trixie, these are the fated mate dragons I told you about. The witch that controlled me got her blood and has been using it to locate Jade."

"Yes, blood is very powerful in all types of magic. It is nice to meet you, Jade, even though it's not under the best of circumstances." Trixie held her hand out to me.

"I appreciate you helping us." I couldn't say it was nice to meet her, because it wasn't. I wished the circumstances had been different and I hadn't needed to meet her at all. But I forced myself to shake her hand.

The witch's grip took me by surprise. She was older, close to seventy, but her grip was strong. I didn't know what I'd been expecting, but it definitely wasn't that.

"And I'm Egan." My mate shook her hand, his face expressionless.

"I expected you two, but who is the other dragon?" Trixie asked as she looked around Egan to Draco.

"Another dragon joined us when the witch started giving us problems. She might be holding a female dragon from our thunder captive, and we're hoping you can locate her," Egan explained.

"I can try, but no promises. A witch that can spell something to control another person is very strong. Not many can do that, and I'm sure she made it impossible to track down the female dragon even with a personal item of hers."

"But if you could try—" Ollie started.

"Of course I will, boy." She patted his arm. "I just hate I can't do more." She faced me. "Ollie told me about that bracelet you grabbed. May I see it?"

Yeah, that wasn't happening. I didn't know this woman, and I wouldn't hand over the one thing keeping Ollie loyal to us. "Not right now."

Her eyebrows lifted, and she opened her mouth to respond, but Draco joined us with the bag, stepping beside me.

I felt sandwiched between the two towering men.

"The moon is high, and Ollie said something about you needing to use your magic at its peak," Egan interjected, changing the subject.

"Yes, that's true." The witch licked her lips and held out her hand to me, palm facing up. "Please put your hand on mine and let me see if I can sense what's going on."

We'd just told her what was going on, but I'd humor her if it got her to help me. I did as she asked, and her hand warmed mine as something passed from her into me. I instinctively closed my eyes, not wanting to watch as everyone stared at me.

The warmth connected with my blood. I guessed it made sense since blood made magic the most powerful. As it threaded inside me, though, it felt cold and uncomfortable.

Is something wrong? Egan asked with concern. *I'm getting a weird emotion from you.*

I had no clue what I was feeling. *I don't think so. I can feel her magic, and it's cold.*

That's because your blood runs hot now with your dragon. Anything outside our norm feels cold. But if you feel any pain or like someone is attacking your mind, let me know.

"Yes," Trixie murmured. "I can feel her all over you. She has a spell on you that informs her where you are." Her hand tensed on mine.

I blinked and found myself staring into the witch's eyes. They were no longer charcoal. Instead, they were a vivid silver that glowed as brightly as the moon and her hair.

"Can you do something?" It freaked me out that Vera became alerted whenever I went somewhere. I'd thought she'd been locating me at certain points in time. I almost felt like my aunt was watching me again.

"Maybe." Her hand gripped mine harder, and more power trickled into me.

My dragon roared and surfaced into my mind. She didn't like what I was allowing to happen, and she wanted me to stop it.

I wasn't sure how to make her understand, and the flames flicked within me like my blood was going to war with the witch.

Something sparked as my dragon attacked the foreign magic. The cold crashed against the increasing temperature. I groaned as my knees buckled, and Egan's comforting arm wrapped around my waist, bearing my weight.

Babe, what's going on? he asked, alarmed.

Her magic just feels foreign. I had no clue what Trixie was doing, but my dragon did.

"What are you doing to her?" Draco asked warningly.

"I'm burning off the magic the other witch linked with her blood." She pushed even more magic inside me.

I sagged against Egan as my internal war intensified. The oddest sensations of hot and cold mixed as the two parts collided.

"Just a little longer," Trixie gasped.

Her eyes were now a blinding, piercing white. I shut my eyes again to find the strength to hold on.

Egan's worry slammed into me. *Maybe we should tell her to stop.*

No. If this was the key to preventing Vera from tracking us, I'd gladly endure it. I only had to hold on long enough for Trixie to finish.

But if your dragon—

The witch released me and staggered away. Her chest heaved, proving she'd struggled as hard as I had.

"Are you okay?" Ollie asked the older lady, touching her shoulder to steady her.

"Give me a moment, and I will be." She lifted her head toward the moon, basking in its light. Her hands shook as she wrapped her arms around her body.

The flames inside me roared, trying to keep the cold at bay until the cold tendrils vanished.

Is your dragon calming? Egan kept a firm hold on me, afraid I might fall.

Yeah, she is. Whatever the witch did has either settled or burned off. I didn't know another way to describe it.

Draco stepped closer, his body coiled, ready to attack.

Everyone was on edge, but I had a feeling until we relocated the thunder or found Mindy, we'd remain this way.

Trixie inhaled sharply and lowered her head to look at me. "You're really strong. I almost couldn't finish."

As strength returned to my body, I moved away from Egan to carry my own weight. I loved that I could count on Egan, but I had to stand on my own two feet.

His hand stayed firmly around me. *Don't rush it.*

I'm not. I'm good, I promise.

When he didn't smell a lie, he released his hold while the corners of his mouth still dipped downward. He hated that I had to endure all this.

"Did it work?" If I'd gone through all of that for nothing, I'd be awfully pissy.

"Yes, child. You're free from the witch's spell." More of Trixie's hair had fallen out of her bun during the intense connection we'd shared.

"What about the female dragon?" Ollie asked. "Can you find her?"

"Yes, that won't take nearly as much power." She nodded and pulled on her long brown dress. "But I need something of hers."

"How about hair?" Draco pulled a hairbrush from our shared bag. "We took this from her room."

"That will work perfectly." She took the brush and kneeled on the ground. She reached into her pocket and pulled out a knife and a paper map.

Her outfit hadn't impressed me, but now that I realized it was a dress with pockets, I kind of wanted one of my own.

The metallic scent of blood pulled me back to the moment, and I realized the witch had cut her palm.

She'd laid the map flat against the ground with the brush sitting on top. She rocked as she chanted, "*Locum tuum revelare.*"

After repeating the words three more times, she placed her hand over the brush and map and let several large blood drops fall on both items.

The wind picked up, and thunder crashed despite the cloudless night. Then the ground shook, and Trixie flew backward several feet.

Lightning hit the map as another bolt raced toward us.

CHAPTER EIGHTEEN

Draco lunged, knocking Egan and me to the ground as the lightning barreled over our heads.

If I'd felt sandwiched between the two men earlier, I'd been grossly exaggerating. My front lay flat against Egan with Draco draped over my back. Smushed between their bodies, I struggled to breathe.

The quaking earth rattled us, and their bodies jostled me, making my teeth clatter together. Vera was pissed and letting everyone know. And hell, she probably wanted to instill some fear in us.

I was thinking we were goners until the thunder tapered off and the world stilled. The silence was almost deafening after the chaos.

Neither Draco nor Egan moved—like they were waiting for the mayhem to start again.

I can't breathe. I squirmed, trying to get up, but I could barely move an inch. My head spun, warning me I wasn't getting enough oxygen. Before now, I hadn't thought it was possible to get too close to Egan. But boy, was I wrong.

"We're good," Ollie said, his voice sounding farther away. He had to be checking on Trixie. "Whatever that was is gone for now."

Draco moved, digging his side into my back and pushing me harder into Egan. My lungs screamed for air. After another second, his weight disappeared as he kneeled beside us.

I lifted my head and inhaled sharply, giving my body a moment to recover.

"Dammit," Draco growled.

I jumped to my feet. I pushed away any leftover discomfort and followed his gaze.

The map and hairbrush had disintegrated.

"Trixie." Ollie squatted beside her, gently patting her face.

If I hadn't heard her strong heartbeat, I would've thought she was dead.

A cold breeze churned, icy tendrils wrapping around us. Whatever clung to my skin was bone-chilling and laced with a deep, dark warning.

Draco turned slowly, surveying the area. "The witch is taunting us."

She couldn't have arrived here this fast, or I hoped not. But we had a more imminent threat to worry about—Trixie could be severely injured. I wasn't sure what magic was capable of and whether someone could be harmed from this far away.

Rushing over to Trixie and Ollie, I scanned the witch for any injuries. I couldn't see any, which made me worry more. Internal injuries were often more serious. I brushed her hair from her face, ignoring the breeze growing stronger. "Can we help?"

"Not really," Egan answered, hovering next to me. "She'll have to wake on her own."

"It's getting cold out here." We didn't have time to wait. Between the chill in the air and the threat of another storm, we needed to move her somewhere safe or wake her up so she could protect herself.

Doing the only thing I could think of, I bent at the waist and slapped her in the face a lot harder than Ollie had.

"Hey!" Ollie exclaimed. "Be careful with her. She's old."

Trixie's eyes fluttered. "I heard that, *boy*."

He winced. "I'm sorry. It's just—"

"You don't ever call a woman old, even if it is true," she scolded and opened her eyes.

"Yes, ma'am." Ollie nodded. "I didn't mean—"

"It's fine." Trixie sat up and rubbed her hands along her arms. "You've pissed off someone stronger than I've ever seen. Magic like that ..." She trailed off and shuddered.

She couldn't stop there. "What do you mean?"

"Old magic is much stronger than the kind you find today, but the strength of her power isn't possible."

"Not possible?" Egan's forehead lined with confusion.

"Strong witches still exist in the world but not nearly as strong as what they used to be." Trixie gazed at the stars. "As with most things, our bloodline has become more diluted, taking some of our power away. The power she has means she's pure-blooded or really old."

"Do witches live a long time?" Ollie asked, curiosity getting the better of him.

"We have a normal human lifespan, unlike shifters, which makes me think she's the purest witch I've ever encountered." She gestured to the charred ground. "I couldn't do something like that."

"I'm assuming there's no way to find Mindy." Draco gazed at where she'd pointed.

"So Mindy must be the girl I was trying to locate," Trixie said.

"Yes, it is," Egan said as he placed a hand protectively around my waist.

I stepped into his side, wanting to be closer.

The witch gestured to the ashes of the map and hairbrush. "There's no way now, and honestly, I wouldn't be thrilled about trying again. She tried connecting with my magic, but I held her off, barely. I'm not sure I could fight her off again."

Egan's face fell. "We don't want you to get hurt. You've done more than enough." *I'll need to help relocate the thunder and inform Mindy's parents that we can't find her.*

You? If he thought that would fly over well with me, he was dead wrong. *Nope. We.*

But if Mindy gives up the thunder's location, you could be in harm's way.

I faced him, allowing my rage to surge between us. *Let me be clear. We are partners and equals, which means we stick together. If you don't stop treating me like I'm delicate, we're going to have a serious problem.*

Feeling the gravity of my words, he frowned. *It's not that I think you're delicate or weak, I just don't want anything bad happening to you. I couldn't live with myself if you got hurt or worse.*

And you think I could live with you getting hurt? Don't be an egotistical, selfish prick. If you can put yourself at risk, so can I. I turned my back on him and closed our connection. He would only continue to rationalize why he was acting that way, and I wasn't interested.

I focused back on Trixie as the wind howled. "We need to get you inside."

"I'm fine." Trixie patted Ollie's hand. "You need to go. That's the only way this will calm down. She's making sure I don't attempt the spell again."

Draco glanced at Egan. "I don't sense anyone physically here, and the longer we stay, the greater the risk to your thunder. We should go now."

"All right." Egan sighed and brushed against our connection.

Nope, I refused to let him try to talk me out of going with him. He'd only piss me off more and make me more determined to prove myself by likely doing something stupid. For my sanity and his, he best back the hell off.

"Thank you for everything," I said to Trixie then arched an eyebrow at Egan. "I'm going to change." I grabbed the bag and rushed toward the woods, ready to strip down and shift into my dragon. I hated wasting time to change, but I refused to meet Egan's parents in the nude. I didn't give a damn if they were shifters.

The three guys followed closely behind me, and Egan said, "Ollie, you need to go back to the pack house and let them know what happened. Vera may attack them since she can't locate us anymore. They need to prepare with as many capable hands as possible."

"Got it," Ollie agreed. "I'll head straight there."

I stopped and faced them. "Maybe I should—" I reached for the bracelet in my pocket.

"Look, I get you don't trust me, but give me a chance to earn it." Ollie frowned. "We both want the witch to die."

He was right. I hadn't given him a chance, and I knew what it felt like not to be given a second chance. "Fine. Don't make me regret it."

He headed off into the woods to shift with Draco following close behind.

I hid behind some trees and undressed, putting my clothes and bracelet in the bag. My dragon surged forward, the flames licking my mind. With little effort, and more quickly, my body began to change. She and I were connecting and working together as one. As I turned fully beast, Egan joined me. He pulled out his cell phone from the bag and typed a message.

I opened the connection between us. *Are you texting your parents?* I didn't know why, but I hadn't even considered messaging them to let them know how dire the situation was. In my mind, we had to race there to let them know what we'd discovered.

Yeah, and Sadie. I want them to know what's going on and that Ollie is heading back to them. If he doesn't show up, we need to know.

I wasn't concerned about Ollie since he'd proved he was still under the control of the bracelet. He couldn't hear my words earlier, and I doubted he would've willingly kissed or hugged the witch. My shoulders shook with laughter, remembering her expression. Nonetheless, it didn't hurt to have some reassurance.

Done with his phone, he tossed it and his clothes into the bag, and soon, his huge dragon form stood right beside me.

We returned to the clearing and found only Draco waiting. The witch was gone, and Ollie was halfway into the sky, flying north.

The wind had calmed. Either the witch had focused elsewhere, or she was waiting for us to take to the air before attacking again. Neither option was ideal.

Egan linked as his wings flapped. *Keep an eye out.*

I'd planned on it, I bit back as I ascended.

The entire way into the sky, I had to keep reminding myself to breathe. I kept holding my breath as if I could hear an attack coming better, but it only made my head loopy. If the witch attacked, I needed to have a clear mind.

When we reached a high enough elevation in the cloudless sky so humans couldn't see us, my heart steadied. We'd already warded off several attacks, so maybe the rest of the trip would be smooth sailing.

A girl could hope.

The guys flanked me as we flew back toward Tennessee, and I realized I was clueless about where we were heading. *How long until we get there?*

Only a couple of hours. Our thunder is an hour north of Knoxville, in the mountains near Gatlinburg.

I'd expected them to be halfway across the world, not so close to Kortright University. Maybe it was the slight accent he and Draco had that had given me the impression.

The moon descended during our flight. Every mile we traveled made my dragon side feel even more antsy. I wasn't sure what was going on, but she was on edge.

We're only thirty minutes away. Egan linked, almost startling me.

For the past several hours, we'd flown in silence. *Is there anything I should know before we arrive?*

I don't think so. He flew closer to me, his golden eyes locking on mine.

How many are in your thunder? Are they okay with Draco coming? Are there any other ex-girlfriends or betrotheds I should know about?

More questions almost tumbled from my lips, but I held them back. Those were more than enough for now. The problem was there was no telling what I was walking into, and the unknown unsettled me.

Egan chuckled. *I should've known you'd have a ton of questions. Our thunder is around two hundred but dwindling. There hasn't been a new birth since me. My father was the last dragon allowed to find his fated mate before me.*

How is that possible? I thought dragons had been in hiding for several centuries.

He looked forward as we approached a large mountain. *Dragons can live for hundreds of years. My parents had me when they were in their sixties. They weren't in a hurry to start a family until after my grandfather died.*

Wait ... *How old are you?*

Don't worry, I'm only twenty-two years old. Dragons age like humans until they reach their mid-twenties.

My relief caught me by surprise. Dating a forty-year-old man who looked twenty would've bothered me. *Thank God. But that means your parents are in their eighties.*

But they look like they're in their mid to late thirties. So, we won't have to take care of them any time soon. He winked.

I stared at him in awe. Dragons could wink!

And they know Draco is coming. In fact, Dad expected him to come. He fell silent.

I realized ... *Is there a reason you're dodging the ex-girlfriends question?*

Not at all. I just have nothing to share on that front. You are my first in all ways, Jade, he said gently.

All of my earlier anger against him dissipated. How the hell could I stay mad at him after he'd said something like that? *I had a horrible first kiss, but everything else is the same about you.*

Annoyance flared inside him. *You kissed other guys?*

Only one, and it was horrible. My stomach revolted at the

memory of all of the drool. *I've never done anything else with anyone and definitely never felt this way for anyone.*

Good, he rasped. *I'd hate to have to kill a human.*

A chuckle bubbled inside me right before raw panic slammed into me. The urge to turn around grew so strong it stole my breath. *We need to turn around. Something's wrong.*

Dammit, I forgot about this. Egan sounded tense. *Jade, it's just the barrier. We use magic to stay hidden, and the barrier repels anything that isn't part of our thunder.*

But I am. Were they rejecting me?

After you've passed through the barrier once, this won't happen again. I need you to stay strong and trust me.

That was a huge ask, but I knew what I had to do. I clutched onto my dragon tightly, and we resolved to push through this obstacle.

Egan descended, and Draco and I followed suit. Draco didn't seem to have any issues passing through the barrier.

Why isn't he struggling? Draco wasn't part of his thunder either, so he should have been struggling too.

The same magic protects all the thunders. Once you're recognized by a barrier, your signature is known by all.

We were so close to the mountain that I could make out the leaves on the trees. Each wing flap increased my urge to flee. Right when I thought we were going to land, I ran into resistance and plummeted.

CHAPTER NINETEEN

My wings flapped, keeping me elevated, but everything inside screamed that I was dropping. My dragon surged forward in a panic, and I focused on the fact that everything was fine. We were only a couple hundred yards from landing on the mountain.

Just a little bit longer, Egan assured me.

As we reached the treetops, the surrounding air churned and spun. A sphere-shaped vortex pulsed before me, and the land blurred.

All of the colors mixed, and the sensation of falling hit me harder.

Egan! I cried. I couldn't make anything out.

Frustration laced his words as he said, *It's almost over. Hold on. I'm right here.*

His presence was the only thing keeping me together. If it hadn't been for him, I'd have already given up.

Disoriented, I continued my steady trek forward. We should have been landing. We'd been so close seconds ago.

I tensed, bracing for impact, but the churning stopped, and the overwhelming sensation of falling dissolved. Colors came back into focus as the mountain view vanished.

I couldn't believe my eyes.

A large cave surrounded by the woods appeared. The opening faced the sky, surrounded by green moss covering the rocks, and was large enough for us to enter in our beast forms one at a time.

What is that? I asked Egan, thankful that the intense feelings had disappeared. They'd been so fierce that I wasn't sure how I'd fought through them. They had vanished just in time because I wasn't sure how much longer I could have ignored the urge to turn away.

The entrance to the thunder. Egan descended with Draco and me right behind him.

Animals scurried loudly in the woods as we approached the opening. *Why is it so much louder here?*

No one travels through here because we rarely leave, and no outsider has ever made it through the spell. The animals aren't scared like they are outside of here. They've been protected the same way we have.

That was interesting. This was what our world would sound like if fear didn't exist.

Egan expertly fit through the opening, and Draco held back, allowing me to go next.

There was no telling what waited inside, but I couldn't let my trepidation hold me back. This was my new life, and coming here to help them evacuate was the way I needed to help my thunder and Egan's parents. I had to be strong, especially since Egan wasn't thrilled about me tagging along.

My dragon took more control, wanting to navigate a little while longer. I was more than happy to oblige. Having her mostly in control wasn't as worrisome as it had been at the beginning.

She took root in my mind and flitted us through the opening. Her excitement was contagious. Her meeting the thunder was the next most important thing to bonding with Egan.

Once inside the cave, I couldn't believe my eyes. I'd expected to find a dark, cold hole, but the cave was the opening to a huge valley at least a hundred miles wide. Next, I spotted an area comprising a village of large log cabins. A huge river ran through the outer section of rolling grassy hills. Next to the river lay vast farmland where all types of crops grew along with pastures containing cows and pigs.

I looked over my shoulder as Draco entered. The hole was the only way in or out but also seemed to be the way for the sun to shine into the valley.

I'd never seen anything so beautiful in my entire life. *I was not expecting this.*

Egan's happiness flowed into me. He faced me as he replied, *I'm glad you approve, and I wish we weren't rushing everyone to leave. I really wanted to share my childhood home with you.*

Maybe you can. Hopefully, Mindy would surprise us and refuse to give up the thunder's location. We had our doubts about her after she'd hidden instead of fighting alongside us, but maybe when she was forced to stand and fight, she would. I prayed, for all our sakes, that we were just being extremely cautious.

I hope so, but we can't chance our entire thunder on that. Egan headed toward the cabins.

There had to be over one hundred houses. A few people stood outside, looking directly at us, with at least fifty bags at their feet.

Egan flew past them and headed to the house in the center. People were focused on me and Draco, their faces lined with concern.

Oh, great. We were outsiders, and they weren't thrilled with us invading their thunder. I knew those looks all too well. That was how everyone in my aunt's entire neighborhood and the school I'd attended had treated me. Anyone outside their clique was treated with mistrust.

In other words—stranger danger. That concept mostly applied to little kids and held merit, but not when adults treated a child with prejudice. I shuddered at the memories. *That's a warm welcome.*

It's more at Draco than you. They know I'm mated and you're part of this thunder. They'll treat you like one of us; they just need to get to know you first.

He was probably right. My negativity stemmed from childhood baggage. What were they supposed to do, run up and throw their human arms around me? They probably couldn't due to my huge-ass frame anyway, and then I'd be freaked out because they'd touched me. These people couldn't win in my mind, and I worked to turn my perspective around. Combine that with the imminent threat of an attack, and of course, they were coming off as indifferent.

As we drew closer to the center house, I realized the doorway was huge. Our dragon forms could easily fit through it.

I guessed that was a perk of living in a thunder. The houses had been made to accommodate our beast forms.

My mate landed, and the door opened, revealing a woman with the same shade of blonde hair as his but pulled back into a long braid. She was an inch shorter than me in human form, which somehow comforted me. I figured I'd be the smallest one in the thunder, but maybe I wouldn't stick out after all.

Her moss-green eyes locked on me, and a smile broke across her face. "You must be Jade." She stepped toward me before stopping. She sighed. "I guess you should shift so we can actually talk and formally meet before welcoming you with open arms." She stepped aside to allow the three of us in.

I stepped into the house, and the sheetrock interior startled me. I'd expected the walls to be made of the same logs as the outside of the house, but it reminded me of all of the homes I'd lived in growing up. The three of us fit comfortably in the foyer. and a human-sized doorway to the right led deeper into the house.

Egan turned to a large door on the left and jerked his head. *Come on. It's the shifting room.*

Of course, they'd have a room designated for that.

The large, empty room took up the entire side of the house, but it was barely big enough for the two of us. Egan moved his wing to drop the bag, and his eyes dimmed as his dragon receded.

Knowing we needed to hurry, my dragon withdrew, and within minutes, I was back in human form.

Egan's eyes perused me.

No. There would be none of that. His mother was right outside the door. I refused for her to hear, see, or smell what he was doing in here. *Get dressed. We have a thunder to save, and we're in your parents' home.*

Not giving him a chance to complain, I snatched my clothes from the bag and dressed.

He sighed in exasperation and retrieved his clothes from the bag. *Fine. You're just tempting is all.*

And to think I once considered you gentlemanly, I teased. I still did, and he was. Our mate sides were just coming out. He always treated everyone with respect.

When he was dressed, he kissed me and laced his fingers with mine. *I would never want to make you feel uncomfortable, especially around my parents. And I'm sorry about earlier. You're right. You deserve to be here with me. It's just my natural instinct is to protect you.*

I struggle with the same thing, so I understand, but you need to realize my aunt made me feel weak, and when I left her, I promised I'd never allow myself to feel that way again. I need you to treat me like I'm your equal in every way. I couldn't hold his earlier behavior against him. My dragon wanted to fiercely protect him the same way.

He cupped my cheek, staring deep into my soul. *You kicked ass against those wolf shifters the other day in your human form. You are a force, and I will never make you feel otherwise again. We will protect each other going forward even if it's hard on us.*

He understood what I needed, proving we were made for each other. He cared about all of me—my mind, body, and soul—the same way I cared for him. *Thank you. I love you.*

I love you too. He tugged me to the door, leaving the bag behind for Draco. *Now let's go help our thunder.*

Words had never sounded so sweet or romantic to me.

Back in the hallway, Egan's dad stood next to his mom. His dad's eyes were the same mesmerizing gold as my mate's, and he had the same striking features. The only difference between them was his father's short cedar hair.

Draco brushed past me into the shifting room, leaving the four of us alone in the entryway.

"Dad. Mom. This is—" Egan started, but his mom cut him off.

"Jade, it's so great to finally meet you." She hugged me and sniffled. "I'm so sorry for what Mindy has put you through and now all this."

"It's not your fault, and everything worked out." I winced. "Okay, 'worked out' might be a stretch. More like fate intervened." Wait, that wasn't much better. My awkwardness reared its ugly head once again. "Not that fate wants you to abandon your home." Oh my God. They were going to hate me.

His mother chuckled warmly. "No, I understand what you mean. And you're right. Fate chose you as his mate. She wouldn't let a jealous dragon shifter get in your way."

It caught me off guard that her presence comforted me almost as much as Egan's did. I'd expected someone prickly, especially knowing how good Egan was. I wasn't good enough for him.

"And it's nice to be introduced to our daughter." His father wrapped his arms around both Egan's mother and me.

The warm greeting shook me. "It's nice to meet you both."

"Please, call us Mom and Dad." His mother beamed.

"Uh ..." I'd just met them. That was a little uncomfortable.

"She means call them Ladon and Kayda." Egan shook his head, his shoulders shaking with quiet laughter. *I'm so sorry about her. She's excited to meet you and can come off a little strong.*

Kayda rubbed a temple. "That was strange asking you to call us that right away. Ladon and Kayda are more than fine."

"Did you travel here without issue?" Ladon asked, changing the topic, much to my relief.

"Yes. Nothing out of the ordinary happened, thankfully." Egan placed an arm around my waist. "How long until everyone is ready to go?"

"Within an hour," Ladon said and looked over my shoulder. "Draco, it's nice to meet you."

"The feeling is mutual." Draco bowed his head formally.

That was odd. *Is that how dragons greet one another?* If so, I'd probably completely offended his parents.

Egan's brows furrowed slightly. *No, I think it's his warrior side coming out.*

"Are you sure about your friends?" Kayda walked through the small doorway, waving for us to follow.

We entered a homey living room that held a couch, a love seat, and a recliner. There wasn't a television but rather a large bookcase filled with books.

"Sadie and Lillith have opened their parents' homes and the woods between their lands to us. We can make do and build a few houses. With our smaller numbers, we could double up some families and get by with what they have available. A few of Titan's pack members moved to Sadie and Donovan's to establish order after everything that went down a few months ago."

"We're so lucky you found such amazing friends." Ladon gestured to the seats in the living room. "Why don't we sit and talk for a minute?"

"Talk?" That was an odd request when we needed to get moving. "Shouldn't we be gathering everyone and figuring out logistics?"

"She's right." Egan pointed to the two bags against the wall at the base of the stairway. "We can talk later. Right now, we need to help others get situated."

Ladon sat on the loveseat. "We will, but there is something we need to discuss."

"Dad? What's wrong?"

"There's something we haven't told you, honey." Kayda sat next to her husband and took his hand. "We just need a few minutes."

Annoyance wafted off Egan.

Whatever they have to say seems important. I understood where Egan was coming from. This wasn't the best time to sit down and chat, but they seemed like reasonable people. So for them to request this had to mean it needed to be addressed right this moment.

I walked over to the couch and sat in the center. Egan hesitated but followed me over.

Draco stood near the doorway, his shoulders tense.

Whatever they wanted to talk about, Draco knew. The realization didn't sit well with me.

"Son, there's something we've needed to tell you since you were a little boy." Ladon inhaled sharply. "But we needed to wait until you'd found your mate. My father asked me to tell you both at the same time." Something coursed through my blood.

The cold feeling I'd felt with Trixie came back stronger, and my body shook as the magic took hold.

"Jade!" Egan yelled and clutched my arms. "What's wrong?"

CHAPTER TWENTY

The power receded, concerning me more than anything. Vera wasn't concentrating on me anymore, which meant her focus was elsewhere, likely on finding a way in.

"I think the witch tracked us. The coldness coursed through me again, like she was telling me she's here." Trixie had said it worked, but thinking back, she'd never outright said Vera couldn't track us. She'd only implied it. Could she be working with Vera, or was Vera's magic that powerful?

My stomach roiled. If I'd brought her here, that meant I'd essentially sold out the thunder.

Draco started. "But the witch said—"

"I know." He was thinking the same thing as me. "But I don't know what else it could be."

"Maybe she broke Mindy or found a way to control her like Ollie." Egan stood, his body tense. "Either way, it doesn't matter. If she's here, there's no undoing it."

"We need to get you out of here." Draco stepped toward the doorway. "Is there a back way out of here?"

"Yes, but it's not passable." Ladon rubbed his thumb over his bottom lip. "We always use the main entrance."

"Wait." Egan's brows furrowed. "There's a second way out? I never knew that."

"Each thunder only has one person who knows about the second passageway," Draco explained. He rushed to the front of the house. The door opened and closed as the warrior ran outside. He wanted to see what we were up against, giving us time to put a plan into effect.

I still wasn't following. "Why is that?"

"In case of an attack of this magnitude, one person can leave and warn the other thunders. If more than one family knew, it could create a mass exodus, preventing word from getting out that we need help." Kayda hurried over to the bags.

"We need weapons. I'm assuming she didn't come alone to a thunder full of dragons." Ladon walked over to the bookcase and pulled a book out. The house rumbled as a section of the bookcase pivoted outward.

"Why didn't I know about this?" Egan stepped up next to his father and peered inside.

"Because we hoped no one would need to know." He gestured toward the dark room that had guns and ammo lined in a neat row. "Grab a few rifles. Kayda, tell the others what's going on and to bring all the secret stashes of artillery. We need to get ready to fight before they get here."

"On it," Kayda said and raced to the door. "I'll be right back."

"There's no way we can lead all of them to the other exit before the witch arrives." Egan picked up a couple of guns and held them expertly.

"No, that exit is purely for backup. I'm hoping we can leave out the main one. That's our best bet." Ladon faced me with a smaller gun. "Can you shoot?"

"Yeah, but it's been a minute." A few self-defense classes I'd taken wanted us to be familiar with guns. Not to use but to know how to fight if our attacker had one. They'd taught us to only use them in a worst-case scenario. My instructors had made it clear he didn't approve, but learning about them was necessary to survive.

He gave the handgun to me. "Better than not knowing at all."

"I don't understand." I took the gun. It felt like it weighed a ton, although it had to be a pound, max, in my hand. "Why don't we shift into our dragons and fight?"

"That's likely what the witch wants, and we may be very strong in that form, but we'd also be bigger targets." Ladon selected a black holster that could be tied around an arm or a thigh and handed it to me. "In human form, we can lie low and hide. And sometimes, our human forms can be more lethal, especially when we tap into our dragons to amplify our senses."

I'd never thought of it like that. In beast form, we were huge.

"Maybe you and Mom should go out the back," Egan said as he looked at me. "Dad and I can stay back and fight with the others."

No, he didn't. Maybe he really did have a death wish but wanted me to end him instead of whatever threat we were facing.

I stared him down and let my anger punch each syllable. "Don't you start. Remember the conversation we just had?" I jabbed my finger at the shifting room.

"Son, you can't expect her to leave you. Would you be willing to run and leave her here to fight?" Ladon sighed.

"God, no, but—"

"You better think through your next words." My blood was boiling, ready for a fight. I'd rather it be against the witch, but Egan was about to get the brunt of my anger.

Ladon patted his son's arm. "We have strong mates for a reason."

"You're right." Egan kissed my forehead. "And you can hold your own. I've seen you in action."

"Damn straight I can." And I had a score to settle with my ex-roommate.

The front door swung open and slammed against the wall. Kayda yelled, "We've got a huge problem."

"What is it?" Ladon grabbed the rest of the guns, and we sprinted to the front door.

Draco stood next to her in the entryway.

Kayda's face was as pale as a vampire's, and her eyes had darkened to hunter green. The acidic smell of fear blew off her. "The witch brought harpies."

"Harpies?" Ladon's mouth dropped. "But they're from Fae."

"I told you the fae king warned me they were still looking for us." Egan stepped protectively next to me. "Maybe the witch is connected to them. It would explain how strong she is."

"Fae as in Sadie's dad and aunt's realm?" That was still a foreign concept to me. Another dimension sounded straight out of a science fiction novel.

"Yes." Egan frowned. "We hid because they were hunting us down centuries ago."

"Are the others getting their weapons?" Ladon asked as he handed two guns to Draco.

"They're getting them now." Kayda pushed past us, grabbed the two bags, and threw one over each shoulder. "We need to get a move on. At least a hundred harpies are heading this way."

"We need to shoot them. The more we take out before they get within fighting range, the better our chances that more of us will come out of this alive." Draco opened the door and left first.

As the rest of us stepped outside, he stood with his gun pointed at the cave opening, covering us, and I could not believe what I saw. At the word 'harpy,' I'd had no clue what to expect, but it certainly wasn't that.

A swarm headed straight toward us. I tapped into my dragon, and the women came into full view—or they looked like women. They were equal parts human and animal. The top half was completely naked and all human. They each had a long torso, two arms, and large, voluptuous breasts. As if that wasn't striking enough, their cruel, weathered faces and deep-set coal eyes made them truly frightful. Their hair was greasy and tangled, and blood crusted their dry, peeling lips. From the torso down, they looked reptilian. They had large, scaly legs, clawed feet, and knotty fingers. Strong, leathery wings jutted from their backs, giving them a bird-like appearance.

I wasn't sure whether they were more human, reptile, or bird.

Half the flock carried bone-like clubs, while the other half had bows made of bone. Their weapons were of all different sizes and lengths, telling me they'd used many different types of victims to make each bow.

Egan walked beside me as we headed toward the dragons standing in the center of the neighborhood. The entire thunder was here.

Five other men with weapons came running toward us.

It looked like we had enough guns for everyone. There were no children in the mix, so everyone was old enough to handle one.

"What's the plan?" a lady around the same age as Kayda asked. Determination filled her amethyst eyes, and she pulled her plum-brown hair into a ponytail. "Do we shift now?"

"No, Rose. Take a gun and hide. Worst case, we shift into our dragons, but their arrows can penetrate our scales. We need to stay human until we no longer can. The more of us we can group together, the better."

Draco stepped forward, taking control. "We can't stay circled like this, or they'll pick us off.

"You'll stay with them, right?" an older man asked. His thin gray hair barely covered his scalp, but his amber eyes held an intelligence that age couldn't diminish.

"Of course," Draco said and glanced at Ladon and Kayda, then Egan and me. "I'll stay with them."

Uh ... why are they so concerned about us? The odd wording had to mean something.

My dad is viewed as the youngest leader here. Egan stepped closer. "Let's move."

I looked over my shoulder, and the front line of harpies was now only several hundred yards away. Two at the front lifted their bows and pulled an arrow from the quiver they wore high on their backs above their wings.

"They're getting ready to shoot!" Draco yelled.

Our group ran in various directions.

Draco waved for us to follow him as he ran back to the house. He yelled, "We can shoot from the windows."

I ran as fast as I could to keep up with Egan beside me. The sound of flapping wings grew louder as the harpies caught up to us. We had to figure a way out of there.

An arrow whistled through the air, growing louder every second. At least one harpy was targeting us. I spun around to see who the target was, only to see an arrow heading straight for my head. "Duck!" I exclaimed to the others and rolled out of the way at the last possible second. The arrow landed only inches from where I'd been standing.

"Jade!" Egan cried with pure terror as he ran toward me. He grabbed me by the waist and threw me over his shoulder.

Each step he took jarred my body, but I ignored the pain and lifted my head. Twenty harpies veered off from the main group, racing after us.

Egan's home was a little ways away, and they were gaining on us. A harpy reloaded her bow and aimed right past us at the front of the group.

"Watch out!" I warned desperately. With the majority of the harpies after us, Vera's target was clear.

The arrow buzzed over our heads, and I heard a sickening thud. The iron smell of blood spilled into the air.

"Ladon!" Kayda whimpered.

"I'm fine," he grunted. "Keep going."

You need to put me down. Egan carrying me was slowing us down. *I'm fine.*

You stay right next to me, Egan said and paused to set me down.

As soon as my feet met solid earth, I sped toward the house.

Draco opened the door and waved us in. An arrow protruded from Ladon's upper shoulder, but he hadn't slowed down.

Thankfully, the wound looked superficial.

Egan's parents ran inside the house, and we were only a few feet away. The harpies were so close I could hear them breathing.

The sound of another arrow being nocked sent a burst of adrenaline through me. I jumped the last few feet into the house and turned around.

Egan raced toward us, his face etched with pure determination. His golden eyes glowed as his dragon peeked through. Right as he crossed the threshold, an arrow followed, buzzing directly at my head. Shocked, I stood frozen in place.

"Move," Draco growled. He slammed the door shut and locked it.

A thud pounded where the arrow had hit the door instead of my brain. I stumbled back and sagged against the wall. My brain had short-circuited as I glanced at the warrior dragon. "Thank you."

"Don't thank me yet." He rushed into the smaller doorway. "Egan, I need your help. Jade, make sure no one gets through that door."

Of course, he'd leave me with the easy job. I crossed my arms, frowning at the locked wooden door. Did Draco expect them to float through it? Vera was strong, but I doubted she was that powerful.

Something loud pounded on the door, startling me.

What the hell was that?

It sounded again and again. Soon, there were multiple hard knocks on the door.

Holy shit, the harpies with the clubs were trying to break through.

Their noise grew louder as they attacked together. The door shook from the magnitude of the force.

"Uh ... guys." Now I understood why Draco had asked me to stay there. "We have a problem."

I placed my hands on the door to reinforce the wood. Each hit against the door jerked my entire body.

The noise turned into one continuous roar as more harpies joined the barrage. The hinges shook, and the door lurched hard against the metal. "Guys!" I yelled again.

"We're coming," Draco said, barely audible over all the noise.

I wasn't sure how much longer I could hold this. I was clueless about how many were on the other side of the door. They began clawing into the wood, determined to get in.

"Move," a loud voice crowed. "I'll get us through."

Something slammed into the door, and I flew back against the wall.

CHAPTER TWENTY-ONE

Hitting the wall knocked the breath out of me, and I fell in a heap on the floor. The door swung open, and ten angry harpies attempted to get in at once, climbing over each other, desperate to get to me first.

"Keep low," Draco commanded as gunshots fired.

A harpy fell, but the others didn't care. Their eyes were glued to me like they had the overwhelming urge to hurt me.

A war cry pierced my ears as a harpy barreled through the others, her club held high over her head. She swung the bone downward, but a bullet pierced her chest. Her eyes widened, and she stumbled forward then fell, landing right on top of me. Her boobs plopped on my face, and her dirty hair acted like a shield between fresh air and her rancid smell. Warm blood trickled from her chest down my cheeks.

This was worse than any nightmare I'd ever had. Her body convulsed, jiggling her breasts. I felt a serious need to get her off me. Granted, I bet some guys in the world would've loved to be in my position.

I pushed her off me as an arrow plunged into the harpy's side, right where my arm had been. The harpy groaned and flopped on the ground, blood pooling at the corners of her mouth.

My focus darted back to the door. Three harpies had their bows drawn and pointed at me. The ones with the clubs banged on the wood outside, adding fear to an already horrible situation.

This was how I imagined impending doom sounded.

A dragon roared as he flew into view, his dark scales reflecting the rising sun. He darted toward the harpies focused on me. Fire poured from his mouth, lighting up the strange women.

"Protect the royal family!" a person yelled, but I couldn't see who it was with all the harpies standing in my way. "They're attacking their home."

The dragon froze, flames pouring in the same spot, seemingly surprised by the news.

The front door of the house next to us opened, and a man around Ladon's age popped his head out, his hair askew. He stepped out of the house with a rifle. "The royal family lives here?"

Of course, the royal family would live here. We'd led Vera straight to the top. Surely Egan would've told me that if he'd known. We would have been extra cautious coming back.

The dragon shook his head like he was coming to, and the harpies dropped their clubs and ran inside the house, desperate to escape the flames the dragon spewed at anything that came close.

Their screams drowned out the rest of the conversation the two dragon shifters were having.

If we hadn't been fighting for our lives, it would've been an amazing sight, but we had far more important things to focus on.

As they reached the threshold, Draco appeared beside me and fired at them one by one. A few took flight.

There was no telling where they were going. I'd moved to stand when Egan's large arms encircled me and pulled me farther into the house.

They're getting away. I tried squirming out of his hold.

Just give me a second. He raced us to the couch and set me down gently on the soft material.

I looked over his shoulder to find Ladon and Kayda kneeling in front of an open window in the middle of the room, shooting at the harpies trying to get inside that way.

Egan cupped my face. "Where are you hurt?"

His concern pulled my attention back to him. He'd asked me that same question more often than I'd have liked to admit. "I'm fine. It's the harpy's blood." If Roxy had been here, she'd have said something to the tune of, "Oh, the one you copped a feel of," defusing some of the tension. A laugh would've been nice right now.

"Thank God." Egan dropped his hands and clenched them into fists. "We wanted to get the wooden kitchen table in front of the door, but they broke through before we could get there."

Gunshots continued to fire as screams echoed all around.

"It's bad out there." I shivered. "Some dragons are shifting to fight in beast form."

"That's good." Egan faced his parents. "A mix is probably ideal considering how bad the situation is getting."

"This is insane." Kayda reloaded her gun and aimed out the window again. "It's like they have no fear."

I had a feeling that was the case. "Did you know the royal family lives here?" From what Egan had said, only a handful of people knew who they were. I was curious if his father did since he was considered a leader. "Apparently, that family is being attacked hard. Vera must know who they are."

"Wait." Egan tensed and straightened. "The royal family is here? You'd think that would have been brought up before the attack."

At least, he hadn't known. That made me feel better because I'd hoped he would've shared something like that with me.

"Yes, they're here," Ladon snapped, his focus on fighting the enemy that kept coming. The arrow had been removed from his shoulder, and fresh blood made his shirt cling to his back.

"Are you okay to fight?" I asked Ladon with concern. Here Egan was, all paranoid about me when his father was actually wounded.

"It's superficial." He nodded at me, his golden eyes lightening. "I'm completely fine to fight. Once we get through this, I'll get it bandaged."

Glass broke upstairs. The harpies had made it into the house.

"They need to know," Kayda scolded, aiming her gun at the stairs. "Do not try to change the subject."

Okay, I was done being helpless. I pulled my gun from my holster and ran to stand next to Ladon. These suckers had to be multiplying. It had looked like there were only a hundred or so earlier, but their numbers must have doubled. I pointed my gun and fired at the closest harpy.

"Need to know what?" Egan hurried next to his mom and pointed his rifle up the stairs. "Who are the royals? There's no point keeping it a secret now."

"Dammit." Ladon fired again and looked at Egan. "This wasn't how I wanted to tell you, but you and Jade must make it out of here alive. You two are the next king and queen of the dragons."

"What?" Egan stilled, and his breathing tensed. "Is this a sick joke?"

Loud tapping noises drew closer as harpies descended the stairs. For whatever reason, they were running down the stairs instead of flying. My mind was reeling from this brand-new information Ladon had unleashed on us. *This can't be real.*

Unfortunately, I think it is. Egan kept his aim at the stairwell as the harpies came flooding down. There were at least ten lined up on the stairs while three flew overhead. They came fast and hard.

Us being the future king and queen of the dragons was something we'd have to deal with later. Our focus needed to be on survival.

Between the shriek of harpies and the gunfire, my ears rang. I shot round after round, my hands shaking even after the gun had stopped vibrating. They were closing in.

Draco hadn't come back around, and I hoped that was a good

thing. They hadn't come through the doorway, which could only mean that Draco was still alive and fighting.

Four dragons in varying colors of green swarmed straight toward us.

The largest one had glowing amber eyes that contrasted against its fern-colored- scales. It led the group to the harpies attacking us.

Harpies with clubs flew to intercept them and attacked. At least, we had backup, but we needed more.

I wanted to pay attention to their fight, but I couldn't. A harpy flew in front of the window and nocked an arrow. She released the arrow, and it sailed straight toward us.

Ladon was too preoccupied with shooting at the closer harpies to see the looming threat. Not knowing what else to do, I lunged at him, praying the gun didn't go off. I sacked him, my arms going around his waist, and landed right on top of him.

The arrow lodged into my upper thigh. I reached down and clutched the bone, and blinding pain overcame me. "What the ..." It hurt worse than I would've ever imagined. My eyes watered.

"We've got to get that out of her leg. Egan! Ladon! Shoot!" Kayda turned her back on the increasing number of attackers coming down the stairs.

Ladon gently rolled me off him as a harpy flew in through the window. He grabbed the gun and used the butt to knock her back outside before turning it around and firing again.

The pain throbbed up my leg. My leg jerked, making the pain worse, so I clutched it, trying to hold my leg steady.

Kayda grabbed the fletching of the arrow that protruded from my leg.

"What are you doing? You aren't supposed to remove an arrow," I whispered and tried jerking away from her, but she held on tight.

"We have to get this out. It's laced with fae poison. It'll be worse if we don't pull it out," she replied and yanked.

The intense pain doubled me over, and I puked all over their floor. Under normal circumstances, I'd have been embarrassed, but this situation had put things into perspective. If puking was the worst thing that happened to me, I was doing better than most.

"Jade." Egan looked at me. "Baby ..."

That endearment always caught me off guard.

"I understand you're concerned, but you need to focus on the winged hags or your mate will get hurt worse," Kayda scolded as she examined my wound.

Surprisingly, the pain receded by removing that damn arrow. More blood came out, but it didn't hurt as badly. "Wow, you were right. The pain is manageable this way."

"They coat their spears in something that intensifies pain. So Ladon struggled more than he admitted earlier when he'd been hit. The bleeding isn't too worrisome, and it's pushing the poison out of your system. You should be good, but take it easy on the leg."

"How do you know all this?" I asked.

"I was a nurse for a couple of years before finding Ladon." She held up her gun and raced over to Egan just as a harpy hit him in the head with the club.

He stumbled backward before catching himself, and his mother shot the harpy in the chest.

We had to find a way out of the house. There were too many harpies attacking us. I linked to Egan. *I'm going to check on Draco.*

I rose to my feet and glanced back. The three of them were holding off the harpies, but I needed to hurry before they overpowered us again. We might not be able to recover a second time.

Refusing to limp, I walked slower than normal. The bleeding was already slowing, reminding me that I wasn't fully human anymore. A nice perk about being a dragon shifter was quicker healing.

As I turned into the entryway, I prepared myself for the worst-case scenarios. I'd expected harpies to be flooding the house, but Draco fought outside the door with a few dragons attacking the harpies. The harpies tried to go around the dragons and attack us from the windows. Maybe splitting up hadn't been the best decision. "Guys, we need help."

I stepped outside. Fifty harpies were fighting the other dragons, but the rest were focused on us. Now I understood why—Vera wanted to take out the royal family.

"What do you mean?" Draco asked, and his eyes locked on my wound. "What happened?"

"Most of them are attacking from the back." Draco obviously thought he was protecting us, and I couldn't blame him. He hadn't expected a horde to be trying to get inside through the back windows.

Egan, there are a lot fewer out front. It's our best way out.

They're gaining ground. We'll be out there in a second.

Draco's eyes widened. "Why? Unless the witch figured out you're part of the royal family and is targeting you."

"That's what I'm thinking." I wanted to blame Mindy, but if Egan hadn't known, how could she? The way she'd pushed too hard despite Egan having found his fated mate had me suspicious of her intentions.

"Protect her!" Draco called to the two nearby dragons and ran into the house to help my mate.

The two dragons flew toward me, and around ten harpies flew around the house. They gazed at me, and I swore one of them smirked.

They must have heard Draco and decided to check out who he was talking about.

A shrill cackle escaped one, though I couldn't tell which. The harpy that had smirked lifted her bow and arrow, aiming it at me.

My dragon surged forward into my mind. Between my injured leg and my dragon's desperate need to take control, I didn't fight back. Instead, I chose to trust her.

The clothes ripped from my body as I shifted within seconds. Just as the harpy released the arrow, I took to the sky.

Something hot built inside as I flew at her. It unnerved me how each one looked identical at a glance, but I couldn't waste time inspecting them to see whether that was true. Survival was of the utmost importance.

The harpy drew her bow, but I gained ground on her.

I felt heat bubbling inside me, and my dragon pushed it from deep inside my belly. Flames and smoke spewed from my mouth, charring her. As she dropped, no longer a threat, I held the flames in and spun around. Another archer reached for an arrow.

I've got you covered. Egan linked as he raised his gun and shot at a harpy behind me.

My dragon purred. For once, he wasn't trying to protect me or get me to stand down. He was treating me as an equal, and I loved it.

A harpy with a club lowered its head and flew at me, trying to distract me while the other one shot at me. I didn't know what to do or which one to choose. Either way, one of them would hurt me.

CHAPTER TWENTY-TWO

My eyes flicked from the archer harpy to the one charging at me like a bull with her bone club tucked at her side.

Ugh ... which one should I attack? That arrow in my leg had hurt like a son of a bitch, so I should take that one out. With the club, my body wouldn't be susceptible to the poison.

Unless ... I pulled something epic.

To achieve this level of awesomeness, the timing would have to align, but it was the best shot I had to avoid injury.

The harpy drew back her arrow as the bull-like one got within five feet of me. My heart raced, and I hoped I could pull this off.

"Jade!" Draco yelled with alarm from below.

He'd distract me if he kept that up. I now understood how lucky the wolves were to have a pack link. It would've come in handy with the thunder, but dragons didn't have that luxury, and wishing dragons had that was a waste of energy.

The harpy lifted the club over her shoulder like a softball player and aimed for my head. I waited a quick second before ducking and flying upward. She startled as I wrapped my arms around her waist and wings, trapping her.

The club fell, and she screamed and buried her face in my chest. This wasn't much better than the boobs. She tried to bite me, but her teeth couldn't pierce my scales, probably from the amount of decay.

I needed a bath desperately.

A whistle grew louder, and I watched as the other harpy had released the arrow. The poisoned-laced tip barreled straight toward my backside.

I had to move fast. I attempted to spin the harpy around, but she jerked, stalling my rotation. Dammit, these creatures were sturdier than I'd given them credit for. This might've been a bad idea.

Desperation clawed at me, and I tried to move her again, using every ounce of strength I had. With the arrow only inches away, I turned her enough so that it lodged into her back between her wings.

If I'd thought I'd heard their worst screams yet, boy did she prove me wrong. My eardrums felt like they would burst at the magnitude. I released her, and she tumbled to the ground. She flapped her wings, but they barely moved, probably from the pain.

Watch out. Egan linked, drawing my attention to him. He lifted his rifle as absolute terror filled his eyes.

I looked to where the barreled was pointed, and the harpy nocked her bow again. A sick, dark chuckle left her as she released the arrow.

Egan's hand jolted, and a bullet launched from the barrel. My ears rang from the harpy's scream, the gunshot barely audible.

The bullet lodged in the harpy's shoulder, causing her to convulse as she released the arrow. Egan didn't hesitate to fire at her again, and he hit her right in the heart. She fell.

The arrow didn't come close to hitting me and landed several yards away to where no one stood.

Realizing we were no longer in the house, the horde headed straight for us.

"We need to get you to safety!" Draco yelled and turned to a couple of dragons in human form. "Tell the others that plans have changed. Everyone needs to come out and fight. Half should shift, and the other half should stay human to fire the rifles. The harpies don't plan to split, and we need everyone in the fight."

"Yes, sir!" a guy who didn't look much older than us yelled and ran in the opposite direction, toward the houses at the other end.

Fifty harpies moved together toward us, their eyes locked on Egan and his parents. It scared me that the identity of the king was no longer secret. The way they were dead set on Egan's family and me screamed that our cover as regular shifters was blown. But we'd have to sort out the implications later when we were safe and sound.

Draco's jaw twitched, and displeasure wafted off him. "I thought they would have spread across the entire village and not just focused on your home and the ones near it."

From a strategic perspective, I would've thought the same thing. No one could've guessed that they'd know who the royal family was when only a handful, if even that many, in the thunder knew.

"Egan, when the group gets here, we need to split off when most of the harpies are engaged in battle," Draco commanded as if he were the ruler. "You all need to shift. It'll be harder to distinguish you in beast form. But wait until they're preoccupied. It's bad enough that they might know what Jade looks like in animal form."

Egan lifted his chin, anger fueling his movements. "We can't leave our people to fight while we run and hide."

I wished I were standing beside my mate, but if the harpies didn't recognize me since they hadn't been around here when I'd shifted, I didn't need to give myself away.

"It's more important that you survive this," Draco told Egan. "You and your family are the only ones preventing the fae dragon from taking control of this realm too."

How could he know? The dragon was in an entirely different realm. The threat didn't sound that real even though I wasn't a huge fan of anyone dying.

Remember, harpies are from the fae realm. Egan scratched the back of his neck as he gazed at me. *Which means the fae dragon is involved. We've been hiding from him for centuries.*

"Son, he's right." Ladon raised his gun at the horde. "You two have to survive."

Egan snapped his head in his father's direction. "You're the king—"

Ladon shot his gun at the harpies that were within range, cutting Egan's words off.

Kayda followed her husband's lead and fired into the cluster of harpies.

"Kill as many as you can," Draco said and gestured to Egan's gun.

The four of them took down several women flying straight at us. The threat of death didn't deter them, which was damn crazy. Any sane being would have run for their lives, telling me way too much about the fae realm.

Some of the archers stopped their forward trajectory and flew higher into the sky, ready to fire down at us. For the first time, they ignored me as they drew their bows.

I had to do something before Egan and the others got hurt.

I flew forward, and Draco grumbled, "Holy shit. She's lost her fucking mind. What part of 'don't put yourself in harm's way' did she not understand? Balls!"

Despite hiding from the modern world for so long, he was pretty damn versed in the art of cursing. I'd thought people were better-mannered back then.

Egan linked with me, furious. *What are you doing? You're going to get yourself killed.*

I'm attacking the ones in the back that are focused on you. I didn't plan on taking out the ones with clubs. I let the fire build in my stomach, ready to spill it over those who attempted to fight me as I flew by.

The flapping of wings sounded behind me, and I turned to find ten dragons heading our way with men and women trailing behind them.

We were finally getting the backup we desperately needed. I turned around and flew toward the horde. Every three shots, a harpy fell, their numbers dwindling.

When I was ten feet from the others, the four dragons that had been fighting behind the house joined me, two flanking me on each side. Luckily, Egan and the others were able to shoot around them.

Despite not being able to communicate, we were all on the same page. Smoke trickled from their noses as they called on the flames inside them. As we met the horde of harpies, two of the dragons breathed flames over them while the two others and I flew underneath them, hiding under the masses to attack the three archers in the back.

Arrows whizzed as the three harpies attacked our thunder. I pushed my wings harder to reach the harpies before they could launch more arrows. The two dragons with me kept pace, and we shot upward toward the enemies.

I bit the reptilian leg of the one in the middle. My dragon wanted to gag at the overwhelming stench, and my stomach revolted, but I pushed it aside and jerked my head.

Losing all sense of control, the winged creature let out an ear-piercing scream, but I was partially deaf from the other harpy, or maybe more immune to their noises. Either way, I didn't want to claw my ears out, so that was a win.

Reaching up, I trapped her body with my arms and dug my talons into her wings. I slashed through her skin, and warm blood oozed from her injury.

Releasing her, I let her drop and spun around to check on the others. Between the four dragons that had attacked with me and the ten on their way, the fight began to look promising for us.

A faint breeze blew behind me, and I pivoted to find Egan a few feet away in dragon form. For all our sakes, I hoped no one realized who he was. I scolded him, *You were supposed to wait.*

As soon as the five of you attacked, their focus turned to you and the ten dragons. They didn't see me change, but dammit, do you know how hard it was to watch you from down there? His golden eyes narrowed.

If he wanted to make me feel bad, it wasn't happening. *Don't give me that. You were fighting on the ground. You were as likely to get hurt down there as up here.*

But not being beside you was driving me mad. He roared as a harpy flew at us, and he shot flames all over her body.

They aren't very bright.

Egan shook his dragon head. *No, they aren't. Come on, Draco and my parents are waiting.*

But ... I glanced back as more dragons came forward. The harpies were being slaughtered, and there wasn't much risk to the dragons.

Once we get out, we'll hide somewhere, and Draco will bring them to us. We need to relocate because one could escape and tell the others of our location. Egan nudged my body with his. *We wouldn't be leaving them if it wasn't under control. And Dad's right. If they capture us, it'll be worse for everyone.*

He was right, and we had taken the brunt of the attack. Hell, we'd done most of the fighting. *Okay. Let's go.* Maybe if they realized the royal family was gone, they'd retreat.

I followed Egan to a grassy hill that jutted from the edge of the cave. The other side wasn't visible from here.

As we approached, Egan landed next to the last house in the neighborhood. I mirrored his movements and noticed that the dragons were still gaining ground on the harpies. There was no way these fae creatures could win now, and none of them were paying attention to us.

Egan clutched my arm and we made it to the side of the house where the hill started a few feet to the right.

Let's hurry before someone catches us. Egan linked as he nudged me in front of him.

I ran as gently and quickly as possible to the other side. Draco snarled but stopped short when he smelled me ... or saw me.

What the hell? Why would he—then it hit me. You couldn't see shit from this side. But if we stayed quiet, no one would consider looking over here.

Ladon's dragon stood as tall as Egan's, and his scales were a dark army green. Kayda was a few inches shorter than me, and her scales were a shade lighter than Ladon's. The two of them took off, leading the way to the secret passageway only they knew about.

Egan reached my side, and Draco waved us forward, wanting to take the rear.

That was fine, but even if it hadn't been, we couldn't argue without making noise and giving away our position.

We ran along the grass, keeping our steps as quiet as possible. The light gray stone of the cave sat to the right with the grass to the left. Farther up, the greenery grew more sparse and the ground more rocky.

If I'd been in my human form, my feet would have gotten cut, but in this sturdier form, I might as well have been walking on a cloud. Well, okay, that was a stretch, but it didn't hurt.

At the top of the hill, the cave was covered with a series of stacked rocks, with green moss growing all over it. It was thick and growing through the crevices.

This was what Ladon must have meant when he'd said it probably wasn't passable, but with our talons, surely we could make it through.

I moved to attack one side, then felt an all too familiar tickle at the base of my neck. I stilled, and my heart stopped. *Egan, she's here.*

CHAPTER TWENTY-THREE

The tingling increased as Vera's presence drew closer. How the hell had she gotten here? She couldn't walk through the entrance to the cave.

Egan spun away from the escape route. We stood side by side, staring down the threat as Ladon and Kayda worked to remove the vines.

The warrior dragon tilted his head in confusion, then the rancid smell of harpy hit. He stood protectively in front of us, preparing to fight.

The foul smell told me how Vera had gotten here. The fae creatures were working with her as her personal chauffeur. The stench grew stronger. I shuddered and wiped my dragon face where blood had dripped from the boobful of convulsing harpy.

A harpy flew over the hill, Vera dangling from its talons, confirming what I'd suspected. Vera's stringy caramel hair looked clean for once as it blew in the breeze but especially compared to the half-human carrying her. Her eyes were as black as night and locked on Egan and me.

"Lower me to the ground," Vera commanded.

The winged creature obliged, slowly placed her on the ground, and stepped behind the witch.

Irritated, I wished I were in human form so I could tell the bitch off.

"Well, well, what do we have here?" Vera wore her standard Star Wars t-shirt. The only thing missing was her thick glasses that usually framed her face.

The stench of harpies warned me that she had backup. *Egan, there are more near.*

I smell them too, Egan said with disgust.

Not wanting to waste any time, I took a menacing step toward her. The horrible woman needed to die before she hurt anyone else.

She lifted a hand and grinned. "I wouldn't be so eager. I want to say a few things first. After all, don't you want to understand why?"

Two harpies holding bows appeared with smug expressions.

None of us had guns, and the harpies were out of range of our flames. They could shoot at us before we ever got near. We needed to come up with a plan, but the only person I could communicate with was Egan.

Draco lifted his wings like he was preparing to cover us, and Egan's parents moved to stand beside their son.

We were trapped, so we'd have to play along with Vera's game until an opportunity to run or fight opened up. *Any ideas on how to get out of this? We'll have to kill her or she'll track us to the new location.*

Not yet. And you're right. We have to end this or she'll keep hunting us. Egan's dragon was so stiff he looked like a statue.

The danger we were in was unreal. For a moment, I'd thought we were going to come out of this mostly unscathed. This was what I got for my wishful thinking.

"So this is the royal family." Vera tapped her crusty fingers against her lips.

I cringed. I wouldn't be putting my fingers anywhere near my mouth after being near those harpies. At least, I'd been in my beast form when I'd bitten the harpy's leg, but the act had still made me sick.

"I'm disappointed it was this easy to get you." Vera sighed, and her shoulders sagged. "But it's fine. My centuries-old grudge still makes this moment worthwhile."

I blew out a breath, unable to hold back my reaction. Trixie had nailed the fact that Vera was either very old or more pure-blooded than most witches. I wondered how old she actually was.

She chuckled and tilted her head. "Are you surprised? I had to sacrifice a lot to make it this long without dwindling my power."

Draco growled at the implication. Obviously, he had a better idea of what that meant than I did.

What am I missing?

For a witch to live that long without giving up their power means they sacrificed someone they love. In other words, they gave up their humanity for revenge.

The magnitude of the meaning hit me. Who had she sacrificed to achieve this?

"Aw, even in beast form, I can see your disgust," Vera sneered and paced in front of us. "But you see, my five-year-old daughter deserved it. After all, she was the reason Blaize met his fated mate that day in the village."

Five? Now I really felt sick and had more reason to end the bitch.

She paused, letting the information wash over us. Her eyes hazed over each one of us, enjoying whatever she found.

"Egan, your great, great grandfather and I were in love." Her face wrinkled with pain as she frowned. "Well, before he met *her*," she spat.

When this was over, I'd have to catch up on his family lineage. Most girls dreamed of being a princess, but so far, my entire experience with it made Hell sound like an amusement park.

"He found his mate the same day we attended a village event. He didn't want to go; rumors floated that the fae dragon king was growing displeased because even though your family had left the realm, his family could never become the true leaders over the dragons. The fae king's magic wasn't strong enough, and none of the other fae races respected them as much. However, my daughter demanded to go to the event, and Blaize gave in. He loved her as if she were his own." She clenched her hands at her sides. "Her father died within a year of her birth, and the two of them connected."

She didn't sound happy about their bond. Not every man would've connected with a child that wasn't his own, especially back then.

"Within the first hour, he saw his mate. I felt the change in him." She rubbed her arms like she was cold. "When he told me he could no longer be with me, I killed my daughter in front of him. It was the only way I could truly hurt him. When he tried to stop me, I disappeared and watched him mourn my child's death. Then I began my mission. My true calling. I found a fae man who put me in contact with the king, and we planned to ruin Blaize's life like he'd ruined mine."

She'd been a heartless bitch even back then. What kind of mother could kill her own child? She practically glowed from the memory.

"I helped the fae dragon king hunt down the other dragons." The corners of her mouth tilted upward. "Kind of like now."

She was a completely miserable person who wanted those around her to be worse off, and I realized we were up against someone that had nothing to lose. This wasn't a granddaughter following in her grandmother's footsteps; this witch had lived longer than Egan and his parents. She was completely delusional and hell-bent on revenge. The amount of hatred she'd carried all these years was something most would never understand.

"You're probably asking yourself how I couldn't find you until now." She laughed like she'd told a joke. "But I'll answer your burning question first. I killed Blaize and his mate but wasn't aware they'd had a child before I got to them. When the dragons went into true hiding, cutting themselves off completely from the outside world, and the full power didn't transfer to the fae dragon, I realized

I'd greatly miscalculated. I might have killed the man I loved, but his child with *her* lived on, and I couldn't allow that. However, I couldn't locate them since I had no other dragon's blood or possessions to track. I'd killed too fast."

She's wrapping this up. From everything I'd watched and read, after villains wrapped up their spiels, they got to the action. Unfortunately, this was real life, and killing us was high on her priority list.

The two harpies remained focused on us, even though Vera had a crazed look. A victorious smile spread across her face, making her look creepier than the creatures trapping us. "But today, I get my revenge and, in a way, get retribution for Mindy. After all, she and I have a lot in common and bonded over the thought of Jade's death. Mindy let it slip that a former human shouldn't become queen. Of course, I had to agree and was thrilled that she'd confirmed what I'd suspected. The prince was allowed to leave the thunder in search of his mate to continue the royal lineage."

Great, psycho bitch and Mindy had bonded. That sounded about right.

When this goes down, get behind me. Egan inched slightly in front.

Yeah, that wasn't happening, but I had to play along. I didn't want to reveal my objective of not listening quite yet. He'd do something more dangerous before I could. *You're the blood heir. It makes sense—*

And you wouldn't be part of this life if it wasn't for me, Egan said loudly, hurting my ears. He growled deeply, his entire body quaking.

He'd never cut me off before. Shocked didn't even describe what I was feeling. I was teetering between amused, offended, horrified, and surprised. Laughter bubbled out, but it sounded like I was choking in this form.

Vera squinted at me. "What's your problem?"

The harpies zeroed in on me, expecting me to attack.

Okay, I hadn't planned on this, but I'd take it.

Jade, I swear ... Egan groaned. *You're a magnet for trouble.*

That I couldn't disagree with, but since I had their attention, I'd use it to our advantage. I took a large step forward. A harpy hissed and drew her arrow.

"I'd be a little more careful if I were you." Vera waggled her brows, and not in a sexy way. "I may have to hurt someone you love."

She was already threatening to hurt Egan and my new family. Who else could she have?

Vera whistled, and two more harpies came into view, one holding a horrified Mindy, but my heart stuttered when I saw who the second one held.

My mother dangled from their talons, blood dripping down her arm and onto the ground. Her brown eyes were wide with fear, and her brown hair was soaked with deep crimson.

My heart sank. How did they know who she was? And how long had the witch had her? Even though she wasn't involved in my life, I couldn't lose another parent.

Everything inside me screamed to save her. I rushed toward her as Vera bounced on the balls of her feet.

"Yes, feel the panic and terror." Vera cackled. "Do you think you can get to her in time?"

The sheer joy in her voice turned my blood to ice.

Jade! Egan linked, his anxiety pushing mine past my breaking point.

This bitch was unpredictable and wanted to hurt us. I soared into the sky, desperate to get to Mom.

"I guess we'll find out!" Vera yelled gleefully. "Let her mother go."

I roared as the harpy released my mom, letting her tumble to her death.

DRAGON QUEEN

THE HIDDEN KING TRILOGY

CHAPTER ONE

My heart stopped while I frantically flapped my wings to get to her. I roared in my dragon form with both fear and rage as I watched my mother tumble to her death.

Thick, fresh blood soaked her dark hair, and it clung to her face even with the long drop to the ground. Her brown eyes, the same shade as mine, were wide with terror.

I couldn't lose her.

Not now.

Not like this.

"Egan, save me," Mindy pleaded as she dangled from another harpy's taloned feet. Mindy's vanilla-blonde hair looked dirty blonde, and her bottom lip trembled in a horrible attempt to look fearful. The tell was that her honey eyes were calm, and the harpy holding her hadn't dug its talons into her like the other one had with Mom.

If I hadn't been worried about my mother, I'd have been pissed at yet another stupid, manipulative stunt the dragon shifter was trying to pull, but her pathetic need for my mate's attention didn't mean shit to me right then. Not when the people I loved were in danger.

The harpy that had dropped Mom smirked at the show. Each

time Mom screamed, the harpy's coal-black eyes twinkled with amusement. But I hadn't expected to find humanity in these creatures since they were from Fae and working with Vera and the fae dragon king. It was a no-brainer that they wouldn't care about us.

The harpy's chest shook, jiggling her naked breasts. The harpies' top halves resembled that of a voluptuous old woman while their bottom halves were reptilian. Long, sturdy wings sprouted from their backs. Oddest of all, they all looked identical from what I could see.

Vera's cackle pierced my brain. It was like she was somehow talking into my head like Egan could when she yelled, "She might actually catch her. Shoot the dragon now." Some humor had vacated her voice, and hope blossomed in my chest.

Egan used our fated mate link to talk to me as he growled in his dragon form, *Jade, the two harpies are loading their bows. Be careful. I'll try to distract them.*

Under normal circumstances, his request that I should be careful would've made me chuckle, but too much was at stake for me to find anything amusing.

My eyes locked on my mother, blocking everything else out. She was only two hundred yards away from slamming into the ground.

Her body flipped and spun wildly as she screamed. With the way she was panicking, she would faint before she hit the bottom. Maybe that was a good thing.

I pushed my wings harder, refusing to admit defeat. If Vera was siccing the harpies on me, I had to be moving faster than I realized.

God, I hoped so. I felt like I was crawling—or whatever the equivalent was for a flying creature.

Loud roars ripped from behind me as Egan, his parents, and Draco attacked the harpies. Hopefully, they'd catch the harpies and Vera by surprise since they were all enjoying the action between Mom and me.

Renewed determination filled me as I felt somewhat safer with the dragons' diversion. Even the threat of the poisoned bone arrows couldn't deter me from saving Mom.

Inches from her, I reached out, preparing to wrap her in my arms. Since the harpy had torn up the top of her shoulders, I didn't want to risk digging my talons into her skin. I could deepen the wounds, not to mention the amount of pain she had to be in already, and dangling from my talons, she'd be like a flying target for the archers. Having my arms available to fight would be ideal, but in dragon form, they were way less important.

I zipped toward the ground, abandoning my natural urge to slow. Apparently, in beast form, my survival instinct was stronger. Pushing it aside, I connected with my dragon. If I let her take too much control and she let Mom die, I might not be able to live with myself. Some things were more important than my own life.

The world blurred as my dragon stopped fighting and flew faster. I braced myself, knowing Mom and I were likely going to die. The mixture of gravel and grass was getting closer by the second.

Mere feet from impact, I desperately stretched my arms out. This wouldn't work, but dammit, I had to try. I'd expected only to snag air, but my large, scaly hand wrapped around her arm. I carefully adjusted my grip so my talons didn't graze her skin.

Tears burned my eyes, magnifying all of the new colors of the rainbow in this form. I hadn't thought I could get to her in time, but somehow, I'd caught her. Not wasting another second, my dragon jerked her toward me and wrapped my arms around her. When her head hit my chest, I shifted my weight upward, and my wings changed directions, pushing us back into the sky.

"No!" Mom yelled as she jerked against me. "Let me go! I'd rather die than be eaten or abused by disgusting creatures like you."

Her words stung, but I couldn't blame her. If this had been my first introduction to the supernatural world, I'd have felt the same way.

Despite my beast's strength, her resistance caught me off guard. She broke free and dropped once again.

My heart pounded.

No, I'd just had her.

I forced my wings to stop, and I dove beside her. My dragon roared in my mind, unhappy with my dangerous plan.

Since I had five hundred pounds on her, I reached her in a second, this time anchoring her in my arms.

I wouldn't make the same mistake twice.

Jade, fly upward now! Egan exclaimed, and my already panicked heart raced harder.

I wouldn't be surprised if I had a stroke. I blinked, realizing that impact was imminent.

Egan's fear melded with mine so much that I couldn't tell where his began and mine ended. The flapping of wings grew closer, and I hoped to God it was him and not a harpy. I wasn't sure how I could fight with Mom in my arms. I needed to find a safe place to set her down.

She squirmed, but I was prepared for it, and my wings sprang back to work, lifting us higher. As my body adjusted to the change of direction, my legs swung forward, and my feet brushed the ground.

Thank God my scales protected me, or my feet would have been in immense pain. Another benefit of being in beast form.

That had been way too close for comfort.

Duck! Egan screamed at the same time that a whistling noise caught my attention.

Dammit, that was an arrow. I rolled to the side despite Mom's distracting screams. I couldn't blame her; she had no clue the dragon was her daughter. The last time she'd seen me had been before I'd run away to college and met Egan when I'd been completely human.

The whistling grew louder, even though I'd altered my course. I spun around to see three arrows spiraling at me. Each one followed a different path like the harpies had predicted each option I had. I wasn't getting out of this without injury.

Draco flew at a harpy as she drew another arrow. He moved so fast his navy scales distorted, his focus on getting to the horrible creature before she shot at me again.

My only option to avoid getting shot was to curl into a ball. I pulled my huge-ass bottom half inward, trying to make myself as small as possible without injuring Mom. I still wasn't used to my dragon form. Before I could get adjusted, an arrow sank into my leg, close to the same place I'd been injured not even an hour before.

Excruciating pain pulsed inside me, stealing my breath. I directed every ounce of concentration I had on keeping Mom in my arms and my wings moving. All I wanted to do was wallow in pain, but I gritted my teeth, resolved to take Vera down.

Egan raced toward me. *I'm almost there. Just hold on.*

He was only ten yards away, but the overwhelming throbbing grew sharper, weakening my entire body. I wasn't sure how much longer I could stay strong. *You need to get Mom.* As long as she and Egan made it out of this alive, that was all that mattered. They both deserved to live. Mom deserved to find happiness before dying.

Cries and growls raged on behind us, but I didn't have the energy to turn around and see what was going on. At least, it sounded like a battle and not a slaughter. I'd have been more worried if all I'd heard was the harpies' war call.

Agony intensified inside me, and my wings slowed. We descended even faster. My body started to shut down, and I channeled all of my strength toward protecting my mother. If we tumbled to the ground, I could shield her with my body.

A low groan emanated from Egan as his golden eyes glowed brighter. *I'm here,* he said moments before reaching me.

I held Mom out to him, but instead of taking her, he wrapped his arms around us both. His dragon was much larger than mine, but I hadn't expected him to be able to take the brunt of my weight.

Hold on as long as you can. Worry laced each word, and they came off like a command.

Normally, I'd be annoyed, but I understood how he felt, and his concern fueled me, overriding some of the pain.

Egan lowered us to the ground, and I looked over his shoulder at the fight. Ladon fought one of the archers, while Draco took on the other. Every time they used their dragon flames, the harpies would fly out of the way seconds before it could reach them.

Dammit, those harpies had to be some of the smarter ones. It made sense that Vera would want them around her for extra protection.

Each time the guys missed the harpies, Vera threw her head back in laughter. Her once sable eyes appeared completely soulless, and her caramel hair was disheveled more than usual. She watched the fight with a sick, satisfied smirk that was at odds with the white, animated Star Wars shirt she wore.

Egan's mother narrowly dodged a harpy's punch. Kayda's scales were a lighter army-green shade than her fated mate's, and she was slightly smaller like me but still strong in her own right. She straightened, and her dragon flames engulfed the harpy. The harpy let out an ear-piercing screech, but it was cut short as her body disintegrated into ash.

I took that back. Maybe they weren't all smarter, just the two Ladon and Draco fought.

My reprieve vanished as the pain rolled back into my body tenfold. I groaned as my wings slowed to almost a stop.

We're here, Egan comforted me. *You can stop.*

That was all I needed—the reassurance to quit. My feet touched the gravel and grass, and I crumpled to my side, feeling the ground shaking under my weight. I somehow kept from rolling onto Mom.

Looking skyward, I realized how close to the top of the cave we were. We'd landed on the very top of the hill—the very hill we'd used to hide from all of the harpies at the village. We were heading toward a hidden exit that only the dragon king knew about in case something of this magnitude ever occurred.

Mom struggled to get out of my embrace, and I gladly opened my arms. She was scared, and I wasn't in the right mind to fight her, not that I would've anyway. I would tell her everything if we made it out of here alive.

I needed to pull the arrow out from my leg before more poison entered my system, but the pain had immobilized me.

My chest shook as I took in a breath, and my gaze went to the entrance to the hidden village inside the cave.

No more of the winged fae creatures were pouring inside, which calmed some of my fear. I had no clue how many harpies Vera had brought. If these were all of them, most of us should make it out alive as long as we killed the witch before she could do anything else.

"Kayda, please help me." Mindy's voice cracked as she struggled weakly against the harpy's hold.

Her act was wearing on my nerves. I couldn't wait to call her out on her shit since Mindy didn't know that Vera had outed her. Not only had Mindy told the witch who Egan's family was, but Vera and Mindy had also bonded over my future death. Apparently, Mindy was thrilled at the prospect and wanted to kill me like Vera had killed her ex-lover's fated mate, Egan's great, great grandfather. The question bubbled in my mind about how Mindy knew Egan's family was of royal lineage. But that was a question for another time.

Babe. Egan leaned over me, his eyes filled with concern and love. *I'm going to yank this out now.*

I nodded but wished he hadn't told me. Now, I anticipated the moment, knowing it would hurt like hell before feeling better. The longer it stayed lodged in me, the worse the injury would be. *Just do it.*

He grabbed the bottom of the arrow, holding it firmly where it jutted from my leg. *On the count of three.* He sucked in a breath while his dragon hands held the bone arrow just as if he were in human form. *One,* he said and yanked.

Pure shock filled me before the pain. I groaned and sagged against his side as the sharp agony hit then finally receded.

A warning tingled at the base of my neck.

Someone was about to attack.

I spun around, but I couldn't find anything, which only meant one thing. *Egan, Vera's invisible.*

CHAPTER TWO

I searched for something—anything—that would alert me to Vera's whereabouts. Scanning my surroundings, I hunted for the ghost-like apparition that appeared when she astral projected. I was learning that all magic came at a cost or with a penance. For instance, dragons were strong but couldn't connect to their entire thunder. On the flip side, wolves weren't as strong, but their pack link gave them an edge.

However, I didn't see anything out of the ordinary.

Fear coursed through my veins. That was the reaction Vera wanted to cause, and I hated giving her the satisfaction.

Maybe she ran like last time, Egan suggested, but we both knew it was wishful thinking.

She couldn't get out of here without a harpy, and none were missing. She planned on using her disappearing act to kill us.

She had the desperate, crazy gleam in her eyes, the kind there was no turning back from. Vera was here to finish this.

To achieve her ultimate revenge.

To kill every last dragon shifter tied to her ex-lover.

Something sharp stabbed into my leg where the arrow had been.

The piercing pain caused my stomach to roil as the wound deepened and bled more.

I roared, my dragon angry and hurt. She was eager to attack, but we had no target.

Egan breathed rapidly as smoke trickled from his nose.

Aiming for her opponent's recent injury was a sound strategy, I had to give her that, but I refused to sit here idly.

Egan slashed his claws at the area around me, trying to hit Vera, but all he hit was air.

For all we knew, she could have been standing right behind him.

She tried to appear strong and confident, but these were the actions of a weak coward. It proved she feared us even if she pretended she didn't.

Her cowardice should have encouraged me or made me feel like we were on equal ground, but it did nothing. I couldn't fight an enemy I couldn't see. My dragon didn't understand how to fight or handle this situation. Her senses had never let her down before.

My dragon roared loudly as flames bubbled in my stomach. She had no clue where to spew the fire. Nothing indicated or even hinted at where Vera could be. Absolutely no scent or sound. My dragon felt useless, adding to our rage.

Mom stumbled back, her eyes so wide I didn't think she'd ever be able to shut them again. The sour scent of fear swirled around us.

I couldn't spew the flames haphazardly, not with Mom this close. I'd risked my life to save her, and I refused to hurt her because of my terror. Acting irrationally would give Vera the advantage and hurt God knew who else.

We had to stop playing her game. *Calm down.*

I can't, he growled. *She's going to attack you again.*

We have to be smarter than her. This is what she wants. I took a deep, calming breath, following my own advice.

My dragon hissed against my mind, but I ignored her. She had to learn to trust me. I was already beginning to trust her.

Something prodded my arm. Nothing too painful but more like Vera was trying to scare me.

As I'd expected, the ghost-like apparition stood several feet away from my injury. Her blurred face was barely visible, watching Egan attack nothing. She wanted to startle me and make me injure myself even more.

Refusing to give her what she wanted, I forced my body to not respond. My dragon hissed inside my mind, but I ignored her again. I would stay in control.

After inhaling and exhaling slowly several times, some of my panic dissipated, and I pushed a fraction of my calm toward Egan. He needed it more so than I did. If our situation had been reversed, I wouldn't have been able to handle seeing him get hurt, unable to do anything. This was both a physical and emotional game the bitch—I meant, witch—played.

I forced my eyes shut, even though it was the most unnatural thing to do, but my martial arts training was kicking in. Sometimes, taking your sight out of the equation could heighten your other senses. I hoped it would do a whole lot more in dragon form.

My dragon roared unhappily, but I mentally brushed her like she often did against my mind.

I projected reassuring thoughts toward her, and somehow, she understood. Warmth spread throughout me as she took a small step aside, granting my request.

With my eyes closed, the surrounding sounds grew louder. I could hear the fighting in the village as well as every breath Draco and Ladon took as they fought the two harpies.

Kayda chased the harpy that held on to Mindy.

Mom breathed raggedly as silent sobs racked her body, and her footsteps grew farther and farther away as she ran away from us.

Little did she know that wouldn't do her any good. She was only running toward more violence, but on foot and at human speed, she wouldn't reach the village for half an hour.

The ground quaked with each step Egan took. He stood protectively in front of my injured leg, ready to attack at the first sign of an assault. Even though he'd calmed, he was still on edge. We both were.

I tried to home in on Vera's presence, knowing she'd be near me.

A sharp edge dug between two scales on my arm—much like the tip of a knife. My arm twitched to jerk away, but I held it still. This was my opportunity to find her.

She dug the sharp tip deep into my arm, piercing the skin. The tip stung, similar to a bee sting, but I didn't react. I focused on where she had to be standing to dig the knife into my arm.

As the pressure increased, the overwhelming urge to react clawed inside me. The moment I felt as though I couldn't take any more, I noticed a warmer spot next to me. That had to be her. Her body heat wasn't hidden, only her scent and body.

I found her, I alerted my mate as she jabbed the sharp edge deeper, my excitement overriding my urge to react.

Delight flowed through our bond as Egan asked, *How?*

You won't like this, so please don't react. I hadn't told him what she was doing for this very reason, but I couldn't leave him in the dark. *She's stabbing me in the arm. It doesn't hurt too badly, but since I didn't react, she's staying close to taunt me. I can feel her body heat.*

He tensed, annoyance wafting through our bond, but he didn't move like I'd asked. *We can work with that.*

She dug the sharp edge deeper, and I winced. A low scream confirmed what I already suspected: she was enraged that I hadn't moved.

Good, that was the entire point.

I swung my other hand at her, talons extended. I hit something solid and tossed her twenty feet away. She landed with a loud thud. I opened my eyes and saw blood dripping onto the grass. *She's bleeding. She can't hide that.* I couldn't suppress my excitement.

Egan's gaze found the blood that trailed toward us. *When her blood leaves her body, it appears. The magic must be for her actual body. Anything outside it shows.*

It was a small win, but I'd take it.

Vera charged at us without any hesitation. She must not have realized that we could spot her. Whether it was reckless, I didn't care as long as we kicked her ass.

Every three to four steps, another drop of blood landed. I had to time this perfectly. When blood dripped only two feet away, I breathed the flames that had been building inside me.

Her screams of agony confirmed I'd hit the mark. Within seconds, the smell of burnt skin hit my nose. Thankfully, in dragon form, my stomach was much sturdier or I'd have emptied its contents. I continued to push the fire out as Egan charged at her.

Before he could reach her, her cries ended.

Hope that she was dead sprang inside, but her body was still invisible. *Is she dead?*

No, her magic wouldn't be working anymore if she was. Egan lowered his head right where she'd been, opened his mouth, and chomped.

Did you get her? I doubted it since no blood poured down his chin, but I didn't fully understand how magic worked yet.

No, he growled and scanned the area. *She got out of the way.*

Dammit, maybe scorching her hadn't been smart. Now the surrounding air was warmer, and I couldn't gauge her location anymore. *She couldn't have gotten far.* Between bleeding and getting burned, she had to be moving slower.

No, but she'll be more desperate, which doesn't bode well for us. Egan stood protectively in front of me again like that had worked out so well.

I bit my tongue, not wanting to hurt his feelings. He was doing what he could to protect me. The best thing I could do was get off my ass. I slowly stood, gradually putting weight on my leg. It hurt, but I could walk on it, so the muscle wasn't damaged. If I'd been in human form, that would have been a different story.

The ground shook, and the intensity of the vibrations increased. My teeth rattled as the earth quaked and groaned under our feet like an earthquake.

Is that Vera or an actual natural disaster? I asked.

Vera. A natural disaster you'd know. There's a change in the atmosphere before it happens. This is all witch. She's using magic.

That was odd. Why did she wait until now?

My dragon surged forward, flapping my wings. We hovered just above the ground to keep the magic from affecting us.

Egan followed suit. *I don't understand what she's doing.*

Join the club. I didn't understand a damn thing she'd done yet.

A cry of frustration sounded behind us. We turned around to see a flashing Vera standing a few feet away. She flickered in and out of view, and I kind of preferred the out.

Her face had taken the brunt of my flames, and her arms were a little crispy. My scratch marks were visible, but the flames had cauterized the wound.

So that was why the blood loss had stopped. I hadn't thought my plan through at all.

"How can you see me?" she snarled and looked at her hands.

The ground stilled as her eyes locked on me, her breathing hard. "If you would've kept your distance from him, everything would've been so much easier." Egan's nostrils flared, and her face contorted into rage. "I could've hurt you and had him begging me to save you, but no. Ever since you came into the picture, you've been nothing but trouble."

Her anger was completely channeled at me as if Egan wasn't even beside me.

"You freed the falcon. You brought Egan to the restaurant the night Ollie was there to kidnap you. You let the dragon into our dorm room." She wielded her knife at me, swinging it from side to side with every point. "You found the girl he was meant to find in the woods that day, and you burned me, forcing me to use a significant amount of my power to survive. You've ruined everything."

She dropped the knife she had in her hands and pulled out a dagger from a sheath on her calf.

The blade was a dark silver, and the slender handle was rounded at the top with two golden jewels side by side. Black wings sprouted from the handle, and I realized the shape looked like a dragon. The blade was six inches long with smooth edges, and I could tell it could cut through anything ... even scales.

"Not only will I enjoy killing you, but he'll also get to watch you die." She raised the dagger over her head and charged, screaming.

The sun shone into the cave, slanting bright light onto us. The edge of the dagger reflected the light into my eyes, half blinding me.

I blinked and squinted, watching her approach us. Did she really think this would work? She was completely insane.

The fire churned in my stomach, ready for release.

When she was five feet from us, Egan and I channeled our flames at her. Before they could reach her, she raised her other hand, forcing a strong wind in our direction.

The flames blew back against us. I braced myself for the pain, but luckily, the flames didn't hurt. *How the...?*

It's because we're soul mates, and they're our flames, thus part of our dragons. Our bodies have to be resilient to produce it. But anyone else's flame can burn you. Egan grunted as he flew higher.

I trailed after him, but I moved too slowly. Vera was only inches away and swinging her arms downward.

When I winced, bracing for impact, Egan grabbed Vera with his feet and dug his sharp, thick talons into her shoulders. He flapped upward, lifting her off the ground. The dagger tumbled from her hands and landed a mere two inches from my feet.

She screamed in agony as he lifted her higher.

"Please, don't!" she cried, reminding me of Mindy. "I'm sorry. Just let me down."

The fact that she'd even contemplate that we might let her go offended me.

He was a mile in the air when he dropped her. Her face transformed from pure terror to a cocky smirk.

She had something up her sleeve.

CHAPTER THREE

As Vera fell, she held her hands in front of her and sneered. A strong gust of wind sprang to life and blew upward, pushing against her body. Her descent slowed, and my heart sank.

No. How could we fight against someone with magic on her side? If she could prevent herself from falling to her death, there was no telling what else she could do. We had no clue how strong she was.

Egan roared and plunged toward the witch's body. He weighed so much that the wind blowing into him didn't affect him other than maybe slowing him a tad. Within seconds, he reached the witch, whose sole concentration was on slowing her fall.

He opened his sizable mouth, his sharp teeth on display, and chomped into her middle.

Blood poured from her torso as her eyes opened in horror. Her arms dropped to her sides, and the whirlwind she had created weakened with her life force.

My mate jerked his head to the side, tossing her.

She didn't put up a fight or struggle. Blood trickled from her mouth, and her body slammed into the ground with such force that it bounced.

Needing to make sure the bitch was dead, I flew the short distance to her body. I landed gingerly beside her, and the sound of silence comforted me like never before. There was no heartbeat or air filling her lungs. Blood oozed from her body, and her open eyes glazed over as death welcomed her.

Under most circumstances, I'd have said that her soul was free to go to its final destination, but I was sure she'd lost it or used it up during her very long lifetime. Only anger and hurt existed inside her —the essential ingredients of fostering hatred into the world.

Good riddance. I hope you experience the pain you inflicted on everyone around you for all eternity. It had been hard for me to look at every other dead body I'd seen, but not hers. Her mangled body made me want to rejoice, and I wasn't sure what that said about me.

Egan landed beside me, and he breathed flames over her body.

Part of me wanted to look away, which eased some of the concern about my mental wellbeing. At least, I didn't enjoy watching her entire death unfold.

With witches, their bodies need to be burned or their energy will connect back with the earth. Egan continued a steady flow of flame. *We don't want any of her vengeful and spiteful spirit hanging around.*

Ashes flaked from the fire and floated in the slight breeze.

But she used the ashes of the falcon feather to control him. We didn't need someone gathering her ashes and using her power.

Yes, his feather. His body was still intact. Her body and energy are being unleashed into the world. There won't be anything to anchor to her.

Egan's parents and Draco landed beside us. I found Mindy standing in human form, her chest heaving with each breath she took as she watched the scene unfold. The worry on her face smoothed over as relief overtook it.

She thought she was safe, but she was far from it. She'd helped Vera find my mother and revealed who the dragon royal family was. If she thought there was any comeback from that, she was dead wrong.

But I'd let her have her moment. The calm before the storm.

It irritated the hell out of me that our group couldn't speak to each other, but these were the cards we'd been dealt. I'd have to get over it.

As the ash thickened, Egan's flames lessened. When the flames stopped, even her bones were gone. Every ounce of her was ash, the charred ground the only thing marking the location of her death.

Ladon glanced at us and nodded toward the village. He held the dagger Vera had dropped.

Good, it looked special, though I didn't know why. Part of me felt connected to it, though.

He nodded again, ensuring that the message was clear. We needed to check on the others. I turned to look for the harpies they'd been fighting and found three similarly charred places flaked with dust. Maybe burning the dead was a dragon thing.

"Oh, God." Mindy sniffled and placed a dirty hand against her mouth. "I'm so relieved."

I bet she was. She thought there was no one left that knew she worked with the witch to get rid of me.

Unwilling to stay here and feeling the need to check on Mom, I took to the sky. My leg twinged with pain but nothing too horrible. My shifter healing was already kicking in. That perk of my new form was pretty damn nice.

The others followed behind me, and I glanced over my shoulder to see Kayda's eyes filled with annoyance as she gently held Mindy with her dragon feet, carrying her toward the village.

Mindy could've shifted into her dragon form to help us fight, and she could have shifted to help the rest of the thunder if things weren't going our way, but she wanted Kayda to carry her. Maybe to show the thunder that their queen cared enough about her to chauffeur her back home. Who the hell knew?

How's your leg? Egan asked as he caught up to me.

I spotted Mom running toward the houses. *It's already healing, so hopefully, I'll be back to normal soon.*

I'm so sorry I couldn't protect you. Defeat wafted off him.

I hated that he put so much pressure on himself. He couldn't be held responsible for my health and safety. He was only one person. *You did protect me. You killed her before she could hurt me or anyone else again. If it weren't for you, she'd still be alive.* I pushed my love and adoration for Egan toward him.

He needed to realize how I felt and thought about him. He was the best person I'd ever met, and I would've felt that way even if we weren't fated mates. Hell, Sadie and the others thought extremely highly of him too. *You fought alongside Sadie and your friends when it was never expected of you. You protected them because you care. You treat everyone with respect and kindness, which is so damn hard to find in this world. You are the absolute best person I've ever had the honor of knowing.*

Something shifted between us, and his wings gently brushed against mine. He turned his huge head and stared into my soul as he said, *I'm not nearly as perfect as you make me sound, but you make me want to be the man you see me as. I've given you such hell about fighting and defending yourself ...*

I'm thinking it's a shifter quality over their mates, I teased. *But I'll take it. Besides, you only did it while trying to protect me.*

If I can use that excuse, then ... He tilted his head and his teeth appeared in a dragon smile.

Nope, no take-backs.

A loud scream broke our moment. Mom had turned around, and she was looking at us. Her bottom lip shook in pure terror as she watched the five of us approach.

We probably looked scary from her point of view, and having Mindy dangle from Kayda's talons probably made things worse since that was how the harpy had carried her.

Did Mindy want to be carried just to cause Mom more distress? Surely not, but I couldn't shake the feeling. She loved manipulating people and wanted to cause me pain.

Draco flew beside us and waved us on to the village. He patted his chest and gestured to Mom.

He was going to get her. I hated to do that to her, but we didn't need someone else finding her, and they'd have no clue who she was. With the way the dragons were attacked, they might think she was a witch or another threat.

Maybe I should get her, I suggested.

The best thing you can do is get back to the house and shift into your human form. That'll be the only way to calm your mother down.

I hadn't thought about that. Whether it was Draco or me getting her, the outcome would be the same. *Okay. Standing around here naked would just make things worse.*

As Draco flew down to get her, Mindy yelled and patted her shoulder. "That hurts. Please stop."

Between Draco flying toward her and Mindy's comments, Mom ran backward. She stumbled over her own feet and landed on the ground. She placed her hands in front of her face and cried, "Please. Don't. I haven't done anything. Leave me be."

That psycho bitch was going to die. I faced the crazy dragon girl, ready to hurt her like she was trying to hurt me. She wasn't much different from Vera, meaning she was a bigger risk than we'd ever realized.

Don't. Egan flew slightly in front of me, blocking Mindy from my view. *If you attack her, it'll only upset your mother more. That's what she's hoping you'll do.*

Egan, I can't do this with her anymore. Not only had Mindy worked with Vera and tried scaring my mother more, but she'd also purposely tried to keep me from connecting with my dragon under the guise of training me, and she wanted Egan to leave me for her, despite us being fated mates.

Don't worry, we won't. Egan sounded as pissed as me.

What Mindy had failed to realize was when I hurt, so did Egan. He and I were bonded in a way she'd never understand unless she found her fated mate. She wasn't just pitting herself against me but the man she wanted as her own. Talk about backfiring, and Mindy was clueless enough not to get it.

I should've known Egan would feel the same way. He was trying to ensure we didn't scare Mom more than we already had. He always had my best interest at heart.

Ignoring Mindy's antics felt impossible, but I kept my eyes forward and my wings flapping steadily.

Okay, that wasn't true. The only way I was able to do that was with Egan by my side. I was beginning to learn how much stronger I was with him firmly beside me.

Mom cried over and over as Draco grabbed her, and not being there for her was one of the hardest things I'd ever had to do, but I would only make things worse for her, kind of like Aunt Sarah.

When Dad had been alive, we'd been a happy family. Mom and he had been so in love, but my aunt Sarah had always interfered with her controlling, abusive ways. After my dad had died, my life had truly changed. We'd moved in with Sarah, who'd controlled my every movement and would smack me whenever I got out of line. Of course, that had only happened when Mom hadn't been around to see.

It'll be fine when she sees you, Egan reassured me.

I wasn't so sure about that. Some things people could never get over.

The village came into view, and the dragons were on the ground, not in battle. Humans and dragons were dragging dead harpies to the grassy edge outside of the village and throwing the bodies on top of one another.

Uh ... is that normal? It wasn't like we were staying here.

Egan grimaced. *They're easier to burn that way. This is how we handle death when we can. Even though the harpies don't pose a threat, it's just a respectful way to treat the dead.*

The more I learned about dragons, the more I admired their race. They had a distinct sense of right and wrong, except for the few crazies in their midst.

We landed right in front of Egan's parents' log cabin home at the center of the village comprised of around a hundred buildings, and Egan and I hurried into the large entryway and to the shifting room on the left. It was big enough for both Egan and me to enter and change at the same time. Our bag was still there from earlier, and I was glad Egan had encouraged us to bring several changes of clothes in case something like this happened. I'd be shifting right back into my dragon form after I talked to Mom.

Within minutes, we were both on two legs and dressed.

Back outside the house, Mom was beating Draco in the chest with her fists and hands like she expected it to accomplish something.

Mindy stood between an older man and a woman she resembled. The woman had her ash-blonde hair pulled into a bun and stiff shoulders. She laid a hand on Mindy's shoulders, but her milk chocolate brown eyes were tight. Her features were sharp, probably similar to her heart.

The man had short, golden hair, but his striking honey eyes were the same shade as Mindy's. His chin was lifted and proud as he tugged on his navy-blue blazer like he was the most important man there. Clearly, neither he nor the woman had fought. Their clothes were in pristine condition.

Any other time, I'd have laughed, but there was too much going on. Their audacity was completely unnerving.

"What kind of monsters are you?" Mom yelled, bringing my attention back to her.

I cringed. That wasn't a very smart thing to say when you thought you were being held captive. "Mom," I said softly, trying not to spook her.

She stilled and spun around to face me. "Jade? Baby?" She ran over and threw her arms around me. "Are they holding you prisoner, too?"

"No." I shook my head, unsure where to start.

Egan stepped beside me and placed a hand on my shoulder. He didn't say anything, allowing me to handle this the way I wanted.

The problem was I had no clue. Should I just blurt out, "You're calling me a monster too"? At least, my awkwardness wasn't running away all on its own.

"Then how are you here?" Mom blinked, trying to make sense of the situation.

"Here, I'll help you." Mindy's voice was soft like she cared. "Your daughter is a dragon and the very one who killed the witch and who knows how many countless others."

Mom's mouth dropped, and rage flowed through my body. This girl had no boundaries, but dammit, I would give her some.

CHAPTER FOUR

"Wait." Mom stepped away from me, wringing her hands. "You've killed people?"

Her reaction hurt so damn badly. She looked at me like she didn't know who I was and as if I might actually hurt her.

"No, she hasn't," Egan growled and glared at Mindy. "Are you trying to make this worse?"

Kayda and Ladon shook their dragon heads, and Mom screamed again. She was all worked up, and the last time I'd seen her far from sane was the day we'd learned that Dad had been in an accident.

Kayda must have said something to Ladon because they headed toward the house, leaving Egan and me to handle Mindy by ourselves.

I wasn't sure if I was thankful or upset. They trusted us to do what was right, but they were king and queen. Our words might not have as much authority without them beside us.

"Just trying to help." Mindy laughed in a high-pitch voice and attempted to flip her hair over her shoulder, but it was so dingy that it flopped back down where it was a moment earlier. She either didn't realize it or chose to ignore it as she continued, "Jade seemed at a loss for words, which is kind of strange for a future queen, but whatever. I just thought that as her teacher, I should help her."

No, she couldn't have said what I thought she did ... surely.

"You view yourself as my teacher?" I barked out a humorless laugh. I couldn't let something like that slide. Most of the thunder surrounded us, and I couldn't let Mindy treat me like this. If I did, it would help her assertion that I wasn't fit to be Egan's mate.

"Of course, I do." Mindy placed a hand on her heart and looked from her father to her mother. "Jade really struggled, but with my assistance—"

"You mean sabotaging me from connecting with my dragon." I was sick and tired of dealing with manipulative assholes. Between Sarah, Vera, and Mindy, I'd had my fill.

"It may have appeared like sabotage," she said condescendingly, "but I was preparing you the best way I knew how for the supernatural world. I—"

"Shut up," Egan said low and deep.

Mindy's mouth dropped open. "What? How can you talk to me this way? If you had a mate who could—"

No, he couldn't fight this battle for me. "Let me help. You were working with a witch? You told her who the royal family is? Or how about bonding with a witch over the death of a fellow thunder member?"

She blinked, completely caught off guard. Her cocky smile faltered, but she kept her shoulders and back straight. "I ... I didn't ..." She trailed off, scrambling for words.

"You didn't what? Maybe it's just me, but I couldn't hear you." I pointed to my ear, letting my own smugness peek through.

She would have to lie to get out of this or think up some half-ass truth to scrape by. Either way, I'd force her to admit everything. It was my turn to taunt her ass.

"Honey, what were you saying?" her mother asked tightly, her eyes narrowed at her daughter.

Mindy's body shook, and she let out a fake sob. "I ... I don't know.

It's been a horrible past few days. With everything I've gone through, I don't even know what I'm saying anymore."

"Are you sure about that?" Kayda's regal voice asked as she stepped from the house.

"Yes. Vera was obsessed with finding you. And when those harpies came ..." She stopped and shuddered.

Ladon took his wife's hand, and they made their way beside me. Egan was on my left side, and they were on my right.

"Others could come at any second." Mindy's dad rubbed her shoulders. "We should continue this later and focus on finding a place to go."

Ladon arched an eyebrow. "As everyone now knows, we're the royal family and will be giving the orders. We have already chosen a spot, but it is necessary that we address this before leaving, especially if we have a traitor on our hands."

Mom ran her fingers through her drying, bloody hair. She turned around slowly until she faced me again. "Is this some elaborate joke? Please tell me there's a camera hidden somewhere. I don't know how you all did this, but this doesn't seem real."

I wasn't sure who to address first. I wanted to be there for my mother, but Mindy and her family had to be dealt with before we could leave. And I needed to be part of that. Unfortunately, Mom could wait. "Mom, it's not a joke, but just give me a few minutes, and we'll talk about everything."

Kayda gestured to their log cabin. "If you would like to wait in our home, you're more than welcome. There isn't anyone inside there."

"Yeah." Mom nodded and took off toward the house. She glanced over her shoulder, eyeing all of the dragons still in their beast form. Everyone had stopped carrying off the harpies to watch the scene unfold.

Mindy leaned into her mother and whispered, "See, she isn't fit to be queen. They'll all see."

My hands clenched into fists, and I stared Mindy down. Why in the world would she say something like that when we could all hear her?

Egan tensed beside me, his eyes glowing. "She is fit to be queen, unlike you."

"What?" Mindy squeaked. "I don't know what you're talking about."

Her mother stiffened. "She was just telling me something she didn't think anyone else should hear. There's no need to overreact."

Now they were trying to make us look ignorant. "We could hear everything you said."

Mindy laughed uncomfortably.

Ladon and Kayda glanced at us out of the corner of their eyes. Their foreheads wrinkled, but they didn't say anything.

I'm over this. We don't have time for their games. Egan took my hand and lifted his chin, looking down his nose at Mindy and her parents. "It's obvious you somehow found out that we're the royal family, and we want to know how."

"Now listen, it's a little more complicated than that." Mindy's dad lifted a hand, almost in surrender, as his face paled. He knew they were in deep shit and there was no easy way out of it.

"Then enlighten us, Rex." Ladon crossed his arms and stared the man down. "We've been best friends since childhood. You found your mate only a few years before me. How long have you known?"

The older man had the sense to look ashamed. He hung his head and averted his gaze. "Since we were young children. My father told me. I don't know how he knew."

There wasn't the stench of a lie, which was problematic. There was no telling who else knew, but I guessed it no longer mattered.

"Rex," Mindy's mother hissed.

"Oh stop, Susan." Rex waved at her. "They know. There's no salvaging it."

Susan? I almost laughed. I hadn't heard a normal human name, other than Mindy, for a dragon thus far. But Mindy wasn't as common as Susan.

Egan chuckled in my mind. *Don't forget she was human before transitioning into a dragon like you.*

But your mother has a dragon-sounding name.

It's actually a nickname Dad gave her after they mated. It means "little dragon," but the others started calling her that too. Egan squeezed my hand lovingly. *The name took on a life of its own.*

It fits her.

"So that's why you pushed for Egan and Mindy to be betrothed despite us learning that two dragons can't have offspring." Kayda sounded hurt.

"Wouldn't you do whatever you could for your son?" Susan crossed her arms and looked indignant, unlike her mate. "Mindy deserves to rule and have everyone worship her. All these years, you've hidden like cowards instead of embracing what you could be."

"Excuse me." Kayda paused as she closed her eyes to center herself. "We were hiding for survival. The fae dragon king has been searching for our thunder. He would torture each one of you because you live on Earth. We hid to be happy and create our own community. We hid so no one would worship *anyone* and everyone could be treated as equals."

"Honey, it doesn't matter." Ladon kissed his wife's forehead comfortingly. "We don't have time for this, and now we know that our best friends wanted to use us. We have to leave before the fae dragon king sends reinforcements. Egan and Jade will make the final decision on how to handle them going forward."

"Okay, well, we can talk later when things are settled." Susan pulled at her white shirt and rolled her eyes. "We do need to get to safety."

She grabbed Mindy's shoulders and turned in the opposite direction.

They'd taken a step away when Egan said, "There won't be any safety for you."

What are you doing? I had no clue where he was going with this.

Making sure we all remain safe, especially you.

Susan slowly turned around and looked at him. "Excuse me?"

"Let me say it another way. You're not coming with us." Egan's pupils turned to slits as his dragon peeked through.

Don't do something you'll regret. I agreed that they shouldn't come with us, but I didn't want to encourage him. If I did and something happened to Mindy and her parents, I didn't want him blaming himself or resenting me.

"But we're part of this thunder." Mindy blinked rapidly like she was holding back tears.

"Not anymore." Egan placed an arm around my waist. "You sabotaged my mate and helped the witch try to kill her. You've shown no remorse, insulting Jade, your future queen, repeatedly, in front of everyone. You and your parents will go live in the human world on your own and not contact any of us again. You are hereby banished!"

"Ladon, do something." Rex looked at Egan's father. "You're the only one who can make the call."

"You heard me. It's his and Jade's decision." Ladon's golden eyes found mine as he asked, "Do you agree with Egan's decision?"

Even if I said no, they'd smell the lie. Mindy and her mother couldn't be trusted, and by default, Rex couldn't either since they were his fated mate and daughter. I hated to put anyone in harm's way, but Mindy would jump at the chance to hurt me. "I do."

"Then it's settled." Ladon gestured toward a house that had to be theirs. "Get your stuff and leave immediately."

"We've been best friends for as long as I can remember," Rex pleaded.

"I would have made the same call." Ladon pointed at Susan as he continued, "As your mate admitted, you two were willing to do what was best for your child, and I'm willing to do the same thing for not only Egan and Jade but our entire thunder. You don't have the thunder's best interest at heart and are only out for your own self-interest. You have five minutes before we force you out." He glanced at Draco, still in dragon form. "You and the guards escort them out and then come back to help with the harpies. Everyone be ready to leave in the next twenty minutes."

I felt bad for the three of them, but I agreed with everything Ladon had said. He was on the same page as Egan and me, giving me a sense of peace. Banishing them couldn't have been easy if they'd been close friends for as long as it sounded.

"Egan, please." Mindy's voice cracked.

For the first time, I had the feeling she wasn't being manipulative. She was actually scared.

Egan took my hand, turning his back on her. *Come on. We need to go check on your mother and calm her down before we have to shift and carry her again.*

Great, I hadn't even considered that. There was no other way to get her out of there. This was going to be a fun conversation.

We entered the house with Kayda and Ladon right behind us.

"Mom?" I called, wanting to let her know it was just us. At least, I hoped that would provide her some comfort. Who knew with the way she looked at me moments ago?

Silence greeted us, but I could smell that she'd gone through the normal-sized doorway. She'd probably run in there as soon as she'd realized the other room was meant for dragons.

I stepped into the huge living room and found her sitting on the couch, staring at the dead harpies on the staircase. Arms wrapped around her body, she was gently rocking back and forth.

The room didn't have a homey feeling anymore. The loveseat and recliner still looked unchanged as did the ceiling-high bookcase filled with books, but dead bodies had a way of sucking the life out of a room.

Dammit, I'd forgotten about the dead bodies in the house. Kayda and Egan had shot all the harpies charging down the staircase toward us.

Give me a second. I released his hand and slowly walked over to her. I didn't want to spook her, but I needed her to pay attention to me. "Mom?"

She stopped and turned her head a smidgen toward me. Her eyes remained locked on the dead bodies. "I haven't seen a dead body since your father."

I hadn't expected that was where her mind would go. She hadn't spoken about someone dying since God knew when. "I'm sorry." I didn't know what else to say.

She pulled her attention from the bodies to look at me. "Have you really killed?"

At least, this was an easy answer. "No, I haven't. That girl was just messing with you."

"Thank God." Her face fell. "I knew that didn't sound like you, but after seeing you in that crazy form. I mean ... was that really you?"

"Yes, it was." I couldn't lie to her even if it would be easier. I'd learned early on that my life would never be easy.

"But how? For how long?" Her brows furrowed, and she started rocking again.

"Only for a few weeks, and it was after I met my soul mate." I pointed at Egan, who stood slightly in front of his parents. "When we cemented our connection, I became like him."

Mom inhaled sharply and spat, "You three ... I should've known it would be you."

Wait ... Mom knew them. How was that possible?

CHAPTER FIVE

Mom acted like she knew who Egan's parents were, but they'd been hiding here for over a hundred years. That couldn't be possible. She was being pretty rude to my ... hell, what was I supposed to call them? Mate-in-laws? Either way, the entire situation wasn't ideal. "Mom, you don't know them."

I cringed, realizing that wasn't the wisest thing to say to someone who was irrationally upset.

"Like hell, I don't." Mom stood and placed her hands on her hips. "But it's crazy. You don't look a day older than that day on the beach."

The beach? "What are you talking about?" But I knew. I spun around and stared at Egan. Then my focus shifted to his parents. Dad had been desperate for us to move away from Sarah and had found a job in Florida. Those few days down there, with no negative influences over us, had been the best we'd had. On our last day there, we'd gone to the beach. That day had been amazing. We'd played together, jumped the waves, and I'd met a boy close to my own age whom I'd connected with. The very next day when we'd arrived home, Dad had run out to do some errands, and he'd been killed in a hit-and-run accident, so I'd suppressed most of the memories until now.

The little boy I vividly remembered morphed into the man standing right in front of me. "You saved me on that beach."

"You're the girl I pulled from the water," he said with surprise. He glanced at his parents. "Why didn't you tell us?"

"Son, we were going to, but many things were going on, and even though I suspected that it was the same girl before you got here, I wanted to confirm it first." His dad slowly stepped toward us in the same way he would approach a rabid dog.

This nugget of information didn't worry me. In a way, it reassured me. Even when we were young, we'd felt this connection. It hadn't magically happened at random. We'd always been drawn to each other even when we didn't understand it. *This is a good thing. Everything makes sense, but your dad is right. We can talk about this later. We need to focus on calming my mom down and getting out of here.*

Egan's shoulders relaxed, and he turned to me. *You're right. I just can't believe I didn't put it all together before now. All these years, I've been haunted by the memory of you until that day you walked onto Kortright's campus. I thought you'd replaced the girl I'd dreamed about for years, but you didn't at all.*

You do realize that sounds creepy? Please don't say you were dreaming about a little girl in your twenties. People will get uncomfortable.

The corners of his mouth twitched upward.

"So you've been orchestrating this ever since we met on the beach." Mom jabbed her finger at them. "Between the way that little boy catered to Jade and how you were talking about future visits, you freaked out my husband and me. That's why we cut our trip a day short, and now my daughter is suddenly involved with you and has become a dragon. I should've known you were in danger when you ran off the way you did."

We didn't have time for this, but she wouldn't willingly leave unless we had this out. The more we forced her to do something she didn't want to, the harder this would be. "They had nothing to do with me leaving."

"Don't you lie to me." For the first time in over ten years, Mom reminded me of the woman before Dad had passed. "You beat the shit out of your aunt then vanished into thin air. Of course, a man would be involved."

"Stop it. You sound just like Sarah." I was done treating her like a child. It was time for her to open her eyes and see things for how they truly were. "There is no conspiracy theory. I left because I couldn't breathe. Sarah not only emotionally abused me, but she would hit me as often as she could. When she took college away from me, that was the final straw."

"What?" Mom's mouth dropped, and she shook her head. "I ... I don't understand. I saw the bruises."

"Yes, I hurt her, but she attacked me first." I'd never struck first with her. "I left to go to college to make something out of myself. I was so damn tired of not being able to do anything without her permission. She caught me leaving and tried to beat the shit out of me. Even had the neighbors call the cops. I met Egan at the university, not before then. He went there the prior semester. Fate intervened and brought us together."

"This is crazy." Mom took in a sharp breath. "The way they acted and how you just happened to run into him. Are you sure it wasn't a setup?"

"Mom, he's my soul mate. My other half." I patted my chest where my heart beat. "Fate made sure we found each other twice. If we weren't connected, I wouldn't have become a dragon shifter like him."

"Ma'am," Egan said softly and respectively as he wrapped an arm around my waist. "Your daughter is the most important person in my life. Even that day on the beach, I felt a tug to the deepest section of the water and found her drowning. I'd give up my life for hers."

"Oh, God." She collapsed back onto the couch. "This is too much, and it's crazy."

"I get it." Boy, did I. "I almost walked away from Egan when he told me everything, and it was another reason I didn't want to tell you where I was. I wanted to keep you far away from ..." I trailed off, unsure what else to say, so I threw my hands up. "All this."

"There's much to say, and I understand that, but we need to get moving." Kayda grimaced, unhappy to interrupt this moment. "We can take you back home or wherever you want to go, but the fae dragon king could send others this way when he doesn't hear back from the witch or harpies."

"God, more creatures could come?" Mom jumped to her feet again. "We need to get out of here." Fear shone through her eyes.

"I can take her back to my aunt's and meet back up with you." I wasn't sure what else to do. Egan was the only one who knew where Sadie's mom's pack was located and where Lillith and Katherine's nest was, so he couldn't go with me.

"No!" Mom shouted then cleared her throat. "I mean ... I would really like to go with you if humans are allowed there."

"Really?" That shocked me. With how poorly she was handling the situation, I'd thought she'd be screaming to head back home.

"If that's ..." Mom glanced awkwardly at the wood floors. "If that's okay with everyone."

The problem was I didn't know. I turned slightly into Egan and asked, *What do we do?*

I don't know either. He breathed. *Do you want her to come with us?*

Yes. The magnitude of what I'd said rattled me. She hadn't wanted to spend time with me in years. The last time we'd even laughed together had been on the beach. If she wanted to come with us, I'd hate to turn down the opportunity. Who knew when it would present itself again, especially when Sarah got her clutches back on her? *I really do.*

Then we'll make it work. Egan squeezed my waist. "There are other supernatural races where we're going, and it must be kept a secret. If you can't guarantee that, you can't come."

"Other supernaturals?" She shivered and closed her eyes. "You know what? Don't answer that. Of course, I'll keep it a secret. I wouldn't want Jade to get hurt or worse. After what I just saw, I wouldn't want that to happen to anyone."

"Then I guess that means you're joining us," Kayda murmured. "After all, we're family now."

It meant a lot that his parents didn't give us a hard time. Family was important to them, and they were welcoming Mom into the fold. No wonder Egan had grown into such a kind and considerate man.

I almost asked about Sarah but bit back the words. Her name would come up again soon enough, and I didn't want to push it. "You do realize there's only one way out of here, though?"

"What do you mean?" Her jaw twitched, one of her nervous tics.

"You were carried in here by a harpy." My gaze cut to her shoulders. Her dark green shirt was torn where the talons had sunk into her arms. Blood still seeped from the cuts, and we needed to clean those injuries sooner rather than later. Harpies weren't the cleanest creatures.

She shuddered. "Don't remind me."

"Did you pay attention to how you got in here?" The only way inside the valley was through an opening in the cave ceiling. With no rocks providing hand and footholds, the mile-high drop would kill anyone who attempted to climb up the entryway. The opening was wide, allowing the sun to shine through most of the day, and inside the mountainous cave were rolling grassy hills with the village located on one side. It was a gorgeous place that wouldn't be a terrible place to live. Near the hidden second entrance was farmland with some livestock. They'd set everything up to be self-sufficient.

She pulled at her lip uncomfortably. "No, not really. Why?"

This wouldn't go over well. "There's only one way in and out, and that's flying."

Mom's eyes popped wider. "Are you going to bite me and turn me into a dragon?"

Her words took a second to sink in, and when they did, I burst out into laughter.

Egan chuckled silently beside me, trying to keep a straight face out of respect for her.

"Mom, vampires are the only race that actively bites to change people." Apparently, wolves could too, but it was frowned upon because the human often ended up with horrible defects. The only two exceptions were when Sadie and Roxy had bitten their fated mates, Donovan and Axel. According to Sadie, she, Roxy, Egan, and her vampire friends had been worried Donovan and Axel would wind up the same way, but since they had shifter blood, they'd transitioned just fine. "Someone will have to carry you out of here."

"Oh, thank God." She sighed and rubbed her temple. "Not that there is anything wrong with dragons. I just don't want to be one."

Now I understood where I got my awkwardness from. It was clearly hereditary.

Ladon chuckled. "Nope, we can't turn anyone into a dragon unless they are a dragon's fated mate. I'll head out and make sure everyone is ready to go."

"Okay, we'll be right there," Kayda reassured me, making it clear there was not any discomfort talking with Mom.

Mom pursed her lips. "Can Jade carry me?"

"Sure, I can do that." If it made her more comfortable, I was all for it. "But no yelling in my ear."

"That I can't promise," she joked back.

I hated to bring up bad memories, but I needed to know. "How did the witch find you?"

"I'm not sure." She scratched her nose. "Sarah had to run out somewhere for work and asked me to pick a few things up at the grocery store. While I was shopping, the witch came right up to me and started talking. After a few minutes, she asked if I was your mom. I figured she was a high school friend and didn't find it very strange. When I checked out, she asked if I needed help loading the car. I thought she was a sweet kid and took her up on it. I was leaning into the backseat, putting the last bag in, when she hit me on the head. The next thing I knew, I woke up in a small cabin in the middle of nowhere."

If Mom had paid attention to my high school days at all, she'd have known I didn't have friends. But I bit my tongue. Vera would've done whatever was necessary to trick her. "I'm glad you made it out okay." It'd been damn close, but we'd survived.

"We aren't out of the woods yet." Kayda sighed. "Ladon is heading back. Everyone is ready. We have our bags in the center, so everyone shift and get ready to fly."

"Can I wait in here until Jade changes?" Mom asked. "I'd rather stay close to her if possible."

"Of course. We'll shift first; then you two can." Kayda headed to the doorway, leaving Egan and me alone with Mom.

The front door opened, and Ladon joined his wife in the shifting room. It wouldn't take long before it was our turn.

Mom watched Kayda walk off and whispered, "Does it hurt to turn into your dragon?"

I'd expected it to, at first, so it was a good question. "It's strange, but it doesn't hurt. It's more like your senses are sharper than ever, and it's a little disconcerting, but there's no pain."

"And you've been a dragon your whole life?" Mom asked Egan.

It warmed my heart that she was talking to him. She might be scared and uncomfortable, but she was trying to get to know him.

"We don't shift until we're seven or eight." Egan smiled. "But ever since then, yes, and I was born with my senses more dragon-like, so I didn't have to adjust like Jade."

"Interesting," Mom breathed.

Dragon footsteps sounded, and the front door opened again. Egan's parents had already shifted and were in a hurry.

We'd stayed here longer than we should've. "Egan and I are going to go shift. Are you ready?"

She hesitated. "As ready as I'll ever be, but I don't want to be here to find out what shows up next."

Yeah, me neither. The image of the harpies alone would take a lifetime to dull. "We'll just be a moment."

Egan took my hand, and we entered the shifting room. We stripped down and put our clothes in the bag. He grabbed our bag, and within minutes, we were walking out into the entryway in dragon form.

Mom's face turned slightly pale when she saw us. Even though she'd known we'd be walking out in this form, it had to be unnerving to see us like this.

I wanted to comfort her, but there wasn't an easy way to do it in this form. Instead, I opened the front door and waved her out. She slowly followed after me, hiding behind my bulky frame as we met all the other dragons ready to leave. Each dragon carried two large bags of personal belongings.

Ladon looked at his son and motioned for him to lead.

He linked with me. *Get your mom, and let's go.*

Ready to get the hell out of here, I lowered myself and opened my arms to Mom. She stepped slowly inside, and I gently wrapped them around her so I didn't alarm her.

Draco stepped beside us, and the three of us took to the air. We flew around the thick smoke trickling upward from what was left of the harpy bodies. Mom coughed. I pushed away the thought of what we were breathing in.

As we flew out of the cave, the silence of the once brimming woods wasn't lost on me. The saying of the calm before the storm echoed in my head.

A loud cry of pain cracked through the sky, ruining any thought of getting out of here without issue.

CHAPTER SIX

My heart pounded in my ears, and if it hadn't been for Mom in my arms, there was no telling what I would've done. But I couldn't risk hurting her, so I kept my head on straight. *What is that? More fae creatures?*

That's what it sounds like, but the barrier spell is working. They're fighting against the spell and crying out in discomfort. Egan flew in front of me, following behind Draco.

That spell had been brutal, so hopefully, it would help keep the enemy creatures distracted. I glanced over my shoulder and found more dragons exiting the cave.

Mom snuggled deeper into my chest, either needing comfort or trying to comfort me. Either way, I appreciated the gesture.

More cries echoed throughout the woods, putting us on edge. Luckily, they were grouped together, coming in from our right.

Draco flew forward, keeping clear of the noise as the thunder flew hard through the channel.

I focused on the feel of the wind against my scales to keep my anxiety at bay. Nothing good would happen if we reacted out of fear.

The sun shone down on us, and the smell of spring flowers hit my nose. On any other day, it would have been enjoyable, but the fae creatures could breach the barrier at any second.

Waving us on, Draco slowed and moved to the right. He had his tense warrior-dragon face cemented into place, his mouth firm and his nostrils flaring. His gray-green eyes deepened to black, but unlike Vera and the harpies, they weren't soulless. Pure determination and anger shone through.

Numerous stone figures flailed in mid-air. They looked like the gargoyle statues I'd seen in a haunted house Dad had taken me to once. But these were about half my size and bulky. Their faces were scrunched in chiseled stone, and their jagged stone teeth were scary. They were entirely gray except for their bright red eyes.

Gargoyles are real? The more I learned, the more things astonished me about this life. I never would've thought that these creatures existed. But why the hell not? Half-naked old ladies and reptile combinations were real, but I hadn't expected stone to come to life. Would the trees start dancing or attacking us next?

Egan kept his gaze locked on the strange creatures, but he didn't look as concerned. His wings beat steadily. *They're from Fae. They live near the dragons and are born of the stone from the volcanoes there. From what we've been told, every eruption causes a new batch of gargoyles to be born.*

Fae had to be one strange, messed-up place. I'd pass the opportunity to visit in a heartbeat. My ass was staying firmly in this realm.

We passed by all of the gargoyles and flew into a cloudless blue sky, but I refused to get too comfortable. Every time I thought we had a small win, we were attacked, or something equally horrible happened.

I could still hear faint screams, but the thunder was no longer under threat.

Egan took the lead, and we ascended higher into the sky.

No one can see us, Egan explained. *We'll be passing by cities and towns on the way there.*

Trusting him completely, I situated my mother and followed right behind.

A FEW HOURS LATER, my arms were getting tired from Mom's extra weight. The first hour, I'd gotten a little cocky since carrying Mom hadn't gotten to me, but I'd been too cocky too soon. My arms were aching, and each time Mom moved, holding her became harder.

From all of the fidgeting she'd been doing the past little while, I had a feeling she felt as uncomfortable as I did.

How much longer? I officially sounded like a whiny child, but if we didn't reach Lillith's home soon, I'd need a break.

Egan examined me. *We're almost there. Do I need to take her?*

No. If we're close, I'll be fine. Besides, I wasn't sure how Mom would react to someone else carrying her.

Hints of the green mountain greeted me. At this altitude, we probably looked like an enormous flock of birds flying over.

We flew past a small town, and after a few more miles, Egan started a slow descent. He said, *Just a few minutes now.*

The others followed closely behind. We flew beyond the small country roads and over a stretch of thick woods. It reminded me of Trixie's, the witch who'd thought she'd blocked Vera from tracking me. We'd flown over a large section of nothing before landing in the middle of a vast clearing that held a small cabin that had seen better days.

I hoped we would have better conditions here, but I didn't have a dime to my name since quitting Haynes Steakhouse, so I'd have appreciated any kind of shelter.

We hadn't seen any cars driving on the roads for miles, and Egan descended farther, only a mile above the trees. I kept my eyes forward, afraid that if I looked down, I might drop Mom accidentally. It was an irrational fear.

After a few more minutes, a huge mansion appeared a mile away.

It was a symmetrical, three-story brick building with brick steps leading to the tall red door at the center. It looked well kept.

Wow, Roxy had called it a mansion, but I'd figured she was being sarcastic. *Is that it?*

Yes. Egan sounded relieved. *Between the vampires and wolves, there are miles and miles of land. With so much space, I'm hoping we won't struggle to find room for everyone.*

That seemed like wishful thinking. Huge homes usually had more rooms for entertainment and stuff than sleeping space ... or so it always seemed in stories and movies. *How many bedrooms and bathrooms are there?*

Fifteen bedrooms with sixteen full bathrooms. However, between Sadie, her pack, and the vampires, there are only about seven bedrooms available. But they have a living room with two L-shaped leather couches that should sleep four and a few blow-up mattresses. And then we can talk to Titan and see how many homes they might have to offer us.

We had a lot to figure out, but we were better off than I'd dared hope for. *Where will we stay?*

I have a bedroom there with how much time I spent here last semester.

Despite our parents being nearby, I hoped that there wouldn't be a problem with me staying in the same room with him.

When we landed in front of the mansion, the front door opened, and Sadie and the others ran outside.

"Thank God, you're okay." Sadie jumped down the stairs, her rose-gold bob bouncing. Her light blue eyes found Egan then me. "We've been so worried about you." She placed her cell phone in her back jeans pocket, and her coral top inched upward, revealing some of her tan, smooth skin.

"She's been calling you nonstop." Donovan stepped up beside his mate and pulled her shirt down. His cobalt eyes locked on Mom as he ran his free hand through his shaggy dark hair. His muscles contracted, outlined in his white polo shirt. He was huge, but only half the size of Egan. In general, dragons were stronger and more built than wolves.

"Holy shit." Roxy's hazel eyes widened. She fluffed her vibrant red hair and clicked down the stairs in her hunter-green platform heels. She wore a matching green designer dress that accentuated her breasts and small hips. "They brought a human."

Now would be a good time to shift into human form so I could explain why.

"That won't go over well." Axel scratched his buzzed head, and his dark eyes deepened to an obsidian.

"What won't go over well?" Lillith asked as she came out the front door. Her dark brown eyes had a deep crimson ring around the pupils, telling me she'd recently fed. Her jet-black hair was cut like Sadie's, but that was where the similarities ended. Where Sadie normally wore clothes in varying shades of color, Lillith did not. Her outfits were all black, the same color as her hair. The only part of her that was a different color was her pale vampire skin.

She wore trendy black Chucks, so her steps were silent when she walked down the stairs. But she stopped short when she saw Mom. Her hands went to her waist, as a slight breeze made her black skirt rise above her knees and her lace shirt crinkle. "Why is there a human here?"

I wasn't thinking, Egan said slowly.

What's wrong with Mom being here? Someone needed to let me in on the crucial piece of information I was missing.

"Uh ... I'm Jade's mother," Mom said feebly as she tried to get out of my arms, but I held firm. I wasn't letting her go until I knew what the hell was going on.

Katherine's family was turned about ten years ago. Her brothers aren't great around humans yet. Egan winced even in dragon form. He stepped in front of me, blocking Mom from their view.

"Really? You think that's going to hide her smell?" Lillith snapped.

"Hide what smell?" Katherine asked as she ran out the door. Her lighter brown eyes held the dark red center, and her long hair blew behind her. She rushed toward us but stopped short. She sniffed so hard that her chest expanded, making the pink word "Believe" on her black shirt legible. Her hands fell at her sides, brushing against her blue jeans. "Oh, that one."

Lillith turned toward the house. "We need to keep Luther and Athan inside."

"I can leave." Mom leaned forward and glanced at me. "I don't want to cause problems."

"You aren't," Katherine assured her. "My brothers have been practicing, so they won't pose a threat to you."

"Pose a threat to me?" Mom's brows furrowed. "I ... I don't understand."

"You know what?" Sadie cleared her throat and gestured to the entire thunder behind us. "How about you all set your stuff down and shift back to human form so we can figure out sleeping arrangements. After your long night, I know you three," she said, pointing to Draco, Egan, and me, "must be exhausted."

Until she'd mentioned it, I hadn't noticed, but between the crazy fighting, the all-nighter, and seeing Mom, fatigue had caught up.

"Come on ... Jade's mom." Roxy tapped her lip. "What is your name? Or do you wanna go by that?"

"Oh, it's Liz." Mom nearly sounded like herself answering a normal question.

Sometimes, normal was underrated. I almost missed things being as I expected them to be. Not that I would give Egan up.

Roxy sashayed over to Mom and pried my arms from her. "All right, Liz. You can hang out with me. I don't bite, unlike the vampires here."

"Vampires?" Mom's voice skyrocketed to glass-breaking levels.

Things were going swimmingly. She probably regretted wanting to come with us.

"Don't worry," Roxy said, brushing off her concern. "The guys just drank several pints of blood, so they aren't hungry, and the decaying blood smell you got going on in your hair would make even the hungriest vamp think twice before chomping down on you."

"Decay?" Mom parroted and touched her crusty hair. She gagged and wiped her fingers on her jeans.

"Yeah, that's going to help." Roxy rolled her eyes at Sadie and Katherine.

"Dude, sometimes I worry about your mate." Donovan shook his head. "Does she really think that's comforting?"

"Nope, you're not getting me in trouble again." Axel took a few long steps away from his best friend. "Roxy does what she wants. I've learned to stop trying to reason with her."

"See." Roxy pointed at me. "I finally got him trained. I'll teach you the ways with that big lug right next to you."

"Okay." Sadie clapped her hands. "You all go shift, and I'll stay here and protect your mother from them." She waved her hand at her pack and the vampires.

Mom's shoulders relaxed some.

I didn't blame her. Sadie had a calming presence about her, unlike Roxy and Lillith.

Come on. Egan nodded toward the trees. *Let's change and get back to your mom before they make it all worse.*

That sounded like a solid plan.

We rushed off to the woods as the other dragons followed suit. We all spread out, giving each other ample space. Egan dropped the bag and unzipped it awkwardly with his huge, scaly dragon hands, and we pulled out our clothes.

Back in human form and fully clothed, we hurried back to the others. Mom and Sadie were talking a few feet away from the rest.

As we walked up to them, Sadie and Mom stopped, and the group turned toward us.

Egan asked, "What's the plan? We have a hundred and twenty with us."

"How many families does that break into?" Donovan placed his hands into his pocket.

"Around fifty." Egan rolled his shoulders.

Sadie gestured to the mansion. "Between the bedrooms, couches, and the three blow-up mattresses, we can take in fifteen couples easily."

"I'm the youngest here," Egan said. "One reason why I got to leave and look for a mate. Only Mindy and I have been born in the last fifty years."

"Wait, she said she trained younger kids." That was the whole reason she'd been sent to train me.

"She has a handful of them. Kids who came from other thunders. She was given the task to train the young for when we would start having children of our own again." Egan shrugged. "We stayed hidden and mostly traveled from thunder to thunder on rare occasions. Usually, only the leaders of the thunders did it because they already knew where we were located. They brought their kids, the next leaders of the thunder, to meet the others and learn about all the locations."

"The next best news is that Titan's pack has about thirty homes open since a majority of the younger families relocated to our pack." Sadie glanced toward the woods where the other dragons had begun filing out. "As long as a few don't mind bunking together, we should have plenty of room until we can figure out our next move."

Wow, this was a much better plan than we'd realized. It just sucked that we would have to split up.

The front door opened, and a guy around our age popped his head out. His blond hair was a shade lighter than Egan's, and his gray eyes seemed friendly until they landed on Mom.

Fangs descended as he hissed and leaped at her.

"Athan!" Katherine screamed. "No!"

CHAPTER SEVEN

The next few seconds blended together. I hadn't expected an attack, and Athan had stunned everyone.

Egan stepped in front of Mom as the vampire reached her, his teeth ready to sink into her neck. Egan placed his hands on Athan's shoulders and shoved him to the gravel driveway. Rocks bounced from the impact, and a puff of dust surrounded us.

Needing to help protect Mom, I ran over to her and wrapped my hand around her arm. When I tugged, she hardly moved. She was frozen in fear.

I would have to use my supernatural strength to make her budge. I hated to do it, but this was a life or death matter. I yanked on her harder, and her feet stumbled, but she stayed upright. She was now behind Egan and me.

Wings flapped as Draco sped past me, half shifted and racing toward the vampire.

Athan jumped up with a loud, crackling hiss, desperate to get to Mom. He blurred as he tried to go around Egan, and I prepared myself to fight the vampire off. Egan lowered his body and threw the vampire over his shoulder.

The whole point of coming here had been to find safety, not be threatened.

"Stop it," Sadie commanded as she raced to stand beside me. Her light blue eyes glowed brightly.

I'd never heard or seen her like this before. She really was an alpha, not that I hadn't believed it before. She had a strong presence, but she never used it. Everyone naturally gravitated to her and wanted to hear what she had to say. She led by caring about people and encouraging them to embrace her views and thoughts. A leader like that could decimate armies because of the morale they instilled in others.

Despite her words, Athan's eyes turned red as he desperately snarled and struggled. I refused to cower. If he got to her, he'd kill her.

The vampire clawed at Egan's back and shoulder.

"Do not injure the prince," Draco rasped and fisted the vampire's head, holding him up.

His legs dangled, and he cried in pain like a puppy in trouble.

Egan reached to take the vampire back from the warrior and winced, dropping his hand to his side. "He's not used to humans, and he's a friend. Don't hurt him."

"I won't, but he can't be trusted." Draco stared at the vampire, his nose wrinkled with disgust.

That only agitated Athan more. He swatted at Draco, but the dragon was too huge and held him a safe distance away. He rocked, his eyes locked on Mom.

He was completely out of his mind. All the vampire needed to do was reach over his head and slash into the dragon's hand.

"I said stop," Sadie growled and punched Athan in the face.

His head snapped back, and his body went limp, dangling like a wet noodle. Draco dropped the vampire on his back, knocking the breath out of him. His face crumpled in pain as he panted.

I might have felt bad for the vampire if he hadn't tried to eat my mom.

"Athan." Katherine kneeled beside him. "What's gotten into you?"

"You said he'd eaten." Lillith glanced from Athan to Roxy. "He wouldn't be acting like this if he had. Sure, he might be tempted, but that was a full-on hunger attack."

Roxy cringed. "About that. I might have been misinformed."

"Misinformed?" Lillith narrowed her eyes. "You were the one with Ollie, him, and Luther, playing that stupid video game."

"Well ..." Roxy blew out a breath and chewed on her green fingernail.

Axel rubbed his forehead. "Babe, come clean."

The words spilled from Roxy so fast they were almost unintelligible. "The game got intense, and I wasn't paying attention to them, so I don't know if they were drinking the blood. I assumed they were."

"Then why did you tell us that?" Katherine moved the hair out of her brother's face.

Roxy lifted a hand in surrender, her face lined with remorse. "I honestly thought they had and didn't expect them to leave their game. When I saw his reaction, I realized they may have gotten caught up in the game too." She leaned over to see Mom. "I'm sorry, Liz."

My anger deflated even though I didn't want it to. Roxy was usually confident and vibrant, and for the first time, she looked remorseful. She obviously felt terrible and was beating herself up.

"We need to get him inside," Egan said and bent to pick up the vampire.

"I'll get him." Draco cut his gaze to Egan's bleeding shoulder. "You're injured." He picked the vampire up and headed to the front door.

Roxy opened the door. "Here, I'll help—"

"No. You've done enough," Lillith said. "I'll go with Draco and make sure he and Luther drink. We don't need another vampire going crazy." Lillith scowled at Roxy and walked past her.

The look on Roxy's face was devastating. Her head flinched

backward, and her cheeks reddened. If I hadn't known any better, I would've thought she'd been slapped.

In a way, she had been. Lillith hadn't held back her words.

Draco marched past her like he was on a mission. Granted, that was his normal disposition, seeing as he was prepared to protect Egan and me at a moment's notice.

When the front door shut again, Mom peeked around me and whispered, "Is he gone?"

"Yeah, he's back inside." Axel rubbed his mate's shoulder, comforting her. Roxy's face reminded me of a tomato, and she frowned even more.

"How can he hear me?" Mom asked louder, not bothering to lower her voice.

I pointed at my ear. "Supernatural hearing. They could hear you clear as day in the woods."

My eyes went back to the tree line where all of the dragon shifters stood. They all wore troubled expressions after watching what had gone down.

If I'd been in their situation, I'd have felt the same way. Hell, I mirrored their expressions now. I didn't need to feel like there was a constant threat lurking in the background. Maybe Mom should go back to Sarah, but I didn't want to encourage that. Mom needed time away from Sarah's influence.

"Is everything all right?" Ladon asked and stepped out from between two trees. His gaze locked on his son's injured shoulder, and his eyes turned dark gold.

Kayda shoved past her husband, rushing to Egan. "Of course it's not all right." She gingerly reached for his shoulder. "We need to clean this."

"And Mom's too." They had near-identical wounds. Egan had the better end since the vampire looked clean and he had shifter healing abilities. Mom's injuries would become infected without treatment and take weeks to heal. I wanted to check on Egan myself, but Mom was buried against my back. The irony wasn't lost on me that she acted more like the child in our relationship.

"There is no way in hell I'm going in there." Mom stepped away from the door.

"You know what?" Sadie casually strolled over to Mom and wrapped an arm around her waist. "Why don't I take you and the other dragons staying with my stepdad's pack over there to get settled?"

Mom rubbed her hands together, her lips drawn. "Are there vampires?"

"Nope, only wolf shifters." Sadie beamed. "And the dragon shifters who want to stay there as well."

"Of course. Wolf shifters." Mom winced. "I guess nothing should surprise me anymore, but I'm down as long as someone doesn't try biting me."

"I can go too," I volunteered, wanting to comfort Mom.

"We were hoping that you, Egan, and his parents would stay here with us," Donovan said slowly. "There's a library here filled with old books. We were thinking you could assist us with research."

I stiffened, hating for Mom to feel abandoned.

"It's fine, honey." Her focus landed uncomfortably on Egan. "You stay here with your ... uh ..."

"Fated mate," Katherine suggested gently. Her kindness knew no bounds, and she was one of the few here, like Donovan, Axel, and me, who understood what it was like to get thrust into an unknown world that made no sense.

"Right." Mom's brows furrowed, and she tilted her head. "Fated mate and his parents."

Sadie tugged Mom toward the back of the house. "She can stay with Mom, Titan, and Torak. They'll keep her busy and on her toes."

"As long as I'm safe there," Mom grumbled, eagerly stepping away.

A small smile spread across my face. She was handling this better than I'd expected, especially after how she'd reacted back in the cave valley. Maybe she wanted distance between us to process everything. She and I were similar like that.

"Son, how do you propose we split up?" Ladon asked, throwing me off guard.

Ladon was the king, not Egan. Shouldn't that be his call to make? I almost linked with Egan but figured this was something he should handle on his own. Maybe his father was preparing him now that Egan knew his future.

Egan surveyed the group and cleared his throat. He squared his shoulders as he stood beside me and took my hand, presenting us as a united front. "Draco and the oldest dragons should stay here. The remainder of the thunder should go with Sadie and the others to the wolf pack. They have thirty homes available for us to use, so families can choose who they want to double up with for the time being. The fae dragon king will not stop, and our time of hiding is over."

A few dragons close to our age cheered. They could have been in their mid-thirties for all I knew, but the younger generation liked the thought of joining the rest of the world.

The thunder split into two groups without fighting, and everyone obeyed based on age. *Are there a few leaders who will qualify for the pack houses? We don't need the younger ones going and acting wild because of their newfound freedom.*

I'd seen what my fellow classmates had done once they'd arrived at college. Their social media pages contained drunken pictures of them doing embarrassing things I couldn't believe they'd post in the first place, and a few even had friends posting pictures of them vomiting into toilets, clearly too drunk. We didn't need crazy dragon shifters getting loose in the world and drawing unwanted attention here. Sadie and the others had made it clear that their families enjoyed living in a place few knew about. We would respect their wishes and ensure they remained hidden.

Okay, maybe "world" was a stretch, but they surely were new to the supernatural community.

You're right. Egan squeezed my hand lovingly. "Rose and Thorn, will you please go to the pack homes and make sure those from our thunder pulls their weight?"

That was code for behaving respectfully but in a more politically correct way. He had a knack for leading without making others feel insulted.

Rose's stern face transformed with a proud smile. Her amethyst eyes glowed slightly at the request, making her plum-brown hair stand out. She was over six feet five inches tall, one of the tallest women, and even in her jeans and shirt, she looked perfectly put together. "Of course, my prince."

Now that I wasn't expecting, Egan grumbled, not thrilled about the prince part.

She took her husband's hand and broke away from the group destined for the mansion. Her husband had a few inches on her, and where she was bright and colorful, he looked pale. His eyes were a light silver, and he had white, ash-blond hair. His skin tone looked more vampiric than the golden shine of normal shifters.

An older couple from the previous group replaced them.

"Okay, let's do this," Roxy said, still sounding defeated. She hurried to catch up with Mom and Sadie, likely to apologize again.

Were those two an arranged marriage? They acted like natural dragon shifters, unlike Kayda and me. We had more of a human way about us. Not so noble ... or rigid.

Egan nodded and tugged me toward the house. *Yes, they are. How'd you know?*

Between learning about arranged marriages among your kind and the way those two move like dragon-born shifters, I put two and two together. Being observant was the main way I'd survived living with my aunt all those years. I'd had to figure out her moods and what to expect based on how her face was set or the way she stood to know how to proceed with her.

By the time we entered the house, the adrenaline of the vampire attack had worn off, and my feet dragged against the pristine wood floors as we walked down a long hallway.

Egan led us into a huge living room where two L-shaped leather couches were set across from each other with a wooden coffee table in between. Everything was positioned in front of an eighty-inch, flat-screen television, and remote controls for a gaming console littered the floor. The vampire young man sat on the couch, his face in his hands as a teenage boy sat next to him. The teenager looked exactly like a male version of Katherine, except a few years younger.

Standing right in front of them with his arms crossed, Draco glared down at the two of them.

Egan stopped, and I leaned against his side, barely able to stand on both feet.

"I hate to do this, but Jade and I have been up since yesterday afternoon, and we need a long nap." Egan turned to his dad. "Do you mind if we rest for a few hours and rejoin you later?"

"No, but I'm not sure who these people are." Ladon looked a bit uncomfortable.

"That's where we come in." Lillith stepped into the room. "I can introduce you to everyone. Egan already knows them anyway."

"We'll be fine," Kayda interjected. "Go get some rest. You two deserve it."

Even though I normally couldn't sleep with so many people around, I had a feeling once I got comfortable on that couch, sleep would crash over me. I nearly sighed with relief as I moved toward the couch, but Egan's arms slid around my waist.

He asked, *Where do you think you're going?*

To get some rest.

He tugged me toward another hallway and rasped, *You're going the wrong way. Our room is up there.*

Together? In front of your parents? Thank God he planned on us sharing a room. I'd figured we would, but I didn't know if his parents expected us to do whatever ceremony dragons did before staying together. I had no clue how this worked in their world.

He picked me up and kissed my lips gently as he climbed the

stairs. *Yes. Did you think I'd let you out of my sight? We're mated. I won't spend a night without you right next to me.*

Despite my exhaustion, my body warmed at his kiss and touch. Of course, his words didn't hurt either.

At the first door on the right, he paused and turned the doorknob.

All thoughts of sleep abandoned me as I wrapped my arms around his neck and slipped my tongue between his lips.

He stumbled into the room and barely regained his balance. He growled as he matched each stroke of my tongue. *If you keep this up, we aren't taking a nap right away.*

I'm okay with that. My hand slid under his shirt.

Someone cleared their throat. I went still and buried my face in his chest like a coward.

CHAPTER EIGHT

I wished the floor would open up and swallow me whole. The sweet scent of vampire hit my nose, but it was more male. A hint of a bitter undertone counterbalanced the smell slightly. Still, his scent reminded me of cotton candy at an amusement park.

"I'm sorry for interrupting," Athan said. "But I ran upstairs, hoping to catch you before you got into your room so I could apologize to you since your mom isn't around."

Yeah, there was no getting out of meeting his eyes. At least, he was similar to his sister and nothing like Lillith or Roxy. They'd have been using this opportunity to embarrass me.

Hey, there's nothing to be ashamed of, Egan reassured me. *Even though vampires don't have fated mates, they have high sex drives like any other supernatural.*

I rubbed my head into his chest, and my shoulders sagged. *Not helping.*

"I guess I'll leave you two alone." Disappointment dripped from each one of Athan's words.

Not only was I a scaredy-cat, but I was also hurting the poor guy's feelings. He obviously felt bad, which, in all fairness, he should, but sometimes forgiveness went a long way. Or that was what I was hoping for.

Inhaling sharply, I forced myself away from the safety of Egan's arms to look at the vampire. He already had his back turned to us, heading for the stairs. His head hung, making him appear smaller than during the attack.

"I'm being silly." My face warmed, but I tried to be casual. "We were just about to get it on, and you caught us. That's why I was hiding, not because you almost killed my mother."

And here I thought I'd overcome my awkward mouth-diarrhea.

Athan's brows furrowed as he tilted his head. I could see his brain spinning, but I wasn't sure why. "Are you trying to make me uncomfortable as punishment, or did you not mean to say that?"

Egan snorted and broke out into loud laughter. He placed a hand on the base of my neck as he faced the vampire. Between his bouts of laughter, my mate said, "She didn't mean to. She's not like Roxy and Lillith, who thrive off embarrassing and shocking people."

Now I was being laughed at. Great. I might as well have been back in high school. "You two can kiss my ass." Egan could find somewhere else to sleep or think I didn't want him in here with me.

"Hey, wait," Athan called out, and I stopped short. "I'm not laughing at you. You just caught me by surprise."

And I'm not either. Egan wrapped an arm around my waist, pulling me back against him. He rasped, *I think it's adorable and refreshing. I can tell exactly what you're thinking.*

Deciding not to make the situation worse, I ignored Egan's words, trying to stay annoyed, and turned my gaze on Athan. "You came here to say ..." Dear God, please redirect the conversation. I didn't want to say anything else, afraid of what might fall from my lips.

"Right." He rolled his shoulders like he was either preparing for a fight or a long speech. "Of course, I'll say this to your mom ... if she'll let me near her again." He grimaced like he realized he might never get a chance to tell her directly. "But I feel awful about attacking her. I didn't realize a human would be part of your group, so I didn't gorge myself to make sure I wasn't the slightest bit hungry. Between that and not being mentally prepared for a smell that delectable—" He stopped and licked his lips at the memory.

I had no clue what to do. He'd come here to apologize, but he was licking his lips at the thought of Mom's scent. *Uh ... what do I do here?*

Give him a second. Egan's thumb rubbed against my neck. *He really is a good guy. With him and his brother being turned younger, they don't have as much self-control, and the bloodlust is hard for them to overcome.*

Isn't he our age, though, like Katherine? Katherine hadn't batted an eye at Mom.

Women, in general, can control their urges better than men, but when she first attended Kortright, she wasn't very comfortable around humans. She's grown a lot in a semester, being around humans constantly. They've taken Athan and Luther out around humans, but it's very controlled. Obviously, they still have more work to do. Lillith was born a vampire, so she grew up learning how to control her urges.

Born a vampire. Who knew? *Does that make her a purebred?*

Yes, but those who are turned aren't viewed as much less. Egan coughed to snap Athan out of it.

"Right, sorry." Athan put his tongue back in his mouth and rubbed a hand down his face. "This isn't going like I hoped. It's just, I really am sorry, and Luther and I will do everything possible to make sure an attack like that doesn't happen again."

"Please do." I wouldn't tell him it was okay, because one, it wasn't, and two, they'd all know I was lying.

"Promise." Athan placed his hands in his jeans pockets and rocked back on his heels.

An awkward silence descended among us, and Egan pushed the door to our bedroom wider.

"Right." Athan lifted his hand and snapped, "You two were busy. I'll let you get back to it."

This couldn't get any more uncomfortable. Boy, I really hated that he'd proved me wrong.

"So ... see ya." He saluted Egan and raced toward the steps.

Once he'd rounded the corner and was out of sight, I leaned against the doorframe and banged my head against the wood. *Is he going to run down there and tell everyone?*

No. He isn't Lillith or Roxy. Egan pulled me into the bedroom and pressed my back against the wall. His hands trapped me, turning me on more than I'd thought possible.

Egan surrounded me, and even if I'd wanted to get away, I couldn't. The sense of him overpowering me should have pissed me off, but the alpha mood had me primed for him.

He kissed my lips and gently bit my bottom lip. My hands wrapped around his neck as I hooked a leg around his waist.

Any sense of fatigue was gone, my body fueled by a desperate need only he could fill.

What's gotten into you? He was normally gentle, almost too much so.

He stilled. *Am I being too rough?*

Oh God, no. You better not stop. I sucked on his bottom lip hard and grazed my teeth against his tongue.

His hands cupped my ass, his fingers digging into my skin. He groaned as he tore his mouth from my lips and kissed down my neck. When he reached the base, he tasted my skin then gently bit.

I bucked against him and slipped my hands under his shirt. My nails scratched his back as my breathing turned ragged.

His mouth went back to mine, and he kissed me so thoroughly my mind grew dizzy. He spun me around and headed toward the bed.

"No, stop." Of course, this was when my germophobic ways would come in handy. "We're both nasty, and your shoulder needs to be cleaned."

"Then it sounds like we need to hit the shower." He walked across the room, through another doorway, and sat me down on the tile next to a sizable, light gray, stone shower.

I almost whined when he pulled away to turn the shower on

inside but was tempted by the water falling from a double shower head like rain.

The bathroom was dark compared to the rest of the house. A dark-gray double sink sat to the right of the doorway with a matching tub to the left. Between the tub and the shower was a closet full of fluffy white towels. I'd never been in a house this luxurious before.

He pulled out two towels and placed them on the stand next to the shower door.

"Come here." He removed my shirt as he kissed toward my breast. I leaned my head back as his lips released some tension from my body.

His tongue flicked my nipple as he rasped, *God, you taste so good.*

The tangy scent of our arousal killed every single one of my brain cells.

He pulled my crotch right against him and ground against me. Even with our jeans on, the friction built, and my body almost exploded when he nipped at my breast.

There was something primal about him. Something raw. Something I'd never seen before, and it was thrilling. My hands shook with desperation as I unfastened his jeans and pushed them, along with his boxers, to the ground. My hand stroked him, and he shuddered at my touch.

I loved having that much power over him.

He grabbed my arms and pinned them as he quickly removed my pants. He paused midway and grimaced. "Did I hurt your leg?"

Shit. I'd forgotten all about that injury during the flight here. Begrudgingly, I untangled myself from him and glanced down to find the wound had scabbed over. I moved my leg from side to side, and there was absolutely no pain.

"I'm fine." My eyes went to his shoulders. "Let's get you in the shower and clean before yours heals too much like mine." I hoped I didn't get an infection, but the skin wasn't red around the scab. Maybe shifters were immune to infections?

You don't have to tell me twice. He winked and moved to pull his shirt off.

If I hadn't been watching him so closely, I might have missed the grimace that slipped through as the shirt tore over his head.

But my eyes didn't stay on his shoulder wound for long as his naked body pulled my attention away.

His six-pack was damn lickable, and his pecs were defined, each muscle clearly lined. He was four times my size, all muscle, and damn sexy.

He opened the shower door, making me walk backward inside. The water felt like a warm caress. It felt magical and fueled my hunger for him.

Water poured down our faces as he captured my lips and positioned himself between my legs. With one swift thrust, he entered me, and I raised my leg higher, causing him to hit where I needed.

A low, deep groan escaped, and he leaned over my body, slamming inside me over and over again.

Wrapping my legs around his waist, I moved in rhythm with him. He captured my nipple in his mouth again.

My vision hazed as utter lust overcame me. The back of my head hit the tile, triggering discomfort, but the pleasure magnified. I didn't want him to stop and moaned, "Faster."

He groaned as he quickened his pace. He pounded harder, and the pressure built quicker than ever before.

His lips landed on mine, and he used the wall for leverage. His citrus scent surrounded me, mixing with his vanilla taste. I opened myself up to him, needing him to feel how much I cared for him. I loved him more with each passing moment, so much so that sometimes all the emotions he caused actually hurt.

I love you too, he whispered inside my head, letting me not only hear but feel the emotion behind it.

An orgasm ripped through me, and he groaned, releasing at the same time. Our bodies convulsed together as we went over the edge.

When we were finished, he didn't move, the water like a barrier keeping the outside world at bay.

He stared straight into my eyes, piercing my soul. *I didn't hurt you, did I? I'm sorry. I don't know what came over me. But both my dragon and I were desperate for you.*

I kissed him and replied, *That was amazing. I want it like that more often, in addition to your usual sweet ways.*

The desperate, alpha side of him was a sight I'd never get tired of, especially when sex was involved. *You can dominate me here anytime you want as long as you let me be my own person in a fight or when threatened.*

I'm trying. He kissed my nose and stepped back. He picked up the shampoo and motioned for me to turn around.

Unable to deny the sweet request, I turned, and his fingers worked the shampoo through my hair. The orange smell that was part of him hit my nose. Ahh, so that was partly due to his shampoo.

After he was done, I quickly washed him, cleaning the claw marks well. By the time we were clean and drying off, fatigue hit hard again, but I didn't feel on edge. I was completely sated.

"Ugh, I'm going to have to put the dirty clothes back on." We'd left the bag in the woods for Draco, and he probably had it downstairs.

"You can wear one of my shirts." A sexy smirk spread across his face. "I've been waiting for that to happen anyway."

We stepped into the room, and now that I wasn't sex-crazed, I looked around. The room was even bigger than my dorm room. A king-sized oak bed sat in the middle against the far wall with matching oak end tables on both sides. Across from the bed was a dresser, and a flat-screen television hung right above it. A door stood open to the left, leading into a huge closet. There was a chest of drawers in the corner, next to a double window that overlooked the woods. I felt like we were staying in a mansion.

Oh, wait. We were.

The room had light gray-blue walls that were popular at the moment, and a navy blue comforter was spread over the bed.

Egan strolled into the walk-in closet and came out carrying two shirts and a pair of flannel pajama bottoms. He handed a shirt to me and put on his clothes.

We both crawled into bed, and he wrapped his arms around me, pulling my back right against his stomach. I drifted off to sleep.

A LOUD POUNDING on the door startled me from my dreams. Strong arms left my waist as Egan stood. He rushed to the door and opened it only a crack. He said quietly, "Jade is sleeping."

"I'm sorry to bug you, son, but we have a problem," Ladon said with remorse. "This can't wait."

CHAPTER NINE

My body protested, but I forced myself to sit up in bed. I kept the covers over my legs since all I had to cover me was one huge shirt. The last thing I wanted was to flash my vag at my mate's father. Some things couldn't be unseen.

Believe me, I knew.

"Is Mom okay?" She'd been oddly resilient after Athan's attack, which wasn't like her. Usually, she'd break down, and Sarah would have to fix everything for her. I had a feeling my aunt would often orchestrate the whole thing, but I'd never been able to prove it. Sarah was smart. I had to give her that.

Ladon's face smoothed into a gentle smile. "This isn't about her. There haven't been any more attacks."

A weight lifted from my shoulders. I hadn't realized I was waiting for her to have a meltdown until this moment. *Can you run and get a change of clothes for me? I love wearing your shirt, but I'd like to get dressed before heading downstairs to see everyone.*

Yes, I'll go grab our stuff now. Egan winked at me before turning back to his father. "Okay, let me find something for Jade, and we'll be right down."

"Okay." Ladon stepped back so Egan could walk past him.

When he didn't follow his son, discomfort grew inside me. I felt comfortable around his parents—well, as comfortable as I ever had around new people—but I didn't know what to expect. Since meeting them, we'd been thrust into nonstop action, and we hadn't had a chance to formally meet. In a way, that had created a bond between us, but we still didn't know each other, and we definitely hadn't talked without Egan around.

Also, my refusal to stand because I was Porky Piggin' it made the situation even more unsettling.

Oh, God. Roxy's sayings were rubbing off on me. I'd had no clue what that meant until she'd informed me about her time in the woods with only a shirt on. She'd been buck naked from the bottom down—no pants or panties—dragging her dying mate toward a van to get him to safety.

"Are you okay?" Ladon asked, his brows furrowed. "You seem perplexed."

Yeah, I wasn't touching that one with a ten-foot pole. "Just some internal ramblings. Sorry. Are you and Kayda okay?" If I'd been the praying kind, I'd have been down on my knees, thanking God that for once I'd contained my awkward mouth-diarrhea.

He stepped into the room and leaned his shoulder against the doorframe. He rubbed his right wrist and rotated his other shoulder. "I just wanted to say I'm very glad that you and Egan found each other. Egan has always been strong, but I've noticed a difference with you by his side. He's always done the right thing, and he's always been loyal—it's the dragon way—but there's a light in his eyes that wasn't there before. He finally understands his greater purpose, and you two will need that to get through what comes next."

That sounded daunting, but maybe that was just me. We all had to get through what came next, not just the two of us. Egan would die before he allowed anything to happen to his loved ones.

The sheer truth of the thought rattled me. The idea of losing him made it hard to breathe. If just thinking about it hurt this badly, what would actually losing him feel like? The concept petrified me.

"We'll all get through it together." I had to believe that.

Egan's footsteps grew closer as he climbed the stairs. He entered the room, and his eyebrows rose when he saw his dad still standing there. "Everything okay?"

"Yes, I just hadn't had an opportunity to talk to Jade alone." Ladon shrugged and stepped out the door. "I'll see you two in the kitchen." He walked away, leaving Egan and me alone.

That was super awkward. I was here in bed with nothing on. My ass always wound up in uncomfortable situations like these, and I had no clue why.

Egan chuckled as he shut the door and placed our bag on the floor. He pulled out a pair of jeans, underwear, and a light gray T-shirt and laid them on the bed next to me. *He didn't realize that. He thought you were in your pajamas. If he'd known, he'd have been embarrassed and run out the door.*

At least, there was that. It had only been awkward on my end.

I pushed the covers off me and changed. My reflection in the dresser mirror caught my attention. My dark brown hair appeared more lush and vibrant, and my eyes seemed lighter, like they had a tad of gold in them. I ran my fingers along my face, surprised that my skin appeared sun-kissed—more shifter-like. My muscles were more defined than ever, and I'd always been in good shape. Even though I was recognizable, I didn't look quite the same. Maybe a more glamorous version of my previous self. "Do I look different to you?"

"When you connected with your dragon, she was free to be part of you. You're the same, only with her influence over you." He stepped behind me, placing his chin on the top of my head. "But you're still my Jade and just as beautiful as the first day I met you."

"Thanks for calling me beautiful, but I'm not your property." Even though we were mated, I was still my own person. He hadn't hovered over me too much during the last few attacks, and I didn't want to do anything to discourage him from the small progress we'd made. "I can take care of myself."

"Yes, I know." He placed his hands on my shoulders and gently rubbed them while exhaling. "You've made that clear." The spot between his eyebrows creased with displeasure.

"I love you." I spun around, laying my hands on his chest. "But I need to make sure you see me as a person ... an individual. I need you to know I can take care of myself and that I'm not some liability."

He bit his bottom lip and nodded. "I know I've been super protective of you. I wish I could say I'm sorry, but I'm not. I just found you, and the thought of something happening to you ... well, I can't fathom it. But you're right. You are more than capable of handling yourself, and even in human form, you could've taken out several dragons I know."

Smooth talker. I giggled as I stood on my tiptoes and kissed him.

A rumbling moan sounded from the back of his throat as he tried to deepen the kiss.

I pulled away before I lost my mind. Something was going on downstairs that they needed us for. We couldn't be irresponsible and act like horny college kids—even if that's exactly what we were. *They're waiting on us.*

He leaned his head back dramatically and looked at the ceiling. "For once, it almost felt like things were normal."

"I have a feeling this has been your *normal*." Between them handling Sadie's issues last semester and this, maybe this was what our future looked like. One battle after another.

"No, we were in hiding, so this didn't happen. Now that we're not hiding anymore, we have to deal with the centuries-old stuff we've been avoiding. It'll get better." He took my hand and led me to the door. "It has to."

I sure hoped he was right. Always waiting for the next fight was already taking a toll, and I hadn't been part of this world for long.

We entered the kitchen. It had so many white cabinets running along the wall that I couldn't easily count them while a gas stove that had a double oven was placed in the center. The gray island sitting in the middle of the room held the sink, and it jutted out several inches and turned into a bar surrounded by four bar stools.

The dark gray countertop complemented the cabinets and island perfectly as did the dark oak floor. A rectangular oak table sat against a section of glass windows and next to a glass door that led out to a back porch and the woods beyond.

Athan, Lillith, Katherine and who I assumed to be Luther were at the bar, each with a glass of blood.

"Are you okay?" a man asked, sitting cross-legged at the end of the table, and I noticed his khaki pants pulled up an inch above his ankle. He appeared to be in his late fifties. His jet-black hair was cut short, and his dark brown eyes reminded me of Lillith's. Unlike her all-black attire, he wore a light green shirt.

Pulling my attention from the vampires, I said, "Yes. It's just seeing the blood in a glass caught me off guard."

Whenever I'd seen the vampires drinking blood before, they'd used coffee cups to hide it. The metallic smell had alerted me to what it was, but I hadn't seen the crimson. "Girl, same," Roxy said, forcing my focus on her.

She sat between Axel and Sadie and was back to her normal self. She'd either gotten over the situation from earlier or Mom had forgiven her.

The man sitting at the other end of the table caught my interest. He was shorter than the other men here, but his haunting, lavender eyes locked on mine. His matching lavender hair was longer, hitting right at the chin, but his sharp features resembled Sadie's.

This had to be Naida's older brother Rook, Sadie's fae father.

Naida turned in her chair, and her teal eyebrows, which matched both her hair and eyes, rose high. Her long hair was pulled into a low ponytail and contrasted starkly against her white clothing. "Wow, you look good for a former human."

Out of Sadie's crew, Naida was around the least. Apparently, there was a civil war happening in the fae realm. I wasn't too surprised to see her here, but it had been a few weeks since I'd last seen her at Kortright University. "Uh ... thanks?"

"Forgive my sister." Rook stood, revealing his stark-white clothing that matched his sister's. "Even though she's spent time on Earth, her social skills are very lacking. She needs to spend more time here to adapt better."

"Yes, because things are going so well back at home." Naida crossed her arms and turned back around in her seat. "It's not like people are trying to kill either you or Murray."

Wow, maybe things were worse over there than they'd let on.

I took in Kayda sitting next to Naida and Ladon, with Ladon beside the dark-haired man on the end. Donovan was nowhere to be seen. Odd.

A woman with dirty blonde hair and light brown eyes lifted a hand, reminding me of a peacemaker. Other than her eye and hair color, she could pass as an older version of Lillith. "Let's all take a deep breath. We have enough fighting going on without us turning on each other."

Lillith spun around in her chair and muttered, "Mom, that's so cliche. That sounds like something Dad would say." She pointed at the man who'd asked if I was okay.

So my gut hadn't been wrong. They were her parents.

"I'm Jade." That was random, but I hadn't met a quarter of the room here.

"See, that's what normal people do." Lillith's mom pointed at me. "They introduce themselves instead of jumping straight to war talk." The lady placed a hand on her chest. "I'm Dawn, and this is my husband, Cassius. We're Lillith's parents."

"I'm pretty sure she figured that last part out." Lillith sighed dramatically, but the corners of her mouth tipped up.

"And I'm Rook." The lavender-eyed man smiled genuinely. "Sadie's father."

"Do all fae have matching eyes and hair?" I paused. "Well, other than Sadie."

"You gotta remember I'm a hybrid." She chuckled, comfortable with that fact. "But, yes, full-blooded fae have matching hair and cycs."

"Oh, so all the other half-bloods mix it up?" I had to learn these rules so I'd have an idea of who I might be talking to. The only other tell that Naida and Rook were fae was their floral scent. Sadie's was a musky floral, but that was her shifter part bleeding through.

"Sadie's the only halfling. If there are others, they'd be killed upon being discovered," Naida said matter-of-factly.

"Then how are you alive?" Wow. That sounded rude. "I'm glad you are, but how are you the exception?"

Sadie waved my apology off like my question wasn't a big deal. "No, it's a valid question. The only rule stronger than no hybrids is no one of the royal family is allowed to be killed."

"And Rook should've been king." Naida tapped her fingers on the table. "Half of Fae is demanding he take the throne."

"Which is why we needed you down here," Kayda said and placed her hand on Naida's.

Axel placed his arm around his mate and asked, "Should we wait on Donovan to get back first?"

Egan glanced around the kitchen and sniffed. "Where are he, Julie, and Paul?"

"They ran out to get more clothes for you and the others and a ton more groceries," Sadie explained. "I didn't want to tag along since Dad and Naida showed up. We have a lot to discuss."

"Wait." I couldn't have heard her right. "They went shopping, and Lillith and Roxy stayed here?"

"We don't always have to go shopping." Roxy shook her head, lifting her chin high. "There are more pressing matters to attend to."

"Yeah," Lillith agreed and lifted her glass toward Roxy. "We didn't want to go."

The smell of rotten eggs filled the kitchen as it wafted off them.

"Oh, dear God." I dry-heaved. "Just stop."

"They wanted budget items, especially for the amount of

clothing needed." Axel scooted away from his mate like that would make the smell go away. "These two high-end fashionistas weren't allowed to go because they'd double, if not triple the bill."

"Exquisite taste is not a bad thing, and stop using the word 'fashionista.' You know that term annoys me," Roxy grumbled and moved her chair closer to Axel. "And I'm your mate. You must be near me even when I stink."

Ladon glanced over his shoulder at Egan.

I could only imagine what he and Kayda were thinking. They'd been hiding away from everything and were now in a kitchen full of loud, diverse supernatural races.

"I've opened the pack link to Donovan," Sadie said, attempting to calm the chaos. "We can talk, and he'll hear it through my ears."

"Good. We don't have time to waste," Rook said, focused on Egan and me. "Tell me everything."

We filled them in on every detail we could think of. The falcon attacks, the bracelet in our room that controlled Ollie, Vera, Trixie, the witch who tried to remove the tracking spell, Mindy working with the witch, and all of the attacks between the harpies and gargoyles. To think about what we'd gone through in such a short time was crazy.

"Wait, gargoyles and harpies?" Naida rubbed her temples and closed her eyes. "Are you sure?"

"Positive." Ladon sighed. "Over the centuries, we've kept up with fae creatures in case a day like this ever came."

"Then this is all worse than we expected." Naida glanced at her brother. "You know what this means, right?"

My breath caught at the dread in her voice. Whatever it was had to be worse than just the fae dragon king.

CHAPTER TEN

"Unfortunately, I know exactly what this means." Rook rubbed the inside corners of his eyes, and his shoulders deflated.

"I'm not trying to be rude, but would you mind filling me in on what you're alluding to? I'm new to this supernatural world, and most of the time, I have no idea what 'this' means." Starting off a sentence with "I don't mean to be rude" should've given me pause, but I was tired of always trying to fill in the blanks.

Roxy pointed at me. "Girl, you aren't the only one not picking up what they're putting down. I'm all for them spelling it out for us."

Sadie's normally friendly face morphed into a deep frown.

I wasn't the only one who suffered from resting-bitch face. Although this was the first time I'd seen hers, and my face was stuck in that form.

"That's exactly what it means." Naida placed her elbows on the table and steepled her fingers. "You and Murray have to do something. Turning your back on the peoples' protests is allowing the other fae races to make moves."

"The other races working together has just been brought to our attention, Nads." Rook huffed. "It's not like we've been sitting on this information."

Nads? The fact that Naida didn't get upset spoke volumes. She seemed okay with that nickname.

"Yes, her nickname is actually Nads." Roxy beamed, watching my reaction.

Apparently, my face reflected my inner horror.

Egan tugged me to the wall behind Cassius. We leaned against it since all the seats at the table were taken. He linked with me. *I'm pretty sure that doesn't mean there what it means here.*

Naida's gorgeous eyes landed on me before flicking to Roxy. She pursed her lips. "Why does everyone react that way to my nickname?"

Roxy shrugged so over the top that her shoulders reached her ears.

Poor girl. Sadie probably didn't want to embarrass her while Lillith and Roxy enjoyed the situation. Yeah, I had to tell her. "Nads is slang for balls."

"Balls?" Naida asked, seeming even more perplexed.

A loud snort left Lillith, and Roxy's shoulders shook with unshed laughter.

Great. She'd been staying here on Earth and didn't know any of the vernacular. "Uh ... family jewels? Nut sack?"

Her face remained blank, and she blinked, not catching on yet.

Maybe I should stop? I asked.

Egan's chuckles wove through each word. *You've already gone too far. Just finish the job.*

Okay, then. "Brass clankers? Nuggets?"

Laughter erupted from everyone but Naida. Her face turned slightly pink.

I hadn't meant to embarrass her. Maybe I shouldn't have said anything and followed Sadie's lead. "Testicles?"

"Oh my God." Naida's jaw dropped, and I was afraid it'd hit the floor. Her eyes zeroed in on Rook. "You call me that, knowing what it means?"

"Whoa. Whoa. Whoa." He lifted his hands in surrender. "I only learned what it meant. Besides, Mom and Dad gave you that nickname, so don't blame this on me."

Naida turned to Sadie and hissed, "And you didn't pull me aside to tell me?"

"Dad's and Murray's faces are filled with adoration when they call you that. It doesn't mean that over there, so I didn't want to ruin it for you." Sadie sighed. "But I'm relieved Jade explained it. Roxy and Lillith get way too much enjoyment out of it."

"I always wondered why they'd get so happy." Naida pouted and waved her hand. "But we have more important things to address than Earth's odd humor."

"That I can agree with." Cassius cleared his throat, the corners of his lips still tilted upward. "What exactly is everyone split on over there?"

"Half the fae want me to take the role as king since I'm the first-born, despite Murray being crowned." Rook glanced out the window, deep in thought. "And the other half support Murray since I don't want to rule and they already view him as the king."

"It's similar to the wars you've had here over personal freedoms." Naida gestured behind Cassius. "The stuff all your books talk about in the library. We've never had something like that happen in the fae realm, but because of the odd situation we've found ourselves in, now is our time."

"Fae is all about rules and order," Egan explained. "A civil war like that is not a good thing. If they turn away from the rules, that means that they could attempt to kill Sadie for being a hybrid even though she has royal blood."

Katherine placed her glass on the bar top. "Maybe if they turn away from the rules, they'll allow hybrids to exist."

"That wouldn't happen." Rook rubbed his chin. "Fae are elitists.

If anything, they wouldn't care that she's from the royal family and would attempt to kill her. We don't get to choose our destiny."

Wiser words had never been spoken. The weight of the truth punched me in the stomach.

Axel nodded and smiled at his mate. "You're right. Even when what's chosen for us is exactly what we want, sometimes it doesn't matter. You're just lucky it all worked out." He kissed Roxy's cheek lovingly. "Even when she may be the death of me."

"You're trying to get into trouble." Roxy waggled her eyebrows. "I kind of like it. I'll start thinking about your punishment."

Smelling someone else's arousal wasn't nearly as appealing as when it was Egan's and mine.

Sadie waved her hand in front of her nose. "And you used to say I was bad."

Conversations always swung wildly from one topic to another. Sometimes, it changed so fast I got whiplash.

Rook's face pinched, and he clearly wasn't thrilled with whatever thoughts were running through his head.

I had a feeling I knew what they were. Despite just meeting him, I could tell he loved Sadie unconditionally. If the only way to protect her was to become king, I had a feeling that was exactly what he would do. "When I found Egan, I fought it as hard as I could."

The banter went quiet at the table as every pair of eyes turned to me.

Ignoring the uncomfortableness of being the center of attention, I continued. "I mean I pushed him away. I'd tell him I needed space and accused him of only being nice to me to get into my pants, and when he finally told me the truth, it petrified me. He was telling me a world I'd never known about existed and I was destined to be part of something I didn't understand."

Kayda tilted her head as she listened to me. Her poker face was unreadable, making me nervous, but the truth was the truth, whether she wanted to hear it or not. I already knew Egan deserved better than me.

"But when I tried to really step away from him after everything had come out in the open, I couldn't. Like you, fate forced my hand even though I thought it was the last thing I'd ever want." When I'd told him I was all in, I'd meant every word, but I'd been so damn scared. "And hands down, this is the best thing that has ever happened to me. Fate knew what I didn't then. Maybe being the king won't be as bad as you're afraid it will be."

"She has a point." Naida nodded, respect shining through as she stared at me. "If you want to end the civil war, you'll have to step up and convince the half that is okay with you not being king that you want it. Otherwise, you taking your rightful place will be for nothing."

The best thing that ever happened to you? Egan rasped sexily as he placed an arm around me. *You've almost died and been attacked more times than I can count on one hand. I find that hard to believe.*

You are worth it. I lifted my head to see his golden eyes. *If you keep doing what you did in the shower earlier.*

His gaze landed on my lips. *That can definitely be arranged.*

"You got on us and aren't saying anything to them?" Roxy said, pulling my attention to her. Her bottom lip stuck out in a pout. "Why is it okay for them to be horny in front of us, including his parents, but not for me?"

I closed my eyes and buried my head in Egan's chest.

"They aren't having verbal foreplay." Lillith downed her drink. "Not that I enjoy the smell, but at least they're doing it in their mind link and not subjecting us to their kink."

"This is the third time this conversation has come up." Ladon pulled at his shirt collar and shifted in his seat. "Will this continue to be a common theme?"

"Yes." Naida motioned to Roxy and Lillith. "These two always bring up this topic. I can understand the vampire since she doesn't have sex, but Roxy perplexes me. It's like the more she gets, the dirtier and more aggressive she becomes with him."

It shocked me that Naida would speak so bluntly about sex. She seemed so reserved. *Is she okay?*

Egan's thumb gently brushed my side. *Naida doesn't mind openly discussing sex. We earthlings are prudes since we don't have loud, wild sex. Or that's what she told Sadie a few weeks after she and Donovan completed their mate bond. This group has a way of shocking you from time to time.*

Good to know. I'd lock up that useful tidbit for later.

"Hey!" Lillith crossed her arms and scowled. "I might not be getting any, but I guarantee that sometime soon, I'll get a guy to clean out those cobwebs."

"Lillith Rose!" Dawn exclaimed. "Do not talk like that in front of your parents. It's hard enough listening to it from everyone else, but you've gone too far."

"What?" Lillith nodded at Naida. "She started it."

Cassius whispered to Ladon, "See, it always comes back to this."

"All right," Rook said and kissed Sadie's cheek. "Nads and I need to get going."

Roxy giggled.

"Stop it." Naida pointed at her. "Do not laugh at my nickname."

"Come on ..." Rook paused. "Sis. That's a safe one, right?" His attention landed on me.

I gave him a thumbs-up. "That one is good."

"See." Rook stood and touched his sister's arm. "The whole nickname thing can be worked out. But we need to return to the fae realm to warn Murray about our problems and come up with a plan."

"You two, be careful." Sadie hadn't lost her displeasure. She moved between Rook and Naida, pulling both into a hug. "And make sure Murray stays safe too. I can't lose any family."

"Neither can we." Naida returned her niece's embrace. "We'll be back soon, but if we're gone a little longer than normal, don't be afraid."

"And contact us if you need us." Rook patted his daughter's cheek. "You know how to talk to us when we're there now."

"Well, for a few seconds." She stepped back, giving them space. "Love you both."

"Love you," Rook and Naida replied at the same time, and their bodies began to flicker. Then, they vanished.

It reminded me of Vera right before she'd died, even though I was sure they'd left Earth instead of becoming invisible.

The room descended into silence, which I couldn't allow. "Uh ... how are the other dragons and Mom settling in?" Mom had been on my mind since I'd woken.

"We haven't checked in on them yet." Sadie pulled out her cell phone and typed out a message. "Do you want to head over there and meet Titan and his pack and check on the others?"

"That's a great idea." Egan nodded. "And where are the rest of the dragon shifters staying here?"

"After they got settled, they decided to take a nap." Ladon climbed to his feet and rolled his shoulders. "They grouped together in rooms so no one had to sleep in the living room; they should be out around dinner."

"Which will be ready in a couple of hours." Sadie headed to the back door and unlocked it. "We have time to explore the woods so you can get a feel for the area and check on everyone."

"Let's go," Kayda agreed and faced Dawn and Cassius. "Do you need us to do anything before we head out?"

"Nope. You helped us get the rooms ready and blow up the air mattresses." Cassius smiled. "You two go on back, and we'll send Donovan to get you when they start dinner."

"Sounds like a plan." Roxy jumped to her feet. "Let's go see the others. I could use a run."

"Wait, we've got to get Draco first. He'll be upset if we leave without him." Ladon headed out of the kitchen, moving down the hallway in the opposite direction.

He'd probably be upset that we'd had that entire conversation without him, but we could fill him in on the way to the pack.

Draco and Ladon reappeared, and our group, consisting of Draco,

Ladon, Kayda, Egan, Sadie, Roxy, Axel, Ollie, and me, headed outside.

I'd been surprised that Ollie had abandoned the video game, but he'd said his feathers needed air, whatever the hell that meant.

All of the vampires had opted to stay back and give the shifters time to get acclimated, and Athan and Luther had visibly cringed at the thought of seeing Mom again.

I couldn't blame them. The thought of them seeing Mom didn't appeal to me either.

We walked through the thick woods while the sun was setting. The entire day had gone by so quickly. We must have slept longer than I'd realized.

The animals ran, and the forest thrived. It felt like we were separated from the world yet still part of it, unlike at the cave where, once you entered, you were confined to a small part of the world.

As we approached the pack homes, I heard my mother's voice nearby.

"But Sarah, I'm fine." She paused. "I can't. I'm sorry."

She was talking to my aunt away from everyone else. I didn't know why, but I'd thought she wouldn't contact her.

"Sarah, please." Mom sobbed. "Fine. I'll tell you."

No, she'd promised. She wouldn't betray me ... would she?

CHAPTER ELEVEN

If I thought she'd hurt me before, nothing compared to this moment. She'd promised me she wouldn't tell Sarah anything, and in her first conversation with my aunt, she was throwing us to the wolves ... and no, I wasn't trying to be funny.

And who the hell had given her a cell phone? I'd figured she wouldn't have the means to call anyone unless she was with me.

Egan growled and took a hurried step toward Mom, but I snatched his arm.

Let me handle this. She was my responsibility, and I'd allowed her to come here. If anyone was going to confront her, it was me, even if I wished Egan could do it for me.

Inhaling deeply, I forced my legs to move. "I'll be right back," I told the others.

"We can come with you," Sadie offered, sympathy lacing her words.

I hated pity. Always had. "No, I'm fine," I bit out. "Just give me a minute." Maybe I was overreacting, but I had to shut Mom's conversation down and get to her before she blew our cover.

Even though Sarah knowing where we were wouldn't mean

much to her, it could to others. If Vera could find my mother, then someone could figure out Sarah's relation to me. Not that her impending death would have the same effect on me, but it would on Mom.

My aunt didn't like losing control, so if Mom blurted out our location, Sarah would be in her car and on her way here to regain it. It didn't matter if she didn't know the exact location; Mom knew enough to get her close to us. If anyone followed her, she'd lead them right to us. Hell, if they told her they wanted to cause me pain, she'd probably let them ride shotgun the entire way.

"Someone jumped me at the grocery store." Mom blew out a breath. "She had stringy caramel hair and lifeless eyes. That's all I've got."

My feet halted, and hope sprang in me again. Maybe she wasn't betraying me after all.

Egan touched my arm, startling me.

That was how worked up I was. I hadn't noticed he was following behind me. What a great dragon shifter I was turning out to be. I needed to be more aware of my surroundings.

He stepped up beside me. *I was hoping we'd misunderstood their conversation.*

Me too. But the situation reaffirmed something. *The problem is Mom always caves to my aunt. We need to get close and monitor their call.*

Ideally, I'd have wanted Mom to hang up, but the more I tried to come between them, the more Sarah upped her game. I didn't need her harping on Mom more and weaving a stronger web of manipulation around her.

I took his hand, glad he'd decided to come with me. My gut still told me to do everything alone, without considering the fact that I didn't have to any longer. So for him to come without me asking him meant so much to me.

We quietly passed through the trees and came to a small clearing. It led into a series of homes that must have been Titan's pack.

Mom paced in the center, her eyes jumping around her like she expected someone or something to jump out. The slightly acidic stench of fear wafted from her.

"Liz, just tell me where you are," Sarah demanded on the other end of the phone. "This is ridiculous."

"I … I can't." Mom grimaced and stared at her feet. "I'm sorry."

"Then when are you coming home?" Sarah pressed. "And who are you with?"

No, please don't tell her you're with me, I thought. That would make her more adamant about finding us. I ran forward to intercept the conversation.

"I'm with Jade." Mom rushed the words, still unaware I was only a few feet away from her.

The trees hid me from her human eyes, but annoyance bubbled within me. Why in the world would she tell Sarah that?

"You're with Jade!" Sarah's voice rose several octaves. "Who else is with you?"

"Her boyfriend." Mom hesitated. "He seems nice," she added randomly.

"So, she ran off to be with a guy? Were they the ones who jumped you and you're covering for her?" Sarah laughed without humor.

"No, it wasn't Jade," Mom replied. "They saved me."

"It doesn't matter," Sarah replied swiftly. "Either way, it's time you both came home. Now."

"I don't think there's any way Jade will come back home." Mom sounded upset. "But I'll come back soon."

Of course, she would. I'd hoped she'd decide to stay with us, but it was clear that wouldn't happen. The rancid stench of a lie didn't swirl around her.

In a way, I didn't blame her. Her entire world had been stuck in limbo for ten years, but I'd hoped that she'd see life in a different light—one without the parameters she'd believed for so long were in place.

"If you would just tell me where you are, I could come get you," Sarah said, dropping the suggestion again.

"I know, but I ... I can't." Mom's shoulders sagged. "Not yet." Mom turned toward the tree I was behind.

Deciding not to hide any longer, I stepped out from the shadows.

Her eyes widened, and she stumbled back until recognition flickered in them. "I've got to go. I'll talk to you soon." She hung up the phone and placed her hands behind her back as if I would forget the phone existed.

Trying to stay calm, I forced my body to relax. For the past few minutes, I'd been so tense that my muscles were tired. "Already called Sarah?" I tried not to sound accusatory but fell short.

"She hadn't heard from me in a week." Mom bounced the heel of her tennis shoe on the ground. "What did you expect me to do?"

If Sarah had been a normal sister, then Mom's point would have been valid. "I don't know. Realize you two have a very codependent relationship and maybe you could find happiness again if you would just gain some distance from her."

All I'd ever wanted for Mom was for her to be happy, but she was the complete opposite—horribly miserable. She deserved to find another man and fall in love. Not that I wanted her to replace Dad, but she shouldn't have to go through the rest of her life alone.

"You sound just like your father." Mom raised her head to look at the darkening sky. "But Sarah was all I had after our parents died, and I don't want her to be alone either."

The more you push her, the more likely she won't want to stay. Egan stepped from the woods, appearing right beside me.

This time, Mom didn't act surprised or scared.

Mom smiled, but it didn't reach her eyes. "I figured you weren't too far behind."

"Staying apart from your daughter is something I never want to consider." Egan kissed my cheek lovingly. "But if you two need some alone time, I'll go with Sadie and the others to see Titan and the rest of the pack."

"No, I think we're good here," Mom interjected eagerly. "I need to give Winter her cell phone back. She only let me borrow it to call my sister."

Yeah, she didn't want to continue this conversation with me. Maybe that wasn't a bad idea. We would only argue anyway, and at least, she hadn't told Sarah where we were, which was what had concerned me the most.

"We need to check on the other dragons." I looped my arm through Egan's and nudged him toward the homes. As we got closer to the clearing, Sadie and the others came out from the woods where they'd been waiting.

"Everything okay?" Sadie asked as she glanced between Mom and me.

I didn't want to lie, so I said the only thing that popped into my mind. "She needs to give Winter her phone back."

"Sure, let's go find them." Sadie's look of concern smoothed into a mask of indifference.

Not sure how to take it, I brushed it aside. I could talk to her later.

Now that we were closer, I focused on the neighborhood. There were at least one hundred simple, two-story, log cabins with two larger houses in the center. The design was similar to the dragon homes back in the cave, but these were smaller and newer.

Smoke billowed from behind one of the bigger homes, and the scent of cooking meat hit my stomach hard.

My stomach gurgled, and Roxy snorted.

"I'll admit it smells good." She tipped her face toward the smoke. "But Julie's cooking is like vanilla icing on a chocolate cake or peanut butter and chocolate. It's pure orgasmic even for us red meat lovers."

"Orgasmic?" Mom shifted away from Roxy and closer to me.

She wasn't comfortable with loud, outspoken people. That was probably one of the main reasons I tried to not make a fuss. Mom hated it. She'd rather appease everyone and live in a compromise than stand up for what she needed or believed in.

I'd been like that for far too long until I'd had enough, but it had been difficult to break the cycle. The longer you remained complaisant, the harder breaking free had to be.

Roxy either didn't register Mom's discomfort or didn't care as she continued. "Something so good that your legs convulse in pleasure."

I caught up to Sadie and said, "Please tell me that Roxy will eat in her room. I don't want to hear or smell what she's describing."

"You think that's bad." Axel sniffed. "Her legs have never quivered for me."

A peal of laughter tumbled from deep in my stomach. I hadn't realized how badly I'd needed to laugh.

Egan's eyes turned a lighter gold as he watched me. He linked with me. *I need to see you like this more often. You don't smile nearly enough.*

With those two, I've laughed more than I have in the last ten years combined. Axel was more serious than Roxy, but I sometimes saw how her playfulness affected him. He'd spit out something unexpected, sounding more like his mate every once and a while.

"That should tell you we need more practice." Roxy winked and kissed him. "I'm about my legs shaking as often as I can get it."

Mom's face darkened to a deep crimson, and I realized she must have bathed as her brown hair looked normal again.

"Every time you're in wolf form, you're always scratching at something," Egan teased. "So your leg shakes plenty. I'm pretty sure you have fleas."

"Oh, there's the dog jokes." Roxy stuck her tongue out at him. "You could at least try to be original."

"Why would he need to?" I couldn't help but join in. "Those jokes are always around."

Two men headed our way. The older one had alpha power radiating off him, which was somehow enhanced by his short brown hair and full goatee. Both he and the younger shifter were built like Donovan—tall and thick. They had the same forest green eyes, but the younger one had his long black hair pulled into a low ponytail.

"You'd think a dragon would know better than to enter into a pack home, making jokes like that." The older one's voice was deep, but a grin peeked through as he walked over and smacked Egan's shoulder hard several times. "It's good to see you again. I haven't seen you since we took on Tyler at that godawful house of his."

Egan placed an arm around my shoulders and pulled me closer as he responded, "It has been too long, but my mate here was making me chase her."

"This is the notorious Jade that the girls have been talking about." The younger one's eyes twinkled as he held his hand out to me. "I'm Torak, Sadie's brother."

"Brother?" I hadn't expected that. "I didn't realize Rook had two children."

"Oh, he didn't." Torak wiggled his fingers. "There's no fae magic here. Technically, I'm her stepbrother, but that sounds cold." He arched an eyebrow at Sadie. "But I can't say I'm not hurt. You didn't tell her about me?"

"In Sadie's defense, they were too busy pining over each other and being dramatic," Roxy stepped in. "And when they finally got their shit together, we were being attacked left and right. Oh, then there was this jealous ex ..." She trailed off. "I don't know what to call her. She wasn't an ex-girlfriend, but she acted like she was—"

"I think he got the gist." Sadie chuckled and hugged the younger man. "And I would've told her about you when things got more settled. You're the best brother a girl could ever have or want."

"Oh, you're good." Torak ruffled her hair. "I guess I can't stay mad at you when you sweet-talk me like that."

"Well, it's very nice to meet you," the older man said and shook my hand. "I'm Titan, Sadie's stepfather."

"I'm Jade." Every supernatural I'd met had been so nice and welcoming—well, except for Vera and the other crazies.

The door to the other bigger home opened, and a woman stepped out. She strolled over to Mom, her shoulder-length, ash-blonde hair bouncing from side to side. She took the phone and placed it into the back pocket of her blue jean shorts then pulled Sadie into a hug. The two of them were the same height. When she pulled away, her sea-blue eyes found me. "It's nice to finally put a face to the name. It's so nice to meet you."

Anger pulsed through me again as I thought about how Mom had called Sarah already. It wasn't this woman's fault, but my frustration leaked out anyway. "You must be Winter since you took the phone from Mom." I crossed my arms and lifted a brow, staring directly at Mom.

"Oh, was I not supposed to?" Winter asked and looked at Sadie. "I didn't realize—"

"No, I can call whomever I want." Mom's eyes flashed with anger as she spun to face me. "You need to remember that I'm the adult here—and your mother."

Was she being serious? This had to be a joke. "I hate to tell you, but I'm an adult as well, and you haven't acted like my mother in ten years."

Her head jerked back, and she glared. "What did you just say to me?"

This fight had been a long time coming. All of the feelings and resentment that had been bottled up inside me bubbled up. I hated that we would have it out in front of everyone, but I couldn't calm down. I'd felt like I might have a chance of connecting with Mom, but at the first opportunity, she'd called Sarah. "You heard me, or should I repeat it again?"

CHAPTER TWELVE

I steadied myself for her retort. I wanted her to say something back to me. I'd never seen this side of her before. Instead, her face crumpled into a look of pure despair.

"You're right." She sniffled, tears trailing down her cheeks. "I've been a lousy mother."

No, she was supposed to fight me, not fall apart. Sarah made her break down. I didn't want to be like my aunt.

Kayda cleared her throat and looked at Titan. "Do you mind taking us to the others? We want to check on them before turning in for the night."

"Yeah, sure," Titan agreed eagerly. "We can show you to their homes right now."

If their escape wasn't proof that we'd made everyone uncomfortable, I wasn't sure what else could be. At least I wasn't the one feeling awkward for once.

The group hurried off, leaving Mom and me behind; our eyes locked on each other.

Egan stepped toward the others, then stopped. *Do you want me to stay?*

This was a conversation Mom and I had been teetering on for a long time. *I do, but it's probably best if you don't though. I won't be far behind.*

If you need me, let me know. Egan pecked my lips. *I'll be back in a flash. You will always be my priority.*

Sometimes, fate still amazed me. How could someone like him be destined for someone like me? Things didn't add up. I was hard around the edges, had so much baggage dragging behind me, and pushed people away, afraid to get too close. Through all my downfalls, he'd stood unwaveringly beside me. He'd patiently waited for every barrier I'd ever put up to shatter.

I love you, I told him, but those three little words seemed insignificant.

When he'd said I was his Jade, he hadn't meant it possessively. It had been the only way to even partially convey his feelings for me. And at that moment, Egan became mine. Mine to love, to hold, to lean on. Not in the way of him being my property but rather my rock.

The magnitude of what he'd meant crashed over me, and I'd responded so coldly ... defensively ... like he would ever view me in a way I didn't want him to.

I should've known better.

He brushed his fingers across my cheek. *And I love you.* He glanced at Mom silently crying and gave her a small, sad smile. "I'll give you two some privacy." He hurried to catch up with the others.

Everyone had cleared. "Want to take a short walk to get a little privacy? Supernaturals and their hearing ..."

"Yeah, okay." She nodded and strode toward the woods.

We walked in silence, following a worn path through the trees. Neither of us was eager to begin the conversation, so I mustered the initiative.

She hadn't deserved me talking to her like that, but she needed to realize how much she'd hurt me too. "I'm sorry for being so abrasive, but in the past ten years, I've harbored a lot of resentment toward you." Resentment was the perfect word to describe my emotions. "It's like when Dad died, I lost both of you."

"You're right." Mom's head drooped, and her hair fell over her shoulders. "But losing your father, it was like a part of me died too."

That was how I imagined I would feel if Egan passed. "I understand that." Now more than ever. "But I was so young and needed my mother. We moved in with Sarah, and things got worse."

"I know that you and my sister don't like each other." Mom twirled a piece of hair around her finger. "But she gave us food and shelter when we needed it."

"Is that what you think?" Maybe she really was clueless. I'd always thought she was, but lately, I'd begun to doubt that. "That she did all that out of the kindness of her heart?"

Mom's head jerked up, and she met my gaze. "She's never asked us to repay her."

"She manipulates you all the time, and yes, she has asked us to repay her." Between that and taking a college away from me, that was the whole reason I'd run to Kortright. "Remember, I was supposed to go to a local community college last semester, but I had to withdraw and get a waitressing job at an Italian place to pull our weight with expenses."

"You're right." She blew out a breath and averted her gaze. "I forgot all about that. But we'd lived there for over ten years, and I couldn't hold down a job."

"That's because she made sure you were late and guilted you into calling in sick all the time." I had to wake her up. It was time for her to see my aunt for the horrible person she really was.

Mom rubbed her hands over her arms. "Look, I know she's not perfect, but she's all I have, especially now. You have Egan, and he's crazy about you. I just hope you don't get destroyed like I did."

Even though losing him would kill me inside, I would never wind up like her. Not after seeing what it had done to her and me. "I still need my mother." My voice cracked despite my efforts to keep my emotions in check.

"Oh, honey." She stopped and pulled me into her arms. "I'll always be here for you. I wanted to come here and be with you before going back to Sarah."

My heart fractured. I'd hoped she'd want to stay with us permanently, but her admission confirmed my fears. "So, you're going back?"

"I have to." Mom shrugged. "I don't know how to explain it, but she's been there for me for so long. I can't turn my back on her."

"But, Mom, she treated me horribly. She hovered over me and made sure I didn't even go outside to get the mail without her permission. And when I did something she didn't like, she'd beat me." I felt like this was a losing battle.

"'Beat' is a strong word." Mom lifted a brow. "If that happened, I would've seen it. And we were living under her roof. We had to follow her rules. I know it doesn't always seem fair, but life isn't fair. That was what our parents taught us, and Sarah is exactly like our mother. Besides, even if I wanted to get away, I don't have anywhere to go."

This was how Mom had been raised. No wonder she didn't see a different way. Whatever connection Dad and she had must have been stronger than her relationship with Sarah. Mom leaving her for Dad must have infuriated her.

"Yes, you do." I lifted my arms out. "You can stay here with us. There is another way."

"Oh, baby girl." She hugged me. "I'd love to, but this isn't my world. I'm not a vampire or shapeshifter. I need to go back home."

If I wanted to have a relationship with her, this was how things would always be unless something drastically changed. A coldness settled in my blood, but I couldn't do a damn thing to change her mind without resorting to my aunt's tactics. "Okay."

"Okay?" Mom stopped and faced me. "What does that mean?"

"This is something we'll have to agree to disagree on." Those words hurt, but I had to accept that this was the relationship she and I had. I'd rather have a connection with her than lose her. At one point,

I thought I'd have to cut ties with her, but Egan and Sadie were showing me that you could love someone and maintain a relationship with them even if it wasn't the exact one you wanted.

"Jade, I love you." Mom touched my arm. "But sometimes it hurts so much to be around you. You remind me so much of him, but you're right. I haven't been fair to you, and I want to do better."

Her acknowledgment that things were shitty between us, even if she wasn't willing to examine her relationship with Sarah, was a start. Maybe time would fix the other.

"I miss him too." I did so much, especially those nights when Sarah would take out her frustrations on me. Mom and I could share memories of Dad. She had no one else but me to talk to about him.

"I loved when he'd play guitar and sing me to sleep each night." I hadn't let my mind wander back to those precious memories that only appeared in my dreams. While sleeping, I couldn't protect my mind like I did when I was awake.

Mom laid her head on my shoulder. "Or how he'd wake up and make Mickey Mouse cinnamon rolls for you."

"I still love cinnamon rolls." That was a habit I could never break. It was comfort food I sought out when I felt alone.

"Wow, this is nice." Mom wiped her nose with the back of her hand. "I'm a snotty mess, but it's been so long since I've talked about him or remembered him this way."

"Me too." My mind raced with memories. "Do you remember when that girl in first grade told me I wasn't important enough for her to be my friend all five days of the week, so Dad came to school and brought cupcakes for all my friends?" Dad had eaten with me and asked if a few of my friends would like to join us at the special table. When she'd tried to suddenly be my friend, he'd informed her it was Tuesday and not one of her days. The rest of my friends had sat with me and eaten cupcakes. After that, she'd apologized, and Dad had given her a cupcake. He'd told me that forgiveness was key and to never lose sight of it.

But obviously, I had.

The two of us strolled through memory lane for a while longer until Egan's citrus scent tickled my nose. My breathing picked up like it always did around him.

Mom tensed. "What's wrong?"

"We have company." I glanced over my shoulder and found him standing there with a tender grin. "Are you guys already done?" Now I felt bad. I'd told him I would join him but wound up spending time with Mom instead.

"We are, and everything is fine." He came to stand beside me and kissed me. "It looks like you two are having a good time."

"We're reminiscing about Dad." Speaking of memories, I hadn't been able to ask him about that day on the beach. Between that and my exhaustion, it had slipped my mind.

"I hate to interrupt, but we're heading back." He gestured over my shoulder at the musky smell of wolf shifters. Then Egan's parents' scents hit my nose. "Donovan linked with Sadie a few moments ago. They'll be here soon."

"Good. I'm famished." My stomach gurgled again.

"Girl, we got you loud and clear." Roxy snapped her fingers. "And I feel you. Ollie's been whining to go back to the mansion. He must be having withdrawals from the video games."

Ollie shrugged. "I hadn't played since the whole Vera thing. I wanted to do something normal. It's not withdrawal."

Sadie stood between Ollie and Roxy, and when her focus landed on me, her face morphed into a frown.

I needed to make things right with her and might as well do it tonight since I already had my heart on my sleeve.

"Don't let her give you shit." Axel rolled his eyes. "She plays just as much as Athan and Luther when we're there."

"Speaking of vampires, I'm going to head back to the wolves." Mom hugged me. "But I'll see you in the morning?"

"Of course." I hated to end my time with her, but I had other responsibilities as well.

"Good night, everyone." Mom waved and headed back toward the pack.

I didn't want to make her feel weak, but after Vera had captured her and almost killed her, I wanted to keep an eye on her. I waited until she was several feet away so she wouldn't hear me.

"Hey, Sadie," I said quietly. "I'm going to keep watch until she gets to the pack. Do you mind coming with me? We can catch up with the others later." If I didn't get her now, Donovan wouldn't let her out of his sight since he'd been gone for a few hours. I hadn't understood it at first, but being away from your fated mate wasn't fun.

Not me? Egan teased.

I need to apologize for snapping at her earlier. I hope you understand.

Pride wafted off him. *I figured that was the case. I'll give you some privacy.*

Sadie's eyebrows arched. "Uh ... sure. We'll catch back up here in a second."

The group headed toward the mansion as Sadie and I followed slowly behind Mom. She was several yards away, unaware that we were near.

I needed to get this out before I changed my mind. "Look, I'm sorry I snapped at you earlier. You were looking at me with so much pity, and I hate that. That's how everyone has looked at me since my dad passed away."

"You think it was pity?" Her mouth dropped. "Girl, that wasn't it at all."

Wait ... "It wasn't?"

"Jade, I get that you've had a hard life." Sadie patted her chest. "Believe me, I do. I had a hard childhood too, but I had two advantages you didn't."

"A winning personality and good looks?" I quipped, feeling uneasy.

"Well, yeah." She nudged her shoulder into mine. "But you have that too—" She winced. "Well, the good looks part."

I almost said "hey," but she was right.

"But seriously, I had Roxy and a pack." She touched my arm, her warmth easing some of my anxiety. "And I wasn't looking at you with pity. When people love you, they worry about you and want to be there for you. I don't pity you. I want to support you."

The weight of her words slammed into me. I hadn't considered that alternative. "I love you too."

"I know." Sadie tugged me to a stop. "And that's why I'm willing to forgive you so easily."

Mom's scream penetrated my ears, and I took off running. No, I couldn't lose her now. Not after we'd bonded.

CHAPTER THIRTEEN

"Wait!" Sadie called out, but I ignored her.

I needed to get to Mom. Maybe the fae dragon king had found us. *Egan, I need you. Mom screamed. I'm afraid she's in trouble.*

Something unreadable passed through our bond as he replied, *I'm on my way.*

Pushing my legs hard, I felt my dragon brush my mind. Before I realized what was happening, wings sprouted from my back, ripping my shirt. My body lurched skyward, and I flew over the trees.

I found Mom plastered against a tree, a look of pure terror on her face. Her body convulsed as she let out another blood-curdling scream.

A wolf stepped from behind the trees, confirming my worst fear.

We were under attack. Again.

As I swooped downward, the strumming of other wings headed my way. I turned to find both Draco and Egan half shifted like me. They were all human except for the massive, scaly wings protruding from their backs.

Thankful they were so close, I focused on Mom, descended, and grabbed her in my arms. Channeling my dragon strength, I lifted us into the sky.

"The wolf was trying to get me!" Mom screeched as she wrapped her arms around my neck, almost choking me.

A loud roar sounded behind me as Egan and Draco flew past me and lowered to the ground. The wolf stumbled back with the prickly scent of fear.

Yeah, I bet having two dragons coming at you would make anyone feel threatened. Both Egan and Draco were huge.

Draco landed first, stepping in front of Egan.

We had to drive the poor guy crazy since Egan and I didn't like sitting on the sidelines. It wasn't right to ask others to do something we weren't willing to do ourselves, but that made the royal warrior's job harder.

The wolf whined and lowered its head.

A howl from the pack homes pierced the air, and several people ran toward us, including Titan, his face lined with worry.

Sadie raced to join us, her eyes cast skyward at me. She said, "Stop. He's my pack member and means no harm."

Neither dragon heard since their attention was on the wolf while also scanning the area for a veiled threat.

I hadn't considered that another witch could be involved and hiding others, waiting for the right time to attack. But this was a false alarm, and I needed to end this before someone got hurt. "Stop. He's one of Sadie's," I shouted to make sure they heard.

Egan paused and turned to me. When my words soaked in, he relaxed, but Draco remained tense, staring down the wolf as if it might lunge. Draco's chest heaved as he unclenched his hands at his sides.

Mom sobbed uncontrollably as I lowered us to the ground. Warm tears spilled down her cheeks and splattered all over my chest.

"Hey, the wolf isn't a threat. He's part of their pack and must have been out on a run. There's nothing to be scared of."

As soon as my feet touched the ground, Mom pulled out of my

arms and stumbled away from the group, almost falling. Titan and a few pack members rushed into the clearing, three in their wolf forms.

Mom screamed again and covered her eyes. "I'm sorry, but I can't do this. I ... I thought I could, but I want to go home."

Her words fractured my heart. I thought we'd have more time together before she asked to leave. Then there was the whole complication with her actually going back to Sarah's. We'd have to monitor her so she wouldn't get hurt.

How are we going to handle this? I tried not letting my hurt bleed through, but it was pointless. We had our mate bond, and I couldn't hide it from him even if I'd wanted to.

We'll figure it out, Egan reassured me as he faced the wolf pack. "I'm sorry. I didn't recognize his scent, and the fae dragon king has sent wolves to attack us before."

A chestnut wolf beside Titan stepped forward, his teeth bared and growling. He pawed the ground, pulling out clumps of grass. He wanted to attack us because of how we'd treated his friend.

"No, I get it." Titan lifted a hand and glared at the aggressive wolf. "Stand down." Alpha will laced his words. "Remember, he fought alongside my daughter when she needed help. They meant no harm."

This could have gone horribly wrong, but these people surprised me time and time again. "It's my fault. Mom screamed, and I reacted. I'm sorry."

"There's nothing to apologize for. No one got hurt." Titan nodded at me. "When you're always under attack, it's hard to tell who's friend or foe, especially when you haven't met everyone in Sadie's pack. How could you have known? Tomorrow, we need you all to meet everyone in my pack. We don't need someone from either side attacking each other."

Egan hurried over and pulled me into his arms.

When his warm hands touched the bare skin on my back, I glanced down. Just like him, my shirt was ripped to shreds and barely covered my breasts. My bra was still intact, but I was almost giving a peep show.

"We need to get you some clothes," Egan growled and turned me toward the mansion. He frowned at the young wolf. "I'm sorry about that. We're a little skittish, and you scared her mom, and we didn't recognize you. We should've realized you weren't a threat when you cowered, but we've had a witch messing with us. We won't make the same mistake again."

The wolf nodded, and his mouth dropped open in a wolfish smile.

Sadie walked over to the wolf and patted his head. "He said he understands."

"That's enough excitement for tonight." Draco kept his attention on the pack around us. "Let's head back before something else happens."

"I'm going with you," Mom insisted. "I need you to take me home." She walked over to me and touched my shoulder. "I can't stay here. I'm sorry."

"But how do we protect you?" I didn't want to force her to stay here if she wanted to leave, but I didn't want something horrible happening to her either.

"Where do you live?" Titan asked as his pack peeled off back to the houses.

"Indianapolis," Mom answered. "Please tell me that's close by."

He tapped his chin. "It's about four hours away, but I know a pack there. I'll make a call and see if they won't mind keeping watch. If they're up for it, I'll text Sadie."

Egan kissed my cheek. *I'm sorry she's leaving, but at least, Titan knows someone who might be willing to keep your family safe, and we won't have to worry about anyone hurting her for our location.*

As long as Mom doesn't get hurt, I'll be fine. Sarah deserved some pain, but Mom had enough her whole life.

"All right. Talk soon," Sadie said and hugged him.

Our smaller group began the trek back to the mansion. Mom

walked silently beside me, her heart was still racing from the encounter.

I couldn't blame her for wanting to leave. Her introduction to this world was being kidnapped by a witch and carried by a harpy. That hadn't done me any favors.

Egan took my hand, his lips turned down. He wasn't pleased with my outfit. I, however, was more than ecstatic over his. He stood next to me shirtless, and his muscles contracted, making my mouth water. If it hadn't been for Mom walking beside me, scared, I'd have sweet-talked him into a quickie in the woods.

Draco cleared his throat and cut his eyes to me, making it clear he smelled where my mind had traveled.

My face burned. Being called out like that was the equivalent of a cold shower. I needed to get my mind on a different track. *So, what's the plan?*

Once we hear back from Titan, we'll take her home. He squeezed my hand gently. *I'm sorry she's leaving. I know you enjoyed your time with her and hoped she'd stay longer.*

There was no point in lying. He'd know. *You're right. I knew losing Dad broke her, but I hadn't realized the depth of their love. She talked like they were fated mates.*

Your parents must have been soul mates. Not quite the same as fated mates, but it's a human form that's just as strong. Some say that a child from a union like that is almost as resilient as supernaturals, which is required when the human mate transforms into a dragon.

The thought comforted me. My parents had given me the best gift in the world as a result of their relationship. They'd allowed me to have a fated mate and find a love similar to theirs. It was beautiful. *I didn't realize how much pain she's been in. Losing you ... it would almost kill me.*

I feel the same way about you. Now that you're my mate and a dragon, our life is interconnected. If one of us dies, the other will follow soon after. It's morbid but another thing that's different with dragon shifter mates. Because your body changed with our bond, and the two halves of our soul fused together, our lifespans are attached. His voice was low with so much feeling.

Honestly, it's romantic. I stepped closer to him, feeling naked with how his skin brushed against my bare skin. I couldn't wait to get home and take out some of this sexual frustration. *Also, I wanted to say I'm sorry.*

For what? He wrapped an arm around me and pulled me closer like he knew I was cold.

Maybe my bluntness would come in handy here. I wasn't one for long romantic speeches like him. *When you called me your Jade earlier, I wrongly bit your head off. I now understand what you meant and that you weren't acting like a possessive, dominating male.*

His golden eyes glowed. *You understand now?*

Earlier today, when you left me and my mom alone to talk, you became my Egan. I allowed my feelings to flow into him. I wanted him to feel my sincerity. Words were easy to say, but feelings and actions—that was a whole other ball game.

Yes, I am, he rasped, overcome with emotions. *When you linked when you thought your mom was in danger, telling me you needed my help, that made me realize you're embracing who we are to each other. You've always tried to take care of yourself and kept me at arm's length like I had to beg you to allow me to be the mate beside you.*

Wow, I did suck at this relationship stuff. I'd always known it, but I hadn't realized how bad I was. Seeing me from Sadie's and Egan's points of view stung. *Well, I'm done with that. As long as you continue to treat me like an equal, we're a team from here on out.*

I really like the sound of that, he replied, not missing a beat.

Something dinged, and Sadie pulled her phone from her back pocket. She swiped the surface a few times and glanced over her shoulder. "Titan said the pack agreed. We just need her address."

Mom rattled it off eagerly, and I took a deep breath to keep my emotions level. I despised allowing her to go back to that horrible woman, but Mom was right. She was an adult and could make her own decisions.

The mansion came into view, and Roxy, Axel, Donovan, Kayda, and Ladon waited for us.

"I heard you had a false alarm." Roxy smirked, finding the situation funny.

"They didn't know George," Sadie said, standing up for us. "And they've been attacked by witches, wolves, harpies, and gargoyles. You can't blame them for being cautious. Remember how we were when we were attacked wherever we turned?"

"As if we could forget." Donovan rushed over to his mate and kissed her.

I glanced into the kitchen and saw two new people. A petite, middle-aged woman with light blonde hair stood in front of the stove, cooking something in a pan. From the smell, it was garlic and ground beef.

A middle-aged man grinned with adoration at the woman that warmed his pale face. He had the same dark brown hair as Katherine, but his eyes were more gray than brown.

They had to be Katherine's parents, Julie and Paul.

"Is that a new look?" Axel chuckled as he glanced from Draco to Egan. When his gaze landed on me, he quickly averted his eyes, and his shoulders tensed, clearly uncomfortable.

"We all half shifted," Draco said strangely.

"Wait." Kayda tilted her head. "Jade half shifted?"

All of the unwanted attention made me feel uneasy. *Why is that such a big deal?*

Only the strongest dragons can do that, Egan said proudly. *You're the only woman I know who's done it.*

That built up my confidence. "I'm going to go change." This would give me a chance to avoid Egan's parents' attention.

"Got you covered." Roxy tossed me a shirt. "Sadie told me you ripped through your shirt too." Then she lobbed a shirt at each guy also.

That was convenient. "Thanks."

"Wait." I hadn't considered needing to shift to take Mom home.

"Shouldn't we change into our dragons to take her home?"

Egan shook his head. "Indianapolis is heavily populated. We'll have to travel human style and drive."

But if we do that, Mom will know exactly where we are. I trusted Mom, but the more she knew, the more danger she'd be in.

Egan put on his shirt, his stomach muscles contracting. *The wolf shifters won't let anything happen. Titan is a good guy, and he wouldn't contact this wolf pack if he didn't trust them.*

"We're taking a car." Mom beamed. "A normal car?"

Roxy chuckled. "Yeah, we don't have any that can sprout wings or fur ... yet."

Mom's face turned a shade lighter. "But you're working on it?"

Yep, this was the moment I learned my mom was gullible, and if I didn't stop Roxy, she'd have Mom believing that it would be on the market for the hot price of one hundred dollars in the next year. The girl was insane.

"The car is out front." Donovan handed Egan the keys. "Do you want me to come with you?"

"No, I'll accompany them," Draco said formally, but there was a hint of anxiety.

He didn't like us leaving either. When someone who trained in war and strategy didn't like a plan, it usually meant it wasn't a good one.

THE ENTIRE WAY to Sarah's home, Egan and Draco watched the rearview mirror, making sure no one was tailing us. I sat in the backseat with Mom, right behind my mate, and snuck glances over my shoulder at every opportunity. Nothing seemed out of the ordinary, which unnerved me.

As we pulled into the neighborhood, a shadowy figure lingered behind nearby trees. The glow of their eyes followed the car.

They were supernatural.

CHAPTER FOURTEEN

W*e have a problem.* I linked with Egan, not wanting to freak Mom out any more than she already was. *Someone is hiding behind that tree on the right.*

Egan slowed the car and pulled over to the side of the road. The moon was beginning its descent, and the clock on the stereo flashed two in the morning. There was no traffic, and our presence wouldn't alarm anyone except for the person watching us.

"What's going on?" Draco asked softly so Mom's human ears wouldn't hear.

Not bothering to respond verbally, Egan tipped his head toward the trees.

Mom stiffened and looked out the window but remained calm. "Why did we stop?"

She must not be able to see the supernatural. *He has glowing eyes. Does that tell us anything?*

Not really. Egan unlocked his door. "Before taking you to the house, we need to make sure no one is waiting for you. We don't want anyone hurting you for our location."

"I would never tell." Mom rested a hand on her heart. "I wouldn't put Jade in harm's way. But do you think someone else could find me?"

"Not at all," Draco said, and when the sulfuric smell of a lie didn't hit me, some of my nerves calmed. "The witch who knew about you is dead, and to keep her leverage with the fae dragon king, she wouldn't have told just anyone. But we want to be diligent before taking you home."

If we didn't believe she would keep our location a secret, we wouldn't have brought her back here. Correction, Egan and Draco wouldn't have. Egan loved me so much that he would never put me in danger, even if he had to hold my mom captive at the mansion.

In the past, that would've pissed me off, but I'd do the same thing for him. Granted, our parents would be locked inside a mansion with food, water, and a place to hang out. They wouldn't be living in any discomfort or enduring hardships, but being forced to stay somewhere against your will wasn't fun for anyone.

"We know you won't say anything." Egan smiled at her tenderly. "Just making sure you'll be around for the birth of your grandchildren is all."

"Your children." Her voice caught, and she fanned her eyes. "Are you?"

"What?" She couldn't possibly think that. "No!" I'd never thought about having children before. I wasn't opposed to the idea, but I'd never been interested. Given my childhood, who would want to bring anyone into the world to suffer like that? But with Egan, the idea was strangely appealing.

Draco opened the door and stepped out of the car. "I'll take a look around."

"I'll go with you." Egan opened the door as well.

Draco paused like he might argue but reconsidered.

If more men were waiting, he'd be outnumbered. Whether he liked it or not, Egan going with him was his best bet.

Do you mind staying here with your mom? Egan asked. There was so much hope flowing through our bond that I knew exactly where he wanted me: safe inside the car.

Any other time, I'd have demanded to go, but I needed to stay with Mom, and Egan had asked instead of demanded. *No, but if you need me or something goes wrong, let me know immediately. Please.*

His eyes turned liquid gold. *I will.*

They shut the doors, leaving the car running. The two of them walked briskly to the tree line while Mom sat with her eyes forward, a small smile on her face.

"Grandchildren," she whispered. "Do you think you'll have them soon?"

Wow, she was a little too eager. "Mom, I'm in college. Can I at least get through that first?" And through whatever war we were in. My brain knew to keep that last part to myself. I almost patted myself on the back.

But realization settled over me. With Egan's family having him so much later in life, he hadn't gotten a chance to know his human grandparents. I'd like to give my children the opportunity to know Mom before she passed.

"Oh, of course." She placed her hand on my leg. "Egan is a good man, not that you couldn't be with him anyway. He's your fated mate, but even if he wasn't, I'd really like him."

"Even though he's a dragon shifter?" I lifted a brow as I watched him and Draco out of the corner of my eye. At the first sign of trouble, my ass would be out of this car to help them while I told Mom to drive far away.

"Despite it, yes." She chuckled. "At least he can protect you. Your father always tried to protect us and provide for us. He was determined to give us the very best of everything we could afford." Her voice cracked with emotion.

If I hadn't been run through the wringer earlier, I'd be tearing up too. "Dad was a wonderful man and father."

She nodded. "He really was."

Draco and Egan stopped several feet from the tree line, and a few seconds later, the person I'd seen and three other men stepped out from the small batch of trees.

I hadn't noticed the other three. My blood pumped hard, pounding in my ears. How many others could be out in the woods?

Four to two weren't horrible odds. Dragons were strong, but I had no idea what type of creatures they were and if there were more hiding. *What's going on?*

They claim to be from the wolf pack Titan contacted. There was no alarm from Egan. *We're verifying it. Give us a minute. If anything goes wrong, get yourself and your mom to safety.*

Yeah, right. I couldn't leave him like that. But I kept my mouth shut. There was no point in arguing with him when he needed to stay focused.

"Jade, who are those men with Egan and Draco?" Mom turned her entire body toward her window, watching the exchange. Her leg bounced. "Are they supernaturals?"

"Yes, they're from the pack Titan talked to." At least, we weren't under attack. It was a good thing I'd stayed inside. I probably would've attacked without giving them a chance to explain themselves like back in the woods when Mom had freaked out. But that guy had been in wolf form. At least, these guys had known to stay human to communicate with us. Egan and Draco had a lot more patience than my hot head.

"Oh, they're already here." Mom sagged with relief, and her leg stilled. "I figured with it being so late, they would just show tomorrow."

Her assumption annoyed me, especially since we were being cautious and this pack had been willing to help without hesitation. "You do realize by coming back here, you'll be watched twenty-four hours a day, right? It's not like the fae and their helpers would only attack during daylight hours if they found you."

Mom's brows drew together. "They'd do that for us?"

"Yes, they would. I'm learning that the supernatural community is way more supportive and loyal than humans are." Every single one of them had welcomed me with open arms, except for Naida. But from what everyone had said, she was standoffish to everyone, except with Sadie. After she spent time with you, she thawed some, but she was still rigid. From what Egan had said, most fae were that way.

"What do you mean?"

Memories of Kortright flashed through my mind. "At the university, they accepted me before they realized my connection with Egan. And Titan and the vampires all helped without a second thought. They look out for one another."

Part of the reason Sadie and the others had accepted me could have been because I was destined to be supernatural. At first, I didn't feel like I fit in with them, but I didn't fit in with humans either. Finally, I felt secure, even though I was just realizing it.

"I have no interest in being part of this strange, scary world, but you look like you're at peace and happy for the first time since Dad died." Her gaze went back to Egan. "That day on the beach, you had a very similar look in your eyes, which petrified your father."

"Why?" I thought they would've wanted me to find happiness instead of feeling like I was awkward and didn't fit in anywhere.

She rubbed her hands across her upper thigh, over the new jeans she'd gotten from the pack. "Because you were too young to feel a tenth of what your father and I felt for each other, and we didn't want your heart broken. But it's clear we may have reacted too rashly. I wonder what might have happened if we hadn't left the beach that day and headed home."

"You can't play the 'what if' game." That was dangerous. I'd played it way too often growing up with Sarah. All it had done was add more angst and heartache to the guilt I already carried.

Egan and Draco turned back toward the vehicle with the four guys following behind.

They'll take your mom the rest of the way. Egan didn't seem tense, but he wasn't relaxed either. The vibes through our bond were hard to pinpoint, which made me nervous.

Why? Is something wrong?

No. He looked at me as he continued. *But the longer we stay out in the open, the likelier someone will see us. And your aunt is pacing around the house. I don't want her to see us or our car.*

Are you sure they are who they say they are? After everything we'd gone through, we didn't need to hand her over to the enemy.

Egan grinned as two guys spoke to him and linked with me. *That's exactly what Draco said. We called Titan, and he vouched for them. That's what took so long.*

I didn't like dropping her off like this, but I didn't want to see Sarah. And if she saw us and our tags, it meant she could locate the vampire nest. So, if someone showed up who was hunting me down, she'd offer me up on a silver platter, no threats or torture required. "Mom, those guys are going to walk you the rest of the way to your house."

"What? Why?" She picked at her nails as her anxiety peeked through.

I had to tread carefully. "Sarah is awake, and I think it's best we don't run into each other."

"But are they safe?" Mom's mouth quivered.

Now she was getting on my nerves. I'd seen her like this way too often to count, and it had made me determined to be a strong person.

To not need anyone.

But I realized that wasn't the way to be either. You could be stronger with the right people by your side.

I steadied myself before I snapped. I didn't understand how she was okay being this way. "Do you think we'd leave you with them if we thought they were a risk?" I couldn't prevent the hurt from leaking through. After almost dying for her, she should know I wouldn't hand her over to just anyone.

"No, I don't." She sucked in a breath and blew it out. "I'm being ridiculous like always. I wish I could be strong like you. That's why I pushed you into martial arts and everything. You can stand on your own two feet, something I've never been able to do."

She was stronger than she gave herself credit for. "Maybe if you tried."

Mom opened the door and climbed out, leaving me alone in the car.

I wanted to say, "See! You just shut me down. A weak person wouldn't do that," but I bit my tongue. No good would come from it. This was something she would have to work through herself, just like I'd had to.

Following her lead, I got out of the car and walked around the back of the midsize sedan to the others. Mom stood several feet on the outskirts, staring the four men down strangely.

"We'll make sure she stays safe," the one who was slightly older than the others said. He looked in his mid-twenties, but I'd learned you couldn't use appearances as any sort of guidance in this strange, wild world. He could be one hundred for all I knew.

I wasn't sure what to say, so I went with the best I had. "Thank you."

"You're welcome." The guy winked at me.

Egan stepped close to me, placing an arm around my waist.

I almost giggled but swallowed it down. At least, he didn't growl, but he was making it clear I was his, and I loved it.

"You three get on out of here," the wolf said with humor, finding Egan's reaction funny too. "If what Titan said is true, your enemies will be looking for you any way possible. It's best you get back out to the mountain where you'll be harder to find."

Draco frowned. "You know where Titan lives?"

"Don't worry, we don't," the younger one said as he shifted his weight to his right leg. "Just that it's in the mountains and well hidden. We see him from time to time when he visits my dad, the alpha of our pack."

Titan was a very well-respected wolf in the community. Sadie had told me he could have easily taken over Tyler's pack, but Titan was a much better man. He believed that one person ruling over everyone gave certain groups unfair advantages and other groups special interests.

If politicians had taught us anything, I'd say Titan was dead on.

"Your sacrifice is noted, and as my mate said, we're extremely grateful." Egan lowered his head slightly.

The younger one chuckled and took a few steps toward the neighborhood. "Making friends with dragons is always a smart move. We'll alert Titan if anything weird happens."

I hugged my mother so tight she groaned in pain.

Oh, snap. Supernatural strength. I had to remember that. I loosened my hold and took a deep breath of her jasmine scent. Musk laced it, probably because she'd borrowed clothes from a wolf shifter.

"You three head on back. It's late." She kissed my forehead and patted my cheek. "I love you. Call me, okay? I'll get a new phone tomorrow so you can reach me."

"Okay." I gave her a small smile as my eyes burned with unshed tears. "If you need anything, message me. I'll have my alerts on."

Mom then focused on Egan. "You better take care of my baby girl."

"I'll guard her with my life." The sincerity behind his words was evident with each syllable.

Mom turned, and two guys flanked her while the other two followed behind.

As I watched them walk away, an overwhelming feeling settled over me like something was wrong.

CHAPTER FIFTEEN

Everything inside me screamed to snatch Mom and run, but I had no clue why. Titan had vouched for the guys. Vera was dead, and there was nothing out of the ordinary going on. There was absolutely no reason for me to feel this way. Again, my panic had to be taking over.

Is something wrong? Egan asked and took my hand.

His touch calmed me, confirming that paranoia was the problem. When there was an actual threat present, his touch made me feel safer, but it didn't soothe me. My aunt had that effect on me. Every time I thought about her, my skin crawled. *Just wish she wasn't going back to Sarah.*

Me too.

"Let's head back to the mansion," Draco whispered. "They're right. The longer we stay here, the likelier we are to be found."

Why did they keep saying that? "How so?"

"There are many kinds of supernaturals that can track, like vampires, and there's no telling how many there are in Fae." Draco headed back to the car. "The farther we are from a city, the harder it'll be to find us. The larger the population, the more creatures could be nearby, already looking."

I couldn't argue with that. There was still so much I didn't know about this world.

Egan and I followed him, and Draco slipped into the backseat, leaving the front passenger seat open for me. He'd tried to do the same thing on the way here, but with Mom freaking out, we'd all agreed it'd be best that I sit back there with her.

Always the gentleman, Egan opened the door, and I climbed in and put my seatbelt on. By the time I buckled the seatbelt, Egan had slid into the car, and we were heading back to the mountains.

My eyes flicked to the side mirror, watching the neighborhood disappear as he turned onto the road back to the city.

I MUST HAVE DRIFTED off because my car door opened, startling me awake. Familiar sexy arms wrapped around my body, lifting me into a hard, muscular chest.

My eyes fluttered open to find Egan staring tenderly at my face as he headed to the front door of the mansion.

Hey there, sleepyhead. His voice was low and raspy.

I loved it when he used that voice. My body always responded, and already being cuddled right against his chest had parts of me warming. *Hey, you.* I licked my lips inadvertently.

A low growl rattled his chest. He could smell and feel what I wanted. His tangy scent of arousal hit my nose, increasing my own need.

The slight glow of the rising sun told me it had to be around seven in the morning. The light glowed behind Egan, adding to his allure.

"Well, okay. I'm going to go crash for a couple of hours on the couch," Draco said uncomfortably as he opened the door. "Uh, I'll see you two later."

Egan walked past him, his eyes locked on mine. There was no doubt what we'd be doing once we were alone in our room.

Seconds later, we entered our bedroom, and Egan shut the door quietly before lowering my feet to the floor and kissing me.

His tongue slipped into my mouth, and his hands slipped under my jeans, resting on my ass. He deepened the kiss, and all I could breathe and smell was him. His fingers kneaded my ass cheeks like he was trying to force himself to slow down.

I stumbled back toward the bed, dragging him with me. He removed his hands from my pants and wrapped them around my waist right as I fell backward and landed on my back on the bed. He caught himself with one hand while using the other to lift my shirt up. He pulled his mouth away from my lips and gently nipped at my breast. My back arched into him.

Closing my eyes, I slipped my hands under his shirt, feeling his abs. He felt so warm, and I loved running my fingertips along his defined muscles.

His hand slipped to the button on my jeans, and he unfastened them with ease. I lifted my butt off the bed, and he pushed my jeans and panties down. He stood and removed them completely. Then he lowered himself on the bed on his side and slipped his hands between my legs. Between his mouth and touch, the friction built, and a low moan escaped.

He knew exactly how to work my body, and when he slipped a finger inside, I almost orgasmed.

I grabbed his hand, removing it from me, and he growled, *What do you think you're doing?*

If he thought that would make me listen to him, he should've known better by now. *I want to make you feel good too.* I pushed him off me and sat, removing my shirt and bra.

His eyes glowed as he watched me undress. *You're so damn beautiful.*

And he was the first person to make me feel that way. Before him, I'd felt ugly and unworthy. It was why I couldn't believe someone like him would be interested in me. But despite all accusations of him wanting me for just sex, he treated me with respect. *I love you.*

He cupped my cheek and smiled. *I love you too, my Jade.*

Unlike before, those words were like music to my ears. I unbuttoned his jeans and removed them and his boxers. I took a moment to gaze at him. He reminded me of one of those chiseled god statues.

I straddled him and leaned over, yanking the shirt over his head. He groaned and chuckled, helping me, and tossed it to the ground. He fidgeted, getting ready for our connection, but I wanted a minute. I rubbed my hand over his chest, enjoying how the thin golden hair on his pecs felt against my skin. Just devouring his body turned me on almost as much as his hands and mouth.

His eyes followed me as I lifted, drawing him inside me. As I lowered, he moaned and clutched my hips. He said, *I love watching you like this.*

Surprisingly, I liked him watching me too.

Our gazes stayed on each other as I rode him. His chest shuddered, and he moved in sync with me.

The speed increased, faster and faster, and he lifted his hands, cupping my breasts. The friction built as our bodies rubbed against each other, and when he pinched my nipples, the pleasure increased tenfold.

I closed my eyes as I spread my legs farther apart, allowing him to go deeper. The feel of him inside me and his hands on my body had me tumbling over. His body convulsed underneath me as we orgasmed together.

I swear it gets better each time. Egan lifted himself and kissed my lips, pulling me into his arms. He rolled us onto our sides, and I turned to face him, resting my head on his chest. My eyes grew heavy once again.

The next couple of weeks passed by in a blur. March was upon us, and the weather was warming, even here in the mountains.

For once, life seemed normal. Well, as normal as it could get in a supernatural world, but the packs and thunder were getting along. Ollie was growing on all of us, and the vampires felt like family. There were no attacks, and Egan and I spent more time laughing than being broody and tense. If our lives could be like this every day, it'd be damn near perfect.

Roxy yawned. "What do you think we should do today?"

Sadie, Roxy, Lillith, Katherine, Kayda, and I were all lounging on six teal Adirondack chairs on the back porch of the mansion. Each mate sat on the ground next to us.

"We could always go for a run." Axel waggled his eyebrows. "It's been too long since I kicked your ass in a race."

"You did not kick my ass!" Roxy crossed her arms and wrinkled her nose. "I stumbled."

Lillith pursed her lips. "Not that it matters, but from where I was standing, you only stumbled when Axel got too far ahead and there was no way you could catch up."

"You bish!" Roxy bared her teeth. "Whose side are you on?"

"The truth." Lillith chuckled and lifted her head toward the sun. "They say it will always set you free."

"Humans are dumb." Roxy pouted. "They say stuff like that to make themselves feel better."

"I'm pretty sure you got that from Tyler." Sadie waved her finger. "Who wasn't the best role model."

"Even you?" Roxy's mouth dropped. "You're my bestie. What the hell is going on here?" Her hazel eyes found me. "Jade, I can count on you, right?"

I stiffened, and Egan placed a hand on my thigh.

"I'm like Switzerland," I gestured to the entire group. "Neutral."

"Katherine?" Roxy stuck out her bottom lip. "Please don't say no."

"I love you all equally, but you have to admit you might be a tad competitive." She put a small space between her thumb and pointer finger. "Just a smidge."

"Momma Kayda?" Roxy asked with defeat.

"Oh, no." Kayda stood and grabbed Ladon's hand, pulling her mate to his feet. "I don't get involved in disagreements unless I have a vested interest. This is one we won't be getting into. We're going to check on the dragons while you two do whatever this is you're doing." She and Ladon headed toward the back door.

"Sorry, babe." Axel kissed her arm. "It looks like they're all siding with me by not picking a side."

"Traitors." She looked at each of us. "All of you are traitors."

"Stop being dramatic." Lillith yawned and placed a hand over her mouth. "You're wearing me out."

"Oh, please." Roxy stuck her tongue out at the vampire. "You breathe drama."

"I do not," she gasped.

I think we need to go do something. Ever since things had calmed down, Roxy and Lillith had gotten snippy with each other, likely due to the amount of one-on-one time we had with everyone. There wasn't much to do out here except eat, watch television, scan library books, play video games, or hang outside.

Egan and I stayed in the bedroom as much as possible, but it felt too weird being up there as much as we would've liked with his parents close by.

The door opened and shut as Egan's parents walked back into the house.

You're right. Egan stood and raised his hands over his head, stretching.

His shirt crept upward, showing his abs. I enjoyed the view.

"Better wipe that drool off your face—" Roxy snorted. "—before it makes a puddle on your chest. I bet Egan doesn't like being stared at like a piece of meat."

"Don't speak on my behalf." His attention on me warmed my body. "She can look at me like that any time she wants."

"Oh, really?" Roxy turned toward the mansion and said more loudly, "Momma Kayda, you might want to come back out here."

"If you think Mom would give us a hard time, she wouldn't." Egan lifted me off the lounger and into his arms. "She wants grandbabies. Tons of them."

That was the second comment about children this month. *You keep bringing up children.*

Yeah, is that not okay? His forehead creased with confusion.

I had to tread carefully. I didn't want to hurt his feelings. *I want them too, but not now. I want to make sure we're on the same page.*

A grin peeked through. *The fact that you do is enough for me. But I won't say that the thought of having children with you doesn't thrill me. To have something we made together would be the second-best thing that ever happened to me.*

You sweet-talker. I beamed up at him. He made me feel so happy and safe.

Roxy bickered with the group, and I took Egan's hand, leading him behind a few trees several feet away to give us some privacy.

I stroked the stubble on his chin. *I still can't believe you were the boy on the beach. It makes perfect sense, but it's still surreal.*

And you're the girl who made me feel funny things I didn't understand. He kissed me as his voice deepened. *And you turned into a woman who owns me.*

I still hadn't asked him the question that had been burning in my mind for the past few weeks. At every opportunity, I got distracted by sex, which I wasn't complaining about. If everyone else hadn't been around, I'd have been on top of him, claiming him as my own again. *I thought you guys were in hiding. How did we run into each other all those years ago?*

We went to another thunder so I could meet the eldest dragon there at the time. Now I know why. The priest performed a ceremony on me, and Dad said every one of his family members had to go through the same rites. Now I realize it was because we're royalty. On the way back to our thunder, Mom asked to see the beach one last time.

She always spoke of it fondly. Dad obliged but said it had to be quick. Little did we know I'd find my fated mate. Of course, I didn't understand that then, but my parents must have. I think that's why they pushed me to go to college ... to find you again.

I kept forgetting he was royalty. *Is needing an heir another reason you want children?*

Not at all. He pushed a piece of my hair behind my ear. *It might be beneficial for that reason, but I'd want this as badly if we were just plain ol' Egan and Jade.*

It would've been nice to be ordinary people—or dragon shifters.

Lillith stood and clapped her hands. "Okay, this is getting gross, even for me. I don't know what you're doing back there, but if we don't intervene, we're going to start hearing uncomfortable noises coming from behind the trees."

Roxy snorted. "Egan's huge. We'll see everything he's working with if that happens."

"Okay." Sadie cleared her throat. "Let's go for a hike."

They'd managed to embarrass us even when we'd tried to hide.

"That sounds good." I stepped from Egan's arms begrudgingly but moving around sounded nice.

Egan took my hand. "We should tell Draco or we may get in trouble." We joined them again before Roxy and Lillith could continue their tirade.

"I'll go tell him." Katherine jumped to her feet and ran inside.

Donovan frowned slightly. "She jumps at any chance to be around him. She does realize he has a human fated mate out there somewhere?"

"Don't worry," Lillith grumbled, "I'll remind her. We don't need her to get her heart broken."

That was something we could all agree with.

Ollie, Draco, and Katherine came back outside, and our group took off into the woods.

A breeze hit my skin, cooling my body down to a more comfortable temperature. The animals scurried as if they were excited for spring. The scent of budding flowers hit my nose, even though they hadn't bloomed yet. It was like they were preparing for the season, ready to pollinate the area.

We moved quickly and quietly through the trees in comfortable silence.

A few miles away from the mansion, I laid my head on Egan's arm as we walked at a slow, relaxed pace. The sun shone through the trees now that it was high in the sky. I hadn't been this relaxed in such a long time.

But then Egan tensed.

What's wrong? I lifted my head. We were in a thicker part of the woods with trees completely surrounding us. Then I realized the animal noises were gone.

He took a deep breath. *Something is near.*

Draco appeared beside us, spreading his legs into a fighter's pose. He'd recognized the same threat Egan had.

Panic surged through me as I tried desperately to figure out what we were looking for.

A roar sounded only a few feet away from us, and I spun around to see a huge brown bear stepping into view between two trees.

The animal threw its head back and roared again. Then it charged.

CHAPTER SIXTEEN

An awful decaying stench laced with musk hit my nose as the bear approached. The grizzly's ice-green eyes held a human-like quality.

Wait. Intrigue replaced my fear. *Is he a shifter?*

Yes, Egan growled as Draco stepped in front of us.

When this was all over, I'd need a flowchart or diagram of all of the shifters in the world. Hell, maybe even a detailed outline. It was beyond insane how much I didn't know.

"One bear thinks it can take us out?" Roxy chuckled and flipped her hair over her shoulder. "There are four wolves, two vampires, and three dragons."

Ollie jerked his head toward her and scowled. "And a falcon."

"Oh, please." She waved him off. "You don't count."

"In all fairness, he pecked through several girls' eyes and necks." Lillith shrugged, completely at ease like Roxy. "And he pecked through that wire net that held Jade."

They did have a point, but they needed to take the threat more seriously. *I have a bad feeling about this. The bear doesn't seem worried.*

My thoughts exactly. Egan looked at the sky.

At first, I wasn't sure why. then I heard the flapping of several pairs of wings overhead like a synchronized beat. I couldn't tell how many. It could have been ten or hundreds.

"Ollie." I glanced at him, the hairs on the back of my neck raised. If I hadn't known any better, I might have thought I was a wolf shifter, not a dragon. "Go to Titan's pack and get them and the other dragons."

"What?" Katherine faced me. "Why?"

"Listen," Donovan growled. "The bear's not alone. Tell them to bring weapons. We have no clue what we're up against. If they're fae, the iron might help too."

That was all Ollie needed to hear before taking off. We might need backup and quick. Out of all of us, Ollie was the smallest when he shifted and could hide. Whatever was coming sounded huge.

"How is this possible?" Lillith's jaw twitched. "The witch is dead. How did they find us?"

"Mom." My voice cracked. "I need to check on her."

We will, but right now, we need to keep our heads in the game and hope Ollie gets back with everyone soon. Egan lifted his head, looking higher in the sky.

I followed his gaze, and my world stopped. The strangest animals I'd ever seen were flying toward us, which was saying something after the harpies and gargoyles.

Each one looked the same. Enormous, scarlet lions beat long, boney wings that sprouted from their backs. They each had a thick, long, scorpion-like tail tipped with a dangerous stinger as well as numerous stingers along its huge tail. Their red faces resembled an old man with a very long beard that matched the red shade of their bodies.

"What the hell is it with fae creatures looking like old people?" Sadie groaned as she returned her focus to the bear.

"Looking old is a strategic advantage." That was something they'd taught me in self-defense class. "You think of them as weaker and lower your guard around them. Apparently, the fae must think the same way, or they find the look sexy."

"Doesn't matter." Axel bellowed while his bones cracked as he called his wolf. "We'll kick their asses."

Wings sprouted from Draco's body. "It won't be easy. These are manticores. They are some of the toughest opponents. You can only kill them by piercing their bellies or injuring their mouths."

Great. Of course, they'd be straight out of Greek mythology. "We'll have to use branches and whatever else we have until the others get here."

Sadie, Roxy, and Donovan followed Axel's lead, shifting into their wolves. We all needed to be in our strongest forms.

"Do not engage until the others have arrived unless you absolutely have to," Draco commanded. "With our small numbers, they'll focus on eliminating the biggest threat first. Try to wait for our numbers to grow before revealing your strength."

The bear stepped back like he was going to allow the manticores to handle us. Once we kicked their asses, the bear was next on my list.

My dragon brushed against my mind, on the same page as my human side. I latched on to the flames, and the warmth flowed through my body. I took a few steps away from Egan and Draco as my body expanded.

My clothes stretched until they ripped from my body. Egan and Draco had the same plan, and every one of us was now in animal form.

Draco's navy blue scales glistened as he gestured for Egan and me to head back to the mansion.

No, he couldn't be suggesting what I thought he was. *I'm not hiding in the mansion.*

Neither am I. I get we're part of the royal family, but I'm not leaving my friends out here to fight a battle that's happening because of our race.

It thrilled me that he wasn't begging me to go back to the

mansion. If this had been a month ago, he'd be growling at me to go. *So, belly or mouth. That's what we aim for.*

That's the plan. He edged in front of me but not too noticeably. *Anything else before they get here?*

I counted the manticores flying at us. The sky was full of them, but I spotted an end to the group.

One hundred.

We had more people than that. We should be okay.

Yeah, I love you, and don't die. I flapped my wings, lifting off the ground. I didn't want to be sitting ducks and let them come to us. I understood not wanting to start the fight, but we didn't need to make it easy for them to clobber us.

Draco made weird noises that sounded between a growl, a groan, and a roar. I had a feeling he was cussing my ass out super creatively. I wondered what he might call me when this was over. He might teach me a new word or two.

What are you doing? Egan asked as he rushed to catch up to me.

We need to split them up. If they got to us before we had backup, it would be harder to hold them off. Maybe Egan, Draco, and I could make some of them chase us around in the sky.

The odd noises were still gurgling from Draco as he caught up to us. He hovered slightly in front of us as forty manticores split off from the main group and headed our way.

See, we're already splitting them up. My plan was working.

Sadie and the others must have caught on because her pink wolf ran into the woods, away from the others. The other three took off in different directions as well.

The remaining sixty split apart with ten taking off after each wolf, leaving twenty still heading toward Lillith and Katherine.

Now we just needed to play cat and mouse for a little while.

The three of us hovered in the air as the forty manticores headed toward us. Suddenly, the one in the front swung its tail around, despite still being a hundred yards away. Something snapped from its tail, and five stingers spiraled toward me like freaking arrows.

I froze, watching in both intrigue and horror as they darted toward my heart like it was a bull's-eye.

Jade! Egan yelled in my head, snapping me back to the present.

What the hell was wrong with me?

Something hard slammed into my side, and wings wrapped around me. Draco's ashy smell surrounded me. His wings unraveled around me after we'd dropped several feet.

We flapped our wings, catching the wind before we crashed into the trees below.

Egan reached me, brushing his wings against mine. *Are you okay?*

Yeah, but what the hell? I still couldn't believe what I'd seen, but as I looked at the forty manticores, I realized they were now closer, which meant we were screwed. Splitting them up wasn't as effective as I'd hoped it would be, but it was better than the full one hundred coming at us at once.

We could only hope that the others would arrive soon. We'd have to survive until then.

As the manticores grew closer, I noted a slight difference between them. Some had more blue in their eyes while others had gray.

When the closest one got within thirty yards of us, its mouth turned upward in a smile before it bared its teeth.

What I saw scared me more than anything I'd seen from them.

The creature had three rows of sharp, jagged teeth like razor blades. Between those, the lion body, and the stingers, the direness of our situation truly dawned on me.

Draco was always tense. Part of his job was continuously looking for threats and never underestimating the enemy, so in a way, I hadn't expected them to be worse than anything we'd faced before. Not anymore.

We had to fly fast and crazy or we'd be screwed if they fine-tuned their attack. *Move.*

I took off, flying as fast as I could away from Egan and Draco. I darted randomly in the sky, keeping my movements irregular with no hint of a pattern whatsoever.

I spun around and breathed a sigh of relief when I caught Egan and Draco doing the same thing.

Thank God. That was the only way we could all survive.

A stinger whizzed toward me, and I knew what to do. I darted hard to the right, causing the manticore to miss his target.

The one closest to me roared in frustration and flapped his wings faster.

Shit, he wasn't shooting at me anymore; he wanted to catch up. The thought of his teeth pushed me harder to get the hell away.

As I flew higher, bulky figures appeared in the distance.

Dammit, was that more of them? God, I hoped not. We might not survive, but that was the point. The fae dragon king wanted us dead, especially Egan, to eliminate any threat to his crown. It was exactly the kind of thing any power-hungry asshole would do. He wanted to hunt his own kind down to end them just so whatever magic could transfer to him.

What was it with asshole men? He had to be short. From every experience I'd had, the men dying for more power suffered from short man syndrome. It was a real condition.

I blinked a few times, and the figures flying toward me took form. They weren't huge lions but dragons. The thunder was on their way, which meant that the wolves had to be too.

Glancing over my shoulder, I saw ten manticores hot on my trail. That had happened quickly. They flew out in a line, planning to surround me.

If I got caught like that, it'd be hard as hell to escape. I ducked, letting my body drop toward the ground.

Just like back in the cave, my dragon wanted to abort and pull up, but I stayed in control. One backward glance confirmed what I'd hoped: those ten assholes were still almost on top of me and following my lead.

Could I pull it off and make a few of them crash? According to Draco, the impact wouldn't kill them, but I could knock them out or injure them somewhat.

Surely.

Something like arrows whistled closer, and I lifted my head to find Egan zigzagging, dodging stingers. The last one targeted the back of his tail. He jerked hard to the right, and the stinger missed him by less than an inch.

A growl of frustration came from a manticore behind me. A click sounded like earlier, right before they'd launched stingers at me.

I'd gotten so distracted by Egan's attack that I'd stopped focusing on a random flight pattern. I spun in circles as the wind rushed past my immense body. We were still seventy-five feet off the ground, but the trees were getting closer. I only needed to get close enough to one of the trees and stop short so the ten manticores behind me wouldn't have time to react before going splat.

Since the manticore still hadn't fired at me, my flight pattern must have been random enough to hold them off.

Forcing my eyes forward, I found an opening between trees that was large enough for me to fly through and get back into the sky. I darted to the right, needing to time this perfectly.

Leaves were budding on tree branches, again proving that spring was right around the corner. It would have been nice if they'd been in full bloom to hide us from these creatures, but at least it wouldn't be hard to find a good branch to use to stab them with.

Twenty feet off the ground, I sucked in a deep breath. There was no time to hesitate or lose confidence. If I let my nerves get the best of me, I'd slam into the ground like I hoped these manticores would.

The time had come.

I shifted my weight, going right side up again. Spreading my wings, I took flight between the trees like I'd planned. My bottom half was bigger than I'd realized, and as I squeezed through the trees, my body pushed them outward, bending them.

They didn't fall over, and I almost cried with joy when several bodies hit the ground.

At least, one thing had worked out. If they stayed down for longer than a minute, maybe I could find a stick to kill them with.

As I flew upward with confidence, I found myself staring at two manticores no more than twenty feet away. They must have realized my intentions.

One had its tail ready, and several stingers launched directly at me.

I didn't have time to move, so I closed my eyes and prayed.

CHAPTER SEVENTEEN

The stingers hit my scales one after another, jabbing like pinpricks. They fell to the ground, and I waited for intense pain to hit, similar to the harpies' arrows.

But the pain never came.

I opened my eyes as the manticore's mouth turned downward. Or I thought it did. Despite having a human face, the expression was pretty one-dimensional.

Angry and feral.

Are you hurt? Egan linked, letting his intense worry bleed into me.

These creatures were scary, but maybe they weren't as fearsome as we thought. *I'm fine. They sting, but that's it. The pain is already gone.* I flew upright, not bothering to fly in a random pattern.

The manticore that had shot at me roared like that would put the fear back inside me.

Nope. The teeth and huge-ass stingers were enough to frighten me, but I didn't need to worry about the small ones anymore. I flapped my wings, hovering in place while keeping my eyes locked on the manticores flying around.

Below me, five of them had hit the ground and appeared disoriented. Two lay completely still while the other three squirmed but couldn't roll back onto their feet.

At least they weren't smart. That was what I'd been banking on.

Egan flew closer, despite the twenty still on his tail, and linked with me. *It's almost time to fight. The others are only a mile away.*

At least sixty dragons were heading our way, and twenty or so wolves and fifty men were running toward us. The men each held two items: what looked like a sword and a metal pole.

Donovan had mentioned something about iron. It had to be fae related, and now we had multiple weapons at our disposal—or we would when they got nearer.

Our army rushed toward us, and I only prayed the wolves were resistant to the stingers too. Had I been in human form, those would've hurt, and the wolves' hide wasn't much thicker.

A wolf howled, and I spun around. The manticores had Roxy surrounded. Five landed on the ground, circling her so she couldn't get out. She hunkered, her vibrant red fur standing on end.

I had to help her. *It's time to engage.* We couldn't wait any longer. One of our own was in danger.

Not bothering to wait for Egan's reply, I rushed to Roxy. If anything were to happen to her when I could prevent it, I'd never survive it. The others should be here in minutes.

I swooped down with my own manticores chasing after me and almost froze in place when the creature closest to Roxy opened its mouth. The three rows of teeth looked as ferocious as before, but the amount of drool pooling from its mouth made its intent obvious.

These assholes weren't trying to injure us; they wanted to eat us.

One charged toward Roxy and reached her within seconds.

Pushing my wings even harder than I had before, I reached my friend just as the manticore's mouth was only centimeters from her head. From the angle of its attack, the creature was planning to eat her head first.

I opened my own mouth and attacked its neck. My teeth sank in, and its blood poured across my tongue. The creature roared and swung its scorpion tail at me. I released my hold and flew upward, the stinger barely missing my leg.

The manticore flew right after me, its gray eyes turning dark as coal. Between it and the others that were focused on me, I needed to do something. Unfortunately, Roxy wasn't out of danger yet.

Draco barreled past me, his focus on Roxy.

Wow, he's not focused on us? Not that I was complaining, but Draco always made it clear that Egan, Ladon, Kayda, and I were his priority.

Oh, he is, Egan replied tensely. *He knows you'll keep putting yourself in danger if he doesn't help Roxy. The others are here, and it's time to take it up a notch.*

A dark purple dragon roared as it flew past me and attacked a manticore. One dragon after another came to my aid and to help in the fight.

The fact that these people had come to help me without any hesitation made me realize they had accepted me as one of their own.

I'd been so worried because of Mindy, but she'd been the exception. And I had to protect them just like they were protecting me.

Pale pink lights lit the sky like fireworks. I followed the trail to find Sadie running toward Roxy in wolf form and shooting magic from her paws every couple of steps. Every other burst hit a manticore. It would flinch back in pain, but not for long.

When Draco had said these guys were worthy opponents, he'd meant every word. They were ruthless and bounced back from attacks like they'd only stubbed their toes.

The men poured into the area, waving their swords around like the manticores would fear them. But the creatures barely batted an eye.

Egan appeared next to me, so stiff his dragon looked like a statute. If it hadn't been for his flapping wings, I would've thought he was frozen. *We have to figure out how to beat them.*

A manticore shot stingers at a chestnut wolf. I recognized him as the one who'd defended his friend, the wolf Mom had thought was attacking her. The wolf yelped in pain and fell with a loud thud.

I had to do something, but as I headed toward them, the creature rushed over to the wolf and swallowed him whole—bones and all.

No. That couldn't have happened. But no matter how many times I blinked, my eyes confirmed what I'd seen. My stomach lurched, and bile burned my throat.

Holy shit. The wolves were susceptible to the stingers.

Pure rage bubbled inside me, and I roared so loud some of the manticores stopped what they were doing to stare at me.

That's right, assholes. Pay attention to me. I had to save my friends and their pack members.

Lillith blurred across a small clearing with her vampire speed, carrying a sword in her right hand.

A manticore opened its mouth to attack Roxy, but Lillith thrust the sword inside it. The creature screamed as the metal sank in deep, and it sagged.

One down, ninety-nine to go.

We need something to use against them. We had claws, but with their tails and our size, getting close enough to use them was problematic. They could easily take any of us out. We needed to get a hold of a weapon or debilitate their stinger.

Egan nodded slightly. *My grandfather told me a story about these creatures when I was little. Before our thunder left for Earth, the fae dragon king sent these creatures to attack, but the true dragon ruler knew the secret to defeating them: dehydration.*

Babe, I love you, but I think it'll take a long time before these creatures get thirsty. Maybe after they eat all of us. That sounded like a horrible plan.

He chuckled, surprising me given the situation. *What's one way to dehydrate someone?* Some of his confidence clicked back into place, and smoke trickled from his nostrils.

Fire. I hadn't even thought of that. If we lit them up, their skin and bodies would lose their moisture.

A manticore flew near us, and Egan opened his mouth, blowing his flames all over the creature. It cried but continued to fly toward us, then began to slow.

Be careful. If we can light them up, the wolves can kill them. Egan continued his assault on the creature. Its wings slowed, and its elevation dropped.

That sounded like a solid plan. I raced toward Roxy, Sadie, and Lillith. Draco fought two manticores, but he was losing steam. One manticore shot its stingers at him while the other swung its tail.

As I channeled my anger, fire grew and bubbled in my stomach. I motioned for the girls to step back.

Lillith caught on as I opened my mouth and smoke curled over my lips.

"Get back!" Lillith yelled. Sadie and Roxy took several steps back.

When they were far enough away, I pushed the fire from my stomach, aiming at the manticore posing the most significant threat to Draco.

The creature growled and spun around. It charged at me, abandoning Draco. I gestured for Lillith to attack as the manticore took flight, trying desperately to get me.

She was a blur as she ran under the creature, using its body to protect herself from the flames, and swung the blade into its stomach.

A screech of pain left the creature, and Lillith rolled out of the way just before it collapsed.

"That's it!" Lillith yelled, counting on everyone's supernatural hearing. "Dragons, light those manticore asses up. The rest of us, jam the swords in their bellies or deep in their mouths to kill them."

Good, that was one way to spread the word. I didn't give a damn if the manticores understood our plan.

Re-energized, Draco turned on the one shooting stingers at him. He lit the creature up as Lillith rushed to help him kill it.

A low growl alerted me to the oncoming creature, its attention solely on me. He opened his jaws wide, his intentions clear.

But I refused to hesitate or freeze in fear.

Fire spewed from me, hitting the creature's mouth.

Sadie's pink wolf stepped up beside me, and she aimed her magic inside the creature's mouth. Her magic held a continuous surge, similar to my flame.

After several seconds that felt like a lifetime, the manticore stopped struggling and crumbled. Its chest stopped moving, proving it was dead.

I looked for the next target, but the enemy creatures were already fighting with other dragons. Everyone had heard Lillith and were following her instructions.

Most of the wolf shifters hadn't shifted, so we had plenty of people in human form to wield weapons.

I took to the sky to check on everyone and watched as Ollie ran toward the mansion. After all this time together, was he really running to safety? Part of me wanted to follow, but I couldn't leave my people and the packs. We were already at a huge disadvantage.

I linked with Egan, looking for him. *Are you okay?*

Yes, I'm helping Donovan and Axel, Egan replied. *Several shifters in human form are here. Are you safe?*

For the moment. I didn't want to lie to him. None of us were safe with these strange creatures here. *I'm going to see if anyone else needs my help.*

One manticore flew high, stalking the area.

No, I wouldn't allow him to find a target.

Rushing toward the creature, my dragon prepared for the attack. A few yards away, I opened my mouth to hit the creature with flames, but it plunged abruptly.

My flames hit nothing, and I yanked the fire back inside as I chased after it.

I couldn't hit the manticore with my flames with the wind blowing back in my face. It wouldn't touch him.

The creature lowered its head, increasing its speed, reminding me of a bird tracking fish in the water.

I attempted to locate its target, but nothing came into view. We flew past several dragons and other manticores engaged in battle, but they weren't its target.

As we neared the ground, Titan and Winter rushed from some trees. They were in human form, handing out weapons to whomever needed them.

They were the reason we were gaining the advantage. They were rushing to dole out a huge pile of weapons to anyone who lost a sword in the fight or to a straggler looking to help.

Placing myself right behind the manticore, I moved my wings and used my body to increase my speed. Tumbling to the ground, I arched my feet and hands to use my talons for as much leverage as possible.

I rammed into the manticore's back, and I dug my sharp talons into its rough skin. Even though it wouldn't kill the bastard, it would distract it.

Its head jerked backward as it tried to bite me, but I was far enough back that it couldn't reach me. I almost roared with victory, but something hit me hard and lodged into my back, and sharp pain erupted down my spine.

I'd forgotten about its scorpion-like tail.

My grip slipped, and I fell from the manticore's body. As the distance grew between us, the creature removed the stinger from my back.

Jade, what happened? Egan asked with concern.

But I didn't have the time or energy to respond because I was only forty feet from hitting the ground. Using every ounce of concentration and strength available, I channeled my strength to my wings. The stinger must have torn through muscle because when my wings moved, it caused sharp, deep pain. I couldn't flap them fast enough to ascend, but I slowed my fall.

I braced myself for the inevitable impact as my body slammed into the ground. My dragon growled as a cloud of grass and dirt covered our entire body.

But the pain of the impact wasn't as bad as I'd expected.

"We need help!" Winter screamed, and adrenaline coursed through my body, numbing the intense pain from the stinger.

I climbed to my feet and found the manticore swinging its tail around, ready to launch a barrage of attacks on Titan and Winter. Pushing the flames from my stomach, I ran as fast as possible toward them.

The stingers launched before I could blaze the sucker, but I remained focused on the fight. I wouldn't allow it to attack again.

The creature spun toward me, opening its mouth despite my flames in pure rage. As it rushed toward me, a human wolf shifter ran over, using the flames to hide its approach, and threw a sword under the belly, plunging it hard in its skin.

Damn, I wished I had an aim like that.

With a half cry, half roar, the manticore sank. Although I watched the animal die, the crying sound remained.

What the hell?

Then the cry turned into pleading, and I realized it wasn't the creature.

"Help me, please!" Winter yelled. "It's Titan."

I spun around to find Titan on his back, squirming in pain with a stinger stuck in his eye.

CHAPTER EIGHTEEN

The amount of blood pouring from Titan's eye had to be dangerous. Between that and how deep the stinger had dug in, I was worried it might have hit his brain. The stinger was wedged in at an angle, though, so hopefully, it had missed his brain. If we lost him, that would hurt both his and Sadie's packs.

Blood wasn't my friend, but it didn't bother me as much in dragon form. The animal side did come in handy. If I'd been human, I would have vomited my lunch everywhere.

Titan's injured, I linked with Egan, not sure what the hell to do. *And so am I. I can't hold them off on my own.*

He responded, *I'll be right there.*

"Help!" Winter screamed as she fell to her knees next to her mate. "Somebody, please."

The alpha flailed around and groaned in pain like he was unsure what to do.

Pounding footsteps grew nearer, and the familiar scent of Kayda and Ladon blew in the air. They raced into view, Ollie running right behind them.

Ollie hadn't hidden. He'd gone to get help. I kind of felt bad. My gut reaction had been to think poorly of him. Little did he know, I hadn't had the bracelet on me this past week to see how he would act. I needed to know if I had to use it for him to comply. I had it hidden under a floorboard in my and Egan's room since the falcon's sight was better than his sense of smell. And despite my little test, when things had gone south, I'd thought the worst of him.

The oldest dragon rushed to Titan, pushing past his king and queen. The little bit of gray hair he had stood straight up from how fast he'd been moving, and he said, "We have to get that stinger out of his eye before the poison spreads and kills him."

"Wait." Ladon tensed, reminding me of his son. "I thought the stingers weren't poisonous."

"To dragons. But to humans and several other supernatural creatures, they are." The older man placed a hand on Winter's arm. "I'll need you to move so I can get this out before it's too late."

"Of course," Winter said and stood to let the older man sit on the side of the injured eye.

She moved to the other side and stood behind Ladon and Kayda as she reassured her mate, "I'm right here. Long is going to help you."

Long's amber eyes surveyed the injury. "Titan, this is Long. I'm going to yank the stinger out of your eye. It'll hurt like hell, but if we don't, you won't survive."

Wings flapped nearby, and I tore my eyes away to find Egan hurrying toward us. Even in beast form, his forehead was lined with concern. Titan was a man he respected and cared about, so this was hard for him to see.

"Fine, just do it," Titan grunted, his breathing shallow. "The pain is getting worse."

"Ladon and Kayda, hold him down," Long instructed. "The less he fights me, the less risky this will be."

I felt so helpless in this form. All I could do was stand here and watch. *What do we do?*

We do nothing. Egan touched my wing as he examined my wound. *You're injured and need time to heal.*

I'm fine. As long as I didn't move my wing, the pain was manageable. *But we need to prevent something worse from happening to Titan.*

We'll stay here and make sure nothing attacks them while they work on Titan. Egan's dragon hand brushed my arm. *We should be safe since most of the manticores are dead, but we don't need to be careless, especially with your injury.*

I had no arguments there. *Okay.* I scanned the area for threats. The smell of flames and smoke was thick around us, but that was a good sign. That meant there were plenty of us left to fight and proved we'd gained the upper hand. Unfortunately, the manticore had acted out of desperation in trying to take out Titan before they all died in vain. But I didn't understand it all. What in the hell had the fae dragon king promised them to convince these creatures to come here and risk their lives? He had to be either very convincing or leveraging hatred in some way.

"We've got him," Kayda said with determination. "Go ahead, Long."

Winter paced behind them, her fingers pulling at the end of her ponytail. Her sea-blue eyes turned cobalt, and her body shook with emotion.

Maybe Sadie should be here with her. I hated seeing Winter like that. She reminded me of my mom outside of the surgery room when the doctors had been trying to save Dad. That look of heartbreak and fear almost made me feel eight again.

No, she's needed in the fight out there. Egan looked skyward as a manticore raced away, retreating from the battle. *Her fae magic is doing the most damage, even more than the swords since she can shoot her magic from several yards away and hit the same targets all the others are having to get close to.*

I couldn't argue with his point. If she was the reason we were making such a big dent so quickly, removing her from the fight could give the manticores the upper hand, and who knew how many others could get hurt like Titan. *Does she at least know?*

I'm sure one of his pack members told her, Egan reassured me. *Several have taken a protective stance around the area.*

How don't I know that? I looked around for his people and noticed a few wolves had scattered. But it wasn't good that I hadn't been paying attention to this. I'd been more focused on my pain and emotions than the battle at hand. That was how people got hurt.

He took my hand, which was odd in beast form, and replied, *Because I flew over here when Winter was screaming for help. I saw his men come to assist, but the manticores attacked as they got close. It looked like it was a calculated move.*

Yeah, it did, which meant I needed to hand out the weapons. *We need to let the wolves focus on helping Titan while we take over their job. If they run out of weapons, we could lose the upper hand.*

You're right. He let go of my hand.

Titan cried out in pain as Egan and I walked past them and grabbed a few swords lying several yards away from the iron pile.

Do not touch anything in the iron pile. Only the swords, Egan said as he gathered some of them. *They'll drain your power and slow down your healing.*

Good to know. *Got it.*

With our strange dragon hands, we couldn't carry too many swords, but we made it work. I wound up carrying at least twenty by holding them in my arms instead of in my hands. The sharp blades didn't cut into my scales.

Egan examined me, looking for any signs of discomfort. *Are you hurting?*

Even if I had been, it wouldn't have dissuaded me from what we had to do. *No more than when I'm standing, and the pain is receding.*

Good. Your dragon is working overtime. Egan's jaw relaxed marginally.

We ran toward the fighting, and I foolishly looked at Titan one last time before leaving. The stinger was out, but his eyeball had come with it. Veins hung limply from the end, and a large hollow hole remained where his eye had been.

Even with shifter healing, there was no way he could come back from that. We could only hope and pray that they figured out a way to prevent the poison from spreading.

"We need to scrape the inside to make sure we got all the poison out." Long leaned over Titan again.

As we walked through the trees that blocked Titan, the alpha screamed in agony.

A younger man who was swinging a knife at a manticore's mouth turned his head toward the alpha, missing his mark. Before he could regain control of the weapon, the manticore lunged and ate him whole.

That was at least two deaths I'd seen done in this same method. Blood didn't even dribble down the creature's mouth. He'd eaten him entirely.

"No!" Torak screamed and carelessly ran at the creature. He held the sword over his head, hatred reflected in his usually warm green eyes.

Draco landed with a roar and engulfed the creature in flames.

The manticore stumbled forward from the force of the fire and tried to escape the flames. Each step it took, the dragon countered, keeping the flow constant.

Something blurred, and Cassius appeared, knocking down the alpha heir moments before he was about to run into the fire.

Athan appeared beside me and held out his hand. "I need one before Torak does something else stupid."

I quickly moved so he could reach a sword, hoping I wasn't making a bad decision. I didn't want him to get hurt either, even if he had tried to make Mom into a snack. In the past few weeks, I'd realized how hard he was trying and how much he struggled. He still apologized daily over what had almost happened to her.

Athan grabbed the sword, knowing how to hold it, and spun toward the manticore. The dragon halted the flames, and the vampire slammed the sword into its open mouth.

The creature sputtered, and its chest stopped moving.

"Look, they're all flying away!" a guy yelled from several feet away.

My attention turned to the sky. At least ten manticores were flying in the same direction as the other one had.

I wasn't sure if I should be relieved or concerned. If they returned to Fae, they would give the others more information about us, despite our location no longer being secret.

Mom flashed back into my brain. I needed to check on her. She was the only one who could've provided the location. I'd talked to her yesterday, so something must have happened between yesterday morning and now.

"Are we sure they're all gone?" an older shifter asked, glancing around the trees. So many damn manticores littered the ground that clean-up would be gruesome, especially with how huge these creatures were.

"They're gone over here too," someone said from a section of the woods we couldn't see.

One by one, the groups confirmed what we had hoped for. They had left ... for now.

Sadie and her pack ran right by us, rushing to get to Titan. Titan released another blood-curdling scream, and my blood ran cold.

The silence that followed seemed eerier. I'd held on to the hope that his screaming meant he was still alive. But what did the quiet mean? There were no cries of remorse, so maybe they were done doing God knew what to him.

Katherine walked into view and looked at Cassius, the wolf shifters, and the dragons. She said, as her eyes locked on Draco, "There was a bear. I think he led them to us. We need to find him. Now."

I had never seen this side of Katherine, but surprisingly, it suited her. Some thought the loudmouths and those who spoke their opinions were strong. And they were. But people didn't realize the strength it took to remain quiet ... reserved. Sometimes, there was more power in silence. People didn't understand the power that a quiet person commanded when they spoke with authority. Everyone stopped and listened.

And that's exactly what happened. No one questioned her; everyone left to obey.

I linked with Egan. *Let's take to the sky.*

Egan stepped toward me. *Can you?*

I moved my wings, and the excruciating pain was gone. There was still an ache, but I could handle flying long enough to search for the bear. *I'm good. If it gets to be too much, I'll come back.*

He nodded. *We can cover more ground in the air while the shifters and vampires track on land.*

We took to the sky as several other dragons followed our lead. Over half stayed back, and I watched as they blew their flames on the manticores.

They're cleaning up the bodies. Egan flew next to me, but his focus was on scouring the ground. *The easiest way to deal with the bodies is to burn them. We don't need humans stumbling upon their bodies or bones.*

Even though this was private land, the occasional human would stumble through while out on a hike. According to Cassius, it rarely happened. It was one reason they kept supernatural behavior to the hours after dark and close to home.

Attacking manticores was probably at the top of the list, but none of us had control over that.

We hung close to the trees, keeping our eyes and ears open for the bear or anyone that didn't need to see us.

One day, I hoped I could enjoy flying with the thunder. But like now, the only other time I'd flown with the thunder had been while fleeing the cave and desperate to get here. I had yet to experience a flight for enjoyment or relaxation with everyone.

"Over here!" Paul shouted from below.

I turned to the left, flying lower to look for him.

Egan flew right beside me as Draco flanked me on my left. Those two were already in protective mode, but I couldn't complain.

They hadn't hovered during the battle despite us being outnumbered.

I'd expected to find the grizzly bear but, instead, found a naked man hiding at the top of a tree.

The guy had rich, dark brown hair and a long beard that turned more chocolate at the edges. His skin was a dark olive, proof that he spent a lot of time outdoors. His eyes were milk chocolate, and that was where I stopped looking. I didn't need or want to see his dangly bits.

Draco swooped down to the tree and used his back talons to latch on to the man's arms. The guy reached up, trying to dig his fingers into Draco's scales and escape the dragon's grip.

But nothing happened.

It probably felt like a tickle to Draco.

The bear shifter must not have been around dragons before, but if that was the case, how the hell was he working with the fae dragons?

Unfortunately, when Draco flew up, I got an eyeful of the guy's family jewels. I closed my eyes and spun away. When I opened my eyes, Draco flew underneath me, coming in front. I saw the guy's entire naked ass before I could shut my eyes again. I wasn't sure which view was worse, but the backside was a whole lot hairier.

Egan flew next to me. *Well, that was easier than I expected.*

What was he thinking? The bear shifter had been in the perfect position for Draco to grab and fly off with.

He chuckled. *Probably thought he could fight the vampires off if they found him, and the wolf shifters couldn't climb up the tree. Bears are good climbers, so he probably just wanted to get off the ground.*

He could have at least brought some clothes to change into. I'd have nightmares over what I'd seen.

I'm just happy you wanted him to be clothed. Egan winked. *Maybe I can give you a better visual when we get home?*

I purred at the promise. *Maybe.*

We all hurried back to the mansion, and it wasn't long before we were landing.

Once the bear shifter was back on the ground, the back door that led to the kitchen opened, and Torak came marching out.

He shoved the bear shifter hard in the chest, and the man fell on his bare ass. The alpha heir growled, "I'm going to kill you."

CHAPTER NINETEEN

The raw rage in Torak's voice was justified. I wanted to hurt the asshole too, but we needed answers first.

The back door opened with Cassius, Ladon, and Katherine running outside.

"Don't hurt him yet," Cassius said as he touched Torak's shoulders.

"Oh my God." Katherine's eyes widened when she saw the naked bear shifter. She held up clothes and nodded to Ladon. "Thank God we brought extra clothes."

She and I were thinking similarly. I'd seen more than enough of that guy, and I didn't even know his name.

Ladon pursed his lips, making the lines etched in his face more prominent. "Everyone outside of Egan and Jade should go help the others burn the manticores' bodies. Your clothes will be here when you get back. Egan and Jade, take what is yours and shift back so we can talk."

They placed the clothes on the ground. Egan and I picked up ours, and we ran into the woods to shift into human form while the other dragons headed back to help with the dead bodies.

"Put these sweatpants on," Cassius told the bear shifter.

I heard shuffling from that area, and then a deep voice replied, "There. Who would've thought a group of supernaturals would be that uncomfortable around nudity?"

Katherine cleared her throat. "We're more conservative."

"Sounds like where I'm from." The bear shifter chuckled. "I'd think people outside of Shadow City would be more accepting. Or that's what I was told growing up."

What's Shadow City? Yet another place I hadn't heard of.

Egan put the light gray shirt on. *Never heard of it.*

"So you're from Shadow City." Cassius clicked his tongue. "Interesting."

"What's that place?" Ladon asked.

"A supernatural city that was established a long time ago," Cassius replied. "I actually know someone from there."

Shifting back to human was harder than before due to my injury, but once I was back on two legs, the pain receded again.

After I'd zipped my jeans, Egan and I rejoined the others.

Torak's clenched jaw twitched from the strain. His hands were fisted at his sides as he glared at the bear shifter, who was now covered from his waist down.

Donovan and the others were huge, but the bear shifter was bigger than them. He wasn't as large as the dragon men but was stout. His muscular chest was pronounced even under the mass of hair covering it.

I hurried over to Torak and placed a hand on his shoulder to pull his attention away from the bear. Considering the way he was acting, I feared the worst. "How's Titan?"

Please don't say dead.

"He's alive but lost his right eye." His words were thick with emotion as his chest heaved with each breath. "Ollie took a dragon to a witch he knew to see if she can help him."

"Trixie?" Egan asked, standing in front of the bear.

"Yes, that was the name." Ladon nodded. "Son, how do you want to proceed?"

"You're asking me?" Egan glanced over his shoulder and lifted a brow. "Isn't that your call?"

Ladon fidgeted. "No, it's not."

I was surprised that he was asking Egan to decide. He'd done this a few times, encouraging Egan to lead. I'd thought it was because he wanted to help transition him into the mentality of a leader, but maybe there was more to it than that. *We need to focus on the bear shifter. We can talk to your dad later.*

Egan's glowing eyes flicked to mine. *You're right.* He patted Draco's scaled arm. "Draco, shift back to human form. We've got it from here."

Hesitating, Draco hissed at the bear shifter then grabbed his clothes from the ground and headed into the woods.

The bear had grown nervous with our group surrounding him.

"Here." Katherine handed me my cell phone. "I thought you might want this."

For the first time ever, I had the urge to kiss a girl. She'd gone out of her way to get my phone so I could check on my mother, and it spoke volumes about her. "Thank you."

I typed a message out on Messenger to Mom and pressed send. I stared at the screen, wishing those three dots indicating she was responding would pop up.

My mate didn't take any time getting to the point. "Who are you working for?"

The bear shifter sneered. "Like I would tell—"

Torak punched him in the nose, and the bone cracked loudly.

"What the—" The bear shifter pinched the bridge of his nose as blood poured down his mouth and chin onto his chest.

"Answer the question or I'll punch your face again," Torak spat, his hand fisted and ready to strike.

"Look." The shirtless man raised his free hand. "I'm not here to cause problems."

I laughed. I couldn't help it. "Really? You're going to lead with that?"

Something like respect appeared in the guy's eyes. "You've got a point, but this was nothing personal."

"Nothing personal?" Egan growled. "You attacked us. How is that not personal?"

Draco stepped back into the clearing and stood protectively beside Egan, staring the bear shifter down.

My phone buzzed, and I swiped the screen. I was relieved when I saw Mom's reply.

Hey. I'm fine. Is something wrong?

If they hadn't found our location from her, then how? That unsettled me. *Mom is okay and Vera is dead. I just don't understand how it is possible.*

If I hadn't seen the muscle in Egan's neck contract, I would have thought he hadn't heard me. But he finally responded, *We'll figure out how.*

My fear was that there was a spy in the camp, but I didn't see how it was possible. Egan's thunder was at risk, and the vampires and the packs were close and loyal. The alphas would've sensed an uprising, or I hoped so.

"Look, a friend told me that a woman was looking for a bear shifter that wanted some quick cash. I'd just escaped from jail and was desperate. I took the job, thinking it wouldn't be awful." The bear shifter shrugged. "She asked me to track down the wolf pack and lead some creatures to it. That's it. Once the job was done, she'd give me cash."

He kept saying "she," so my first thought was Mindy. Was she still working with the fae dragon king since we'd kicked her ass out? "Light blonde hair, tall, with honey eyes?"

You're thinking it's Mindy too? Egan rubbed his fingers together.

"No, not at all." The bear shifter shook his head, and the blood flow slowed from his nose. "Middle-aged woman with long caramel hair, very short, and light blue eyes that appeared cold. She was all human, which shocked me."

That description sounded so familiar. "Was her name Sarah?" My voice cracked.

"Wait. Yeah." The bear shifter looked at me. "That sounds right. We met outside Indianapolis, and she said dragons were causing problems and hanging around the pack that took down Tyler. Like Tyler would mean anything to me, but she thought it was a big deal."

"Tyler?" Katherine blinked. "A human mentioned Tyler? I'm going to get Sadie and Donovan." She headed back into the mansion on a mission.

"How does a human know about Tyler?" The shock on Egan's face would have been comical at any other time. He was usually good at keeping his emotions close. *Are you sure it's your aunt?*

It sounds like it is based on the city and description. But none of this made sense. Mom was okay, and Sarah was pretty much always home. If she knew about the supernatural world and was involved in it, wouldn't I have known?

"She mentioned that Tyler contacted her once she figured out her niece was a dragon's mate. She acted like he was a big deal. She got a phone call then became a lot less chatty." The bear shifter pursed his lips. "She said some wrongs needed to be righted and needed my services. She gave me a flannel shirt and jeans that had the wolf shifters' scents and told me it should be about thirty minutes east of Darmark. I picked up the scent after a couple of days. Those wolves like to run a lot. Honestly, she's a little crazy, but I needed the money."

But if Tyler had died before I'd made it to Kortright, how had she known I was a dragon's mate. The coincidence was too much, though. And unfortunately, Mom was the only one who knew the town closest to us.

Swiping my phone, I messaged her again. **Did you tell Sarah where we are?**

Her reply was immediate. **Of course not. Did something happen?**

If I knew Sarah, she'd be monitoring Mom's conversations. I had to be careful. I didn't need to alert her to anything and put her in danger. **Nope, just miss you.** *We need to get Mom. If Sarah is involved, we can't leave Mom there.*

As soon as we're done here, we'll go, Egan promised.

Sadie and her pack joined us outside with Katherine.

"I hear Tyler is involved." Roxy's nose wrinkled. "I shouldn't be surprised that he's still causing trouble beyond the grave."

"Why don't you go inside with Titan?" Sadie said, patting Torak's arm. "He was asking for you a minute ago."

Torak glared at the bear shifter for a few long seconds before responding, "Fine, but if you guys need me, just yell." He stalked toward the mansion.

"It looks like we missed some of the fun." Donovan gestured to the bear shifter's nose. "Has he said anything?"

We informed him of everything we'd learned.

"What do we do with him now?" Axel asked, gesturing to the bear shifter.

"Take him to the basement." Cassius gestured to the side of the house where there were stairs. "He won't be able to get out on his own. It's vampire-proof for when we find people who were just changed. I'll call the guy I know in Shadow City."

"Sounds good to me." Draco grabbed the bear shifter's arm and dragged him to the stairs.

Donovan ran ahead.

Sadie tensed, her eyes distant. "Rook and Naida are on their way. I informed them about the attack."

Two figures flickered into view, and the bodies took shape to reveal Rook and Naida. They were dressed in white, and Rook had a crown on his head.

"When you said they were on their way, you weren't kidding." Roxy sighed. "I still can't get used to that."

Sadie chuckled. "That's why I warned you. The few times I didn't, you almost peed yourself."

"Just because I shrieked doesn't mean I dribbled." Roxy lifted her chin. "I have a steel bladder."

"Sure you do, babe." Axel wrapped an arm around her waist.

"Every time I join you all, there is always interesting commentary going on." Naida rolled her eyes. "Sometimes a 'hey' and general pleasantries are completely underrated."

Sadie's brows furrowed. "What's with the crown?"

Rook pulled at the collar of his white robe. "Things were getting out of control, so Murray and I agreed that was the best thing."

"But you didn't want that?" Sadie sounded upset.

"Don't worry, it's for appearances only." Rook rubbed his temples. "I'm the face of the monarchy, but Murray is handling all the affairs like normal. Something had to change to keep the peace in the fae realm, but things are still a little unsettled."

Roxy crossed her arms. "Meaning manticores coming to Earth to attack us."

"Yes, that's exactly what I mean." Rook rolled his shoulders. He obviously didn't like the royal attire. "The fae dragon *king* used Fae's divide to his advantage. He leveraged the location of the true dragon royal family on Earth to make promises to some of the more unfavorable creatures of our realm for their assistance."

"How many of these creatures are we talking about?" Cassius asked. "And do we have any idea of what we need to do?"

Donovan and Draco came back around the house and rejoined the circle.

"He's getting these creatures to attack us while he stays safe back in his realm." Assholes like him were the worst. He wanted whatever power he thought was rightfully his but wasn't willing to fight. "We need to make him come here. But what could make him want to leave to fight us himself?"

"The problem is we have no clue since we've been here for so long." Egan rubbed a hand down his face. "The dragons in Fae are essentially immortal. They live for thousands of years."

"That's true. The one in charge is the original brother who angered the fae gods and caused the split." Rook paced in front of me. "But he's getting older, and he's desperate to gain power. He only has one heir, so that should play to our advantage."

"Angered the fae gods?" I felt like I was always asking questions.

"Yes, they mind their own business, but the younger dragon brother tried starting a war like he's doing now, only in the fae realm. The fae gods punished them by taking away their fated mates, slowing their reproduction. When the older brother saw the destruction his brother was causing, he decided to leave, and the fae gods lifted the curse since they'd proved they cared more about Fae than the dragons that were staying behind." Naida's eyes turned a lighter teal as she told her realm's history. "They can only reproduce by the power of the land. Thus, the fae dragon king only has one heir."

"Which means the heir is our leverage." Egan inhaled sharply. "But we can't go into Fae."

"We need an ally willing to get them for us." Draco looked at Egan then Ladon.

"Is there someone you know who can help us?" Sadie grimaced. "I hate to ask, but Titan has lost an eye because of these attacks, and several pack members were eaten. We're all at risk."

"You have the strongest ally in Fae." Rook stepped to his daughter and brushed his fingers along her arm. "Your father, who so happens to be king."

"Look, I'm all about protecting Sadie and everyone here, but can we risk that?" Naida chewed on her bottom lip.

Grinning, Rook lifted a hand. "What is the one rule every creature in Fae must follow or suffer the consequences? The one law that has saved Sadie from our own kind."

"No one can attack a member of the royal family," Sadie answered.

"Exactly. We'll send guards to capture the dragon princess and bring her here," Rook said and hugged Sadie.

"Maybe we should write a note, making it clear it was us." We needed to make sure the asshole came here. "Add something to make his blood boil."

"I like the way you think." Draco nodded with approval.

"Of course, my guards will be here to help you fight too," Rook said confidently. "They will learn that the fae king backs the true dragon king and queen."

"I hate to do this, but Liz may be in danger." Egan took my hand and stared at the others. "We've got to go get her before Sarah realizes the attack didn't work."

Draco marched over to us. "I'm going with you two."

"Cassius, do you mind if we take your van?" Sadie asked the older vampire. "Donovan and I need to go too. A few extra hands would be helpful since we don't know what we're walking into."

"The keys are on the holder. Take what you need."

"Be careful," Ladon said as he hugged Egan then me. "I'll go write the note. You all go on so you can get back as soon as possible."

My phone buzzed again, and I glanced down to see a message from Mom.

Call me when you can.

CHAPTER TWENTY

We were about an hour away from Indianapolis, and my leg wouldn't quit bouncing. My back was significantly better since I'd sat pretty still, so that was a huge benefit.

The sun was setting, and I felt almost suffocated inside the van. I glanced at my phone again, but nothing else had come through from Mom.

As Egan drove, he reached over the center console, placing his warm hand on my thigh. He linked with me. *Everything is going to be okay.*

You can't know that, I snapped and immediately regretted it. He didn't deserve that. He was trying to comfort me. But it unsettled me that I hadn't heard back from Mom, especially after what we'd learned. Under normal circumstances, she'd have replied within an hour, so for four hours to have gone by made my skin crawl.

I sighed. *I'm sorry. I'm being an ass. It's just my aunt has known about us for God knows how long, and she orchestrated an attack meant to kill us. What if she hurt Mom?* I'd tried calling Mom when we'd left, like she asked, but it had gone straight to voicemail. She'd messaged shortly after saying she'd call me right back, but that hadn't happened.

Draco snored quietly in the back of the van. The faster Egan drove, the deeper he fell asleep. I had to admit, I was slightly jealous. If I could have knocked my ass out, everyone would have appreciated it. My nerves were on edge, and everyone around me felt it.

When the huge dragon had shoved himself past the middle row and into the back of the van, I'd thought it was rather odd. But he'd muttered something about needing rest before another attack and promptly lain down. He'd fallen asleep before we'd even pulled out of the mansion's driveway. I'd never been around someone who could fall asleep that quickly before.

"He better be glad Roxy didn't join us." Sadie sat in the middle row, right behind Egan, and she glanced at me as she gestured to Draco. "Because he'd never hear the end about his snoring."

That was an odd thing to say. "But he's not snoring that loud."

Donovan leaned over from behind me so I could see him. "Have you met Roxy? That girl lives on exaggerating truths and sarcasm. She'd make the rest of the world believe that Draco sounded like a foghorn on a peaceful night."

"Or a jet taking off in the middle of a forest," Egan suggested.

Both analogies sounded like something she would say.

"True, but she keeps things interesting," Sadie said in defense of her best friend. "And she's as loyal and steadfast as they come."

"I'm not arguing that." Donovan lifted a hand in surrender. "You know I love her like a sister, but facts are facts."

"Point taken. I'm surprised she didn't demand to come with us." Egan glanced in the rearview mirror. "She normally goes wherever Sadie is and pitches a fit when she doesn't get her way."

"I asked her to stay back with Torak." Sadie tapped her fingers on her leg. "Someone needed to relieve some of the tension, and we needed them there for when Ollie and that witch came back."

Roxy thought the world of Sadie, so her staying behind made sense. If she knew that staying with Titan would make things easier on her and the rest of the pack, she wouldn't have thought twice about it.

"Don't forget the bear shifter in the basement." Donovan shook his head. "And here I thought all of our enemies and fighting were behind us and we could live a semi-normal life."

Egan frowned. "I'm sorry. This is my fault. This is all happening because of the dragons. I hate that I dragged you into it."

"Hey, that's not what I was getting at, man." Donovan's shoulders dropped. "Of course we're going to fight alongside you. You're family, and it's the right thing to do."

That statement resonated with me. They thought of each other as family, and more importantly, I did too. Sadie and the others were a pack, but if they needed us, I'd drop everything to be there for them. That was what families did. I liked to think I'd been so slow to come to this realization because I didn't grow up in a very supportive one.

In high school, I'd read that family could be formed beyond blood, and I thought the sentiment had been stupid ... until now.

My phone buzzed in my hands with a message from Mom.

With shaky hands, I opened Messenger.

I need you. Help.

I blinked at the message, hoping the words would somehow morph into something a lot less dire. But there they sat, and with each second, the words grew larger and more desperate.

Egan leaned over and read the message. "We're only a few minutes away." He pressed the gas, speeding past vehicles.

"What's going on?" Sadie asked tensely.

"I'm not sure." I forced my lungs to expand. Passing out wouldn't help anyone. "Mom just texted me that she needs our help. You'd think she'd tell me what kind of help she needs." Those words could mean so many different scenarios, but they all led back to the same thing—Sarah.

I chewed on my bottom lip as I looked out my window. "Maybe I should shift and fly over there." I already knew what they would say, but I was desperate to get to Mom.

"Babe, we're getting there as fast as we can, but the sun isn't completely down, and this is a busy city." Regret flowed through our bond. "And that neighborhood isn't exactly remote. We can't risk revealing the supernatural world to humans. It would only put a bigger target on our backs. Besides, we need to be careful that we aren't walking into a trap."

Every word he said was true, but they still irritated me. The thought of something happening to Mom plagued me. I couldn't live with myself if she died when I could've gotten there faster to help her. But if I acted rashly, I would put Egan and the others in danger, and I wasn't willing to live with that burden either. I was damned if I did and damned if I didn't.

"Why don't you try calling her?" Sadie suggested. "If she answers, you could get an idea of what's going on there."

What did I have to lose? At the worst, she wouldn't answer, and my situation wouldn't change.

What the hell.

I pressed the call button, and the line rang. After the fourth ring, my finger hovered over the red button, ready to disconnect, but right before I was about to press it, the other end picked up.

"Hello?" Mom sounded scared. "Jade?"

"Is everything okay?" There was no time for pleasantries.

A soft sob filled the line. "I ... I can't find Sarah."

"What do you mean you can't find Sarah?" I tried to remain calm, but if Sarah had disappeared, it wouldn't be a bad thing. Maybe she'd run away with some supernaturals, leaving Mom behind. In a way, that would be a blessing. Mom could live without the supernatural influence and Sarah's controlling ways.

"She was acting strange all morning. Almost cagey." A door shut on the other end. "And then she got a phone call about an hour ago and started freaking out. She told me to pack some things. Then about ten minutes ago, someone knocked on our door. She yelled at me to go to my room and stay put. I heard her let them in, and they headed out the back, near the window of my room."

I wondered if the phone call had been about the attack near the mansion. Could someone already know we hadn't gotten hurt? Several manticores had flown away. They must have returned to Fae. "Do you hear them talking?"

"No, it's been silent for the past few minutes. I heard Sarah shriek, but that was it." The floor creaked under her weight. "I saw the guy run away. He had oddly colorful hair, but Sarah wasn't with him."

"Oddly colorful hair?" The only creatures that looked human and had colorful hair were fae.

"It was a vibrant yellow-green color like nothing I'd ever seen before." Mom inhaled shakily. "The color seemed to glow, and so did his eyes. They were the same color."

"Fae," Sadie whispered with disgust. "A fae is helping them. I'm going to tell Dad."

Tell Liz to stay where she is. Egan linked. *She doesn't need to stumble on something and get hurt. We're close by.*

For once, I welcomed his bossy side. I was so torn about what to say or do that my brain felt like it was spinning in place. "Stay put. We're less than ten minutes out."

She exhaled in relief. "You're that close?"

"We knew something was off this morning, but I'll explain more later." I needed her to remain calm. "Just hang tight."

"Okay. Call me when you pull into the neighborhood?"

"Will do." I hung up my phone right as Sadie's rang.

"Who's that?" Donovan asked.

Sadie answered the phone and glanced at her mate. "Torak, is everything okay?"

With my supernatural hearing, I could make out every word on the other end.

"No. Something happened at Liz's house." Torak sounded more like himself. "The pack alpha has been trying to call for the last thirty minutes, but Dad dropped his phone when the ... uh ... incident occurred. A dragon heard the phone ring and brought it here."

That must have been when the fae had shown up.

"What did they say?" Sadie asked.

Torak cleared his throat. "He killed two of the three wolves standing guard. The third one barely got away and linked his alpha to inform him of what had gone down. There are more shifters at the house now for backup, but it looks like the fae is gone. They're going to approach the house."

"No, tell them to wait until we get there." The last thing we needed was more supernaturals showing up and Mom thinking she was under attack. "Tell them we're five minutes out and to wait."

"Okay. Call us when you're heading back. I'll call the alpha now." Torak hung up.

Egan got off the interstate, and five minutes later, we were pulling into the neighborhood. We coasted down the street, hoping not to alarm any neighbors more than they might already be.

I typed Mom a message letting her know we would be there in a minute. I didn't want to risk calling her.

"Draco." Sadie turned toward him. "We're here, and something has gone down."

"Yeah, I heard." Draco sat up and yawned. "You all were jabbering, so I listened while resting my eyes."

The less we had to tell him, the more efficient we'd be.

"It's the house on the right at the end of the street." I pointed at the two-story white house. There was a wooden porch just large enough to protect you from the rain if you were standing right at the door. There were two double-pane windows on both sides of the front door.

Egan pulled into the driveway, and I leaped out of the car.

A few men ran over from a few houses down. Their olive complexion and thick, musky smell informed me they were wolf shifters.

Egan caught up to me and looked at the men. "Did you notice anything alarming?"

"There's nothing around," the older one said as he approached.

His gaze flicked to a few neighbors down the road. "But you need to go check out the back." He avoided our gazes. "It's bad."

Yeah, I was done waiting. I raced to the front door and turned the doorknob, expecting it to be locked, but the door flung open.

"Mom!" I rushed into the foyer that led to the living room and to the staircase.

"Jade!" Mom cried, and her footsteps pounded from her room toward us. "I ... I think something is wrong. A few minutes ago, I saw three strange men in our backyard."

Ugh, Torak must not have caught the shifters in time, but at least they weren't in animal form. "No, they were the wolf shifters that have been keeping an eye on you two." I was being nice by including Sarah in that, but in a way, it was true. If Sarah got hurt, that would put Mom at risk. And unfortunately, that had happened.

Her mouth dropped, and her head tilted. "They were still keeping an eye on us?"

The urge to smack her upside the head almost overwhelmed me.

Almost.

Egan stepped up beside me, so huge his body brushed against my side. "Of course. They were going to watch you until the whole dragon thing had settled."

"I ..." Mom seemed flabbergasted. "I didn't realize."

"It's fine." She needed to focus. "What happened?"

"I told you everything on the phone." Mom gestured to the back door. "I can't see her out there, but she hasn't come back inside."

From what the guys had said, I figured Sarah had been injured in the backyard. There was no telling what we would find. "Okay, stay right here. We'll go check it out."

"I'm going with you." Mom crossed her arms, lifting her chin. "She's my sister, and I need to go look for her with you."

Out of all of the times for her to decide to be strong, it would be now, when I had no clue what we might find outside. I'd opened my mouth to tell her no when Egan linked with me.

Babe, let her be part of this. She wants to be, and she's an adult. She at least waited on us.

He was right. Next time, she might not be willing. "Fine, but stay behind us."

She nodded. "Okay."

Egan took the lead, heading where Mom had gestured. A sweet floral smell trailed in the same direction.

We walked through the small mint living room, where a single brown leather couch sat against the wall, and toward the flaky white door. Egan opened it, and the stench of rust overwhelmed me.

My stomach hadn't been prepared to smell blood again today. It roiled as I found Sarah. She lay close to the side of the house, next to the white plastic chairs. Blood pooled under her body, and her caramel hair was fanned around her head.

If it hadn't been for the faint heartbeat and the way her cruel eyes found me, I would have thought she was dead. One hand clutched her stomach, but she had enough energy to lift her other one, despite it shaking. She said, her voice deep and filled with disgust, "You."

CHAPTER TWENTY-ONE

If I'd ever questioned how my aunt felt about me, I no longer did. Her face twisted, and she sneered. Pure hatred filled her ice-cold eyes, turning them a shade darker to sky blue. "You've ruined everything."

Mom took a hurried step toward the door to follow me out, but Sadie walked out the back door and told her, "Wait here for a second. The guys are checking the area one more time for threats."

"But ..." Mom hesitated.

"Just a few minutes," Donovan reassured her, stepping up next to Sadie. "You are human, so we need to make sure we don't have to protect both you and your sister, especially while she's injured."

The smell of their lie hit me hard, but I appreciated what they were doing. I didn't want Mom to see Sarah like this.

After a long sigh, Mom said, "Okay, but once it's clear, I need to get out there."

Not needing to worry about Mom, I dropped to my knees next to Sarah. "Where are you hurt?"

She jerked away. "You're the reason this happened."

Somehow, that stung even more. She was bleeding out, yet she was still so revolted by me that she didn't want me to touch her.

Egan growled as he placed a hand on my shoulder and glared at her. "How is she to blame?"

The gate to the privacy fence opened on the other side of the house, and Draco stepped around the house, his eyes scanning the scene, stopping on Sarah for a few seconds before he glanced at Egan. Draco shook his head slightly.

The message was clear.

Sarah wouldn't survive.

"Because she was supposed to be my ticket to power." Her voice grew louder until she was almost yelling. She hadn't noticed the other man who had entered the yard since she was focused on me. "I sacrificed everything for you."

My hurt morphed into anger. She'd sacrificed for me? She had to be living in an alternate reality.

I refused to let that be the way her story ended even if only in her mind. I jerked to my feet, enraged. "By controlling my every move after Dad died? Or beating me when Mom wasn't looking?"

"Why do you think your dad died in the first place?" she shouted, blood mixing with her spit. "When your mom told me about the strange people you met on the beach and how the little boy acted around you, I knew exactly what they were and what you were to them."

The most alarming fact was how long she'd known about Egan and me. "How the hell could you've known that?"

"Because I've known about the supernatural world since I was a little girl."

Her words stunned me. Obviously, she knew about the supernatural world, but for that long? That couldn't be possible. Humans were forbidden to know.

She chuckled. "Your expression is almost comical. You're so clueless and gullible, just like your mother. Thankfully, you took after her instead of your dad." Her face hardened, the smile morphing into a scowl. "That's why he had to go."

She was throwing out so much information that my brain protested. My natural inclination was to go numb, but I couldn't afford to do that. This was our only chance to get whatever information we could out of my aunt, so I couldn't shut down.

My dragon surged forward, easing some of my angst to help me focus. I didn't know which piece of information to latch on to. Where did I even begin? I wasn't sure how much time she had left, so I needed answers to the most important questions first, but hell, I couldn't tell which one I should address first.

"No." Mom stumbled outside and stood beside me. Her body shook, and her face was lined with confusion. "You wouldn't hurt Jeff. You wouldn't do that to me."

"Mom, why don't you go back inside?" She didn't need to hear this. I'd rather she mourn the death of a sister than struggle with the fact she hadn't known Sarah at all. "Go wait in the van for us. We won't be long."

"But ..." Mom glanced at me and then Sarah.

"Yes, be a good little robot, and do what you're told," Sarah mocked. "Lord forbid you have to listen or deal with anything unpleasant."

"I ... I can't leave." She needed answers like me. "Not until she tells me she didn't hurt Jeff." She held out a shaky hand and begged, "Please, just tell me that."

Sarah's hands were slick from the blood pouring out of her wound. "I had to kill him."

Mom gasped and wrapped her arms around her body. "You caused the car wreck?"

"I planned it." Sarah shrugged then winced from the pain. "When you called me on the way to the airport after you left the beach, and told me about the strange occurrence, I had time to set things up for him to die the next morning on his way to work when he planned to turn in his notice."

Draco stepped closer but stayed several feet back. He was watching the scene, keeping his focus on Sarah like she was still a threat.

But how could she be with the state she was in? The only potent thing she still harbored was raw hate for herself and those around her.

"You killed her husband and my mate's father because of me?" Egan rasped. "Why was finding a dragon that important?"

"I stalked Tyler and pinpointed him to a city. I ran into him at a restaurant that a local pack owned, and he was impressed with my ambition even though I was human. And he promised me power." Her eyes lightened with a wistful glow. "Promised that I would rule his kingdom next to him. Of course, he'd have to turn me into a wolf once I proved my worth by locating a dragon."

She had lost her mind. And maybe I had, too. My body felt numb to touch and emotion. "How did you even find out about this world?"

"I stumbled upon it one night years ago." She looked at the darkening sky. "I watched a vampire drain the life out of someone. It was amazing to watch. They held no remorse and enjoyed the act so much. I wanted to feel something like that. To dominate others and control their destiny."

This woman was so much worse than I'd realized. There was no telling what kind of monstrous acts she had committed to get to this point. Bad enough for the fae dragon king to want her dead after failing.

"So, I began researching and stumbled upon all these websites in my twenties." She coughed several times. Sweat beaded on her paling skin.

She knew she was dying. That was why she was telling us all of this. She wanted someone to know her story, her fall from grace, even though she might not see it that way.

For so long, I'd wanted to know why she acted the way she did, but now I was scared for her to continue. Yet, if we left before I heard it all, I would regret it.

I needed to hear her reasoning for everything she'd done.

It was strange watching Mom stand over Sarah as she bled out. Mom's chest heaved, the only sign she was struggling as she waited to hear everything just like me.

"Oh, God," Sarah groaned and wiped her mouth with her arm. Blood streaked across her skin. "This hurts so damn bad."

If she thought she'd get sympathy, she was clearly mistaken.

Egan cleared his throat. "So you learned about Tyler, then? I'm assuming you stumbled upon articles about him?"

"Yes, his family was revered." Sarah grinned. "And most importantly, feared. But after our first run-in, he refused to meet with me again. That was until my dear sister called to tell me about these tall, beautiful people who sounded like they were from another world. Liz babbled on about your family's mannerisms, but the biggest clues that narrowed my suspicions were the glowing eyes and a child so strong he could easily pull a girl from the water. Add in the facts that he catered to her and talked about how amazing it was to fly. I put it all together."

"I forgot all about that." Mom blew out a breath as she looked at Egan. "But you did. Jeff stayed close while you two were playing in the sand where the waves had crashed over you. You were telling Jade all about visiting another group of your kind that you'd never met before and how flying was amazing. I always thought you meant family and that you'd been in an airplane. But I remember it made Jeff so uncomfortable he wanted to go." Mom shuddered. "Your parents tried to explain that there was a storm while you were on the plane, but it didn't really make sense."

Egan ran a hand through his hair, and his shoulders deflated. "Dad jerked me aside and told me about the human world and how you would be at risk for knowing anything about us. He explained there was no way to protect you and warned me to be more cautious. He hadn't expected that I'd click with a human, so they hadn't considered reminding me, but the damage was done."

Remorse slammed into me through our bond as Egan linked with me. *I caused all this. I'd recently shifted and was so thrilled with my first flight and meeting others of my race that I didn't even think about not sharing it with you that day. But I was careless, and you've suffered and lost so much because of it.*

You did not cause this. My anger spread through my body, making my blood boil. Sarah would not make us doubt ourselves or manipulate us any longer. I was so damn tired of it. My dragon brushed against my mind, lending me some of her strength. *This was all Sarah's fault. Her choices. Her decisions. You were a child and did nothing wrong.*

I clenched my hands as I stood to look down my nose at her. How dare she try to make anyone feel accountable for her actions. "You used that to get Tyler to take you seriously and promise you the world. But how does the fae dragon king come into this?" That was the piece I was missing.

Sarah took in a ragged breath, her skin turning white. "Tyler was working with him. That's how he captured the fae king heir that he was holding hostage. Tyler's daughter—" Sarah paused and held a shaky finger at Sadie. "—failed him by not securing the dragon. Then the dragon helped take him down. But I had something Tyler didn't and was able to leverage it upon his death." She smiled. "I had you—the very weapon to take down a dragon and force them to disclose the location of the royal family. Little did I know you were mated to the prince himself." Malice dripped from her words. "You. Like you deserve to be with someone like that. You're too weak and pathetic."

A low growl rattled Egan's chest, but I touched his arm and said, *I need to stand up to her. I have to do this for myself.*

Okay, but if she tries anything, I'll kill her. His eyes glowed liquid gold with promise.

He always had my back, and it gave me the strength to face my demon in the face. Straightening my shoulders, I lifted a brow and scoffed, "Yet I'm not the one who's on the ground, bleeding to death.

In fact, my mate, my friends, and I kicked the manticores' asses, which is probably why you're here dying."

She laughed, her teeth tinged with blood. Crimson leaked from the corners of her mouth. "Maybe I underestimated you, but it doesn't matter now. There's no way you'll survive. They all know where you are, and they won't stop until you're dead. I'll die peacefully knowing that."

Mom screamed and kicked Sarah in the jaw. My aunt's head jerked back from the force then flopped to the side.

"You killed him and hurt my daughter repeatedly," Mom screeched and kicked Sarah in the side. My aunt curled into the fetal position and groaned with the intense pain.

We have to stop Liz before she does something she'll regret. Egan stepped in front of me and grabbed Mom by the waist. He pulled her away from Sarah, and Mom fought against him, trying to attack her dying sister.

"I trusted you!" Mom screamed as tears rolled down her cheeks, contrasting with her red face. "And you did everything possible to hurt me and my family." Mom lurched desperately against Egan's hold again to get back to her. "How could you!"

I almost wanted to tell Egan to let her go, but I couldn't let Mom live with the regret.

"Jade," Sadie said gently as she stepped behind me. She placed a hand on my arm, diverting my attention to her. "Egan needs help calming your mother down."

That snapped me out of my shock, and I shook my head as the gravity of the situation crashed over me like torrential waves. Thank God my mate had stepped in because, if he hadn't, Mom would've finished the job of killing Sarah. He was right; she wouldn't have been able to live with herself once her sense of betrayal had simmered down.

"She's not worth it." In reality, I wanted my aunt to die slowly and painfully. Killing her quickly was too merciful for everything she'd inflicted on the world. I wasn't sure what kind of person that made me, but I'd examine it on the ride back to the mansion.

Mom continued her attempt to break free to attack Sarah.

She must not have heard me. She was only focused on hurting her sister. "Mom," I said loudly and pivoted to block Sarah from her view. "You need to calm down. This is what she wants."

"What?" Mom blinked and inhaled sharply. "She wants this? Why?"

"Don't you see?" I cupped her cheeks while keeping my voice calm. "She thrives on anger and pain. She wants to hurt us. Don't let her win."

Mom's bottom lip quivered, and she took faint breaths through her mouth. "You're right." She ran her fingers through her dark hair. "She's always been like this. Why didn't I see it before? You tried to tell me."

"Because you wanted to see the good in your sister." There was nothing wrong with that. In a way, I wished I could be more like Mom. Maybe I could be after all this shit was behind me. I was so tired of thinking the worst of people. Egan and his friends and family had taught me that not everyone out there was bad. In fact, most of them were good. "You need to tell her goodbye and head to the car. Don't do something you'll regret."

Realization flashed in her eyes. "She's going to die."

I nodded, not strong enough to say the words out loud.

"Okay." Mom looked over her shoulder at Egan. "You can release me. I'm good now."

Egan arched an eyebrow. *Should I let her go?*

Yeah, I guess we should give her that. It warmed my heart that he was allowing me to make this decision. He trusted me. *But stay close in case this is a bad call.*

He released his hold on her, and Mom stepped around me to stare at her sister. "I grew up idolizing you and didn't listen to Jeff or Jade when they warned me about you. I loved you and stood up for you. But I'm done lying to myself. I only hope I can earn Jade's forgiveness and that you burn in Hell." Mom spun on her heel and marched into the house. Egan and I watched her leave.

"Do you think I'm going out like this?" Sarah yelled. "If I'm going to Hell, I'm taking Jade with me."

"Watch out!" Draco yelled.

CHAPTER TWENTY-TWO

I spun around as Sarah lunged at me with a small knife in her hand. The faint glow of the sun glinted off the tip, but that wasn't what concerned me. Sarah's face set with grim determination as she used the last of her strength to strike at me.

People claimed that near-death experiences slowed time down, but that wasn't my truth. Everything accelerated like a fast-forwarding movie. All the actions blurred and didn't make any sense.

She aimed right at my heart, and Egan had been focused on Mom like I'd been, so he couldn't react in time.

My dragon took control, and I willingly submitted. Instead of shifting, I caught her wrist inches from my chest, ignoring my back screaming from my injury, and kicked her in her stomach. She released her hold and crumpled. The knife plopped to the ground.

She landed hard on the grass as blood gushed from the wound I'd made worse.

Draco stopped a few feet from me with a deep scowl. His nostrils flared in anger, but I wasn't sure why.

Hands pulled me in the opposite direction. Egan held me tight and rubbed my back where the manticore tail had wounded me. *I thought she was going to hurt you, and neither Draco nor I could get to you in time.*

Hey, it's fine. I kissed his cheek and stepped from his arms. *You have to remember I do have some training and a dragon that can come to my aid.*

He sighed. *You're right, but that doesn't make seeing you in danger any easier.*

I couldn't disagree there, but I had a sorry aunt to contend with.

She rolled her head slowly toward me. Her skin was almost white, and her heartbeat was very faint. "You won't win."

"Maybe." Who really knew? We had a lot to overcome to even get the fae dragon king to come here. "But you won't be the one to kill me. You never became powerful, and you never dominated me. You were just a pawn. I believe that makes you the dense and stupid one."

"I—" She coughed, blood pouring out of her mouth and down her cheeks. "—was not."

I squatted next to her, but for once, I didn't feel anger. I felt pity. Her entire life, she'd hated herself and spewed it everywhere. "If Tyler had bitten you, you would've died." I was being cruel, but maybe she'd finally see things for the way they were. "Over ninety-nine percent of people don't survive a bite, and the one percent who do have severe disabilities. You were never going to be queen or powerful. You got played."

Her eyes widened as the realization settled over her. Something like regret reflected back at me. She blinked as her breathing slowed. "Tell Liz ..." Her heart sputtered, and she sucked in one last breath. "Sorry."

Glassiness set in her eyes, and her body stopped moving even with her blood still pooling underneath her. Sarah had died, and it infuriated me that she'd used her last bit of strength to talk about Mom. Obviously, a piece of her had cared about her sister, but her greed and hunger for power had won until her last breath.

A heaviness weighed on me that I didn't understand. I'd hoped to feel relief. "We need to call 911."

A wolf shifter stepped from the house and asked, "Do we really want to bring that kind of attention here?"

"This is a neighborhood. If we don't, it'll bring more attention."

For some reason, my feet were glued in place. I couldn't look away from Sarah.

Donovan joined us on the back porch. "She's right. I was human long enough to know that if someone finds her dead out here with no call in, reporters will dig even deeper."

"Are you three okay handling it so we can get back to the others?" Egan asked. He took my hand, pulling me toward him and away from my aunt. "There's a lot going on back at the pack house."

"Yeah, go." The shifter pulled out his phone. "We can handle it. Torak mentioned that Titan lost an eye in a fae attack."

"We appreciate everything you did." Donovan patted the shifter on the arm. "If you ever need anything, you know how to get a hold of us."

"We'll take you up on that." The shifter glanced at me. "It's best she gets out of here. Sadie took the other lady out to the van."

Egan stepped toward the door, but I stopped him. I faced the shifter, my voice thick with emotion as I said, "Thank you for protecting my mother."

He averted his gaze. "I'm sorry we couldn't do more."

"You did more than enough." They didn't have to keep an eye on my family. "You lost two of your own. Thank you."

The guy smiled. "Just know when we call in the favor, it'll be to both of you, not just Titan."

Egan bowed his head. "And we'll gladly return the favor."

Donovan, Egan, and I entered the house with Draco on our tail. I could hear the shifter calling in the accident as we walked out the door.

The other two shifters were out front, keeping watch. They'd propped themselves on the side of the house, appearing casual to any passing humans. But with the help of my dragon, I noticed their jaws clenching and the way their eyes scanned the area for threats.

Mom paced in front of the van, wringing her hands together. Her hair fell limply over her shoulder as she swayed with each step.

Sadie turned toward us, her mouth pressed into a line. A stark contrast to her normal friendly demeanor. "Are you ready?"

The question sounded innocent, but the real question was whether Sarah had died yet. Everyone knew it, even Mom because she stopped in her tracks and stared at me.

"Yes, it's time to go." There was no time to sugarcoat things for her. Mom needed to stand on her own two feet. She had no one else to rely on, especially if she didn't want to stay in our supernatural world. I met her gaze. "Where should we take you?"

Her eyes were bloodshot from all the crying, and she inhaled another shaky breath. "Can I stay with you for a few days?"

"Of course you can." Sadie smiled. "You can stay with Mom and Titan like before since you probably don't want to stay with us at the mansion."

"Sounds good." Mom nodded and opened the passenger back door to get into the van.

Egan asked, "Do you want to grab some things before we go?"

I already knew her answer.

She paused. "Actually, I do." She ran back to the house.

Everything told me to follow her, but I couldn't move. I didn't want to go back inside again. That chapter of my life had been pure hell, and this incident with Sarah had solidified that I'd never step foot inside again.

"I'll go with her." Egan kissed my cheek and went after Mom.

Thank you. That man proved over and over he'd do anything for me. I wasn't sure how I'd gotten so damn lucky.

He looked over his shoulder at me, his eyes smoldering. *Of course. I love you.*

"Hey, are you okay?" Sadie winced. "Well, obviously not, but can I do anything for you?"

"You and Donovan being here is more than enough. And thank

you for taking Mom out here. I'm so glad she didn't see her sister like that." Sarah's pale, bloody face was seared into my memory.

Draco popped his knuckles. "Jade, I'm so sorry."

"What?" I faced him, completely confused by his comment. "Why?"

"I didn't protect you back there." His words were strained. "If you hadn't reacted the way you did, you'd be dead, and it was all my fault."

"You tried to get to me." I'd always known that Draco took his guarding job seriously, but he was putting way too much pressure on himself. "Egan couldn't even get to me."

"Egan shouldn't have been in the position to try." Draco's hands fisted at his sides. "That's the whole point. I failed you both."

"No, you didn't." He didn't need to beat himself up. "You were standing guard. You expected the threat to come from either inside or around the house. We all thought that. No one expected a dying woman to use her last bit of energy to try to kill me." Actually, now that I'd said that out loud, that didn't surprise me. Sarah had been certifiably insane. "There is no way to predict every possible situation. And part of my and Egan's responsibility is to not be completely helpless either. You can't protect all four members of the royal family at one time."

He tilted his head and scratched the back of his neck. "I never really thought of it that way."

"Jade has a way of making us think about things differently." Sadie bumped her shoulder into mine. "Especially with Egan."

Faint sirens sounded. The ambulance was on its way.

How much longer? The ambulance will be here soon. I hated to rush Mom, but we were running out of time.

The front door opened, answering the question for me.

Mom held a book close to her chest, and Egan followed behind her.

"Sorry, I had to get my journal." She climbed into the back of the van and sat, clutching the book as if her life depended on it.

Draco moved to climb in after her, but I stopped him. The poor guy was almost too big to sit back there alone, never mind with Mom. "Sit up front. I'll take my turn in the back."

"But you don't—" He stopped. "You want to be there for her. Okay."

Not wasting any time since the ambulance was growing closer, I climbed in the back as everyone else settled in. Egan pulled out of the driveway, and we made our way out of the neighborhood. The ambulance passed us as we turned onto the main road.

The van remained silent. So much had happened that no one had a clue what to say.

After thirty minutes, Mom lowered the book to her lap. She turned it to the side where there was a clasp, but it was broken. "Dammit," she said loudly. "I should've known." She dropped the book on the floorboard.

Her random act of anger startled me. I wasn't sure what had triggered it. "What's wrong?"

Mom turned to me. "Did something happen to bring you here?"

I couldn't lie to her, but something had caused her to ask. "We were attacked earlier. I was worried they might have gotten to you."

Mom sighed with defeat. "All this time, I stood up for her and turned a blind eye to everything wrong she did. I let her come between your father and me. That was why he was moving us away. Then when he was gone, I let her come between us. And all she did was hurt and betray me and those I love the most, over and over again."

What happened? Egan asked with concern. *She randomly got upset.*

I have no clue. It's like her journal pissed her off. The final piece of the puzzle clicked into place. *She realized the lock is broken.*

Sarah must have done that. "Mom, when did you start keeping a journal?"

"Right after I got back." Mom laughed, but it was devoid of humor. "She told me I should talk to a therapist after I was kidnapped and refused to talk to her. The therapist suggested I write down my thoughts and feelings about my experiences in a journal. She broke into it, and that's how she found you."

"You put our location in your journal?" I tried to keep the surprise from my voice. Mom had been manipulated; it wasn't her fault. A licensed professional had told her to do it, but I wanted to shake her. She should've known better.

"I only referenced Darmark." She placed a hand on my thigh. "When you drove me home, I realized you were staying thirty minutes east of there. Your father and I visited the waterfall on the outskirts of the town on our honeymoon."

"That was why she hired the bear shifter." Sadie groaned. "Because she knew our general location, and bears have the best sense of smell."

"I'm so sorry." Mom's shoulders shook. "I didn't know. Did anyone get hurt because of me?"

"There's no reason for you to apologize." Egan focused on the rearview mirror as his hands tightened on the steering wheel, his knuckles white. "You didn't do a damn thing wrong."

"Dude, Egan just cussed," Donovan whispered to Sadie like we wouldn't hear. "I've never heard him cuss before."

He'd said it loud enough that even Mom could have heard.

Sadie chuckled. "I know."

This was only the second time I'd heard him cuss too, but I loved that about him. "Like Egan said, you aren't held responsible. You had no idea it would happen."

"But I should've." Mom sniffed and turned away from me. "That's the thing."

I'd moved to slide across the bench to her when Egan linked with me. *Give her a second. You're a lot like her, and she needs time to process it first.*

And that proved he understood me better than I did myself.

The rest of the ride home had been in complete silence. It was around one in the morning when we rolled up to the mansion. All of the lights were on. Everyone was awake and probably on edge.

"I'll go in and tell the vampires Liz is here," Sadie said as she opened the back door and ran to the front of the house.

She was gone in a flash as the rest of us climbed out.

Mom held the journal in her hands as she shifted her weight from leg to leg. "Should I head over to the pack?"

"Sadie and I planned on taking you." Donovan yawned. "But she's heading this way with Winter, Titan, and Torak."

"He's okay?" I'd been worried about him, but I'd been afraid to ask in case something bad had happened and Sadie wasn't ready to share.

"Yeah, Trixie was able to help him." Donovan turned to the front door as it opened.

The four of them walked outside. Titan had a black patch over his right eye.

"But not like we hoped," Titan said, his mouth set in a firm expression. "But she made sure the poison was out of my system and healed my eye socket so it wouldn't take days to heal on its own."

"And it's better than you being dead." Winter took her mate's hand. "It could've been a lot worse."

"You're right." He lifted her hand to his mouth and kissed it. "We're heading back to the pack. There's a lot we need to take care of now that I can't be alpha."

"You can't be alpha?" My heart broke for him.

"No, not like this." Titan patted his son's shoulder. "It's time to hand over the reins. I've been thinking about it for a while now anyway. I'm getting old."

"And speaking of leading, Ladon and Kayda want to meet with you two." Torak lifted a brow. "They're waiting for you in the kitchen. We'll take care of your mom from here."

"Thank you," Egan said as he walked next to me. *I have a feeling I know what this is about.*

Me too. I turned to Mom and hugged her. "I'll come see you in the morning. Get some rest, and if you need me, I'll have my cell phone on."

She hugged me hard. "I love you."

"I love you too."

Mom walked off with Titan, Torak, and Winter, leaving the rest of us standing under the moonlight. When they stepped out of view, Egan focused on me. "Are you ready?"

"As ready as I'll ever be," I replied and stepped toward the house. I lifted my chin and squared my shoulders. I was done cowering and running. Our futures were about to change rapidly once more. I felt it in my bones. And this time, I wouldn't run away.

CHAPTER TWENTY-THREE

Egan and I walked hand in hand into the kitchen with Draco following right behind us. Sadie and Donovan peeled off, heading toward the living room where everyone else was.

If the entire group giving us privacy wasn't a neon sign warning that something was waiting for us up ahead, I wasn't sure what else could be.

We found Ladon and Kayda sitting at the rectangular kitchen table with their backs to the windows. They watched us sit in front of them. I was right across from Kayda while Egan took the open chair next to me in front of his father.

Ladon tapped his fingers on the table. "Was Liz in danger?"

I wanted to shut him down and get straight to the point of this conversation, but he seemed concerned. Snapping at him would have been rude and wrong, given the circumstances.

"Not really, but a fae attacked my aunt." I rolled my shoulders, trying to keep the strange, remorseful feelings at bay. "She died shortly after we got there." A lump formed in my throat, and I tried swallowing it down with no luck.

Kayda leaned forward, her hair falling into her face. "Is Liz okay? I know how much she loved her sister."

My eyes burned, which was insane. Why was I getting choked up over this? My aunt had been awful to me. She didn't deserve any remorse.

Not wanting to risk a breakdown, I linked with Egan. *I'm sorry. I can't.*

He squeezed my hand comfortingly. "Many things came to light, and unfortunately, they were a little shocking to Liz. But she'll come around. She's stronger than she realizes."

"Yes, she is." Kayda smiled sadly. "But losing a family member is hard, especially when you grew up around them. I am truly sorry for your family's loss."

"Thank you." My voice cracked, and I cleared my throat. I hoped no one had noticed, but the concern etched around Kayda's eyes informed me they had.

Draco joined us in the kitchen, standing by the doorway. "Do you need me to stay, or should I join the others in the living room?"

"Please stay." Ladon squared his shoulders as his jaw ticked. "You should hear this as well."

Nodding, Draco stood stiffly by the door. Katherine's laughter filtered into the kitchen, and Draco flicked his attention in her direction.

He must have felt the same attraction as she did.

I only hoped neither of them got hurt.

"Your mother and I have been wanting to talk to you about this for a very long time, but we needed to wait until you'd found your mate." Ladon gestured at us. "Had we known we would be under a threat like this when you found each other, we would've started training Egan at a much younger age, but there isn't much we can do about it now."

Egan ran his thumb along my wrist. "We can start now. Yes, war isn't an ideal time, but we'll do the best we can."

"You're right." Ladon nodded. "War isn't the best time, but this is when the transition begins."

"Transition?" I wanted to hear him say it to ensure we were all aligned.

"Yes." Ladon took his wife's hand and placed it on the table. "The transition of the crown from us to the two of you."

There it was. The words I'd been expecting. "Now?" The timing was horrible.

"I know it's abrupt," Kayda said, "but this has been in the plans for a long time. Your father and I feel that we're not the right people to lead."

"Genetics say differently." Egan leaned back.

"That's not true," Ladon said sternly. "Every dragon king passes the torch when they feel their reign should be over, and there are two reasons we want to do this now. First, I've never wanted to be king. It's never interested me. The day I learned I would be taking over, I realized no one knew who I was except for a small handful with access to that privileged information."

"It's true." Kayda patted her mate's arm. "I'd only been part of the thunder for a week when your grandfather dropped the news on your dad. I thought he'd cry right then and there."

"So you'd like to pass that burden on to me?" Egan arched his brow.

Ladon sighed. "Which brings me to the most important point. You were born a leader. Your peers looked up to you. Look at the strong alliances you've made during your short stint in the human realm. You are sharp, strategic, and have such a good heart. And with Jade by your side, you've grown into a stronger leader than I've ever been, and she's a solid rock beside you. If we're going to make it through this next battle, you and Jade need to lead the charge. You're our best hope."

I had to give him that. Egan was an amazing person. His presence alone made people feel safe and at ease. He had a natural charisma that made others want to follow him.

"But Dad—" Egan started.

"This isn't a question." Ladon made a slicing motion with his hand. "Effective immediately, you and Jade are the dragon king and queen." His attention turned to Draco. "Alert the other thunders and make the announcement. There's no point in keeping it secret any longer since the fae dragon king knows who we are."

Egan opened his mouth to argue.

If he doesn't want to lead, maybe we should take over. The last thing we needed was for Egan and his dad to be at odds. It wasn't like his dad would disappear. *If we fight with each other, the fae dragon king will win.*

He blew out a breath. *It just happened so fast. I feel like I have whiplash, and we didn't even have time to focus on us before a whole kingdom got thrown at our feet.*

And there was the real reason. He wanted time to focus on us, and I had to admit that sounded pretty damn amazing. *I don't want it either, but if we're supposed to protect our people, don't they deserve for us to step up? Especially if your dad doesn't want to?*

Turning toward me, he cupped my cheek. "Jade and I are in agreement even though we aren't thrilled with the timing."

Sadie shouted, "Egan! Jade! You may want to come in here."

Her voice contained no fear, which was the only reason I wasn't losing my mind.

Our group ran into the room to find Sadie, Donovan, Axel, and Roxy on one couch and Cassius, Dawn, Julie, and Paul on the other. Katherine, Lillith, Luther, and Athan sat in front of the fireplace under the television with Ollie and Trixie standing off to the side.

The witch's charcoal eyes locked with mine, and a smile twisted on her face, looking menacing with the deep wrinkles of age. Her hair spilled from what had once been a bun on top of her hair, and silver wisps hung in her face. Her brown dress was lined with sweat as she rocked in place.

But Trixie couldn't be why Sadie had called for us. I was

searching for what had made Sadie shout when Rook and Naida flickered into view with a strange woman standing between them.

She was pale like the other fae beside her, but with a faint reddish hue and thin scales instead of skin. Long, pale cyan hair cascaded to her ankles, the color matching her eyes. She stood as tall as Egan and wore a dark green robe with a tiara made of turquoise stone.

"What are you?" The word vomit had already begun. I wished I could take the words back, but they'd flown out before my brain could process what I'd said.

A hint of a smile peeked through, making her breathtaking. "And all I heard back in the fae realm was that humans lied and played games of the brain. But she asked a direct question with no disdain."

"Playing games of the brain?" This had to be a dream or a nightmare. I wasn't sure which way it would go.

Her forehead creased. "Manipulate to get what you want."

Rook chuckled. "She means mind games."

"That makes so much more sense." Roxy tapped her head. "I was really confused for a second."

"Please excuse these two." Naida glared at Roxy then me. "They sometimes don't know how to behave. This is Libelle, the fae dragon king's daughter."

"And you didn't chain her up?" Draco rushed past Egan and me to stand in front. "We need to restrain her now."

"Actually, we don't." Libelle crossed her arms, and smoke trickled from her nose. "I came here willingly."

"Why should we believe that?" Lillith stood as if the move would put them on the same level, despite the dragon princess having almost two feet on her.

"Fair question." The princess walked around the room, taking in every detail. "My father has been a dictator since before I was born. He starves those who anger him, treats everyone as if they are his slaves, and when bored, he enjoys beating his own people." She ran a hand over the wall. "Even his own family isn't off the table. He does whatever is necessary to instill fear and has broken the spirit of our entire thunder."

"When she says thunder," Rook added, "she means every fae dragon. They don't live apart like you."

Ladon stepped beside Egan. "We didn't until the fae dragon king began hunting us."

"I remember the day my father began reaching out for human contacts." Libelle walked next to Roxy and touched the leather couch with her finger. "It was after the harpies had laughed at him when he'd told them to leave the lands outside our volcano. They informed him that no one revered him and that many wanted the fake fae dragon king, Otin, dead since he didn't possess the true dragon king power. After that, things got worse for all of us, me included."

"So you want us to kill your father?" Donovan said carefully. "Because that's what it'll take to end this."

"Of course I do." Libelle stared at him. "It doesn't bring me joy to say it, and I refuse to do it myself, but he's lived for over two thousand years and had a full life. He's shown cruelty to everyone, and my people are already speaking of rising against him before he gets more powerful. With all the turmoil, he's made some allegiances, making him more ruthless. The more power he gets, the crueler he becomes."

She didn't smell of a lie. Rook and Naida seemed comfortable around her, so maybe we could trust her.

"I understand it's hard to believe, but I want the best for my people." She placed a hand over her heart. "My people have tried rallying for him to let me step up and lead, but he killed the ringleader and told me if I tried to overthrow him, he'd kill my best friend. We're all at his mercy, and his terror must end."

"I understand that all too well." Sadie leaned over Roxy and placed a hand on her arm. "I've lived a life similar to yours, and sometimes doing the right thing isn't easy or fun."

"Same here." Maybe that was one reason Sadie and I had connected from the beginning. We'd both grown up with people who didn't love us and punished us for just breathing, and it had made us see something in each other, similar to how we could see something in Libelle now.

"My guards informed me that she was dropping information on Otin's plans for attacking the kingdom while the civil war was going on." Rook lifted a hand toward the princess. "She's been helping us, and it's why we regained control so quickly once I took the throne. I believe we can trust her."

Do you think she's telling the truth? Egan asked.

Taking my time before answering, I watched her a little more. *Yes, but that doesn't mean we trust her blindly. I say Draco and a few other dragons stay close and guard her. She seems genuine, and if she is, we want to make sure she trusts us in return.*

Nodding, Egan inhaled sharply. "Then we appreciate your help. Draco, please contact the thunders and tell them to make their way here. If Libelle is staying with us, I'm assuming her father won't be far behind."

"You're correct." Libelle took in the entire room. "My capture will make him look weak. He won't tolerate it. I suspect he'll attack before a day cycle."

"Day cycle?" Katherine asked and scooted closer to Draco.

Naida sighed. "Within twenty-four hours."

"I'll text them now." Draco pulled the phone from his pocket and typed a message.

Libelle watched, her head tilting so far I was afraid it would fall off. "This is such a strange, wonderful place."

"It is a lot different from back home," Rook said.

Naida stood stiffly and on edge like always. "Rook, you better go back and ready the guards. Sadie or I will alert you when it's time for the guards to come."

"And the rest of us need to get some sleep while we can." Egan tugged me toward the hallway. "Draco, why don't you, Ollie, Trixie, and Libelle sleep here? I'm sure we can get blow-up mattresses for you all."

"I'll grab some now," Dawn said and hurried from the room.

"Jade and I are going to get some sleep. She got injured earlier and needs time to heal." Egan held his hand out toward me. "Call us or come get us if anything happens."

"Wait." Trixie took a few shaky steps toward me. "Let me heal her so she can rest better."

Just like last time, I felt extremely uncomfortable around the witch. "After what you did for Titan, I'd hate to put you out."

"Nonsense." Trixie circled me. "Where is the wound?"

"On her back," Egan said and touched my arm to calm me. *It wouldn't hurt to let her heal you.*

I don't trust her. I didn't know how to explain it, other than that.

He pointed to my back where I was hurt. *It's only because her magic is different than ours.*

I hoped that was the case because before I could move, Trixie's hands touched my back, and magic pooled inside me.

My flames flared, fighting back, and my head grew light. Something was wrong.

CHAPTER TWENTY-FOUR

My dragon roared as the flames increased. *Something feels off.*

Egan tensed. "She says something feels off."

"You know why." Trixie pushed more magic inside me. "Do you really think I'd do something stupid in a house full of supernaturals?"

"Maybe," Egan growled. "If you have a death sentence."

Flames licked my skin as my dragon fought against the foreign magic. I wouldn't be surprised if I spontaneously combusted. My mind screamed to move, but between the two warring magics, I was mercilessly stuck in place.

"I may be old," she tsked, "but I'd like to live as long as Mother Nature intends me to."

The magic receded, and I sucked in a breath. I'd been so focused on the warring parts inside me that I'd forgotten one of the most basic survival techniques. Maybe my gynecologist had been right all along. He always reminded me to breathe during my annual exams, and I'd thought it strange until now. Granted, this had been way more invasive than that.

After a few seconds, she removed her hand. "There. She's physically healed."

Her choice of wording was correct. Maybe I was healed on the outside, but I was completely drained inside. My dragon coursed through my body as if she was waiting for another magical attack.

I sagged against Egan, more exhausted than ever before.

"Do you have everything you need?" Egan asked as he lifted me and cradled me in his arms.

His touch soothed my dragon, but not enough. The fire still licked my skin, and in my weakened state, I could barely hold off the shift.

"Yes, get her to bed," Sadie said. "It shouldn't take long before we all can get a little bit of sleep."

"The thunders are moving." Draco sounded almost excited. "Everyone is eager to meet their new king and queen and remove the fae threat that's kept us in hiding for so long."

If all of the places were beautiful like where Egan's thunder had stayed, I wouldn't consider it a horrible sentence. But if I'd had no option but to stay there, I'd have felt trapped too.

"Good." Egan headed toward the stairs. "We'll need all the energy we can get to make it out of this alive."

"Word of advice," Roxy interjected. "Don't tell them that. It's a real morale killer."

"I hate to agree with Roxy." Lillith snorted. "But a little bit of 'go team' would be ideal in this situation. Don't be a dream crusher."

"I'll consider your suggestion," Egan said seriously, but I felt a trace of humor through our bond.

Out of the corner of my eye, I watched Katherine and Draco slip away, hand in hand. I tried not to worry since it was clear they were interested in each other, but I cared about them deeply and hoped no one got hurt.

Roxy cleared her throat loudly. "That makes me part of the royal decision-making. I should probably receive a formal title."

"Now's not the time." Julie chuckled. "Go take care of Jade, Egan."

The group bantered, and with each step, their voices grew farther and farther away.

Seconds later, Egan sat me on the edge of the bed and brushed my hair from my face. "I'll go warm the water for you."

A warm shower didn't sound appealing. *Can you make it cool? My dragon is still agitated.*

Of course. He gathered our things and headed into the bathroom. The sound of running water trickled into the room.

Gaining distance from the witch had helped, but some of her magic remained inside me, maybe finishing up the job, so my dragon wouldn't completely calm because of it.

I slowly undressed. Thankfully, my shoulder didn't scream or twinge with pain as I pulled off my shirt. I dropped my clothes on the floor and entered the bathroom.

"I was going—" Standing by the shower, Egan turned around, and his eyes glowed as he scanned my naked body. In a low, husky voice he linked with me. *Turn around.*

Obliging him, I slowly turned and pulled my hair over my shoulder so he could see my back.

He closed the distance between us, and his fingertips brushed along where my wound had been. "You're completely healed. There's not even a scar."

Even in my exhausted state, his touch ignited warmth inside me. The very kind that a shower wouldn't extinguish.

Only he could.

I spun around, and my breasts brushed his hands. The amount of need coursing through my body took me by surprise. I'd always wanted him, but this bordered on desperation.

My hand clutched his neck, yanking his mouth to mine. Not bothering with foreplay, my tongue slipped inside his mouth, showing him what I wanted.

Jade, it's been a hell of a day. Maybe you should take it easy. But his body responded despite his protests. His fingers pinched my nipples, and I moaned.

I stepped forward, wanting to dominate him. I needed him and wanted control. *I need to feel you. Make me feel alive.*

I'll do whatever you need me to. The tangy scent of his arousal and his consent charged me more than ever before.

Get naked, I commanded and stepped back, unbuttoning his pants and pushing them from his body.

He stepped out of them as his back hit the glass door of the shower.

Not wanting to step away from him again, I grabbed the top of his button-down shirt and ripped the buttons off, shredding the fabric from his body.

There was no way we were making it into the shower. I couldn't wait. I climbed him and wrapped my legs around his body. His hands moved to my ass, and his fingers kneaded my skin.

He slid down the glass wall until he sat propped against it. I eagerly straddled him. The tile cut into my skin, adding to my desire. Egan sucked on my nipple as I slipped him inside me.

There was no time for slow as I rode him. I gasped as his teeth nipped, and I groaned in pure ecstasy.

Using the glass as leverage, I spread my legs wider, wanting him as deep as he could go. He thrust in sync with me and leaned his head against the glass wall supporting him.

Lowering my head to his neck, I grazed my teeth against his skin. I wanted him to experience what him being rough with me felt like. I always thought he wanted to be gentle, but I refused to give him that tonight.

A low, deep growl rumbled from his chest. *Damn, that feels good.* His emotions poured into me—love, arousal, and pure pleasure.

Emotions only I could invoke, and I felt powerful.

I sucked on his neck, not giving a damn if I left a mark. He bucked against me in a frenzy, and the pleasure built between us.

Maybe he'd realized that gentleness was overrated sometimes.

He pinched my breasts, and I fell over the edge as he slammed into me. Responding, I dug my teeth deeper into his skin, leaving a slight metallic taste on the tip of my tongue.

He groaned as he climaxed, bringing me further over the edge. My body quivered as the largest orgasm ever rolled through me.

My body sagged against his as we came down from wherever the hell we'd been. Our breathing was ragged and somehow in rhythm. As the world crashed back over me, I glanced at the bite mark I'd left on his neck. *I am so sorry.*

Don't be. He kissed my lips gently. *That was amazing.*

I couldn't argue with that, but pure exhaustion hit. I wasn't even sure I had the energy for a shower. *I love you.*

I love you too. He kissed the tip of my nose and grabbed my waist, lifting me off him gently. *You're exhausted. Let's clean up and get some sleep.*

We climbed into the shower, and Egan washed me. I'd never realized a man could be so loving. The pure joy radiating off him from taking care of me made me fall even more in love.

I hadn't even known that was possible.

Fate knew what she was doing. He was my perfect match. Even if we hadn't been mates, I would've fallen in love with him. It just would've taken a whole hell of a lot longer. And I was so glad it hadn't. I never wanted to experience another moment without him.

Minutes later, we cuddled in bed and fell fast asleep.

SOMETHING cold and unsettling charged through me, waking me. Egan's breathing grew rapid as he released me and sat up in bed.

You feel it too? Maybe I hadn't lost my mind.

He looked at me. *Yes. I have a feeling the fae king may have arrived on Earth.*

Of course he had. I threw the comforter off and stood. "Then we have no time to waste."

We ran to our closet, each picking out old jeans and a shirt. We didn't have any armor, and we'd be shifting soon, so we didn't care what we wore.

Throwing our bedroom door open, Egan yelled, "It's go-time. The fae king has arrived."

Sadie's door opened. Just like us, she and Donovan were dressed and ready to go.

"Yeah, I felt their arrival too." Sadie shivered. "It was faint but malicious. It was almost a sinister feeling as he arrived in our world."

"If we can feel him, why didn't we feel the harpies and manticores?" Some things still didn't make sense to me.

"They probably didn't transport close to us. Fae travel to Earth all the time, and we only pick up on their energy when it's close to us." Sadie headed toward the stairs.

That only raised more questions. "But I don't feel anything with Rook and Naida."

"That's because you knew Naida as human before you shifted into a dragon. Since they're my family, you recognize their energy, and that's why you don't register the dizziness that warns of fae. If someone you don't know transports over, you'll grow dizzy."

"She's right, although it's very faint," Egan said and followed Sadie as Roxy and Axel's door opened. "Maybe if it's the same race as us, we feel it more prominently."

"I don't know if I should be relieved or upset that I can't feel anything." Donovan waved his hand, indicating I should go next. "All I know is that it's time to kill some assholes. We warned Titan's ... I mean, Torak's pack."

Axel and Roxy joined us in the hallway as Axel shook his head and said, "Dude, that change will take some getting used to."

"Ah, just don't say it too much." Roxy rolled her eyes. "Or Torak will get an even bigger head."

I hurried after Egan as Donovan chuckled. "He's not bad at all. Several others have a bigger ego than him."

We entered the kitchen, and it was packed with all the dragons, vampires, Ollie, and the witch. Libelle, Cassius, Ladon, and Draco were at the door leading outside.

"Did everyone feel them come over?" I asked, surprised our group was already assembled.

"All the dragons did." Cassius inhaled. "They alerted everyone."

Good. Us being split across the house had come in handy.

Sadie scanned the group. "Where's Naida?"

"She transported to Fae to get the guards." Libelle pursed her lips. "My father striking this early isn't a good sign."

Egan took my hand, and we moved toward the front. He asked, "What do you mean?"

"He must know not every dragon is here yet and he's trying to capitalize on it." The princess's skin turned a shade darker, making her scales more prominent. "How far away are they?"

"I'm not sure." Draco frowned. "They're on their way but in dragon form. There's no way to communicate with them."

"You can't communicate with them?" She tilted her head as the corners of her eyes crinkled in concentration.

"No, only wolves can pack-link when they're in the same pack," Egan explained. "Dragons can't unless it's with their fated mate."

"I can't hear my father either." She moved her head from side to side like she was trying to catch a frequency. "I felt him and figured he'd reach out to me, wanting to know everything about you. I'd hoped to play that to our advantage."

"Maybe the fae realm allows that sort of connection." Ladon chewed on his bottom lip. "And Earth prohibits it. There are different rules between the two worlds."

"That makes sense." Libelle glanced out the window. "I'm already feeling weaker from being here."

"At least, we have that to our advantage." Ollie pursed his lips. "Is there a way to drain the fae dragons faster?"

"Make them use their magic." Libelle shrugged. "It's the only way."

Katherine drank from a blood bag. "Will the iron work?"

It was strange watching her drink like that. They always used cups, but we were in a hurry. Then I noticed that all the vampires were drinking.

Egan must have felt my confusion since he explained, *Vampires are strongest after they eat.*

Gotcha. We needed everyone at their peak. I'd carry the blood bags personally if that would make us win.

"Iron?" Solid scales formed around Libelle's nose as she squinted. "What is that?"

"A material that drains the fae." Sadie lifted a hand. "I discovered it when the fae were trying to kill me."

"Ah, yes, since you are a half-blood." The scales became less visible, and her face smoothed. "If that works on them, it's worth trying on the dragons. Our magics are similar."

"Good." Donovan sighed. "The pile they brought during the manticore attack is still in the clearing. We should head out and get it before it's too late."

A roar rocked the mansion, and I looked outside to see the strangest sight ever.

If I'd thought our dragons were huge, I'd been wrong.

So wrong.

These dragons were at least twice our size. They were varying colors of light pinks, yellows, purples, and blues. They were gorgeous, but their faces were contorted. Eyes narrowed, they bared their teeth with smoke trickling from their noses.

In other words: pure rage.

"Outside!" Draco yelled. "Before they set the mansion on fire."

They were out to demolish us.

Ten circled the house as blue flames poured from their mouths, hitting various points of the mansion.

Shit, we had to move.

Draco opened the door, and we poured outside, which was exactly what they wanted.

"Your Highnesses, stay close to me," Draco commanded as he

stood in front of us. He looked at Katherine, and then his gaze flicked toward me, making it clear he wanted her with us too. "My family will be here soon, but until then, I have to keep you alive. Otherwise, the fae king will get what he wants."

Katherine stepped toward me, listening to his silent command ... or was it?

Did they mind link? I had to be seeing things. They were different species. But hell, so was I.

That should be impossible. Egan sounded confused. *Maybe she just understood his physical cues.*

The magnitude of the situation washed over us as more dragons flew our way. There were hundreds.

They were here to wage war and win.

I only hoped we could survive until the others got here.

CHAPTER TWENTY-FIVE

Blue fire erupted from all sides of the roof as the fae dragons concentrated their attacks. One of the manticores must have seen Ladon and the others run from the mansion during their escape back to Fae and informed Otin.

My dragon surged forward, wanting me to shift, but I pushed her away. We all wanted to shift, but it would put us at a severe disadvantage. "Don't shift. Stay human so we can use the trees as coverage."

The trees had budding leaves that would partially hide us as we ran to the supply of iron and waited for the other thunders to arrive.

"Listen to the queen's orders!" Draco shouted and motioned for us to run in front of him. "And follow her to the others."

"Libelle, keep close to Ladon and Kayda," Draco commanded. "I need to protect you as well."

Even though his words were sincere, he also wanted to keep an eye on her. Since this was her thunder attacking, we didn't need her to tell them our plans.

Wait. He wanted to move in front. *I thought he wanted us to stay behind?*

That was before more dragons came. We'll be safer in the woods.

He can guard us better from behind. Egan chuckled even though humor didn't flow through our bond. *He'll want to get in front again soon enough. Don't worry.*

A cyan dragon flew down from the house, heading after those running into the woods. Not all of us would make it into the woods before it reached us. We had to do something, or people would die in the first few moments of battle. "We have to hold him off."

I stopped and spun around, staring the crazy-ass dragon in the eye. I searched for something, anything to protect our people.

"Dammit, Jade!" Draco spat. "Run."

Sadie rushed over to me and touched my arm. "I've got this, and Naida is on her way."

Did she expect me to leave her? She was one of the most important people in my life. "But I don't want you to get hurt either."

Egan held me in place, "I promise she has this handled," Egan rasped. "I wouldn't leave her behind if I wasn't sure."

Smoke trickled from the fae dragon's nose; he was close enough to spew flames. He roared, blowing Sadie's pink bob behind her and filling our noses with the stench of brimstone.

Naida and several other fae flickered into view, and Sadie lifted her hands. Pink magic spilled from her palms. The flames charged toward us, but when they hit the pink barrier, they blew back in the dragon's face.

The dragon roared again, and I braced myself for a smell that never came. Not even Sadie's hair blew from the breeze.

My mouth dropped. "What the hell?"

"It's like a force field." Egan moved toward the iron. "She's been practicing her magic with Rook, and she's gotten stronger. Just shy of pure-fae-blooded levels."

Draco stepped beside us and frowned. "We need to get to the other dragons before it's too late."

Donovan walked over to us. "I'll stay here with her and the fae. We'll catch up to you, but I'll let them drain the dragons as much as possible before we leave."

I felt stupid for not wanting to leave her since she was more than capable of handling herself. "I'm sorry, I didn't know."

"There's nothing for you to be ashamed of." Egan brushed his fingers against my cheek. "You didn't know, and you love her. Any one of us would've done the same thing."

He was right. I'd lost any concern I'd had about growing too close to any of them. They were my family, and I was willing to risk my life to protect them.

My life had changed so drastically, and I wouldn't alter it for anything. "Okay." I turned and ran back toward the woods.

Ladon, Kayda, Libelle, and Katherine had stopped to wait for us, probably due to Draco requesting it. He wanted us together, which wasn't a very strong plan.

We ran quickly with the other dragons toward where we'd fought the manticores.

Egan and I needed to be in agreement before we got to where the battle would truly begin. *The four of us sticking together isn't smart. All it'll take is one strike, and the whole royal line will be wiped out.*

You're right. He replied as a few of the fae dragons flew overhead. *Let's split up from my parents, but Draco will have a fit.*

It doesn't matter. I understood that Draco wanted to protect all four of us, but there was only one of him and hundreds of fae dragons. *This plan is the best way to ensure our people stay safe.*

"We're heading right," Egan informed Draco.

The warrior's head snapped in our direction. "No, stay the course. I can't protect you if you're over there."

"That's the point," I butted in. We didn't have time to waste by not fighting in the battle. "Focus on keeping Ladon and Kayda safe. Egan and I will protect each other."

"But ..."

"Let them go," Katherine said softly. "It's better that way, and you know it."

Blowing out a breath as a muscle in his neck pulsed, Draco nodded stiffly. "Fine, but if you are attacked, let the dragons closest to you help fight. Once my family arrives, I'll come looking for you two."

"Wait!" Libelle shouted. "Hold me captive so Dad will ignore me." Libelle's eyes glowed pink. "If he suspects I'm working with you, he'll kill me before I can help. Once we get to the clearing where my people can see me, I'll take a stand beside you."

"You want to be our prisoner?" Egan asked slowly. "That means we'll have to restrain you."

"In other words, we're both taking a leap of faith with one another." Libelle let the truth of her words settle over us.

Egan lifted his hands and wiggled his fingers. "I don't have any rope."

"This should work." Ladon pulled out the dagger Vera had tried to use on me back in the cave. The rising sun reflected off the dark silver edge, and the two golden jewels at the top of the slender handle glowed, making the black wings that sprouted from the neck appear to move.

Libelle stumbled back. "Where did you get that?"

"From the witch that attacked us in the cave." The memory of her attacking me with it still gave me nightmares that I refused to admit to anyone.

"I wasn't sure you could win." Libelle's gaze stayed on the dagger. "But you have the one weapon that can kill any fae. You could succeed."

We deserved a break after everything we'd been through. "What do you mean?"

"That's the fae realm dagger." Libelle lifted a hand like she was considering touching it. "I can't believe Dad gave it to that witch. He's even more power-hungry than I realized."

"Vera was crazy." Egan ground his teeth. "She was all about killing us."

"Everyone thinks he hid it somewhere, so scratch my plan." Libelle grinned. "I'll show him I'm on your side to completely piss him off. His anger will make him more ruthless—that's why I wanted us to hold off—but we have this. We need him crazy with rage so we can use this to our advantage."

"Then I'll need that so I can kill him." Draco took the dagger and sheath from Ladon and placed it through his belt loop.

"The plan doesn't change." I nodded to the right. "Egan and I will catch up with the dragons that ran off that way."

Draco sighed but grunted his agreement.

I hated to cause him more grief, but we all knew this was the best plan. Before he could argue, Egan and I ran to the right, straight toward Long and a few members of the thunder. Cassius and Dawn were right beside them with Ollie and the witch only a few feet behind.

It surprised me that the older witch could keep up, but hey. She might creep me out, but I didn't want something bad to happen to her. She'd only helped me ... so far.

Our group pushed as fast as we could, and after a few more steps, paws pounded the ground. I turned to find a vibrant red wolf and a darker brown one racing toward us. Roxy and Axel were keeping up and informing Donovan and Sadie about what was going on.

We were less than a mile away from the spot we were aiming for. It was between the pack house and mansion but, most importantly, where the iron was. Even though we dragons couldn't touch it, the vampires and wolves could, which would hopefully give us more of an advantage against the fae dragons.

Several fae dragons flew overhead, but unlike the others, they were flying lower, searching in between the leaves. They circled the sky like a flock of birds.

Mind linking would have been amazing, but unfortunately, that wasn't happening. I wanted to tell them to slow down, but I couldn't without giving our location away.

Egan and I crouched behind a tree, hoping that they wouldn't see us.

"Hide!" Long shouted as the dragons circled back.

The others scattered towards safety, but the dragon's eyes were latched on to the older dragon.

He was sacrificing himself for us.

We've got to help him. We couldn't hide and let the poor man die for us.

I jumped to my feet, and Egan was right in sync with me. He linked with me. *I want to help him, but he's saving us.*

Long's silver eyes widened, and he shook his head as I tried to reach him in time. I had no clue what we would do, but I had time to figure something out.

Jade! Egan yelled in my mind as he raced toward me.

When I was only twenty feet away, something slammed into my back, and I fell into the brush. Egan landed next to me, and I realized Roxy and Axel had tackled me.

I fought against their hold and glanced at the older man. Relieved that the wolves had taken us down, he mouthed the words "thank you" as a buttercream dragon swooped toward him.

Bucking against the wolf on top of me, I watched in horror as the dragon bit into the older man's back and stomach. The dragon's teeth thrashed through his skin, and the sickening sound of flesh ripping and bones breaking hit my ears. The dragon released its hold, and Long's body split in half.

I'd never seen a sight so disgusting or heartbreaking in my entire life. His slashed organs hung outside his body.

The urge to vomit overtook me, but I swallowed the bile back down. The buttercream dragon flew higher in the sky with blood dripping down its mouth.

After a few seconds, Roxy and Axel got off me. Tears rolled down my face.

Egan pulled me into his arms. "You can't do that again. Those dragons would have found us. Long saved us, and his sacrifice would've been in vain if Roxy and Axel hadn't stopped you."

"But he died." I wiped the wetness from under my eyes, knowing

I had to pull myself together. We were at war. I didn't have time to break down.

"Because he was old and wanted to protect us." Egan kissed my forehead. "We'll fight too, but we can't be reckless. If we die, our people will fall under Otin's rule, and Libelle told us how it is there. His own daughter is turning away from him."

He was right. I'd been careless.

I don't like it either, but it was his call to make. Egan intertwined our fingers. *Now, let's make sure his death has purpose.*

His words invigorated me; he knew exactly what to say to drive his point home.

The other dragons reemerged as Ollie and the witch caught up to us. We all took off, and soon, we were approaching the clearing. I glanced to my left and found Draco and the others a hundred yards away.

"Let's shift!" Egan shouted. "It's time to fight."

All of the dragon shifters called their animals forward, and we all stepped into the clearing, ready to fight.

Fae dragons approached from every direction in the sky. Each flap of their wings sounded like a battle cry. The pack and the other dragons broke into the clearing on the other side, already shifted into their dragon forms. Half of the wolf shifters were still in their human form, racing to the iron along with our vampire friends.

Most surprisingly, Ollie flew out in his falcon form with the witch right behind.

Only Libelle was missing.

Where's the princess? She'd been so steadfast in joining our fight and helping us win.

I don't know. Egan rasped as our group formed a circle, our backs facing one another. *But it doesn't matter. At least, we know what the dagger is.*

The dagger.

I glanced at Draco, wondering where the dagger was now that he was in beast form.

Katherine stood beside him, wearing the dagger peeking out from her waistband. She wouldn't leave his side, so he'd have easy access to it.

The fae dragons flew into the clearing, their eyes locked on Egan and me. A limestone-colored dragon flew at me and opened its mouth. Blue flames shot out, and my own fire bubbled inside. I blew my red flames out and prayed I would survive.

CHAPTER TWENTY-SIX

Our flames collided, crackling loudly. When I didn't feel immediate pain, I opened my eyes to something amazing. The red and blue flames connected, neither one advancing, creating a vibrant purple that would have been breathtaking under normal circumstances. Various hues of purple sparked from the connection and hit the ground. The grass quickly went from brown to black.

My eyes remained locked on the beauty of the chaos until the fae dragon roared and pushed his flames harder toward me.

All of the other dragons followed his lead and attacked the others with a vengeance. I'd hoped to get some help, but that wouldn't happen.

I was on my own.

Shit, I had no clue how to fight a dragon. *Only your flames don't hurt me, right?* A lot had happened, but I vaguely remembered Egan telling me that. The fae dragon was determined to set me on fire, but I'd assumed a lot about this world and was usually wrong.

Any fire outside of mine will hurt. Fear and determination wafted from Egan and slammed into me. *Hold on. I'm coming.*

I found Egan in a battle of his own with a peach-shaded dragon.

Instead of attacking my mate with flames, he leveraged his size. The mammoth dragon dug his talons into Egan's shoulders. Blood dripped from the puncture wounds, and Egan clawed at the enemy dragon's feet.

The crackling turned into sizzles, bringing my attention back to my own battle. The dragon had pushed his flames closer to me, and a few sparks hit my large, scaly hands. The sensation reminded me of the sparkler injury I'd gotten on the Fourth of July when I was six years old. I'd screamed in pain, and Dad had rushed over with water, telling me that was why we didn't play with fire.

I chuckled at the memory of his words. Little had he known his little girl would grow up to be a fire-breathing dragon.

As the blue flames receded, I fixated on the fae dragon again. Even in his dragon state, his forehead lined with confusion, and he turned his head side to side slightly as if looking for an attack.

He had to think I was crazy to laugh in the middle of a battle unless I had the upper hand.

Finally, my strange personality was coming in handy. I laughed harder, which sounded like a cross between choking and burping in beast form.

Maybe that was why he was confused. He wasn't sure whether I was about to attack or die.

Egan turned his head to me, distracted from his own fight. *Are you okay? You're laughing.*

Aw, at least, he knew not to ask if I was insane. His mom, Sadie, or I must have trained him well. Maybe it had been a group effort. *Yeah, just a random memory, but it's confusing the fae dragon, so I'm using it to my advantage.*

The peach dragon attacking Egan dug his talons back into my mate's shoulders.

Pay attention and fight. I'm fine. I focused back on the limestone dragon, needing to end this. If Egan became severely injured, we would be hurting. At least his current wounds would heal relatively quickly.

Taking my own advice, I locked eyes with the enemy dragon, who still seemed unsure.

Projecting my fire toward him more, I concentrated the rolling liquid inside. I wasn't sure what to do, but I was letting my beast side take over more than usual.

My dragon's hot magic coursed inside me, spreading through my body. My skin grew hotter than ever before.

A loud *kak* sounded overhead as Ollie's white feathers flew toward the limestone dragon. Compared to the dragon, the falcon looked like an ant, but Ollie didn't falter as he flew right at the beast.

Ollie had lost his mind.

He had joined the fight without me commanding him to. I regretted ever doubting the guy, but right now it didn't matter.

I had to survive.

The falcon flapped his wings and landed on the limestone dragon's nose. The blue flames extinguished.

The bird perched on the dragon's face, fluffing his feathers. Taunting.

This couldn't end well.

The dragon roared and swiped at the bird, but Ollie hopped over to the dragon's eye and pecked.

A screech echoed in the clearing as the dragon stumbled backward. The limestone-hued dragon bared its claws, his intent clear.

No, I couldn't let Ollie die after he'd risked his life for me.

I flapped my wings, lifting off the ground. My flames erupted and hit the limestone dragon in the chest. I continued a steady stream as the dragon tried charging toward me.

He hesitated, not knowing which attack was more lethal.

Ollie jerked his head back and dropped an eyeball. Blood spilled down the dragon's snout. He ignored the blood like it was nothing out of the ordinary, hopped over to the other eye, and got to work.

And I'd thought seeing the girls without a throat and eyeballs on Kortright's campus had been bad, but seeing him in action was even worse. At least, my beast form eased some of the trauma.

This time, he was on our side, and injuring an enemy was the same regardless of whether it was through their chest or eyes.

The dragon cried for help, and the peach dragon fighting Egan paused.

Egan threw the peach dragon to the ground, jarring the earth. Within a second, Egan was on top of the enemy dragon, sinking his teeth into its neck. He jerked his head to the side like a wolf and ripped the dragon's throat out.

Peach scales hung from Egan's mouth, contrasting with his dark olive complexion. He looked furious and dangerous in his current form. He spat out the scales, and they landed next to the dying dragon.

I'd always heard that war was ugly, but I'd never understood the meaning until this very moment. This was more gruesome than all of the other attacks. Maybe because they were dragons like us and didn't know any better since they were fighting for the only king they'd ever known.

The limestone-colored dragon fell on its back, desperately searching for anything or anyone beside it. Ollie had managed to remove both eyeballs.

No longer under direct attack, I surveyed the area.

I saw Torak and his pack still in human form, wielding iron poles like they were their sole chance of surviving.

Maybe they were.

The few shifters that had been in wolf form were scattered throughout the clearing, dead, and Long had given up his life to protect us. I didn't see Roxy or Axel's bodies, but only the unshifted wolves, vampires, and dragons seemed to remain. I had to believe they were somewhere else fighting.

Still, my heart broke. We'd lost so many in a short amount of time, and the only fae dragons that were injured or dead were the two Egan, Ollie, and I had fought. This was a fucking massacre, and my heart felt ripped in two.

We were losing and fast. We needed help.

Mom, Winter, and Titan were absent, which gave me some comfort. Not everyone I loved was at risk.

A low rumble filled the air as a light red fae dragon flew overhead. She turned her head side to side, making sure everyone heard her call.

My dragon acknowledged the sound as one of battle.

It was Libelle.

But I wasn't sure if she was rallying her troops or pinpointing who to attack.

Stay close to me. Egan linked as he stepped beside me, our sides brushing.

Libelle darted toward Egan and me, and we both tensed. My heart pounded, ready for the fight, but I hoped it wouldn't come down to that. I chanted internally, *Please be on our side.*

Wings flapped loudly behind me. It had to be a larger dragon. *Stay focused on Libelle,* I commanded as I spun around and found a sand-colored fae dragon flying at me.

Now would have been a great time to have the dagger, but I couldn't reach Katherine before the enemy dragon caught me.

The enemy dragon flew at me with purpose. Its matching sand eyes revealed a cruelness I'd only ever found in Vera's. Each move was calculated like we were playing a game of chess.

Inhaling sharply, I steadied myself. Overreacting would get me hurt. My years of martial arts training had taught me not to overreact. That was when a fighter got careless and lost.

My biggest advantage was my fire. That should hold him off long enough for us to determine which side Libelle was on. If it was ours, Egan could step in and help.

The magic churned in my stomach as I prepared to expel the flames, but Libelle flew over my head and landed right in front of me.

She expanded her wings, blocking Egan and me from the dragon's onslaught.

The fighting around us paused as several enemy dragons turned toward their princess. Even though we couldn't speak, their confusion was clear by the shaking of their heads and their hesitation.

Libelle rumbled again and paced around Egan and me.

Is that equivalent to a dog marking its territory? I hoped his answer was yes.

Egan chuckled. *I'm not sure.*

The enemy sand dragon roared and threw his head back in disgust. Libelle stood her ground protectively in front of us.

He stomped then charged. His mission was clear.

He would attack us, no matter what.

Libelle's blue flames covered the sand dragon, and his body dropped. He didn't even attempt to fight back. Instead, he tried getting away, but she countered each move.

She's killing one of her own. When she'd said she didn't want to kill her father, I'd assumed she'd meant all fae dragons.

Egan turned his attention to the other dragons watching the show. *He looked like a warrior dragon like Draco. She's showing that she's standing against her father, and we're under her protection.*

Thank God. *So, this is over?*

No. Egan was so tense a strong gust of wind couldn't have blown him over. *It means things are about to get nasty, and we have to wait for an attack to know who isn't on our side.*

His words made me feel raw.

We would be on the defensive since there was no way for us to know which fae dragons were on her side and which ones weren't. I'd thought her help would strengthen us, but I hadn't processed the risk. *There has to be some way to tell a friend from foe.*

Every opponent had a tell that signaled their next move. We just had to figure out what the fae dragons did when they were about to attack.

A scarlet enemy dragon roared as he flew toward the clearing. He was easily the biggest of them all and wore a white-gold crown on his head. The crown reflected off the scales, giving off a sinister vibe.

That had to be the fae dragon king—Otin. Based on Libelle's

description, the scarlet red with the gaudy crown fit the asshole perfectly. His skin reminded me of the blood bags the vampires drank from.

His evil eyes locked on Libelle, and he pointed at her, baring his long, pointy teeth. He made the same rumbling sound and threw his dragon hand toward her.

They'd made their stances known. We'd soon learn how many people were loyal to Libelle and not her father.

All of the fae dragons glanced at one another, unsure what to do until an ivory dragon lunged at Luther fifty yards away.

The suddenness of the movement gave the enemy dragon leverage. We couldn't reach him in time.

As blue flames were about to engulf the vampire, Luther swung his iron pole in front of him in the nick of time. The flames blasted into the iron, almost like a vacuum. The enemy dragon tried flying away, but it was like the iron was anchored to the core of its magic.

Luther's eyes widened as his hands shook from holding the pole. "Uh ... this works."

"That's the trick!" Torak shouted enthusiastically. "The staff has to be the center focus."

Sadie and Donovan flickered into view, her arms wrapped around her mate. She'd teleported him along for the ride. She glanced around the clearing, taking note of the dead, as the rest of the fae appeared. They were spread around, their eyes locked on Otin, ready for war.

Otin roared like a general declaring war, spurring the dragons into action.

"No!" Sadie cried as she lifted her hands at the enemy dragons about to attack. "Only attack the ones who try to hurt us. Libelle and the other fae dragons should remain safe."

"You heard her," Naida said, supporting Sadie's order. "Now protect the Earthlings and take down the evil tyrant who has been hurting our own kind."

One by one, the fae shot their magic at the attacking dragons.

Maybe we could win this without anyone else on our side getting harmed.

Three figures ran from the woods to join the battle. My heart dropped when I recognized them.

Mom, Titan, and Winter.

No, they were supposed to stay back where it was safe. Mom and Titan shouldn't be here in their state.

Wearing his eyepatch, Titan rushed over and grabbed three iron poles. He passed them out to Winter and Mom. The three of them stepped onto the battlefield.

I wanted to fly over there and strangle Mom.

I linked with Egan as I lifted into the air. *I've got to get close to Mom.* I couldn't let her get hurt. She'd gone through so much already.

Egan screamed, *Jade, we'll go together!* He caught up to me, flying beside me.

Despite the battle raging around, we dodged all of the fighting.

When I reached Mom, her eyes widened with fear. "Jade!"

Something hot and soul-splintering hit my back. My wings gave out, and I fell.

CHAPTER TWENTY-SEVEN

I'd never felt pain like this before. The sensation was indescribable, and I crumpled face-first into the ground.

Egan roared with rage, and pure hatred flowed from him and into me.

He was pissed and scared.

"I've got this!" Mom yelled, and her footsteps pounded toward me.

Not wanting Mom to come near me and become more of a target, I forced myself back onto my feet. Every time I attempted to move quickly, pain ripped through me, and my core felt scorched.

Mom tugged on my arm like she could help. "I haven't been there for you in ten years, and it's time I make up for it."

Under normal circumstances, her dedication to mend the bond between us would have elated me, but I was injured. If I didn't steady my feet, I could fall over and hurt her. Her tugging put me further off balance.

Forcing myself to balance, I glanced over my shoulder. Egan was attacking the lavender dragon that had injured me. The enemy dragon kept spewing blue fire at my mate, who was barely dodging it.

He was forcing the dragon to pay attention to him instead of attacking me and Mom, but I couldn't allow him to get hurt. Mom had to get to safety.

Pink magic shot at the enemy dragon. Sadie had to be close by. I found her and Donovan running straight at us with Trixie in tow.

"Go heal her while we help Egan," Sadie said, gesturing to me. "Any funny business, and Donovan will be right on you."

"If I was going to hurt you, I would've done it by now," Trixie grumbled, rushing to me. "Damn shifters. They always think the worst of us."

My gut screamed not to trust her, so maybe she had a point, but witches like Vera didn't help that stereotype.

Mom stepped in front of me, blocking the witch. "Is this safe?"

"Of course it is," Trixie pushed by Mom. The witch touched me, and her foreign magic pulsed inside. Everything in me wanted to attack. My dragon cringed like a caged animal. I inhaled sharply as Donovan stood close by, splitting his attention between his mate and me.

"Here." Winter ran toward him with iron. "This works with their flames if you hold it in front of your body like a conductor."

"Thank God." Donovan took the metal from her. "At least, there's something our kind and the vampires can use."

Sadie blasted the lavender dragon in the chest, and she flew backward into a tree. The tree wobbled from the dragon's weight before tipping toward the clearing. The enemy dragon lay unconscious under the tree.

"Watch out!" Winter cried as Egan flew past us toward the enemy dragon.

The tree roots cracked, removing the tension that held the tree up. It started to fall, and Egan reached the tree moments later. He groaned as he pushed the dead weight in the opposite direction. For a scary moment, the two of them came to a standstill, then the tree straightened before toppling away from us, preventing so many injuries on our side.

Trixie removed her hands from my back. "All done. That went a lot faster in your beast form. I've never healed someone during their shift before."

Her magic receded from inside me, and I stood, feeling almost brand new. All of the commotion prevented me from focusing on the witch and the suffocating feeling her magic caused.

I'd say this was how she should always do her healing, but this was a unique situation. Besides that, I hoped I'd never need healing again.

Egan landed beside me and examined my back. *Are you tired like last night?*

No. But I'm pretty sure it was the entire day, not just her magic, that had exhausted me. That was not a day I ever wanted to relive. *But the pain is gone.* Several fae dragons were fighting their own kind. Libelle's followers were coming through.

I'd been worried they would fear her father too much to take a stand.

"Help!" a shifter yelled several yards away. Three dragons were attacking, and he couldn't use his pole. All of the fae warriors around him were engaged in battle, so Sadie rushed to them.

Mom screamed, and I spun around to face her. She charged the unconscious dragon, her face the same scarlet color as Otin. She raised the iron over her head and yelled, "You hurt my daughter! I'm going to kill you."

Dammit, I had to get to her before something happened. I pushed my healed wings while Egan followed right behind.

I understood why she was angry, but throwing herself into a supernatural fight or killing something wasn't the healthiest outlet.

Later, she and I would have a serious talk about acceptable risks.

Now I understood how Egan had felt when I'd been mostly human, determined to fight beside him. He hadn't seen me as weak; rather, he knew the strength the supernaturals held. I'd been too arrogant and self-righteous to see the real concern he had for me.

Titan dropped his iron and caught Mom as she ran by him. She swung her weapon down, unaware of who'd grabbed her.

The former alpha caught the iron before it could strike his head. "Liz, it's me. You need to calm down. This is war. You can't lose your head."

I didn't know Titan well, but that right there solidified my undying loyalty to him.

She tried jerking from his grip, but he kept his hold steady, and she sagged in defeat. "You're right."

The thunders. Egan linked as he looked at me. *They're here.*

Four hundred dragons were heading this way, all in varying shades of greens, browns, and blues, contrasting drastically with the fae dragons. It was easy to see which ones were tied to Earth.

A roar of warning emanated from a fae dragon close by. The larger dragons glanced skyward in trepidation, drawing the attention of the shifters and vampires too.

Bright yellow blurred as an enemy dragon attacked. Its blue flames erupted over Athan.

Athan yelped in surprise, and then the sound quickly changed to heartbreaking agony.

The other enemy dragons charged, their fighting more desperate and determined.

We would soon outnumber them.

"No!" Katherine yelled, watching as her brother rolled on the ground to extinguish the flames.

But the dragon kept pouring them on, burning his flesh, which smelled like burnt cotton candy. I had to help him before it was too late.

A few feet off the ground, something hit me solidly in the side, and claws pierced my arm. I stumbled and caught my balance as Egan appeared beside me in a flash. He sank his teeth into the offending dragon's wing. The enemy dragon spun toward my mate and lunged for his neck.

Not happening.

I blew flames at the enemy's back, relishing that he'd know how it felt. My flames engulfed him, and Egan slashed the fae dragon's neck with his claws. Blood poured out as the dragon gurgled in pain.

I found Athan motionless and doused in fire. Enemies picked off every shifter that tried to get to him.

Katherine's face morphed into pure rage as scaled, black wings ripped the shirt from her body. Her pale skin turned scaly, and her body grew, splitting her pants from her body. The dagger fell beside her.

My eyes had to be playing tricks on me, but every time I blinked, nothing changed.

A black, smaller dragon-like creature stood where my sweet vampire friend had been.

I'd say she and Draco were definitely fated mates.

Roaring, she picked up the dagger and took flight. She flashed across the field, and stopping behind the attacking dragon, she stabbed him in the back.

The dragon's scales thinned as it roared in pain, and its scales disintegrated into sand.

As the blue flames lessened, what once had been Athan came into view. Only a pile of ash remained.

"Athan." Julie's voice cracked as a sob left her chest. "No."

My heart hurt for them, but if we disengaged, we wouldn't make it out of this alive. To end this, we had to go after Otin.

But first, we had to find him.

Of course, he wouldn't fight in his own war. He'd hang back and reap all the rewards, though. *That means he's hiding in the woods where he can watch without putting himself at risk.*

Paying attention to the tree line, I found a patch of scarlet behind Titan, Winter, and Mom. *I see Otin close to the tree that almost fell over.*

There were more enemy dragons concentrated in that area than the rest. They were protecting their king.

Our thunder reached us and engaged in battle.

Only a small portion had been trained for battle since they'd planned to remain in hiding. But dragons were natural fighters, so they weren't completely defenseless. Going forward, Egan and I would change that. We needed our people to be strong.

There would always be someone looking to tear us down, and it was our responsibility to protect our people and, most importantly, ensure they could protect themselves.

Two navy blue dragons flanked Egan and me, their stature similar to Draco's.

I'm pretty sure that's Draco's family, Egan confirmed.

Good, we needed warriors. *Let's go.*

Please stay close to me, Egan asked. *These people want to kill us. We're what's standing between their king and the throne.*

I promise not to be careless.

We took off with the warriors staying close to us. Libelle fought another dragon. It tried to get away, not fighting back at all.

I had to be missing something. *Why aren't they trying to take Libelle out?*

The best way to solidify your reign is to have an heir. Egan sounded disgusted. *Even though they don't want to kill her, her father will punish her.*

By killing her best friend. No wonder Sarah and the king had gotten along. They were the same type of people, using whatever they could to force others to their knees. That was probably why Libelle had been hesitant, so we couldn't lose. She had just as much, if not more, at stake.

Every fae was engaged in battle, and it took several wolf shifters to hold their own against a single dragon, even with the iron. Our dragons had gone straight to battle, but the enemy dragons had training.

It made sense that Libelle had questioned our abilities. Otin obviously never paused their training.

We flew across the field, avoiding any fighting since our people had the lead.

As we flew closer to the tree line past Mom, five fae dragons flew from the woods, swarming us.

This had to be the king's personal guards.

The warrior dragons went straight on the offensive. Each fae dragon charged our warrior dragons, but that left three to focus on Egan and me.

Crap, this was what the fae king wanted. He'd held several dragons back, hoping to split us off from the others and attack. We'd walked into his trap.

What do we do? I linked with Egan. *We're outnumbered.*

Stay close to me, and we fight dirty. Egan's voice held an edge I'd never heard before. *Do whatever it takes to make it out alive.*

Fight dirty.

I could do that.

If I could figure out how with these creatures.

The three enemy dragons circled us. Two locked eyes on Egan, and the eggshell-colored dragon extended its talons, making its way toward me.

Squaring my shoulders, I prepared for the impact and pain. If I could reach his neck or injure his wing, that would put us on more even ground. I was already a slightly smaller dragon than the others because I'd been human.

But when it flew over my head, avoiding me, my blood ran cold.

He wouldn't have let me go unless something horrible would happen.

I spun around right as the enemy dragon swooped down and picked Mom up by his talons.

"No!" Mom swung the iron like a bat, desperately trying to hit the dragon. "You aren't hurting me or my daughter again."

Terror took hold of my gut as the memory of the harpy holding her exactly like this blasted through my mind. The harpy had dropped her from two hundred yards high, letting Mom spiral to her death.

I almost hadn't caught her that day, but I had, just like I would today.

I spread my wings, ready for a game of cat and mouse. Unease pulsed through me when the dragon stayed put.

Mom pounded the dragon's feet with the iron. The dragon seemed to droop as his eyes focused on me.

He had to be growing weak and couldn't get away.

But that would only make him more dangerous. I wanted to yell at Mom to stop. If he took off with her, I wouldn't have a chance at saving her unless I left Otin alone. But if he didn't move, he'd get desperate and be willing to do anything.

He dug his talons deeper into her shoulders, and Mom sucked in a painful breath. She stopped moving her arms and faced me, tears filling her eyes. "Jade, I'm sorry. I love—"

The dragon spread Mom's shoulders apart, cutting off her words. Bones cracked, and blood oozed down her arms. Her body went slack, and the dragon released her.

Hot rage consumed me, and my vision hazed as a roar racked my body.

They'd killed my mother.

Pain consumed me, mixing with the loss of Dad. Now I had no parents left. No one to see my children or stand beside me during birth, telling me I'd be okay. My heart shattered, and I couldn't breathe.

Tears threatened my dragon eyes, but I blinked them away. They would not get the pleasure of seeing me fall apart.

That was what they wanted.

And there was one thing I was good at—retribution.

I'd mourn her when this was done, but I had to focus on serving justice to these assholes.

I relinquished all of my control to my dragon for the first time in my life. Letting her flames consume my blood, I felt on the edge of combustion. I encouraged the feeling, allowing it to grow.

I trusted her a whole hell of a lot more than I did the king.

It was time to bring that bastard to his knees.

CHAPTER TWENTY-EIGHT

When I opened my eyes, the world seemed sharper ... clearer. Even the bond between Egan and me had amplified. Strength pulsed through me as I roared with rage and pain.

Egan's own pain mixed with mine, making the void and anger that much stronger.

Spinning toward the mango-colored enemy, Egan grabbed its neck and jerked it hard to the side. His bones cracked, and he dropped dead.

Without missing a beat, Egan spun to the other fae dragon and expelled orange flames instead of the normal red. The enemy responded with his blue, but Egan's easily cut through it, covering his opponent. The heat from his new fire pulsed hotter than before.

Something had happened. He was stronger too, like me. But how? *Do you feel different too?*

You let your dragon completely free with our thunder here. Egan watched the two warrior dragons fighting the fae. *The true royal power got transferred to us. This is what Otin is after. It makes us stronger.*

Good. We needed it.

Satisfied with how the warriors were fighting, he linked again. *You handle the dragon that killed your mother, and I'll go after the king.*

Sounds like a plan. Both of them had stolen too much from us to make it out alive.

Please be careful, and let me know if you need me. He flew off into the woods, searching for the fae king.

I hunkered down to charge at my target. *I will be. You be careful too.* I scraped the ground with my claws and clutched fistfuls of dirt. I wouldn't allow this bastard to die with dignity. It'd be gritty and nasty.

The kind of death he deserved.

Forcing myself not to look at Mom, I stared at the enemy and ran. I could see each breath he took and hear his heart even from farther away than normal. I welcomed the insight into their emotions.

He inhaled, planning to spew flames, so I jumped.

His eyes followed me, and smoke seeped from his nose. His focus flickered to the ground, telling me he planned on hitting me as soon as I touched down.

Nope. Not today.

I flapped my wings at the last second, and his flames missed my feet by inches. He threw his head back, chasing me with his fire as I flew higher. He was determined to end me with magic.

But I was faster than him. Before his flames could catch up, I hovered over his head and threw dirt in his eyes.

His fire cut off as he rubbed his eyes. A rumble, followed by a choking sound, escaped him as he pawed at his eyes. He shook his head back and forth like that would make the dirt fall out.

I flew behind him and extended my talons, slashing his wings in one slick movement.

His cry for help hurt my ears, but I wanted to debilitate him one agonizing inch at a time.

I waited for the joy of victory to come, but it didn't. Watching him be helpless didn't comfort me because the pain he felt wouldn't come close to losing Mom, and it wouldn't bring her back.

The truth slammed into me. I didn't want to do this ... become this. Taking pleasure in someone's death was wrong, even if they were cruel. If Otin had taught me anything, it was that revenge was pointless and would only get me hurt.

Ready to end the eggshell dragon's suffering, I slashed his throat with my claws. The crying cut off as blood poured down his throat, onto his chest, and dripped onto the grass. I'd made sure the cut was deep so there would be no coming back from it.

He stumbled, dropping his hands from his eyes to the more serious injury. He wrapped his dragon hands over his neck, but they slipped.

"Jade!" Winter yelled. "Egan needs you."

Those words chilled me. My head jerked toward my mate.

Egan and Otin were engaged in hand-to-hand combat. They charged each other, throwing punches and trying to bite each other.

Blood oozed from bite marks on Egan's neck and thick scratches down his arms and wings.

Dammit, we might have king and queen power, but that dragon was thousands of years old and from Fae. They weren't an even match, which meant we needed leverage. Libelle's earlier words repeated in my brain. The easiest way to kill a fae was with the dagger.

I needed to find Katherine.

Finding a vampire dragon shouldn't be hard.

I turned around, and as expected, I found her within seconds.

She and Draco fought their own dragon side by side. Katherine wielded the dagger and used her extremely long and pointy teeth to thrash some throats along the way.

Throwing my head back, I roared and stomped on the ground to get her attention. I couldn't leave Egan.

But she was too focused on her pain and anger. Her normally brown eyes were deep red, almost like she'd finished drinking blood, but the pure anger of her movements conveyed her rage. Where I wanted to slowly hurt the dragon that had killed Mom, Katherine wanted to hurt every enemy she came into contact with.

Either reaction wasn't healthy.

Our loved ones weren't coming back.

Lillith stood a few feet away from Katherine with an iron pole in her hand and smacked a fae dragon engaged in battle with Sadie over the head. As she turned to look for the next fae to help, her eyes locked on mine.

I could count on her help.

Pointing at Egan, I only hoped the vampire would understand my message. Not being able to speak in this form was a huge pain in the ass.

She looked at my mate, and realization dawned on her face. "Katherine, Egan and Jade need you."

But it was like Katherine couldn't hear. She stabbed the next fae dragon instead of acknowledging her friend.

"Oh, hell no," Lillith hissed as she flashed over and smacked Katherine on her arm. "Your friends need your help." Lillith wouldn't be ignored.

Katherine spun around, her long teeth dripping blood. She went to strike her best friend but abruptly stopped like what she'd said had sunk in.

"Bitch, you better be glad your ass didn't bite me," Lillith warned. "Now, go help Jade."

She nodded and turned to Draco.

The warrior dragon glanced at me, and they flew over the clearing toward me.

They had to be mind linking. There was no question they were fated mates.

Knowing they were on their way, I flew past Draco's family still engaged with the fae dragon warriors. It looked like they were gaining the upper hand.

As I rushed to my mate, Otin bit into Egan's shoulder and shoved him into a tree. Egan's head bounced against the trunk, and he tried to claw at Otin's face, but the king fought his hands off and sank his teeth deeper into Egan's scales.

Lowering my head, I steamrolled Otin in the head, making his jaw pop. Growling, he released his hold on my mate and turned his blood-red eyes on me.

Jade, I've got this, Egan said and slowly climbed to his feet.

Nope, he was worse off than me. Trixie had healed me, and I barely had any injuries.

Otin bared his claws and swiped at my chest. All of my martial arts training kicked into gear. I'd grown up with hand-to-hand combat.

I ducked his attack and rammed my head into the asshole's stomach, throwing his large frame over my shoulder. I intended for him to fall on his back, but he clutched my wings, stopping his movement, and pulled at them until the scales couldn't give any longer.

The asshole was going to rip the wings off my back.

No! Egan shouted as he flew over my head and sank his talons into Otin's shoulders. He flapped his wings, lifting him and Otin into the air and off me.

When they'd elevated several feet into the air, Otin flapped his wings, and Egan lost his balance. Otin swung his feet toward Egan's face and cut deep into his cheeks.

My mate fought back, but Otin flipped him over. He landed on his back with a thud.

I moved to reach him, but the Otin bared his claws and swung at Egan's throat.

No! I was hurrying to him when something black darted past me, but I didn't care.

I had to save my mate.

No matter how hard I pushed myself, I wouldn't get there in time. *Egan!*

As the claws were only inches from killing my mate, the dragon king sagged forward, landing on top of Egan and revealing the dagger plunged into his back.

My legs gave out when I saw Katherine standing over them.

Otin cried as his scales turned to dust.

I dropped next to my mate. Tears dripped down my cheeks and splashed across his dark olive scales. *You asshole.* I sobbed and snorted at the same time. I was pissed at him for putting himself at risk but so damn relieved he was alive. *I thought I was going to lose you.*

Never, Egan groaned and brushed his hand against my arm. *Even death couldn't steal me away.*

The sounds of the fight quieted, and Libelle's roar echoed through the trees.

I crumpled near my mate.

Thank God. The fight was over.

Three Months Later

"I STILL CAN'T BELIEVE you decided to live here and not near us!" Roxy pouted as she stood in front of Egan's and my brand-new, two-story brick house.

She'd been giving us shit about that since we'd agreed to buy a spacious section of land from Cassius and build a neighborhood for our thunder. "You live too close to the city. We can't fly, even under the cover of night, like we can here." This was the hundredth time I'd explained that to her.

In moments like these, with Egan by my side and our best friends surrounding us, I felt a sense of peace. The loss of Mom and Dad still hurt, but they'd given me so much. Dad had tried to save his wife and daughter and give them the best life possible, and Mom had found the strength to stand on her own.

Kayda told me what finally made peace with her parents she'd lost too soon was to find the best in them and hold that close to her heart. That doing that would allow me to carry them throughout life. Even though Kayda would never replace my mom, she and I had grown closer over the past few months while building the homes in our new neighborhood. Egan's family was now my own.

"I'm just pissed that Katherine is living here too." Lillith crossed her arms and arched a brow at her best friend. "Just because you're half dragon doesn't mean you can't still live with us."

"No," Katherine giggled. "But being mated to the lead warrior protecting his king and queen made that decision for me." She looped her arm through Draco's and stared lovingly into his eyes.

At first, we'd been confused about how those two could be fated mates, but Cassius had come up with a theory. A vampire who never killed anyone retained their soul. Because Katherine had kept her humanity, she could forge the bond with Draco. Since their souls had connected, Draco had taken on a few vampire tendencies too. Just like I'd become a dragon, both he and Katherine had merged into hybrids. Katherine had been thrilled that she could get rid of her all-liquid diet now that she could taste food again.

"Leave them alone," Sadie said, wagging a finger at Roxy and Lillith. "Besides, we're all heading back to Kortright in the fall, so it's not like we'll never see them."

"Let's not forget that your nest lives ten minutes away." Donovan shook his head. "I think you're good."

"For many reasons, we will not be living in the dorms." Draco surveyed the group. "We will rent a large house and stay together. Trying to protect you two in a dorm building would be a strategic nightmare."

"Don't forget to add that we'll be sleeping with our mates." Axel pinched Roxy's ass. "And might have some pissed-off roommates if they don't agree to let us bunk together."

When Draco had realized we all wanted to go back to college, he'd gotten excited. He'd always wanted to get an education, so convincing him to come along hadn't been the difficult task I'd imagined. Egan's parents agreed to look after the thunder while we integrated more with humans. It wouldn't be a hard job now that Libelle had proven to be a very supportive ally, and the other fae races respected her position since Egan and I had given her our blessing to rule over the dragons that had decided to remain in Fae.

Also, things had settled down for Rook and Murray. For once, everything appeared to be calm in the fae realm and on Earth.

Our entire group would get to have a somewhat normal college experience, despite being responsible for a thunder with over four hundred members.

Katherine pursed her lips. "I'm still shocked they let us come back for another semester."

"Money has a way of making people agreeable." Sadie frowned. "Though I hate it was Tyler's money."

"Hey, you grew up with that bastard." Roxy huffed. "And he swore you were his daughter. You deserve it. And you've put it to good use by helping restore the packs Tyler and his minions tore apart and bribing our way back into college over and over again."

"Let's not make the latter a habit." Donovan wrapped an arm around his mate's waist. "Next semester, we promise there won't be a creepy bird pecking people's eyes out or a rabid vampire gorging on Hidden Ridge locals."

"Now that's something I can agree to." Lillith lifted an imaginary glass in a toast. "Even if I'm the only single one surrounded by couples." She shuddered.

"Don't worry, girl." Roxy winked. "I got you covered. I already ordered you a body pillow you can cuddle."

The vampire scowled as we laughed.

This was love. This was family. And we'd all make it through together.

Hey, I want to show you something. Egan linked with me. *Follow me?*

Always. I'd go anywhere with him.

"Where are you going?" Lillith hollered. "I need all the backup I can get."

"Just give us a second," Egan said as we entered our brand-new home. He shut the door behind him.

I stepped into the living room. Rose petals covered the rosewood floor. In the center of the pale-yellow room, four candles surrounded a seashell on the coffee table.

"What's all this for?" Today was special since we were officially moving in together. Alone. No one else in the house but us. Something we'd never had. But I hadn't expected him to go all out.

"I wanted to do something to signify what this day means to me." Egan cleared his throat and walked over to the table. His khaki pants almost matched the candlelight, and he pulled at the collar of his green dress shirt. "You see, this shirt is jade, which is my favorite word in the world." His face turned a shade of pink as he pointed at the candlelight. "And the flames remind me of our bond now that our souls are connected."

"Okay." I couldn't keep the smile off my face. This might have been incredibly cheesy to some, but the effort he'd put into this and his sincerity left me breathless.

"The rose petals represent my love for you." He picked up the shell, cradling it in his hands. "And this seashell reminds me of the first time I laid eyes on you."

"I love you." I waved my hand around the room. "You didn't have to do all this to prove anything to me."

He raised an eyebrow. "Will you let me finish?"

"Of course." I placed my hands on his.

He laughed nervously. "We kind of did things backward. We didn't really date. We more or less danced around each other then went all in. The time we spent getting close involved constant threats. And now we've already completed the mate bond and will live together."

This was taking a drastic turn. "Are you saying you don't want this?"

"What?" His mouth dropped. "No. That's not it at all."

He removed something from the center of the shell and bent to one knee.

Oh, my God.

"Jade Storm, I want you in all ways. As a fated mate and as a wife. Will you marry me?" He held out a white-gold band with small diamonds that surrounded a three-carat diamond in the center.

Yes. I linked since I couldn't speak, my throat thick with emotion. *Of course.*

A huge smile filled his face as he slipped the ring onto my shaking finger. I hadn't realized how badly I wanted this, but like always, he knew me better than I did.

His lips landed on mine, and my heart felt full. Exactly the way it should.

The End

ABOUT THE AUTHOR

Jen L. Grey is a *USA Today* Bestselling Author who writes Paranormal Romance, Urban Fantasy, and Fantasy genres.

Jen lives in Tennessee with her husband, two daughters, and two miniature Australian Shepherd. Before she began writing, she was an avid reader and enjoyed being involved in the indie community. Her love for books eventually led her to writing. For more information, please visit her website and sign up for her newsletter.

Check out my future projects and book signing events at my website.
www.jenlgrey.com

ALSO BY JEN L. GREY

The Marked Dragon Prince Trilogy

Ruthless Mate

Marked Dragon

Hidden Fate

Shadow City: Silver Wolf Trilogy

Broken Mate

Rising Darkness

Silver Moon

Shadow City: Royal Vampire Trilogy

Cursed Mate

Shadow Bitten

Demon Blood

Shadow City: Demon Wolf Trilogy

Ruined Mate

Shattered Curse

Fated Souls

Shadow City: Dark Angel Trilogy

Fallen Mate

Demon Marked

Dark Prince

Fatal Secrets

Shadow City: Silver Mate

Shattered Wolf

Fated Hearts

Ruthless Moon

The Wolf Born Trilogy

Hidden Mate

Blood Secrets

Awakened Magic

The Hidden King Trilogy

Dragon Mate

Dragon Heir

Dragon Queen

The Marked Wolf Trilogy

Moon Kissed

Chosen Wolf

Broken Curse

Wolf Moon Academy Trilogy

Shadow Mate

Blood Legacy

Rising Fate

The Royal Heir Trilogy

Wolves' Queen

Wolf Unleashed

Wolf's Claim

Bloodshed Academy Trilogy

Year One

Year Two

Year Three

The Half-Breed Prison Duology (Same World As Bloodshed Academy)

Hunted

Cursed

The Artifact Reaper Series

Reaper: The Beginning

Reaper of Earth

Reaper of Wings

Reaper of Flames

Reaper of Water

Stones of Amaria (Shared World)

Kingdom of Storms

Kingdom of Shadows

Kingdom of Ruins

Kingdom of Fire

The Pearson Prophecy

Dawning Ascent

Enlightened Ascent

Reigning Ascent

Stand Alones

Death's Angel

Rising Alpha